Don't Make Me BEG

JERÉ ANTHONY

Copyright © 2025 by Jeré Anthony
www.jereanthony.com

Don't Make Me Beg
Ashford Falls Series, #2

Cover Designer: QAMBER Designs & Media
www.qamberdesignsmedia.com
Editor: Sherry Shafer, Creative Heart Editing
https://creativeheartediting.com/
Developmental Editor: Becca Mysoor
https://www.fairyplotmother.me/

ISBN: 978-1-967555-03-1

ISBN (ebook): 978-1-967555-01-7

PLAYLIST

Listen to the full Don't Make Me Beg playlist on **Spotify**

Loved You A Little — The Maine, (with Taking Back Sunday
and Charlotte Sands)
Silence — Marshmallow, Khalid
Your Guardian Angel — The Red Jumpsuit Apparatus
Have Faith In Me — A Day To Remember
Getaway Car — Taylor Swift
I Did Something Bad — Taylor Swift
Nobody's Home — Avril Lavigne
Bad Things — MGK, Camila Cabello

Airplanes — B.o.B, Hayley Williams
Lonely is the Muse — Halsey
Never Be the Same — Camila Cabello
Who Knew — P!nk
I'd Do Anything — Simple Plan
Take on the World — You Me At Six
Shapeshifting — Taylor Acorn
Iris — The Goo Goo Dolls
Closing Time — Semisonic
Scars — Papa Roach
my tears ricochet — Taylor Swift
I Love You, I'm Sorry — Gracie Abrams
Afterglow — Taylor Swift
Pain — Three Days Grace
Figure You Out — VOILÁ
If It Means A Lot To You — A Day To Remember

*To all the Good Girls out there that need a little extra *spice*
with their praise kink...*

AUTHOR'S NOTE

PLEASE BE ADVISED...

While Don't Make Me Beg is a fun, hilarious, and *spicy* romcom, this story delves into some heavier topics. If that's something you are sensitive to, please pay attention to the following **content warnings:**

— Mention of **emotional abuse** as well as **strained parental relationships**.

— A **descriptive and intense de-virging scene**, *which is 100% consensual.*

— **Light BDSM play**, touches of a **humiliation/degredation kink,** as well as a **pain kink**. *Again, all of which is 100% consensual.*

— Use of **marijuana** recreationally.

— Characters **engaging in explicit sexual conduct while under the influence** of marijuana/alcohol. *Consensual*

If you're still here after all of that then, happy reading!

XOXO

Jeré

ASHFORD FALLS BUSINESS DIRECTORY

Adult Store --- Scarlett Pitman

Market ------ Fergus Fletcher

Restaurant ------ Jett Kingsley

Flower Shop ----- Lily Hewer

Inn -------- Colleen Quarry

Colleen's Husband -- Old Man Melvin

Boutique ------- Annie Mercer

Bakery -------- Lucy Miller

Bookstore ------ Paige Ledger

Coffee Shop ----- Hazel Perkins

Handyman ------- Clyde Collier

Auto Shop ------ Big Dan Jones

Big Dan's wife --- Susan Jones

Hardware Store -- Hank McKinney

Doctor ---------- Dr. Arthur Stone

Mayor ------ Eleanor Stone

Meteorologist --- Dr. Richard Drizzle

PROLOGUE

LUKA

Eight years ago...

The music blares all around me and my drunken classmates as I make my way through the crowded pool party, my eyes searching for a petite, brown haired girl in glasses.

My best friend isn't really the partying type. If she had things her way, we'd be celebrating graduation in the comfort of my living room. Probably rewatching one of her favorite old horror movies that I still have to pretend don't scare the shit out of me.

I swear, she's such a little weirdo...not that she looks like it from the outside.

She's a good girl in every sense of the word, a literal seventeen-year-old Girl Scout—I know, I can barely handle the irony—and I'm just the bad boy next door neighbor her parents can't wait for her to move away from.

Too bad for them, getting rid of me won't be that easy.

Little do they know, it's not just graduation we're celebrating tonight...I've been buzzing with excitement all day. And now that the festivities are over, I finally get to tell her my good news.

I got into the arts and technology school that Scout and I have been dreaming of attending since Freshman year.

My acceptance letter came in the mail this morning. I'd almost given up hope after Scout received hers back in November. Apparently, there was a glitch with my application. Better late than never, I guess.

I'm just excited for all the fun we're going to have over the next four years, now that Scout won't have her parents constantly breathing down her neck. You never know, I may even manage to break out of the friend zone if I'm lucky...

My phone buzzes in my pocket, and I freeze as I read the message.

SCOUT

I'm pulling the best friend card tonight. I need your help with something illegal, but you can't ask me what it is or why.

You know I wouldn't ask you if it wasn't important...

You in?

I'll be there in ten.

"Just up here. You can park in the alley," Scout says, pointing to the dark, narrow alley off our small town's cobblestone street. I'm far enough away not to draw attention to her, but close enough that she can still sprint to me if something goes south.

I know this is reckless, but this is so out of character for her. Scout doesn't do shit like this. She doesn't break rules for the hell of it. Her father is the town judge and a strict one at that. Image is everything to her family, so I can't imagine what must've happened to push Scout past her breaking point.

The question is on the tip of my tongue, but I can't make myself ask. I clench my jaw and breathe deeply before my imagination can conjure anything too crazy. Maybe it's better that I don't know... If I'm going to be her getaway driver, the last thing I need is to be distracted by my blinding rage.

Right now, I've got to keep a cool head. Scout's never asked me for something like this, and I'll be damned if I let her down when she obviously needs me the most.

The black face mask sits atop her head, rolled up like a beanie, and her light brown hair hangs in a long braid down her back.

It's not how she usually wears her hair, and I can't seem to stop staring. She's so fucking pretty with those sparkling hazel eyes that look extra green tonight, and her full pink lips. Her oversized gold-rimmed glasses only add to her innocent appearance. Her soft, feminine features are contrasted by her baggy dark clothes—my clothes actually—because everything she owns is light or pastel colored.

I've already had to bite my tongue about a thousand times to keep from telling her she looks like an angry Care

Bear cosplaying. Somehow, I don't think that'd go over too well. As cute and harmless as she seems, the girl has a hell of a temper. Luckily, it's never been directed toward me, though I did witness her wrath firsthand when she blew up on my little brother, Guy, in middle school. He wouldn't stop teasing us, trying to get us to admit we liked each other. I'd never heard such a creative string of swear words used together, but she managed to hit every single one of his insecurities—even gave him some new ones that he still thinks about to this day. That was the last time he teased her, and it didn't take long for the word to get around. No one ever bothered us again after that.

I don't know why, but I love that about her. Maybe it's because I'm the only person she trusts enough to be her true self. I love that people underestimate her, that she's got this fire in her belly fueling her through life. I think passion is the hottest attribute a person can have; it doesn't even matter what it's for. And Scout Sinclair has it in spades, especially when it comes to her art.

People don't know this about her, but she's a vicious little thing. All sweet and unassuming on the surface, but she's got a darkness inside her. Like recognizes like.

I probably don't know half of the secrets she keeps from me, but I know they're there. I can see it in the way she keeps herself so in control, the way she's put together on the outside without a hair out of place. From the outside, she seems so meek and polite, but her art tells a whole different story.

It's dark and gritty and almost scary. It's like overhearing someone grieving in another language. I don't have to know what's being said to feel the pain. It's a vibration, an undeniable energy that evokes so many contrasting emotions you almost feel like you've been hit by a truck after being in a room full of her paintings.

She doesn't let people in easily and she keeps her circle small —ie. Just me. I'm the circle... and maybe my mom too. She's sort of adopted her into our family... unofficially, of course. We're next door neighbors, best friends... basically family at this point.

I can only hope that one day she'll trust me enough to fully let me in. That she'll allow me to help her fight her demons...but until that day comes, I guess I'll have to settle for being her getaway driver.

I can tell from her flushed cheeks and the way her nose is swollen and pink that she's been crying. And that's another thing about Scout, she never cries when she's upset—now, when she's watching Disney movies, that's a whole different story. Which means that whatever has her this upset is really bad.

My fist clenches tightly around the steering wheel, and I grit my teeth to keep myself from prying. Scout's never been one to complain, though based on what I know about her family life, she's got plenty of reason to. They treat her like shit, always expecting perfection and refusing to tolerate anything less. Sometimes I feel like she thinks she owes them something for simply existing.

I know I basically hit the parental jackpot so it's not exactly a fair comparison, but the Sinclairs are not the nicest people. They've lived next door to my family for over ten years and haven't once attended any of my mother's parties. They're too caught up in maintaining appearances at their country club in the next town over to be bothered with mingling with their neighbors—or anyone else in Ashford Falls for that matter. Honestly, I think the only reason they've stayed this long is because of her dad's high status in the community.

My thoughts are interrupted by the sound of the clinking tin can as she digs through the plastic bag sitting at her feet, and my ears perk up. She pulls the black knit ski mask over her face, shoving the extra cans of spray paint in her cargo pockets like she's preparing for battle. It's not hard to put the clues together as to what she may be up to, but I still don't know why she's doing it.

I open my mouth to ask her what's going on, but she cuts me off before I can get the words out. "Keep the car running and try to lay low. I shouldn't be more than twenty minutes."

I suck in a breath, flaring my nostrils as I hold back the ever-growing need to ask her why she's doing this and simply nod. "Be careful. And make sure you don't leave any evidence or whatever. Call me if you need me."

A silent moment passes between us as I stare into her eyes, feeling a rush of something oddly protective washing over me. My eyes flash to her, the cutout of her mask revealing her pouty pink lips, still swollen from crying. And when she wets her lips, I have the strangest urge to lean in and kiss her.

Everything around us seems to disappear, and time stands still. My heart pounds in my chest so hard that it vibrates off my bones, sending ripples of electricity between us. I know she feels it, too, because her pupils are dilated and her heavy breathing falls into rhythm with mine.

Maybe it's the rush that we could get caught, or maybe it's because I'm seeing a new side to her, wanting to hurt whoever's behind her being this upset, but there's definitely something happening right now. It's not that I'm not attracted to her; she's the prettiest girl I've ever seen on the inside and out, but she's always seemed out of reach, uninterested. She's made my position of being in the friend zone abundantly clear over the years, correcting anyone before they can even ask, and I've never questioned it.

Rather than acting on my impulses, I reach to adjust the mask around her oversized, round-framed glasses. I don't miss the way she sucks in a sharp breath before quickly backing away.

She shakes the can of spray paint in her hand and whispers in an almost raspy voice, "Wish me luck."

The car door slams behind her, and then she's gone, leaving only the scent of her vanilla perfume behind.

I watch as she crouches down and bolts through the alleyway, before jumping the wrought iron fence to cut through the graveyard. I keep my eyes trained on her for as long as I can until she eventually disappears into the darkness.

"Good luck, Girl Scout," I whisper to myself as I feel my goofy grin stretch across my face. It's odd timing, I know, but I can't help the sense of pride I feel for her in this moment. Seeing her finally let out some of that anger she keeps locked up so tight. Maybe this is a turning point for her? I can only hope.

My leg bounces with nervous energy as I stare at the twenty-minute timer on my phone, impatiently waiting as the seconds tick by.

After fifteen minutes have passed, I can't take the silence anymore. I type out a quick text to check on her.

A couple of minutes later, my phone buzzes with a response.

I tap my fingers to the beat of the music that's barely loud enough to hear as I try like hell to keep my mind from going to the worst-case scenario and tell myself she's fine. But when I catch sight of a white car speeding by out of my peripheral vision, my spine goes ramrod straight. There's a sickening feeling twisting in my gut, and I break out in a cold sweat—my fear tightens like a noose around my neck.

Two seconds later, another car passes by, going just as fast, heading in the same direction as Scout.

"Goddammit," I hiss as I shift into drive and take off after them, turning down an adjacent road so I'm hopefully unnoticed.

Turning onto Main Street, I see Scout busy putting the finishing touches on her painting. It's hard to make out exactly, it's large and definitely more intricate than I was expecting. The bright green eyes catch my attention, and I immediately know it's the Phantom.

The second thing I notice is the building where she's spray painting. It's the abandoned church smack dab in the middle of town... A *historic* church that's still standing, despite its ramshackle brick walls. The building's nearly as old as Ashford Falls, one of the very first built here.

You'd think someone would've bought it and fixed it up by now, but since it's a historical building, the city's more protective of it. I guess they're waiting for the right person to swoop in and fix it up like it deserves. I don't have time to figure out why Scout chose this building of all places, but knowing her, I'm sure she had her reasons.

I see the police cruiser turn down the block, and I pull the car to the side of the road, and I'm already out of my car, running to her, not even caring that I'm illegally parked in a fire lane.

"Scout, we've got to go!" I whisper-yell, waving my arms to get her attention.

She looks over her shoulder and drops the can of spray paint at her feet, as the bright blue lights of the police cruiser start to flash.

She takes off toward me in a sprint, reaching me just as the second cop car rounds the corner. "Oh, shit. What do we do?" Her round eyes go wide as she looks up at me, and my heart shatters into a million pieces at the sight of the fear on her face.

"Come on, we need to hide." I take her hand and lead her to the back of the building, just as the cop's bright lights illuminate the space. The siren's wailing now, as if we didn't already know we were screwed.

I hear the sirens grow louder as the second cop pulls up. Gravel crunches beneath the tires as another bright spotlight flashes around the building.

We lay low, our breaths coming out in heavy pants as I try like hell to formulate a plan. We can't run, we've got cops on both sides of us, and there's no way we'll be able to get past them at this close of a distance. I look above me and see the broken metal ladder of the fire escape. It's the only way.

Before I can talk myself out of it, I pull Scout to her feet. "You need to get up there. The fire escape goes all the way up to the roof. You can jump to the vacant building next door and climb down the other side. Then, you need to hide. I'll come for you, okay?"

She nods, her eyes wide as saucers, as her whole body shakes in my hands.

"You can do this, Scout," I reassure her before pulling her into a tight hug, wrapping my arms around her small frame. She hugs me back with all her strength, and when I pull away, I see her eyes are rimmed in tears. The dam in me breaks.

I press my lips to hers as the years of pent-up tension comes crashing to the surface, the gigantic waves washing my feet out from under me. I lose myself in the feel of her soft lips as she grips my shirt and pulls me closer. Nothing has ever felt more right than this. My hand moves behind her head as I cradle her against me, my neck cranes down almost painfully because of our height difference.

Her lips are incredibly soft, and she tastes like a mix of strawberry lip gloss and peppermint gum. My body is a live flame burning hot as desire rips through me. I grip my fists in the fabric of her t-shirt as I pull her into me, needing to feel her more than I need air in my lungs.

And she's kissing me back with just as much vigor, her fingernails clawing at my back just as desperately. Like she's wanted this just as much as I have, and I can't help but wonder how long we've deprived ourselves because we were both too afraid to act.

We lose ourselves in the kiss, drowning in all the promises we've already made and everything that's to come. It's a promise, a vow, a revelation all at the same time.

And when I finally find the will to pry my lips away from hers and tear our bodies apart, she lets out the sexiest whimper of protest. She blinks several times as awareness slowly comes back to her, and she slowly places two fingers against her lips.

I don't have time to react before I hear a voice shouting in the distance. "Who's back there? You're already caught, kid, so you can do this the easy way or the hard way...it's up to you," the cop's deep voice echoes through the megaphone, and I feel my heart drop to my stomach.

"Come on," I say, just before I grab the can of spray paint from her pocket, then I'm hoisting her up before she can argue. I lift her over my head with ease, adjusting her so she can climb up my shoulders. When I feel her weight lift, I glance up and watch her quietly pull herself up the rest of the way. She pauses for only a moment, like she's trying to tell me something, then she takes off, climbing up to the roof.

I let out a sigh of relief, then uncap the can of spray paint and rub a little on my fingers. With my hands held above my head, I slowly walk to the front of the building as the cops rush toward me. I follow their orders to get down as my face is pressed into the asphalt and my hands are cuffed behind my back.

I know I said I'd try to get away, but we're already busted. Better to turn myself in than have them come searching and find both of us, besides, all the evidence is already here.

It's only when they pull me up to lead me to the back of

the cop car that I remember the joint in my pocket...and I know I may have just royally fucked up.

CHAPTER ONE

SCOUT

Your image is everything. It doesn't matter what is true, only what is perceived to be. Stay out of trouble—once your reputation is marked, it's nearly impossible to wash the stain out. My mother's words haunt me as I choke on another full-body sob.

This shouldn't be happening to me...but no matter how hard I pinch myself; I still can't wake up from this nightmare.

I never thought that I, Scout Sinclair, valedictorian of Ashford Falls High School, Student Council President, Girl Scouts of America Gold Award recipient, and all-around good girl in every sense of the word, would be expelled from law school...for plagiarism of all things. But as of two o'clock this afternoon, those are the facts...whether I like them or not.

Arguing was pointless...not when the stack of evidence was all there.

And like my mother says, *it doesn't matter what is true, only what is perceived to be.*

Call me naive, but I always thought there was a higher probability of my fiancée cheating *on* me...rather than *from* me.

And now I only have myself to blame. I guess I'll just add it to the heaping pile of parental disappointment I'm already carrying around on my shoulders. What's one more going to hurt?

The lump in my stomach churns as if answering my question for me. Yeah...I'm not exactly expecting a welcome home party, but once I explain myself, maybe we can figure out a plan... Besides, it's not like I have anywhere else to go. My immediate expulsion meant losing my scholarships, my on-campus housing, my internship...not to mention the engagement I broke off after I realized what I'd been accused of. In only a matter of a few hours, I managed to lose everything I've worked my whole life for.

All I have to my name is the leased car I'm driving, which my parents routinely threaten to take away should my grades ever dip below a 4.0, and my ever-practical capsule wardrobe that easily fits in a single carry-on suitcase. At least it made packing easy.

A wave of panic rushes over me as I pull into the gated subdivision and see that there's a guard working the gate. I do a quick double-take of my GPS, making sure I typed in the right address.

What does it say about me that my parents have lived here for three years, and it took my being expelled from school to finally come back here to visit them?

I don't have the energy or the time to psychoanalyze my

avoidance of my hometown right now... There are too many reasons to count, but the most obvious one comes to mind straight away.

I push his name to the back of my mind like an overstuffed linen closet and quickly close the door, knowing it's only a matter of time before all the clutter bursts through.

As I approach the guard, I attempt to get myself together, smoothing my tear-soaked hair from my forehead and wiping the bleeding mascara from underneath my swollen eyes.

"Good evening. I'll just need to see some identification..." His eyes widen ever so slightly as he takes in my disheveled appearance, but he clears his throat and quickly recovers. "Who are you here to see?"

I give him the most confident, artificial smile I can muster as I pass him my ID. "Oh... um...well, I'll be staying with the Sinclairs. I'm their daughter."

He doesn't look up as he types something into his computer, then he passes back my ID. "Mr. and Mrs. Sinclair live just over there, at the end of the cul-de-sac."

"Oh...uh, great. Thank you for your help. Have a great day." I can't get away fast enough as I pull through the large iron gates and make my way to the end of the street.

Rows of stark white, modern houses line the streets, void of any character or unique charm. The newly constructed homes, with their harsh edges and cookie-cutter design, scream sterile and rigid—it's nothing like the house I grew up in.

I feel my chest begin to constrict as I desperately look around for something that feels like home. My mother's signature pearl white Lexus sparkles in the sunlight, and I let out a tiny sigh of relief. It's not much, but it'll have to do.

My stomach feels like it's full of rocks, and sweat makes my palms slide on the steering wheel as I make the turn. I've never been so nervous in my whole life...well, maybe just once... Why is my brain so determined to torture me today? This is exactly the reason why I don't break rules. My guilty conscience can't take it. I mentally press my shoulder into the closet door, holding off the demons inside for a little while longer. I need to deal with the situation at hand, *then* I promise I'll sort through the closet of doom...eventually.

I can do this. I just need to talk to them. I'm their only daughter, they love me. It's all a big misunderstanding. Once I explain, we can start working on a plan to fix this. Everything is going to be okay.

Straightening my shoulders to look more confident than I feel, I climb out of my car and march up the freshly paved walkway, my fist hovering in front of the matte black door, but before I can knock, the door swings open.

And there stands my mother, her sandy, shoulder-length blonde hair is styled to perfection, as if she's just come from a blowout. She's dressed to the nines in a pastel pink pant suit with modest nude pumps. She's the picture-perfect image of put together...apart from the twin streams of mascara running down her face.

"Hey, mama, I know you probably already heard, but I can expla—"

My words splinter as the sharp sting of her palm cracks across my cheek.

"Do you have any idea what you've just done?!" she hisses under her breath, always careful not to make a scene before pulling me inside and slamming the door behind me.

I flinch at the sound of the door slamming, rubbing a

hand over my throbbing cheek. I can practically feel the disdain dripping off her as she glares at me with her arms folded across her chest. I figured they'd be upset, but I was hoping the anger they felt would be directed more toward Jimmy, considering this is all his fault.

"Mama, I didn't do it. You have to believe me. This was all Jimmy—"

"That's enough!" I hear my father's booming voice before I see him. When he turns the corner and comes into view, the look on his face tells me he doesn't care what really happened, only the mess he's left to clean up.

"Daddy, you know I'd never do something like this—"

He points a finger in my direction. "You are going to fix this."

I shake my head. "What are you talking about? Daddy, I didn't do anything wrong—"

"Unbelievable. Not only did you get yourself kicked out of school, at the end of your final semester...but you had to go and make a scene on top of it." He shakes his head. "Was it not good enough for you to embarrass yourself? You had to humiliate Jimmy, too?"

At the mention of Jimmy's name, I feel my whole body tense, and I jerk my head to look between my parents, both of whom look angrier than I've ever seen them. I blink at them in confusion before I finally find the words to speak. "Wait... You're mad that I broke up with Jimmy? That's what this is about?"

My mother throws her arms in the air in frustration. "Of course, we're upset about Jimmy! Do you have any idea how embarrassing it is to be accused of something as serious as plagiarism in front of your peers? And then you had the nerve to publicly break off your engagement without even giving him the courtesy of having a private conversation?"

I stare at them both, clearly feeling like I'm missing something, because why the hell are they defending him? Not to mention the irony of their words. "Are you serious right now?"

"Watch your tone, young lady," my mother warns.

My father begins massaging his temples, like the whole idea of this conversation is stressing him out. "For the love of God, Scout. Are you trying to screw up your life? Is that what this is? Because you're doing a damn good job of it."

"You're upset because I ended my engagement with someone who plagiarized my paper and got me kicked out of law school," I say, trying to make sure I'm clearly understanding what's going on right now.

"We're upset...because you've disappointed us. You have a certain reputation to uphold, and today you caused a scene," my mother clarifies, rolling her eyes like it's the most obvious thing in the world.

"But I didn't do anything wrong. You know I don't need to cheat to pass my classes, especially not from Jimmy—"

My mother cuts me off before I can finish. "Ok, now that's enough. There's no need to insult the man. This isn't about Jimmy. We're talking about you, young lady."

I can feel my blood growing hotter, all my feelings of guilt and shame quickly being replaced with white hot anger. I shake my head. "I can't believe this. Here I thought you two would be on my side, but you're really going to defend Jimmy over me?"

My father drops his hands from his temples with a sigh, then, as if trying to take a gentler approach, lowers his voice and says, "Listen, honey, we can talk about this and figure out a plan after I have some time to think. But right now, can you please just call Jimmy and apologize?"

My mother places a hand on my shoulder. "There's no reason for a misunderstanding to come between you two. The wedding's only six months away, and we've already sent out the invitations. Let's not add any more drama than what's already been done."

Of course, that's what this is about. For the past two years, Jimmy's and my mother have been planning this massive wedding—despite all my protests about not wanting anything big. If she'd listened to me, and didn't invite over five hundred guests, and let me have the small wedding I'd always dreamed of, she wouldn't be stuck uninviting all her guests.

I don't know why I thought it'd be any different. It's always the same with them. They don't care about what I want. All they are concerned about is that I make them look good. I can't believe that it took getting kicked out of law school for me to finally see it.

I shrug her hand away and take a step back, feeling emboldened to finally stand up for myself. I can't believe I've listened to them all this time, thinking they had my best interest in mind.

"No. I'm not going to apologize for anything because I didn't do anything wrong. Jimmy *should* feel embarrassed. Imagine how humiliated *I* am right now? This is all his fault, and I'm not going to bow down this time." I let out a deep breath and slowly take another step back, my pulse racing as I gauge their reaction.

My parents don't even try to hide their shocked

expressions as they stare back at me like they don't even recognize me anymore.

And honestly, I can't blame them; I'm just as shocked as they are. In all my twenty-five years, not once have I ever stood up to them and stuck up for myself.

I turn to leave, slowly making my way to the door. I'm not even sure where I'm going, but I feel like we all need a little space to process the events of the day. I'll give them a chance to cool off and then, hopefully, we can talk about this rationally.

But I stop dead in my tracks at the sound of my mother's voice.

"Where do you think you're going?"

Before I can answer, my father clears his throat, then says, "Whatever this rebellious act is needs to stop...because you are going to marry Jimmy. Do I make myself clear?"

My eyebrows furrow in confusion as I look at my mother to see if I heard him right. But she doesn't even flinch, just stares back at me with a stone cold look on her face.

I take another step back and scoff. "No, I'm not. I meant what I said today. I can't marry someone who'd betray me like that... And why would you want me to?"

"The decision has already been made. This is not up for debate," my father snaps back.

I cross my arms over my chest, feeling my blood boiling with a whole new level of rage. "No. I'm. Not. And you can't make me." I may sound like a stubborn five-year-old, but I don't care. Maybe if he hears himself, he'll realize how unhinged he sounds right now.

He takes a step forward. Then another.

The look he gives me is cold and controlled; it's nothing short of terrifying, and I have to will my feet not to move.

"Are you sure about that? Because I think we both know exactly how this ends."

He's threatening me now?

I swallow hard, forcing down the lump in my throat, and meet his gaze like my whole body isn't trembling in fear. "I won't do it. I'm sorry if that upsets you, but this is my life... and I'm done. I can't do this anymore."

"You're done?" My father mimics my words, scoffing a laugh as he shares a look with my mother.

If there was ever a moment to backtrack, this is it, but I find myself strangely feeling braver than I ever have. At this point, what more do I have to lose?

I make my way toward the door, but I stop in my tracks at the sound of my father's cruel tone. "Give me your keys."

I glance behind me to see him holding out his palm as he tries to mask his shock with anger. "The keys, Scout. Give me your keys," he says again, voice clipped, his patience fraying at the edges.

With an exaggerated sigh, I fish the lone key from my back pocket and press it into his palm. "Happy?"

"Oh, thrilled," he snaps. "Nothing delights me more than watching my only child throw her life away."

The look he gives me is nothing short of disgust, and for a split second, I find myself wondering where it all went wrong. How has my seemingly happy life managed to change so quickly?

I take a step through the door, pausing just long enough to glance back over my shoulder—hoping, stupidly, that they'll stop me. That they'll say something, or apologize...

But they don't move.

Their faces are locked in those same tight scowls, and that's when I feel it. Somewhere deep inside, something shifts. Like glass breaking. And I know my life will never be the same...

It's only when I hear the door slam, punctuating their words like a nail in a coffin, that I realize the pain feels oddly like relief.

I breathe in the fresh air, filling my lungs for what feels like the first time as I start my trek back into town.

I have no idea what I'm going to do next, but I guess I'm about to find out.

A rush of cool air and the mouthwatering scent of cheeseburgers hits me the second I push open the door, washing over me in sweet relief. My feet are screaming, each step of that three-mile trek to the bus station still echoing through my bones, and I've never been so happy to be inside air conditioning.

After leaving my parents' house, I wasn't sure where to go or what to do next, so I followed my hunger pangs, which led me here.

At Restaurant—yes, that's its actual name. Luckily, it's easy to avoid confusion, considering it's the *only* restaurant in town.

Let's just say the founders of this small town weren't exactly the most creative when it came to naming local businesses. Everything is named for exactly what it is, and there's no place in the world quite like my quirky hometown of Ashford Falls.

I let my eyes scan the open dining room, noting all the tiny details that've been added over the past five years.

Much like the town itself, this place has managed to maintain its historic charm while still managing to feel updated and improved. It's one of the things I love most about this town. It's full of charm, full of history. No one's trying to erase the past and start fresh like I'm used to seeing in bigger cities. Because they don't see their history as something to be ashamed of, despite the real pain and devastation that was once present here. Instead, they value the stories these buildings hold and all the memories tied to them.

It's like seeing someone for who they truly are and loving them *because* of their imperfections, not *despite* them.

What must that feel like?

I feel my throat begin to tighten with emotion, my eyes slowly filling up with tears. How pathetic can I be, feeling jealous of a building?

"We're closing early this evening, so we don't currently have a waitlist, but you're welcome to take a seat at the bar," the friendly young hostess says, pulling me out of my emotional spiral.

I make a quick attempt to wipe the unshed tears from my eyes, suddenly remembering why I came in here to begin with. I was so lost in my own thoughts that I didn't even see her approach.

My stomach takes that moment to let out a ravenous growl, and my eyes follow to where she's gesturing at the last empty seat at the bar.

I force a smile, feeling my heart rate begin to race. "The bar is perfect. Thank you." My hand clenches around the handle of my suitcase as I roll it behind me, feeling the curious stares of everyone I pass.

It's not every day the hometown girl who's been gone for nearly a decade without even saying goodbye, comes back with a suitcase and her tail between her legs. I can only hope the word of why I'm back isn't what they're whispering about.

I perch myself up on the tall barstool, using my oversized menu as a shield as I try to calm myself down. It's not exactly convenient that my emotions are so visible on my skin.

"What can I get you to drink, hun?" A raspy female voice asks from behind my menu, and I feel my shoulders sag in relief that she doesn't know who I am.

"Can I get a Cherry Coke? With extra cherries if you've got them. And I'm ready to order my food if that's okay?" I tell her my order, and she scribbles it down, then disappears to refill a drink on the other end of the bar.

I'm grateful for the loud music and dim lighting as I do my best to look and act nonchalant despite feeling like I'm sitting underneath a spotlight. I find myself fidgeting, tugging at the stiff fabric of my pants, and feeling completely out of place.

It's not that I'm overdressed per se, there are plenty of people in here who have obviously come straight from work. It feels more like I'm wearing a costume.

Don't be ridiculous, Scout. No one here is judging you...or even thinking about you. You're not that special.

As if on cue, the friendly bartender appears, sliding my fruity, nonalcoholic drink down in front of me. "One Cherry

Coke with extra cherries. Let me know if you want a shot of whiskey to add to that," she says with a wink.

I slide my favorite nostalgic drink toward me before taking a long gulp. The ice-cold bubbles burn, coating my throat in the sweet syrup on the way down, and I already feel so much better.

Okay...so what? I like what I like, sue me. Besides, after the day I've had, I could use all the comfort I can get.

Thirty minutes later, I'm sipping on my second Cherry Coke, mindlessly doodling on the damp bar napkin, when a server slides a burger in front of me. My mouth instantly waters at the sight of the cheeseburger—another indulgence for me tonight, and I don't hesitate before diving in.

The savory flavors explode over my taste buds and I let out a not-so-polite moan, not even waiting until I've completely swallowed the bite in my mouth before taking another one.

Damn, it feels good to be home.

Maybe it's the comfort food, or the feeling of blending into the bustling, dimly lit restaurant that makes me feel like I'm alone but not *lonely*, but I'm starting to feel better.

I still don't know what my next steps will be, and I hate knowing how angry my parents are with me after our fight. Still, I'm cautiously optimistic that things will sort themselves out...eventually.

We all just need to take a little time to cool down. My parents will come to their senses and realize how ridiculous they're being by expecting me to go through with the wedding. They just need a little time to process.

I shade in the heart, adding little reflective stars to the cartoon Phantom's eyes as I scribble my doodle on the bar napkin, feeling ten times lighter than I did when I walked in. I can't remember the last time I got lost drawing either. Heck, I can't remember the last time I even held a pen. These days, all my notetaking and work is done on a computer.

The ballpoint pen in my hand feels like a magic wand, transmuting my worries and pain into the only language I've ever been able to express myself with.

Who knew all it takes is a cheeseburger, a cold soda, and doodling on a bar napkin to completely turn my mood around?

I did, actually. But I can't remember the last time I let myself indulge in any of it.

In more ways than I realized, coming back to Ashford Falls feels a lot like coming back to myself. It feels good to remember who I used to be. I can't help but think maybe I needed the reminder more than I realized...

I see his retreating figure running behind the barrier of the bar before bursting through the metal swinging doors that lead to the kitchen, followed by a clanging of pans. And if I didn't already know that gait anywhere, the sound of his voice pierces through the din of 90s music and chatter. "Jett. Dude. I'm begging you. Please help me out here! When was the last time I asked you for anything?"

"Three weeks ago. When you asked me to cover for you so you could get out of the charity auction Mom was throwing. Now move your ass—"

There's a loud bang. Then he's flying back through the door, his feet slipping and sliding until he steadies himself with his back braced against the bar top. My gaze zones in on the veins in his forearm as his strong hands brace himself up.

I'm mid-sip of my soda, and when I swallow, the bubbly

liquid goes down the wrong pipe. I have to hold my breath to contain my cough.

Jett bursts through the doorway, his white apron disheveled and smeared with marinara sauce, fisting Luka's shirt before shoving him back.

"God forbid you're asked to do *one* thing out of your comfort zone. Welcome to the real world, Luka. It fucking sucks, and there's always a list of shit you don't want to do." He points a finger toward the narrow gap behind the bar. "And how many times do I have to tell you, no one's allowed back here. You're going to slip and crack your head open, and I don't have the time or energy to clean up that mess." He crosses his arms over his broad chest as he waits for Luka to make his way behind the narrow threshold of the bar's entryway.

Luka throws up his hands. "There. Happy?"

Jett's only response is a grunt.

My eyes water, and I can't hold it in any longer. My body takes over, jerking forward in an exaggerated heave before a full-blown coughing fit consumes me. It's the exact opposite of blending into the background. Slowly, they both turn my way, and their reaction to my presence couldn't be more different.

Luka's eyes widen for only a second, then his expression turns hard.

Meanwhile, Jett's hard jaw relaxes, his lips twitching like he's trying to hold back a smile as he silently looks from his brother and back to me.

It's the first time I'm able to get a good look at him, and my chest tightens as I take in every new detail. He looks older, obviously, but it's more than that. The sharper lines of his face, the weight in his eyes... There's something different in the way he carries himself, like a quiet kind of confidence that wasn't there before.

He's changed a lot in eight years, and there's a part of me that's sad that I missed out on watching him grow from a boy to a man.

He looks exactly like I imagined. But somehow...better.

His dark brown hair falls in soft waves over his ears, like it's styled to perfection, but knowing him, it probably just dried like that after he went to bed with it wet.

I feel the heat of his gaze—those dark, emerald-green eyes locked on mine with an expression I've never seen before. It's intense, like there's a current sparking between us, running just beneath the surface.

Does he feel it too?

Does he hate me for what I did to him? Does he still think about that kiss the way that I do?

His chest rises and falls with strained breaths, and I wet my lips as my eyes drift further, my inner artist itching to paint him. His once lanky frame is now replaced with sculpted muscle, which fills out the button-up white dress shirt he's wearing. My eyes roam over his exposed forearms where black inked tattoos disappear beneath his rolled-up shirt sleeves. I can't make them out in this dim light, but I find myself wondering when he got them and what the story is behind each one.

Knowing Luka, there's definitely a story.

The top two buttons of his shirt are undone at the collar, making me think he's come straight from work. When I drag my eyes down further, I expect to see trousers and dress shoes, but instead, I find that he's wearing fitted, black cargo pants and leather boots.

What does he do for work?

I should be ashamed that I don't know the answer to that most basic question. There's so much I don't know about him...not that I deserve to. I can only hope that while I'm here, he'll give me the chance to apologize...for everything.

Luka's gaze drops to the suitcase sitting by my feet before slowly dragging back up to meet my eyes. I give him an apologetic smile, feeling my coiled muscles begin to sag from the relief of seeing him again.

He clicks his tongue with a humorless laugh. "What the fuck are you doing here?" His voice practically drips in disdain, and all the floaty, happy emotions I was just feeling come squealing down like a deflated balloon.

I guess that answers my question. He most definitely still hates me.

Not wanting him to see that his harsh words have affected me, I wipe my mouth with my napkin and force myself to sit up a little straighter. "Just stopping by to visit my parents. I've been meaning to visit and haven't had a break in my schedule—"

He narrows his eyes into slits. "What's with the suitcase?"

His question catches me off guard, and I shift in my seat, suddenly feeling like I'm being interrogated. "Oh...uh...my parents are renovating their guest bedroom, so I'm staying at Inn while I visit. I don't want to be in the wa—"

"Is that right?" he snaps, voice low and biting. "And does *Colleen* know about that?"

Who does he think he is? I don't owe him an explanation

about where or how long I'll be staying. I may not be a Kingsley, but Ashford Falls is my home just as much as it is his.

For the first time today, I'm thankful to be wearing a turtleneck. I can feel the heat rushing up my neck, and I don't need Luka seeing how much he's getting to me. I cross my arms over my chest in annoyance and lie, "Yes. I've already prepaid for the week. Is that okay? Because I didn't realize I needed your approval."

Just then, the bartender appears, sliding my debit card back to me without a receipt. "Do you have a different card? This one keeps giving me an error..."

My brows furrow in confusion, and I shake my head. "No. That's the only card I have. Can you try to run it again? There's plenty of money in my account; it must be your computer."

She offers me a sympathetic smile, then leans in and lowers her voice. "I'm so sorry, but it's not the computer. I've tried at least ten times. It says the card's declined."

I feel the color drain from my face as panic coils in my stomach. I fumble for my phone and open my banking app. It only takes a few seconds to load, but it feels like an eternity.

Available balance $0.00.

My jaw falls open as I stare at my phone, then back up at the bartender as the panicked realization hits me all at once.

No. It can't be. They wouldn't....

"Why don't we call this a welcome home present?" Luka says before passing his card to the bartender.

A new wave of shame and embarrassment washes over

me when I come back to my body and realize he just witnessed everything.

When I turn to face him, he's biting his lip as if he's trying to fight back a smile. And it absolutely kills me knowing how much he's enjoying this. He scribbles a one-hundred-dollar tip on the receipt, then glances back at me with a wink.

Arrogant jerk.

And to think, I was worried about how I'd apologize to him, worried I'd somehow ruined his life. Looks like he's doing just fine to me.

He pulls out his phone and types something, then pockets his wallet before silently spinning on his heel to leave. He's almost to the door when he calls over his shoulder, "Welcome home, Scout. I'd say it was nice running into you, but unlike you, I'm not a liar."

My lips quiver and my eyes burn, but I refuse to give him the satisfaction of seeing me break. I've already punished myself enough for one day, and he has no idea why I did what I did. I don't owe him any explanations, especially when it's clear he's already made up his mind about me.

The music fades, then the song, *Closing Time*, cuts in over the speakers, and I take my not-so-subtle cue to leave.

CHAPTER TWO

LUKA

Bells chime announcing my arrival as I push through the heavy glass doors with a little more force than necessary to find the room chock full of friendly faces. More like nosey gossips, if you ask me. Fuck, why does everyone in this town have to be so involved?

Of course, the whole town shows up to hear who's taking the lead for this year's annual Phantom Festival.

With our family's company so integral to the community, Kingsley Industries has always elected a festival chairman from within. That job is usually reserved for my middle brother, Roman—he's the one that has the right attitude and charm for shit like this.

But after putting it on for several years in a row, and since no one else is exactly lining up to volunteer to take his place, we decided the only fair way to choose this year's chair was to put it to chance.

So, thirty-six hours ago, my brothers and I settled it the most civilized way possible: a rock, paper, scissors tournament.

Naturally, I dominated.

Jett came in dead last.

So you can imagine my confusion when, approximately one hour ago, Roman dropped the bomb in our family group text, announcing me as the head of the festival committee.

Talk about getting blind sided.

I don't know what the hell happened, but I don't appreciate them switching it up on me at the last minute, that's for damn sure. No one in the town takes me seriously as it is, and they really think putting me in charge of the most important fundraising event of the year is the best option?

I need to know whose shit list I landed on to deserve this type of torture because if I'm going to suffer, I'd at least get my money's worth.

Honestly, I blame my oldest brother, Leo. If he hadn't drawn so much attention to the event last year, then there wouldn't be such big shoes to fill. And now he's fucked things up for everyone.

Okay, so maybe he didn't exactly fuck things up by falling in love and planning the most successful Phantom Festival this town's ever seen...but he didn't have to set the bar so goddamn high.

I do hope he's drowning in all the pussy he's getting for following his girlfriend to the other side of the world so she can chase her dreams. Especially since his decision came immediately after he was named the new CEO.

Seriously... I wouldn't mind if he suffocated in it just a

little...just enough to scare him, shake him up from time to time...

This kind of thing is totally out of my wheelhouse, and I know everyone in this room feels the same way.

I'm the fourth-born son of Frank and Mary Kingsley, CTO of Kingsley Industries—only because I'm wicked smart and equally lazy, a powerful combination in the tech world.

I also happen to be the only Kingsley with a criminal background.

I'm a twenty-five-year-old tech guru—the lazy gamer nobody takes seriously unless they have a computer problem —and the most apathetic of the bunch. I know my place, and I know what I bring to the table...and leading a group of volunteers for the largest charity event of the year is not one of them.

It's not that I don't care about the town or raising money for charity, I do care about those things and want this event to be a success. I just don't share the same drive to achieve as the rest of my family. Good enough has always been enough for me. I don't get caught up in chasing perfection or childish fantasies.

Not anymore.

Irritation flares in my chest as those pretty hazel eyes flash through my memory. I clench my fist at my side. It's been eight fucking years, and of all the nights for her to waltz back into town, it had to be *this* one.

Impeccable fucking timing.

Idle chatter shifts, thinning into hushed whispers as I move through the room, making a beeline straight to Roman.

His smile grows wide when he sees me. "Glad you finally showed up."

"Sorry, I'm late. I didn't want to come," I scoff. "What the fuck happened, dude? You know I won fair and square."

A smug smile tugs at his lips as he claps me on the shoulder. "Exactly. I wasn't expecting you to fight so hard for it, but you've earned this honor. Congratulations, little brother."

My mouth falls open, and I glare daggers in his direction.

Roman just laughs and gives my shoulder another pat. "Oh, were you under the impression that we were fighting to *not* take the lead?" He leans in, voice low and smug. "You really need to start paying better attention. You know, I think this is going to be good for you. Maybe we should've put you in charge years ago—"

I slap his hand off my shoulder like I've just been electrocuted. "Fuck off. You knew what you were doing. You assholes set me up." My eyes scan the crowd until they land on Jett, and I give him one more silent plea. "Please. I'll do anything you want!" I mouth, clasping my hands in prayer.

He rolls his eyes and shakes his head, exaggerating his silent words, "No way." Then, with a mocking smile, he offers two enthusiastic thumbs up.

I bite my lip and shake my head. The sight of my broodiest brother acting so uncharacteristically goofy almost makes me crack a smile, but when Roman clears his throat and asks everyone to find their seats, I'm quickly cemented back to reality.

Realizing my protests are useless, I shove my clenched fists in my pockets and step aside, allowing Roman to kick off the meeting. Let's just get this over with.

"Welcome, everyone," he begins, flashing his signature

dimpled smile. "I'm sure you're all excited to hear tonight's announcement, so let's jump right in, shall we?

"As you all know, the popularity of the Phantom Festival has grown exponentially, and our goal is to continue that explosive success to make the biggest impact possible. So, this was not a decision that was made lightly.

"After a lot of thought and careful consideration, I am pleased to announce that this year's Phantom Festival will be led by none other than...our very own Luka Kingsley!"

Gasps of shock and whispered disgruntlement fill the silent room while Jett provides the sole clap of encouragement.

Well, damn...tough crowd. I wasn't expecting a parade or anything, but a guy could use a little enthusiasm...

"You can't be serious!"

"Is this a joke?"

"All right, all right, let's all settle down. There's no need to panic, I promise you're in good hands," Roman, says as he taps the gavel to get everyone's attention.

"Do you really expect us to be happy about this? Is he even qualified?"

"Is that even legal?"

I snap my eyes toward the back of the room, and judging by the way everyone's glaring, it could have been any one of them who made the comment.

Not that it really matters. It's obvious they're all thinking the same thing.

"No offense, but are we sure that's the image we want to portray? I mean...do you think businesses will feel comfortable associating with a *criminal*?"

"All right, everybody, calm down. My brother is more

than capable of putting together a successful event, and you all know his past mistakes have nothing to do with his leadership or organizational abilities."

"What about Inn? In order to accommodate the town's growing needs, I've had to close for the renovations and expansion. If we screw this up, all of the lost months of income and costs to expand could be sunk!" Colleen calls out, using a folded flier to fan herself.

"Last year, Miss Ivy set a certain *expectation*. Do we really want to disappoint everyone by dropping the ball?" Big Dan, the owner of Auto Shop, asks, not even trying to hold back his glare.

"Trust me, your balls are safe in my hands," I assure them, but my joke doesn't even get as much as a snicker. Instead, the room falls silent as everyone exchanges worried looks. Except for Jett, who's watching the whole thing with wide eyes and the closest thing to a smile his face can muster.

Roman cuts his eyes at me and not so subtly elbows me in the ribs. "What he's trying to say," he says with a tight smile, "is this is a team effort and while Luka is *technically* the new chairman, *your* voices are just as important." He taps the gavel again, this time more for show. "Now, why don't we spend the rest of our time focusing on something productive. Let's open it up. Does anyone have any ideas? Feel free to shout them out."

"Maybe keep him away from the historical buildings," someone else calls out.

"Unless they need a new coat of paint," another voice adds, followed by a ripple of laughter.

I shove my clenched fists into my pockets and rock back on my heels, trying not to look bothered by their digs.

Would it even be a town meeting without my past being thrown in my face? After all these years, you'd think I'd be used to it, but the truth is that it still catches me off guard at times.

It's not that I really care what these people think of me... Hell, half the time, I benefit from it. I like keeping a low profile. I like knowing that no one expects more of me. The bar that they judge me by is basically underground, and that suits me just fine.

It means nobody bothers me or expects me to do anything more. And despite being part of the most influential family in town, I have the privilege of carrying zero guilt.

Everyone already assumes I'm a fuck up. Might as well enjoy all the perks.

But I'm only human, and I'd be lying if I said that there weren't moments where I wish I could wipe the crimson stain off my name and start over. Not just for me, but for my family too.

I'm almost relieved when the bells above the door chime, giving everyone something else to focus on.

Until I see who just walked in.

A wave of gasps and surprised murmurs sweeps through the room—noticeably different from the reaction I just received a few moments ago—as everyone realizes who has joined us.

"My goodness, is that who I think it is?"

"Well, would you look at that. Our favorite hometown girl has finally come back."

Scout smiles and offers an awkward wave, somehow looking even more innocent and meek than she did at seventeen.

I don't know what I was expecting her to grow up to be like, but it sure as hell wasn't *this*.

She doesn't look anything like the girl I remember, all muted neutrals and stripped of individuality. She's wearing high-waisted khaki trousers and a cream turtleneck top. Her arms are crossed as if she's trying to use her bulky tan cardigan as a shield.

Her mousy brown hair's pulled neatly back in a black velvet bow, making her bright red cheeks that much more noticeable.

I don't know why, but I get a small rush knowing she wears every single emotion on her skin. It's probably why she's gone to such great lengths to cover herself... It's hard to lie convincingly when your body gives you away.

"Come over here and sit by me. We've got room," Hazel calls, as she shuffles over to make enough room for Scout.

"Sorry... I didn't mean to interrupt... Please continue. I'll just—" She offers everyone an embarrassed wave before ducking her head and weaving through the crowd, settling into the empty seat beside Hazel.

"It's good to see you, Scout," Roman says smoothly, picking up without missing a beat. "We were just talking about how Luka's been elected to lead this year's Phantom Festival. Now, does anyone have any ideas?"

I'm relieved when I see Miss Scarlett's hand fly up. The town gossip and owner of Ashford Falls' one and only Adult Store is sure to have some interesting ideas that will take this meeting in a much-needed new direction. Besides, out of everyone in this room, she probably hates me the least. Which makes sense considering I'm single-handedly responsible for keeping her in business.

"I think our downtown could use a little more excitement. It'd be nice to brighten things up a bit. All the dark colors are so dreary and boring—"

"Some might say that's what sets our small town apart from all the rest," Jett cuts in, already annoyed and defensive. "We've worked hard to maintain the integrity of our town's history."

Here we go.

Jett's obsession with Ashford Falls and the integrity of its image is something that should be studied. I swear, sometimes I think he's in love with his building—not that I'm judging... everyone has their kinks...

"Scarlett's right," Lucy, owner of Bakery, adds. "We need to create a vibrant downtown area. We can't depend on the old folks to keep the spirit of the Phantom alive. We need to appeal to a younger crowd. We need to give them an experience they can't get anywhere else."

"We agree," her friends, Hazel and Paige, say in unison.

"I don't know. I don't see anything wrong with our downtown. I think it's nice," Fergus pipes in.

"No offense, Fergus, but I think your opinion just made my point," Miss Scarlett says with a shrug.

"What's that supposed to mean?" He snaps back.

She whips her head around to glare at him. "It means you're too old to get it, and if you like it, then it's obviously outdated."

"That's rich coming from you. Last time I checked, you and I graduated the same year—"

Roman holds up his hands. "Everyone just needs to take a breath. There's no need to get heated. Remember, all ideas are welcome here."

"You're still mad that I turned you down on prom night. You're never going to let me forget that, are you? Imagine still holding a grudge after all these years because I chose to lose my virginity to Roger Cline over you—"

"Really, Scarlett, you want to do this again? He was my best friend, and you only did it to get back at me. It's been fifty years, and your're still bitter because you missed out... Hell, you had to go start a whole sex store to satisfy your needs—"

"I am passionate about sexual pleasure, and I will not apologize or explain myself to you for that!"

He shrugs, crossing his arms over his chest, looking pretty damn proud of himself. This man seems so confident and sure of himself and judging by the way Miss Scarlett's neck is flushed, I'd say he isn't too far off the mark.

"Can you two have this discussion privately? Sounds like there's some history you need to deal with, but that's not why we're—" Roman's words are interrupted as Miss Scarlett and Fergus start firing insults back and forth, everyone chiming in with their own opinions on the matter and talking over one another.

"Can't you see what you've done?" Fergus calls out. "The moment we all learned the festival's fate would be in the hands of a punk kid all order flew right out the door. We're fighting each other because we're worried about everything falling apart!"

"Are you sure you won't reconsider? There must be a better option..."

"We're all doomed. Have you even stopped to consider the real repercussions of this? How will the Phantom react when this whole thing blows up in our faces? Is that really a gamble we want to take?"

Oh, Christ. Not this shit again.

My eyes land on Scout, who at least has the decency to look ashamed.

By all means, Miss Perfect, please speak up. Why don't you clear the air and tell everyone who the real criminal in this room is?

But of course, she says nothing.

I hold my stare in challenge, but she never looks up. That's probably for the best. I've already paid the price, and people are going to believe what they want to believe. I'm not dumb enough to think I can persuade them otherwise.

"Okay. Okay. Now that's enough." Roman says, finally stepping in to rein in the chaos. He elbows me to say something, and I wince, rubbing the sore spot on my ribs.

I hold up three fingers and place a hand over my heart, like the good little Boy Scout I've never been. "Look. I'm not any happier about this than you are. But it looks like you're stuck with me, so I suggest you either find a way to accept it..." I click my tongue, eyes locking on my old pal. "Who knows? I might surprise you."

A tense beat passes before I clear my throat and glance toward Roman. "Why don't we all go home and cool off. We can pick up where we left off next week."

I don't know why she's back, but her lie about where she's staying and that suitcase, she's rolling beside her, tells me all I need to know.

CHAPTER THREE

SCOUT

My leg shakes with nervous energy as I try to disappear in on myself. The last person I thought I'd see in one of these town meetings is Luka Kingsley, let alone leading the damn thing.

After I left Restaurant, I went to Inn to see if I could beg Colleen for a room for the night. However, I was stopped short by a large orange sign posted on the door that read: *Closed for renovations until further notice.*

So that's what Luka meant when he called me a liar. I hate that he so easily caught me in the act. I've never been a good liar; I've always worn my emotions right on my face—or my traitorous neck—it's why I opt to wear turtlenecks in high-pressure situations. I don't need everyone knowing how nervous I am. That's not exactly considered a strength when you're training to become an attorney. I'd hoped that by now my body would become desensitized to dealing with conflict, but if anything, the stress of arguing and high-tension situations has only made it worse.

It feels like a cruel joke that I've all but tortured myself to finish law school with a 4.0 GPA, pursuing a career that goes against my very nature, only to end up disappointing my parents anyway.

It's not fair.

I try harder than anyone I know. I fight fair. I work hard and study. I have virtually no time to myself, always using every free moment to better myself in some way. Whether it's studying, reading boring books with zero romance in them, or attending the many events with either my or Jimmy's family.

I've kept sweet. I've played the part like the innocent angel of a daughter my parents have always expected me to be. Even going as far as accepting a proposal from my father's best friend's man-child, just because I knew it would make our parents happy.

And to top it all off, after I've spent the last eight years working toward a career I never wanted, all I have to show for it is an un-finished law degree, a tarnished reputation that no law school would even consider touching with a ten-foot pole, and a measly work wardrobe I was able to fit in my suitcase.

Money isn't something I've ever had to worry about before. I know that makes me privileged, but I never considered myself to be entitled.

I didn't expect the fallout of fighting with my parents to be easy, per se, but I never expected they'd go this far to teach me a lesson.

I drag my suitcase behind me as I weave my way through the fired-up volunteers until I finally spot Colleen. She's in conversation with Lily Hewer as Old Man Melvin dozes in and out on her arm.

"Colleen!" I call to her as I break through the crowd.

Colleen's smile widens as she pulls me in for a tight hug. "You look so lovely, dear. What brings you back to Ashford Falls?"

Lily brushes a plump hand over my cheek. "How long's it been? Six? Seven years?"

Miss Scarlett taps her lip. "Let's see... It's got to be at least eight...that's when—"

Paige not so subtly elbows her friend in the ribs. "Welcome back, sweetie. I hope you'll stop by the store. We've completely renovated the romance section. You do still love reading, don't you? I can hardly remember a time when you didn't have your nose in a book."

"Unless she was painting or drawing," Hazel adds. "I still have some of your old artwork hanging on the bulletin board for people to enjoy while they wait for their coffees."

"I always thought you'd grow up to be an artist. You were always so quirky and free-spirited. A weird bird who danced to the beat of her own drum," Lucy says, then quickly adds, "But I'm just an old woman whose greatest skill in life is baking cookies—certainly no psychic."

Old Man Melvin lets out a loud snore, then Colleen shakes him with the arm she's using to hold him up with. "Melvin. Wake up. You're still standing up for heaven's sake. Can you at least try to wait until we get home?"

She starts to leave, pulling Melvin along with her, and I realize I still haven't asked what I came over here to talk to her about. "Wait. Colleen. Before you go... I was wondering if you have anywhere for me to stay tonight. I know you're technically closed for renovations, but I didn't know if maybe you could make an exception...just for the night?"

She's quiet for a moment, twisting her lips as she thinks, and I feel all their pitying eyes fall on me. I have no idea how much they know, but I don't want to add any more fuel to the rumor mill than I already have by showing up here with my suitcase.

Leaning in, I whisper, "I don't have any money to pay you right now. But I'm sure I'll be able to get it...or I can work it off if you need help. Really, anything you can offer. I'd really appreciate it..."

"Oh, honey. Of course. It's not much, but if you're that desperate, you're more than welcome to sleep on the sofa in mine and Melvin's room. It's the only habitable room right now since we've just demo'ed the back external walls and had the roof removed to add more floors."

I swallow the lump in my throat, not wanting to appear rude but really wishing there was another option...like *any* other option...

A throat clears, and then I hear, "Why don't you stay with me? I know you're broke and clearly have nowhere else you can go." I blink in confusion when my eyes land on the source of that voice. Luka stands just a few feet away, looking casual and nonchalant, like he hasn't been sending me death threats with his eyes for the last thirty minutes.

He gestures to my suitcase that I'm clinging to and adds, "I've got plenty of room. Besides, what are friends for?"

My jaw falls open, and I don't know if I'm more shocked that he witnessed my pathetic begging or that he offered me a place to stay. Either way, I find myself running after him as his long strides carry him back outside.

"Thank you for the offer, Colleen," I call behind me, not wanting to appear rude for refusing her offer. Though it wasn't ideal, I do appreciate her willingness to put me up for the night. I'll have to stop by tomorrow and see if she needs any help.

Bursting through the doors, I find Luka standing beside a motorcycle as he slides on his helmet.

I stop dead in my tracks, causing someone to run into me from behind.

"You ready to go?" A cocky smile spreads over his face as he holds out a white helmet to me.

I fold my arms over my chest and take a step back as I look around, hoping someone will appear and give me a third *safer* option. "What are you... Luka, what is that?"

He looks down at himself, then back up at me. "Uh...my motorcycle?"

"Do you really expect me...to get on *that*...with *you*?"

"That is normally the way it goes when someone offers you a ride," he says with a shrug.

I shake my head, crossing my arms over my chest. "I'm not riding on that thing. How do I know you won't hit a bump just to make me fly off and fall down the edge of a cliff or something?"

He quirks a brow. "Do you really think so little of me? Why would I do that?"

"I don't know...but judging by the way my day's gone, I don't think it's out of the realm of possibilities. Don't you have another vehicle around here somewhere? Something with doors and a roof?"

He ignores that question, throwing a leg over the motorcycle, then makes a show of looking around. "Oh, I'm sorry, I thought you needed somewhere to stay...but if you're too good to accept my help, then I guess I'll be on my way..." He starts to roll the bike backward from the parking spot, and I leap forward to stop him.

"Wait. I'm sorry. I just... I..." I bite my lip as I look at the tiny seat behind him. How the heck am I supposed to fit back there? And how on earth is this considered a legal form of transportation?

The opening of his face guard's flipped up, and his eyes crinkle at the corners, telling me he's wearing a smile beneath. And when he revs the engine and winks at me, I feel a shockwave of electricity ripping straight through me. "Come on. It's perfectly safe. Unless you'd rather spend the night with Colleen and Melvin. You know he's a sleepwalker, and I hear, during the summer, he gets so hot he's resorted to sleeping in the nude."

"Why are you offering to help me? I thought you hated me?" I finally ask, needing to know what his angle is here.

His eyes narrow, then he lets go of the handles and sits up. "Oh, don't worry, Scout. I do hate you. But that doesn't mean I want you sleeping in the park. You are my oldest friend after all. Consider this a favor that I will undoubtedly cash in at my earliest convenience."

I don't like the thought of Luka having something else to hang over my head, but am I really in a position to be picky right now? He may be angry with me—justifiably so, but I know Luka, and he would never hurt me.

"What about my suitcase?" I nod to the small rectangular ball and chain I've been dragging around with me all day.

"I can make it work." He climbs off the bike, takes my suitcase, and attaches it to a small rack with a couple of rubber straps. He pulls the straps tight and jiggles the suitcase, adjusting it until he appears to be satisfied. "It's not ideal, but it'll hold for the ride home." He, once again, offers me the white helmet. "Now put this on. I've had a hell of a day and I'm ready to get home."

Yeah, that makes two of us.

I try to hide the shake in my hands as I take the helmet and slowly slide it over my head. I don't know if I'm more nervous about riding on the back of that death-machine or that I'll be forced to be so close to Luka while I do it.

"Here, let me help. I don't have all night," he says, swatting my hands away so he can buckle the strap under my chin. Every accidental graze of his finger over my skin has my heart beating faster. *You're just nervous, Scout. Don't make it out to be a bigger deal than it is.* When he's finished, he slaps the glass of my face mask down, and all the outside noise goes quiet. That is, until I hear his voice directly in my ears through the speakers in the helmet.

"I think it's safe to assume you've never ridden on the back of a motorcycle?" He doesn't wait for me to confirm before throwing a leg over the bike, holding it steady as he gestures for me to climb on behind him.

I let out a deep breath before following his lead, propping myself on the very edge of the seat as if to put as much space between us as possible.

"Yeah. That's not going to work, Girl Scout."

I don't have time to decipher the rush of emotions that spring forward from the sound of Luka calling me my old nickname before he revs the engine, sending me flying back. I reflexively tighten my arms around his middle, holding on to him with all my might as the bike launches forward.

"That's better. Hold on just like that. Follow my lead."

I let out a little squeak of surprise as my arms cling tighter around his rock-solid core. His little adjustment has me pressed against him, impossibly closer, making me keenly aware of every inch where our bodies connect.

The engine purrs louder as Luka takes off down the street, my trembling hands clinging to him with a steel-like grip.

I feel so helpless—completely out of control as the powerful engine vibrates beneath me, propelling us through the dark inky sky. The warm summer air feels heavenly against my skin as my heavy-knit cardigan flaps around me. I have no idea how fast we're going, but as we drive out of town, hitting the highway that leads through the mountains, I finally feel my shoulders relax.

It's not like me to completely surrender control like this, certainly not at the expense of my safety, but there's something about the wind. It encompasses me on every side, and if I close my eyes, I feel like I'm flying. Is this what it feels like to be a bird? No wonder they're always singing.

Luka slows his speed, leaning to the side as he makes a sharp turn, and I do my best to match his movements. I can feel his heart beating beneath my palms, the hitch in his breath as my hands move over his chest, as I find a more comfortable grip.

"Holy shit," I whisper under my breath, and I feel Luka's back shake with silent laughter. Dang. I forgot about the microphone thingy.

"That good, huh? I have to admit, I have that effect on women. The vibrations don't hurt either," he says with a laugh.

Great, just what he needed, an ego boost. "I was talking about the view," I quickly lie.

"Sure you were," he teases, picking up speed as we hit a straightaway through Phantom's Reach.

I feel a flush of embarrassment heat my neck at being so predictable. He's probably used to girls throwing themselves at him, having them plastered against him on the back of his motorcycle. It's obviously why he carries an extra helmet with him.

I try not to think about how I'm just one of many—not to mention his hatred of me. Instead, I let all my worrying thoughts drift away, as if the wind is washing me clean of my every flaw, my every problem, my every sin.

The trees grow denser, framing us on each side of the road as we make our way deeper into the forest, and when Luka takes a sharp left turn on the narrow, secluded road, a million memories flood my mind all at once.

Where is he—?

There's no way...

Surely he's going to turn...

My silent questions are answered when he pulls up to the all too familiar Victorian house...only it's not the same faded yellow that I remember...

My eyes go wide and my heart plummets to my stomach as I take in the sight before me...and it looks nothing like I remember.

The once faded yellow siding has been updated and painted white. The wraparound porch is sporting new railing, and all the windows are updated as well. The front door is painted charcoal instead of robin's egg blue. The bones of the house are mostly the same, but it's nothing like the sweet little dollhouse I grew up in, the one I still try to visit in my dreams...

"Wait...this...is your house?"

Luka steps off the bike and opens his arms wide. "Welcome to Casa de Kingsley—"

I shake my head, feeling my eyes already stinging with tears. "You bought my childhood home?"

He shrugs as he unfastens my suitcase. "What can I say, I've always loved this house and it's right next door to my parents. Honestly, it was too good of an opportunity to pass up."

CHAPTER FOUR

LUKA

Scout tries to keep a neutral expression as she takes in the home before her, but the tears welling in her eyes give her away. It's easy to see that she's upset. I can see it in her stiff movements and how she refuses to look me in the eye.

I can practically hear her heart breaking as recognition hits. She doesn't even have to step inside to know what I've done.

Her childhood home is virtually unrecognizable and knowing I'm the one who took this from her feels even better than I imagined. For the first time in years, there's a momentary reprieve from the dull ache of betrayal that's become my constant companion.

Sure, there are plenty of old homes I could've restored in Ashford Falls. Hell, I could've built my dream home anywhere I wanted. But I have a lot of great memories here, and the thought of taking something that was so precious to

Scout and completely gutting it was too good of an opportunity to pass up. I never dreamed that I'd get to witness her seeing it.

Is it cruel of me? Absolutely. Could I have warned her prior to offering her a place to stay? Also, yes. But then I wouldn't see the moment all her childhood memories crumbled right in front of her.

Besides, how was I supposed to know her parents hadn't told her? I mean, it's been three years since I approached them with an offer well above market value, and they couldn't say yes fast enough. I guess I'm not the only one who doesn't seem to care about preserving Scout's childhood memories... I know it had to wound their pride to sell it to me—the most hated Kingsley of the whole bunch—but at the end of the day, money talks and it's not like her family enjoyed living next door to mine.

I'm not sure where and when the tension between our families began. All I know is that the hatred has always seemed one-sided. The Sinclairs have made no secret about their disdain toward us, always complaining about how noisy we were or my parents' eccentric hobbies outside. The two houses share a five-acre lot, but they might as well have been on top of each other, from the way her mother was always complaining.

They hated Scout's and my friendship and made every excuse they could to pry us apart... but there's only so much you can do when you live next door to each other. We were inseparable from the time we started Kindergarten up until the night we graduated.

Of course, their hatred toward me was only magnified after my arrest. Scout's father, Henry Sinclair, has been the town judge for the last thirty-five years, and he took every opportunity he had to lengthen my sentence, giving me the maximum punishment for anything he could grasp.

It didn't help that his buddy was the head prosecutor against me, the same bastard whose son Scout got engaged to her first semester in college. She didn't even wait six months before she moved on with her life...with the son of the man who ruined mine.

They colluded against me, charging me with everything they could dig up.

The vandalism charge was made worse by the fact that the building had been deemed historic.

The joint I'd stowed in my pocket didn't help, nor did the weed in my system.

They tacked on a DUI just because I'd driven there, stacking the deck against me like they'd been waiting for the excuse.

They then tried to come after my family's company, making a huge deal about the toxic material in the spray paint harming the environment. My parents had to fight the rumor mill for years after that to repair their reputation.

In the end, Judge Sinclair got his way. I went to prison, serving the maximum time of three years, while Scout moved on with her life and went away to school.

They finally succeeded in separating us. But even that wasn't good enough.

After they'd fucked me over, it was like they'd made it their mission to make my parents' lives miserable, too. After I was released from prison, my parents were so stressed by the whole ordeal that they were considering moving from the home that'd been in my mother's family for over one hundred years.

There was no amount of mediation or compromise that could fix it, so, I took matters into my own hands and offered them a more-than-generous cash offer for the house and everything inside it.

They were moved out by the next weekend.

And I'm guessing by the way Scout's looking right now, she never got the full story. Either that or she's too naive to think her parents capable of any wrongdoing. I don't know how she can't see it...but Scout's always been that way. She sees the best in people, no matter how many times they prove her wrong, even when it's at her own expense.

Oh well. It's not my problem anymore. It's not my job to help her see the truth when she's so clearly determined to ignore it. I don't need to defend myself, nor do I care if she's angry with me. Honestly, I hope she is. Because as much as I did it to help alleviate the stress my parents were feeling, I'd be lying if I said it wasn't my need for revenge that sealed my decision.

Heat flickers in my chest as I watch her try to hold herself together, to keep from falling apart right here in front of me. For a second, I think she might crack—but somehow, she finds the strength to swallow the tears back down.

Damn, I guess she's stronger than I thought. Good thing I have plenty more surprises hidden up my sleeve.

"I thought the old place needed a little sprucing up. What do you think?" I say, gesturing to the newly renovated Victorian.

"Oh yeah...looks great...I hardly recognize it," she

mutters under her breath, dragging her suitcase behind her as we head inside.

As we step inside, the lights turn on automatically and we're greeted by a friendly robotic voice. "Welcome home, Mr. Kingsley. I see you're entertaining a guest this evening. Shall I prepare your play—"

"No. That won't be necessary." I cut my AI assistant off before he can go any further. "Miss Sinclair isn't that type of guest. L.O.K.I, this is my...friend—"the word is bitter on my tongue—"Scout. She's going to be staying here for a while...in the guest room," I add for extra clarity. It shouldn't be necessary, but I know how curious he can be when he's bored, and I don't need him stirring the pot or meddling. I may have programmed him to be my home manager, but my AI assistant has adopted a few personality quirks over the years that I've grown attached to. These days, he feels more like a friend with no filter than a robot.

Scout's eyebrows furrow as she looks around, as if she's trying to figure out where the voice came from.

I make a gesture with my hands. "L.O.K.I's my AI home assistant. He controls everything around here and is available to assist you with anything you need. All you have to do is ask—"

"It's nice to meet you, Miss Sinclair. Please call on me any time you like." L.O.K.I quickly adds, and I breathe a sigh of relief that he's on his best behavior tonight. Normally, I prep him for things like this, but I didn't exactly see any of this happening tonight.

"Loki, as in Thor's brother? I guess it was the natural next choice since Jarvis was already taken." Scout scoffs a laugh, clearly irritated, though she's doing a pretty good job of playing nice.

Too bad I see right through her mask. This is going to be even more fun than I realized.

I tilt my head, not even trying to hide my smirk. "Technically, it's short for *Luka's Original Kick-ass Invention*...Though if I knew his name would turn out to be a self-fulfilling prophecy, I might have chosen differently."

"Would you also like me to start referring to you as Tony Stark now...or do you prefer Iron Man?" She says without missing a beat, this time she doesn't mask the annoyance in her tone, and when her eyes meet mine, there's no hiding the glassy sheen to them.

Poor thing looks like she's on the verge of tears.

Good.

I hold her stare, silently begging her to push me. To give me a reason to blow up and unleash all this pent-up rage I've been carrying.

But, of course, she's too much of a coward. She clears her throat and looks away. "So how does that work?" She gestures to the house. "Isn't the whole AI thing bad for the environment? It kind of goes against your family's whole eco-friendly movement, doesn't it?"

I click my tongue and shrug. "L.O.K.I.'s the first of his kind, he runs off sustainable resources... A mixture of solar power as well as kinetic energy from the falls." I take a step closer and she instinctively takes a step back. "It was sort of a passion project I developed while I was locked up," I say with a wink.

Scout's eyes drop to her feet at the mention of my prison

sentence. Well...that's one way to shut her up. Good to know she feels guilty at least.

I should probably leave well enough alone, but selfishly, I'm enjoying watching her squirm. "Did you have any more questions, or..."

Scout just shakes her head, but she doesn't say anything.

"I find it curious," L.O.K.I. chimes in, "that your lady friend is wearing a turtleneck sweater and dress pants, considering the current outdoor temperature. Does Miss Sinclair have an aversion to air conditioning I should be aware of? Should I calibrate the guest room to accommodate her...peculiar preferences?"

Rather than answering for her, I quirk a brow and wait for Scout to respond.

She swallows thickly then finally says, "Oh...um...no thank you, L.O.K.I. That won't be necessary."

"Noted. Please let me know if you change your mind. I will begin prepping the guest room now."

Scout looks around in confusion. "Is he still watching us?" she asks in a hushed whisper.

I just shrug. "Probably. He's a nosey little fucker." I slip off my shoes and hang my bike gear on the rack.

But when I glance back at Scout, I see she's preoccupied looking around.

"Well, what do you think? It's barely recognizable from when you lived here, right?"

"Yep... You've certainly made it your own," she says through gritted teeth as she kicks off her shoes.

I almost laugh at her painful attempt to stay polite, despite how obviously pissed she must be. The fact that Scout can be so justifiably furious with me and still have the manners to leave her shoes by the door only confirms what I've always known. She hasn't changed a bit...

Hell, if anything, she's even weaker now than she was back then. And somehow, that realization only stokes the hot coal of fury already burning inside me.

I study her for a moment as she shrugs out of her cardigan, folding it over her arm rather than placing it on the hook. Her cheeks are flushed pink as she pushes her emotions back down to wherever she keeps them hidden away, and I find myself growing more curious about the circumstances that led her back here. What is she hiding in that pretty head of hers, and how can I provoke her enough to finally get her to break?

Without another word, I make my way to the kitchen, Scout following closely behind me as we both carefully step over the loose wooden plank that, despite all my upgrades, I couldn't make myself fix. I don't have to give her a tour; she knows the layout of this place better than anyone.

Scout clenches her cardigan to her chest, standing awkwardly like she's waiting on direction...or permission for what to do next.

I make my way over the bar cart. "I don't know about you, but I could use a drink." I don't wait for her request; just make her the same gin and soda that I'm having, adding a few maraschino cherries to her glass before handing it to her.

It's a small, thoughtful gesture, but old habits die hard, I guess.

She gingerly accepts the drink, and I hold out my glass. "To reconnecting with old friends," I say, clinking my glass to hers before throwing back half its contents in one long gulp.

In contrast, Scout takes a tiny sip, coughing in surprise as she swallows.

"I may have gone a bit heavy on the gin. I hope you're not still a lightweight," I tease, and then I notice the slightest tick of her jaw and even more intriguing, the flicker of challenge flashing behind those pretty hazel eyes.

Maybe there's a little bit of the old Scout still in there after all...

Good. Get mad. Tell me how much you hate me. Tell me how you wish we had never met. How you regret everything we shared that night. Give me all your pent-up rage so I can finally let go of this grudge and move on with my life.

I wait, but her expression shifts, melting back into that pleasant, neutral mask she's always been trained to wear.

"Why don't we have a seat, and you can catch me up on what you've been up to?" I gesture to the living room, kicking away a dirty pair of jogging pants to clear our path. "You'll have to forgive the mess. I wasn't exactly expecting company," I say as I take a seat in a leather armchair. Scout takes a seat in the other armchair across from me, rather than the sofa that's in the middle.

She sits perched on the edge of the seat as she sips her cocktail, surveying the cozy living room for every new detail. "Wow, that's a big TV. I didn't realize they made them that big..." It's a dig—a polite dig—but a dig, nonetheless. Judging by her stark change in appearance, I'd bet her love for horror movies is just another thing she's abandoned along with the outdated version of herself.

I hate that that bothers me so much. What's it to me if she's changed in eight years? Lord knows I have, though I don't think the core of who I am has changed much, but I've hardened up a bit…grown up a hell of a lot.

"You know I love a good movie night, so when I was furnishing this place, I had to have the best setup I could get my hands on." I kick my feet up on the coffee table and sink into my seat. "And let me tell you, the sound system on this baby is incredible. It really makes the experience."

She shifts in her seat uncomfortably, and I take it as my cue to tease her a little more. I sit up, propping my elbows on my knees as my gaze zones in on the bare finger where her engagement ring should be. "So how's wedding planning going? I hope you'll send me an invite. I've always loved weddings."

Her posture is rigid and forced, like sheer determination is the only thing holding her together—much like the pretty velvet bow in her hair, uselessly clinging to the wild, windblown strands.

I love seeing her so disoriented. It's as if karma is finally on my side; all of the pieces that had been used against me are finally falling into place. All it would take to unravel her is one deliberate tug of the ribbon…

Her throat works as she takes a large gulp of her drink. "We…uh…we recently broke up, actually."

I can't deny the feeling of relief that washes over me at that confession. It's not like it really matters, but at least that walking shit-stain doesn't get to keep the girl, too. Scout may have lost all her sparkle, but I don't have to know him to know she's still too good for him. The version of her I used to know, anyway.

She pauses for a moment, then finally adds, "It's sort of

the reason why I'm here. It's a long story, but I hope to get things sorted out soon."

"Oh, man. I'm sorry to hear that," I lie, biting my cheek to hold back my grin. "Well, at least you have your parents to fall back on." I barely manage to get the last part out without laughing, and this time, Scout zones in on it.

Glaring daggers at me, she tosses back the last of her booze, slamming the now-empty glass down on the coffee table and shooting to her feet. "You know what? Screw you, Luka. I knew I shouldn't trust you after the way you treated me back there. I get it, you hate me. But I guess you're going to have to get in line behind everybody else."

She sucks in a sob as she rushes back through the kitchen, depositing her empty glass in the sink before stepping back into her shoes.

"Hang on. Hang on. Don't be so dramatic. It's nearly ten o'clock at night, you have no money, and we're ten miles outside of town. Unless you plan on spending the night in the woods tonight, I don't know where you think you're running off to."

"Then I guess I'll have to take my chances sleeping in the woods. It can't be any worse than staying here with you."

"I'm sorry, all right?"

"Sorry for what?"

"I'm sorry I provoked you about your failed engagement and then immediately pointed out how shitty your parents are. Okay? Just don't...don't go..."

"Why shouldn't I? It's not like you care about me. You've made that abundantly clear tonight."

I drag my fingers through my hair in frustration. "Seeing you has brought up a lot of old feelings, that's all. But that doesn't mean I want to see you put yourself in danger. Just... stay here tonight and we'll figure out a plan in the morning."

"Fine. But I'm leaving as soon as I get my money and card situation sorted out.

I tense as a strange sense of disappointment sinks in my stomach at her threat. I guess that alcohol hit me faster than I realized; it has my body acting on its own accord. "Come on. I'll show you to your room," I lead her through the hallway, pausing as we pass the stairwell. "You can stay down here. Stay as long as you need, but just don't go upstairs."

"Why? What's upstairs?"

"That's where I keep all my shit. It's none of your business," I snap.

She holds up her hands in defense. "Okay... Jeez. I won't go up there." She crosses her arms over her chest, her heated stare meeting my gaze.

I notice the slightest tremble in her chin, but she bites the inside of her bottom lip to fight it off. She's acting tough, but I know it's all for show, and I almost start to feel sorry for her... But then I remember the sting of her betrayal, how devastated I was when I learned she'd just moved on with her life, leaving me to deal with the mess she made. And any pity I had for her instantly vanishes.

I clench my jaw and nod. "Good."

Then, without another word, I spin on my heels and make my way upstairs, putting as much space between us as possible.

What the fuck am I doing?

Before I can talk myself out of it, I'm pulling out my phone to text the only person who could actually understand me right now.

Are you up?

JETT

I am now

What's going on? Please tell me you're not in trouble again…

No. Nothing like that

JETT

Then what the hell do you want? I've got six hours before I've got to be up

I need some advice

JETT

Seriously? What, are Roman and Guy too busy or something?

No. I wanted your opinion on something

JETT

That's a first

Is this about Scout?

Yes

JETT

Of course it is.

It's a bad idea, bro. Save yourself the heartache now and WALK AWAY!

I can't exactly do that, considering I offered to let her stay with me…

JETT

Why the fuck would you do that?

I don't know. Moment of weakness, I guess.

JETT

Pussy

My bartender told me her card was declined earlier. What the fuck is going on?

I don't know, man…but she told me she called off her engagement.

JETT

Fuck, dude. Any idea why?

No clue.

JETT

Tread carefully, little brother. I'd hate to see you get your heart broken a second time.

Trust me. I have no intention of ever getting that close to anyone again.

That's what they make sex toys for.

JETT

Yeah… I guess we'll see about that.

I'm serious, dude. My plans are far more sinister than that.

JETT

Now you have my attention

What are you thinking?

I'm not sure yet. I need to figure out what the hell she's running from first…

JETT

If you need some ideas, you know where to find me.

Thanks, dude.

JETT

I'm invested now. If you're going to drag me into this shit, then you'd best know I expect an update the moment you figure out what's going on.

Don't worry, I wouldn't dream of keeping any juicy gossip from you

JETT

Good. Now leave me alone. Some of us have to wake up early in the morning, and my head still hurts from that stupid town meeting tonight.

Oh yeah, I feel terrible for you. That must've been so hard to sit through 🙄

Jett Kingsley has silenced notifications.

I laugh at the automated message and hit *notify anyway* before rolling over and turning off the light.

CHAPTER FIVE

SCOUT

"No. That can't be right—" I clench the phone in my hand.

"I'm sorry, but there's nothing I can do here. The account was created by your parents, and you've since been removed. It sounds like they're the ones you need to be calling right now."

Believe me. I've tried.

I drag my hand down my face in frustration, trying to compose myself. I know it's not her fault my parents are being so difficult, but I'd hoped she'd be a little more helpful. "Are you sure? Can you please check one more time?" I plead, not caring how pathetic I sound. After everything that transpired yesterday, I'm feeling a whole new level of desperation.

The customer service lady lets out an exhausted sigh. "No. I've already told you, there's legally nothing I can do here. I do hope your luck turns around, Miss Sinclair."

My face falls as I scratch through the last item on my *attempt to fix it list* and accept my defeat. "Okay. Sorry about keeping you so long. Thank you for your help. Have a good—"

The line goes dead, and the dial tone hums in my ear before I can even finish my sentence.

Well, isn't that just fantastic. I was hoping the bank could help, by finding some kind of loophole, since the account is in my name. But instead, all I've learned is that my parents are even more dangerous than I realized.

Apparently, they're the primary account holders on all my accounts. Which means I'm officially more screwed than I thought.

My fist clenches around my phone as it buzzes with a fresh wave of incoming texts.

DAD

I can't believe I'm hearing this. You left the town meeting last night riding on the back of Luka Kingsley's motorcycle?

Are you purposely trying to fuck up your life, Scout? Because you're doing a damn good job of it.

I didn't exactly have many options for a place to stay, considering you shut me out of all my credit cards...

DAD

Oh, so that's what this is about? You're trying to teach me a lesson?

No, Dad. I'm just saying, I didn't exactly have many options. Would you rather I have spent the night on the park bench?

DAD

Don't spin this on me. We both know that you're the reason you're in this mess.

MOM

All those years I spent trying to teach you to be a lady have gone right down the drain. Do you have any idea what people are saying about you?

DAD

You need to get your ass back here this instant before things go any further and Jimmy changes his mind.

What are you even talking about? I told you; Jimmy and I are done. It's over! I don't care what he thinks of me.

DAD

Well, I do. So stop acting like a spoiled brat and bring your ass home and fix this before it's too late. Unless you want me to take matters into my own hands.

What does that mean?

DAD

It means that you can either marry him willingly…or unwillingly…Either way, the result will be the same.

You can't do that…

DAD

Can't I? You have until tomorrow afternoon. Don't test me, Scout. I'm tired of your shit.

I don't know what I'm going to do now. I have no money. No place to go—I can't expect Luka to let me stay here forever, and besides, being around him doesn't exactly elicit warm fuzzy feelings. I can't go back to school, and any chances of transferring are out of the question. And now he's giving me until tomorrow to come back home...and what, agree to marry Jimmy?

How is this happening right now?

I bite my trembling lip as a fresh wave of tears fall down my face. I've never felt more hopeless—and knowing my parents hold all the power is almost more than I can take.

Is my father really capable of doing what he says? And if he's telling the truth, then what's the point of fighting? Am I just making it harder for myself?

It's absolutely terrifying knowing there's nothing I can do to stop them. Up until yesterday, I thought I was the one in control of my life. But now it's clear that I'm no more than a chess piece, and it's my father who's calling the shots.

I bury my face in the pillow and let out a blood-curdling scream, feeling my last bit of hope fly right out the window. My eyes are scratchy and swollen from crying all morning, and I can't imagine how pathetic I must look.

Thank God, Luka's not here to see my breakdown.

"Miss Scout... I can't help but notice that you seem a little...upset. Is there something I can do to provide you with a little comfort? Perhaps a bubble bath or a cup of tea?"

The sound of the AI's voice sobers me, and I sit up, trying to regain composure. How the hell could I forget about Luka's talking house?

Goddammit. Can't a girl have a mental breakdown in

peace without having to worry about the house robot spying on her?

I use the hem of my shirt to wipe my tears and snot. "You know…maybe a cup of tea wouldn't hurt."

"Coming right up. I'll have it ready for you in the kitchen momentarily."

I make my way to the bathroom and splash my face with cold water. It does little to hide the fact that I've been crying all morning, but at this point, I don't really have the energy to care about that.

I get dressed for the day and make my way into the kitchen, where I find two cups of steaming hot tea sitting on the counter.

"I didn't know if you took honey in your tea or not, so I made one of each," L.O.K.I. says.

"That's very considerate of you, L.O.K.I." I reach for the one with honey and take a small sip.

"Your preferences have been noted. Enjoy your warm beverage, Miss Scout. Please let me know if there's anything else I can do for you."

"So… L.O.K.I. Uh… Exactly how much of that did you see this morning?"

"If it's your emotional breakdown that you are referring to…then probably 90 percent," he answers flatly. "I'm programmed to give guests their privacy but also to respond to emergencies. Your crying seemed quite upsetting, so I sent a recording to Mr. Luka for his records."

"You…you sent a video to Lu—"

My words break off at the sound of the door slamming against the wall, followed by Luka's heavy footsteps as he stomps inside.

"What the fuck happened? Where is she?" I hear his voice disappear down the hall like he's checking the guest room, before he stomps back toward the kitchen.

I blow out a sigh, feeling embarrassment heat my cheeks.

When Luka finally makes it to the kitchen and spots me, he stops in his tracks. His breathing is strained, and his fists are clenched at his side. If I didn't know any better, I'd almost think he sounded worried about me.

I see his eyes widen before he rushes to me. "What the fuck is going on, Scout? Are you okay?" He lifts my chin to meet his eyes, and my stomach erupts into nervous flutters.

"Yeah. I'm fine," I lie, "Sorry about that. I was just feeling a little stressed... I didn't realize I was under surveillance."

His eyes roam over my face, no doubt noticing my swollen eyes and splotchy skin from crying. He opens his mouth to speak, but the string of incoming texts blowing up on my phone catches his attention.

Shit, I didn't realize I left it face up.

His eyes widen as he reads the new message, and I grab my phone to hide the screen.

"What the fuck is he talking about? Are they threatening you?"

"Nothing. It's just my parents freaking out about me leaving on your motorcycle. They'll get over it," I lie.

He reaches for my phone, but I jerk it away and shove it in my pocket before he can grab it.

"Scout, give me the phone," he warns, his voice low and threatening.

"No. It's none of your business."

"I don't give a fuck if you think it's my business or not. If that message is anything close to what it looks like, then I need to know. Now give me the phone."

I try to push him away, but he overpowers me with ease, grabbing both of my wrists in one hand and holding them over my head before reaching into my pocket and pulling it out.

He points the screen toward my face to unlock the phone, and his jaw hardens as he reads the string of texts.

"He's threatening to forge the paperwork on the marriage certificate himself if you don't come home by tomorrow. And your piece of shit ex is fine with it..." He flips the phone and shows me the newest text message, this time it's from Jimmy.

JIMMY

Scout, I just got off the phone with your dad...

I hope you'll do the right thing. I'd hate for our marriage to start off on the rocks, just because you let your emotions get the best of you.

You know this was always how it was supposed to be. I don't really need you to like me, but it certainly will help make better pictures...

I just wanted you to know, I'm signing either way.

Luka's eyes search mine, and for a moment, I can't breathe,

"So am I supposed to congratulate you now or what?" He drops my hands and takes a step back, breaking the tension between us.

There's a simmering in his eyes. "What are you going to do?"

I shake my head, my throat tight as a fresh wave of tears rises to the surface. "I'm not sure there's anything I can do..."

"So that's it? You're just going to let him bulldoze you into a fucking marriage? You're not even going to try to fight back?"

"What's the point? I know he's capable... He's clearly proven that already. Why do you care, anyway? At least it'd get me out of your hair..."

Luka shakes his head, looking disappointed as he backs away. "So fucking pathetic. You know, there was a time when I actually thought you'd grow a fucking backbone and stand up for yourself. But I guess I didn't know you at all, did I?"

"What's that supposed to mean?" I call after him as he rushes to the door.

He shrugs on his leather coat. "Whatever. I don't have time for this shit." And then he's gone.

CHAPTER SIX

LUKA

Coffee in hand, I drag my ass into the conference room and fall into my seat with a sigh.

Normally, I'd tell my brother to go fuck himself if he even thought about putting a seven-a.m. meeting on my calendar, but since it's for Ivy, his firecracker girlfriend who will someday be my future sister-in-law, I let it slide.

She's chasing her dreams in Romania and hates that she's not here for this year's Phantom Festival, so filling her in on the details of what's going on is the least I can do. Even if it means dragging my exhausted ass out of bed on only a couple of hours of sleep.

Sleep isn't something I usually struggle with, so this exhausted shit is new for me. But ever since I brought Scout home, I haven't been able to sleep for shit. It's like I can feel her presence in the house, even though our bedrooms are on different floors.

I find myself alternating between frustration *with* her and wanting to fight on her behalf. I still can't get over those text messages I saw yesterday. What the fuck is her dad thinking? He can't be serious with that shit, can he?

And even if he was...why the fuck would her douchebag ex go along with it?

When the thought of her safety comes to mind, it takes all my strength not to drive over there right now and handle this myself.

You don't need another criminal charge, I remind myself.

So instead of acting on my impulses and doing something I'll most likely regret, I take a huge gulp of my scalding hot coffee and remind myself that Scout's problems are none of my business. Just because I saw a few text messages, it doesn't mean anything. There are two sides to every story...

"Was it a long night or an early morning?" Guy's question slices through the war zone in my mind. I glance down at my wrinkled shirt, realizing the buttons are all misaligned and the collar's slightly twisted.

I huff out a grunt, working to re-button my shirt as Roman takes a seat across from me. He gives me an incredulous look, then looks to Guy, as if silently asking what he missed.

"You look like shit, dude," Roman says after getting a better look at me.

"Jesus, I was in a rush, okay. I didn't realize you two worked for the fashion police."

Guy holds up his hands in mock surrender. "Hey, I wasn't judging. Don't worry, your sour mood tells me more than enough." He places a palm on Roman's shoulder and leans in. "If you want to talk about your sexual hardships, I'm sure Roman will be more than happy to commiserate with you."

Roman slaps his hand away, looking offended. "What the fuck's that supposed to mean?"

Guy levels him with a get-real look as he quirks a brow. "Do I really need to spell it out for you? Nobody who's getting steady pussy is wound that tight."

"I'm not wound tight."

"You spent an entire afternoon last week arguing with the design team about fonts..."

"Fonts are important. Just because you don't give a shit about your work doesn't mean everyone else cares too much." Roman fires back, flipping his yellow notepad to a new page with a little more force than necessary.

Guy's eyes widen, but he just looks down at his own notepad, clearly feeling like he's made his point.

I'm relieved for the interruption when Leo and Ivy's faces pop up on the large screen on the wall.

Ivy's face lights up the moment she sees us, her face splitting into a beaming smile. "Hey, guys! It's so good to see you. Thank you for coming in early so we could do this today."

Leo wraps an arm around her and smiles, looking so fucking proud to be the one sitting beside her right now. "Ivy's been worried about what's happening with the festival...no offense, Luka."

"Leo, I told you to be nice," Ivy hisses, slapping my brother on the chest.

He jerks back, looking confused. "What? That was nice. I said *no offense.*"

Ivy just rolls her eyes and directs her attention back to us.

"Anyway... I heard the news about Luka taking over the festival...and I just wanted to check in and see how things were going?" She pauses, her eyes narrowing. "Luka, is everything okay? Maybe it's the lighting in there, but you look...a little more tired than usual..."

Guy offers me a smug smile and shrugs. "Now, who are you calling rude?"

"Oh, yeah, I'm great. Just had a long night last night—nothing too crazy is going on." I try to sound casual, but I can feel their eyes on me.

"Uh huh," Leo says.

"How are you feeling about leading the festival? I know you're probably nervous, but I want you to know I'm here to help you in any way I can. I'll send you all the vendor contacts from last year, and the template for the schedule I created, so all you have to do is fill in the blanks..."

I scribble down notes while she's talking, trying my best to seem like I'm paying attention, but when her words trail off, the room goes quiet.

"You seem oddly...focused on this," Leo cuts in. "What's going on with you?"

I drop my pen and lean back in my chair. "Seriously? Now I'm acting like I care too much?" I look at Roman and Guy, who both just nod in agreement.

I catch the faintest hint of a smirk at the corner of Roman's lips before he says, "Does this..." He gestures to me... "Have anything to do with Scout by chance?"

Ivy's eyes grow wide as she looks at Leo and then back to us, and clears her throat. "Ahem, who is Scout?"

Oh, great. Here we fucking go. So much for brotherly secrets, I guess.

"She's his childhood best friend who lived next door to us growing up..." Roman supplies.

"He was in love with her, but after he got arrested, she ditched him and never looked back," Guy adds.

"I thought we were here to talk about the festival," I say, trying to steer the conversation away from my personal life.

"That was before I found out your long-lost childhood lover just came waltzing back into your life," she says, waving a dismissive hand. "The festival can wait." Then she turns to Leo. "When were you planning to tell me about this?"

Leo shrugs. "I didn't realize any of it still mattered." He leans closer, his voice softening with concern. "So...she's back in town? What's the story?"

Guy props an elbow on the table, grinning as he gives me his full attention. "Is there a better way to start the day than with a little morning gossip?"

"If I remember correctly, she's also engaged, and the other night, Luka offered for her to stay at his house," Roman adds that key detail. I kick him under the table with the toe of my boot. To his credit, he doesn't even flinch.

"Wow. Okay. Sounds like there's a lot to unpack there," Ivy says, blinking slowly. "And, judging by the dark circles under your eyes and your overall annoyed expression... I'm going to take a wild guess that things aren't going great for you?"

"You could put it that way." I admit. A memory of Scout's red, swollen eyes flashes through my mind, and I feel my jaw clench tighter. I don't know the full story behind why she's back, but the text messages I read yesterday told me more than enough to know her situation is a little more than desperate.

I stare down at my clenched fists and sigh. I had no plans of sharing any of this today, but maybe a little female advice wouldn't be the worst thing.

"Long story short is, her parents have always been hard on her. I'm not sure what happened, but from what I've gathered, she upset them when she broke off her engagement.

"Yesterday, L.O.K.I. sent me a video of her crying. She looked pretty upset, and it scared me. I thought somebody died or something, so I rushed home to check on her. When I got there, she looked so fucking broken. Her face was red, and her eyes were all puffy from crying for who knows how long. Her phone was sitting face up on the table, blowing up with incoming texts. I caught a glimpse of one of the messages that was concerning, so I forced her to show me the rest of them.

"From what I gathered, it seemed as if her dad was threatening her to come home and apologize. That if she wasn't back home by this evening, then he was going to forge her signature and file the marriage paperwork himself."

Ivy's mouth drops open, and she slaps a hand over it. She looks at Leo and then back to me. "Can he do that?"

"I'm not sure. But Judge Sinclair was the reason I went to jail for the full term. He's got a lot of connections and knows his way around a loophole. I wouldn't put it past him."

"So what are you going to do?" Ivy asks.

I shake my head. "I don't think there's anything I can do. Besides, it's not really my place. Scout hasn't asked me for my help."

"But you can't just let them get away with that!" Ivy says. "You can't let them force her to marry someone she doesn't want to be married to. What if he hurts her?"

"Trust me, I've been worrying about the same thing. But

apart from driving over there and getting myself a couple of assault charges... I'm not really sure how to stop it. Hell, if anything, me showing up will only make things worse. I don't think her parents could hate me any more than they already do." I sit back in my chair with a sigh.

"So that's it? You're not even going to try to help her?" Ivy asks.

"Like I said, her father is an evil man who knows how to get what he wants. I'm not sure there's anything I can do."

Roman chuckles under his breath. "Unless you married her first."

I feel my spine stiffen, my whole body going on alert.

"For Christ's sake, Roman, don't give him any crazy ideas," Leo snaps.

Guy lifts a brow and nods. "Actually...that could work."

"I don't care if it'd work. That's insane. He's not going to get married just to beat her dad to the punch. There's got to be another, more rational way to help her...like I don't know, calling the police and reporting it," Leo says.

Guy snorts, rolling his eyes. "Because historically the judicial system has always favored Luka..."

"Should we also not forget another important detail... Luka hates her. Does no one else remember how heartbroken he was after he got out of prison and realized she had ghosted him?" Leo says, trying to be rational.

Ivy smacks him in the chest. "Oh, Leo. Why do you have to be such a buzz kill? Have you ever heard of the term enemies to lovers?" She looks back at me with stars in her eyes. "I think it's romantic. You have my full support... For what it's worth."

Leo's not wrong... I do hate her... but I hate Judge Sinclair more.

How fucking pissed would he be if I pulled something like that on him? All he's ever cared about is his stupid reputation. His family's picture-perfect image.

He'd lose his shit if somebody like me, an actual criminal, defiled his angel of a daughter.

"I'm sure Judge Sinclair will come to his senses and he and Scout will be able to work out their differences without the need for any extreme measures," Leo says. "Now, where were we? Luka, do you have any ideas for this year's festival?"

We fall back into conversation around the festival, and I catch them up on the first town meeting, but I can't seem to shake Roman's words from my mind.

Is this my chance to finally get back at that bastard?

CHAPTER SEVEN

SCOUT

I'm so exhausted I don't know what to do with myself. I tossed and turned all night long, as I lay there watching the hours on the clock tick by, as if watching a countdown of my last moments of freedom.

I glance down at the time on my phone. If what my father said was true, then I have about eight hours until I have to crawl back home with my tail between my legs, accepting defeat—either that or he drags me back kicking and screaming.

Either way, it seems like I'll be marrying Jimmy whether I like it or not.

You'd think I'd be more upset...shocked, even. But I had an entirely sleepless night to come to terms with my fate.

Trust me, I did try to think of a way out of this mess, but it's no use. My father is a very powerful, well-connected man, and there's no use in trying to go against him. It'd just hurt me more in the long run, and I think I've sufficiently pissed him off enough already.

That doesn't mean I intend on going home early. I may have accepted my fate, but I don't plan on telling him that until a moment before I have to. The least I can do is make him sweat while he waits.

It may not be much, but it's my only card left to play, my last act of rebellion.

So, I've decided to make today as good as it can be. I'm giving myself one last hurrah. One final day of freedom where I don't think about my problems, and I spend the whole day doing whatever feels fun.

So naturally, my first stop is Bookstore, which also happens to be conveniently attached to Coffee Shop and Bakery.

I pull open the heavy glass door and step inside. I instantly feel my stress dissipate as the rich scent of freshly ground coffee and warm cinnamon surrounds me.

Coffee Shop, Book Store, and Bakery are all owned by widowed women in their sixties, and since they all share a wall anyway, they decided to connect the businesses by adding a door inside. The three women are more like sisters than friends and work to help each other every chance they get.

Hazel spots me from behind the coffee counter and gives me an excited wave. "I'm so glad you stopped by." She finishes steaming the drink in her hand, then wipes the machine clean with her rag. "I didn't have a chance to catch up with you the other night at the town meeting before you left on the back of Luka Kingsley's motorcycle..." Her words trail off, and I know it's an invitation to explain.

A moment passes, and then she adds, "Tell me, dear, is there something going on between you two? Is that why you're back in town?"

Her question catches me off guard, but I'm quick to catch myself. The last thing I need is to seem uncomfortable. Looking guilty will only fuel the rumor mill.

"Now, Hazel, I don't remember you being one for gossip," I tease, giving her a knowing look as I turn the question back on her. If there's anything Hazel hates, it's being compared to Miss Scarlett. The two may be cordial in public, but there's definitely more to their story.

She waves me off. "Oh, I was just repeating what everyone in town's been saying. I didn't figure it was anything more than two old friends reconnecting." She gives my cheek a playful squeeze. "I figured as much. You're a good girl and too smart to settle for someone like that...especially given his criminal history." She blows out a breath and shakes her head. "I can't imagine your daddy would ever allow something like that to happen."

Her words sear into my brain like a scalding hot fire poker as a wave of guilt rises in my chest. I think back to the concerns they expressed at the town meeting, how everyone treated him like he'd committed a far worse crime than spray-painting the side of a building.

That just goes to prove how powerful my father is. Not only did he successfully send him to prison, but obviously, his smear campaign worked even better than I realized.

I had no idea things were this bad for him... After all this time, why wouldn't he try to defend himself? Surely it's not to protect me.

"Watch out, hot pan coming through!" Lucy calls out as

she backs through the swinging metal door, carrying a large metal pan full of freshly baked cinnamon rolls. Her eyes light up when she sees me, and I give her a friendly wave.

"Fancy seeing you here. I almost didn't recognize you the other night," Lucy says as she uses tongs to move the pastries into the display window. "What brings you back to town? It wouldn't be—"

"Oh, stop interrogating the girl," Hazel scolds, giving her a stern look. "You're going to scare her off thinking everyone in town's talking behind her back."

Lucy's brows furrow as if confused, but then she must read between the lines because she nods and presses her lips into a tight smile. "Never mind that. We're just happy to see you again."

"Is that Scout?" I hear Paige call out before popping around the corner carrying a tall stack of books. "Thought you'd forgotten all about us." She waddles toward the door, the heavy books nearly crushing her petite frame. "You should see the romance section. It's nearly taken over my whole store. Sales have been so good, I'm considering pivoting to solely carrying romance." She grunts, adjusting the heavy pile of books in her arms, and I rush over to help her.

"Here, let me help you before you hurt yourself."

She waves me off. "Oh, this is nothing. I've been working out hard in the gym." She flexes a thin, fragile-looking bicep. "I can easily carry twice this much."

"Oh, for heaven's sake, Paige. Just use the rolling cart like a sane person before you give yourself another bulging disk," Lucy huffs, wiping her hands on a towel before chasing after her friend.

"Never a dull moment around here," Hazel says, blowing out a sigh of exasperation as a wave of new customers begin filing in.

I take it as my moment to escape, politely waving before sneaking off to sift through the shelves of books in the next room over.

The vibes shift from the dimly lit, cozy Coffee Shop to a brighter, more upbeat energy as I make my way through the rows of bookshelves straight toward my favorite genre. The romance section.

I can't help but smile as I drag my finger along the rows of brightly colored books.

Paige wasn't kidding. She's got quite the selection here. All the books are separated into their respective sub-genres, ranging from cute contemporaries all the way to dark romance. There's even a special section dedicated to the most recent Phantom romance novel, which is where Paige and Lucy are currently standing, fighting over where to hang the banner.

I smile to myself as I flip through what I thought was a manga monster romance but quickly realize it is actually an erotic graphic novel. A warm blush heats my cheeks, and my eyes nearly bulge out of my head at the detailed image of the monster gripping his massive tentacle-like dick as a woman kneels before him.

It's vulgar and borderline disgusting, but for some reason, I find myself captivated as I stare at it. It's one thing to read erotic romance...but seeing it feels like something else entirely.

I can't help but feel in awe of the way the artist was able to bring the image to life, noting all the fine details in the monster's expression that may go unnoticed by the untrained eye. The way he looks down at her with such need and desire, it's carnal and primal, like there's nothing in the world he needs more than to have her.

It's certainly not the type of love that was modeled for me growing up, and I'm not quite sure it even exists outside the realm of fiction. I can't help but wish the man I marry would look at me like that. Maybe that's my naivety talking, but that's the kind of love I always dreamed of having—not with a monster per se—but to be the object of intense desire.

At least the universe got the monster part right...

Maybe I need to be more specific next time I make a wish.

Then, as if on cue, I nearly throw the book in the air when I hear a familiar voice talking on the phone. "Yeah, thanks again, Judge Sinclair. Don't worry, we'll find her... Trust me, she's going to come home. No, that won't be necessary, I'll take it from here. I'll let you know when I find her... Okay then, goodbye."

My heart falls to my stomach, and I feel the blood draining from my face, hearing the sound of Jimmy's voice. I can't believe he's here, and from the way it sounds, he's looking for me.

I bite my cheek as I consider my options. Sure, I was planning on going home this evening, but I'll be damned if I am going to be treated like some runaway child who needs to be brought to heel.

Did he talk to Hazel? How does he even know I'm here right now?

Heart pounding in my ears, my eyes scan the room, searching for an escape route. I won't be able to go through the front entrance because I'll have to cross in front of him, not to mention anyone else who may see me.

Since the three buildings are connected, my only other option is to go back through Coffee Shop, then I can use Hazel's front door or make my way over to Bakery, which is probably the least busy during this time of day.

I breathe in a calming breath as I drop to my knees, leaning forward to peer around the bookshelf to see if he's in view. I'll need to be fast, but if I can get on the other side of the Phantom display, it'll be easier to get away unnoticed.

Crawling forward, I shake out my hands, leaving my position behind the monster erotica graphic novels, and dive to the next aisle.

Relief floods me as I successfully cross the aisle going unnoticed, but it's quickly replaced with panic when I hear Jimmy's voice, even closer now. "Excuse me. I'm looking for Scout Sinclair. Have you seen her in here today?"

A moment passes when I finally hear Lucy's voice. "Nope. I haven't seen her."

"I haven't seen her either," Paige says in agreement.

Why are they covering for me? They know Jimmy—well, they know *of him* at least—and I certainly haven't told them what has been going on in my life. Is my female intuition really that terrible that I agreed to marry him?

I don't have time to answer that question. Right now, I just need to get out of here.

I'm giving myself a mental pep talk to make a run for it when I hear a throat clear behind me. I slowly look up to find Luka smirking down at me, looking like the devil himself.

He's wearing a button-up dress shirt with a skinny black tie and the same black cargo pants and boots combo he was wearing the other night. His shirt sleeves are rolled up to his elbows revealing his tattooed forearms, emphasized by the way he's got his arms crossed over his chest.

Hell, he looks like he just stepped out of one of the dark romance books.

"Who are we hiding from?" he whispers as he crouches down beside me.

Suddenly, my tongue feels too big for my mouth and anxiety rushes through me when Jimmy comes back into view.

"Ahh, I see," Luka says, still crouched beside me. "I suppose this means there's still trouble in paradise?"

"Shh." I reach to cover his mouth, which only makes his smirk grow wider. "Can you just be quiet. I'm not ready to go home yet..."

His eyebrows knit together, and he narrows his eyes. "*Yet*? Does that mean you're going through with it then? You're going to marry him?"

I shrug, rolling my eyes. "I don't exactly have any other options, do I?"

He bites the corner of his lip, looking hot as sin as he seems to consider something. "But you don't want to go through with this? You really don't love him?"

"Of course I don't," I scoff, feeling my lip curl in disgust as I study him. Jimmy looks like a frat boy finance bro in his boat shoes and khaki shorts. His bright blue polo shirt is tucked into his shorts, and his sandy blond hair is cut neatly, not too long or too short, just the perfectly acceptable length. He's the epitome of clean boy aesthetic...if that's even a thing.

Luka's eyes shift from me and then back to Jimmy, and I can see the wheels turning in his mind. "Luka... What are you... Please don't make a scene," I plead, grabbing for his arm the moment he begins to stand.

But he just brushes me off. "There is one other way out of this." He clicks his tongue as he tilts his head to the side. "But you're going to have to trust me."

I blink at him in confusion before realizing I'm still awkwardly on my knees and push myself up to stand. "You want *me* to trust *you*? Last time I checked, you seemed to hate me." I cross my arms over my chest as I scowl at him. "For all I know, you're the one who ratted me out to begin with."

Luka chuckles, not even trying to keep his voice down now. "Oh, believe me, I do." Then he leans so close to me that his lips barely graze my ear. "But I hate your prick of a father more," he whispers, and I feel a shiver shoot up my spine as goosebumps break out across my skin.

His eyes flick down to my lips and then back to mine, his smirk growing impossibly wider, clearly proud to have gotten a rise out of me.

I blow out a huff and roll my eyes. "What's your plan then?"

But rather than answering me, he turns around and pushes a pile of books off the display table, then grabs my hand and pulls me toward him.

The books crash to the ground with a heavy bang as Luka and I stand beside the table; he leans toward me and drapes his arm around my shoulder.

I stand there frozen as Jimmy turns around, his blue eyes flashing with something that looks like relief. He rushes over to me. "There you are. Your father and I have been looking everywhere for you—"

His words break off when he reaches for my arm, but Luka slaps his hand away. "Don't fucking touch her."

"She's my fiancée. I guess I'll touch her when I damn well please," Jimmy snaps back, reaching out to grab my arm again.

Luka pushes me behind him, then takes a step closer. "Lay a hand on her and see—"

"Or what?" Jimmy shoves Luka in the chest, but Luka doesn't so much as move. "You gonna hit me? Are you missing your boyfriends down at the county jail already? If you're looking to go back, all you had to do was say something."

Luka glares down at him, his fists clenching at his sides, and I'm not sure what he's going to do next. He told me to trust him, but I won't let him go back to jail for me...not again.

"Luka, he's not worth it." I grab his arm to pull him back, realizing we've now got the attention of everyone in the store, and I have no doubt Jimmy knows it. He's baiting him on purpose, trying to get Luka to throw the first punch.

"Come on, Scout. Come with me before you embarrass yourself any further," Jimmy says, trying to act like he isn't shaking like a leaf under Luka's death glare.

I take a step forward, wanting to end this before Luka does something he'll regret. But he holds out a hand to block me. "She's not going anywhere. You can run home and tattle all you want, but you don't have any claim on her...not anymore."

"Is this guy serious?" Jimmy scoffs a laugh, then his eyes find mine. "We're engaged. Sorry, bro, but she's already taken—"

"I didn't see a ring on her finger when she had her hand wrapped around my cock last night," Luka retorts.

"What the fuck did you just say?"

Luka's smirk grows wicked. "Oh, I think you heard me." He wraps an arm around my shoulders and pulls me into his chest, then plants a kiss on top of my head.

Jimmy looks to me as he says, "Then I guess we're going to have to do this the hard way." He turns to leave; his phone already in his hand before he makes it to the door.

I spin around and face Luka. "What the hell was that? You know he's calling my dad right now. Now they're definitely going to go over my head and file the paperwork—"

"Not if we beat them to it."

"What do you mean?"

"I mean...legally you can only be married to one person at a time."

I stare at him, blinking. He can't really be suggesting what I think he is...

His cocky smirk returns, and then he drops to one knee right there in the middle of the monster romance section. "What do you say, Girl Scout? Are you going to marry me or what?"

CHAPTER EIGHT

LUKA

I think I just did the second dumbest thing I've ever done...

Of all the impulsive ideas I've had, proposing to marry my sworn enemy, the woman who got me sent to prison, has to top the list.

But even more shocking is the fact that she even agreed to it.

I guess that shows just how desperate she is.

Luckily, I planned ahead. I knew we couldn't file in Ashford Falls without it getting back to Judge Sinclair, so I had L.O.K.I. do a little digging into the staff at the county clerk's office in the next town over.

That's how I learned that Anita—the lovely woman in charge of issuing marriage licenses—is a die-hard fan of the Ashford Falls Phantom, and, judging by her role as the founder and mod of the secret online forum community,

"*The Phantom Phuckers*," some may even say she's his number one fan.

Given the information, it wasn't hard to come up with the perfect *incentive* to make sure the paperwork got expedited before the end of the day.

I knew it was a long shot, but that's what I was doing when I ran into Scout at Bookstore. I figured it'd take a hell of a lot more convincing on my end. But it turns out, Jimmy made it a hell of a lot easier than I expected.

"All right, all the paperwork's been filed. Here's your marriage license," the clerk says, sliding the official document across the counter.

"And as promised...one early copy of *Falling for the Phantom*." I slide the brown paper bag under the small opening in the acrylic window.

She snatches the bag eagerly, sucking in a gasp as she peels it open and sees the book.

I tuck the envelope into the inside pocket of my leather jacket. "Thanks again for helping us with this, Anita. I hope you enjoy the book."

She clenches the book to her chest, beaming. "Oh, I will! I can't wait to tell everyone in my...uh...bookclub." She leans in, lowering her voice. "Okay, but seriously... How did you get this?"

"I've got my connections..." I say with a wink. "But I think it's best that they stay a secret."

She blushes and waves me off. "Of course. You know my lips are sealed."

One down...two more to go.

"I can't believe that worked," Scout says.

"I don't know if that's meant to be a compliment or an insult."

She shrugs. "Neither do I."

I pull out my phone and send a text to Jett.

> I'm calling in my favor.

> I need your help with something, and you can't tell anyone.

JETT

Goddammit.

What's going on?

> I'm getting married this evening, and you're going to be my best man.

JETT

Fucking hell, Luka. For what it's worth, I think this is a terrible idea.

What do you need me to do?

> We need rings. Stop by Jewelry Store and pick out something classy. Gold, not silver. Nothing gaudy but make sure the diamond's big enough to make a statement.

JETT

I really hate you right now. I hope you know, after this, we're even.

> Trust me, I know.

I used the ride over to make the last of my calls, and lucky for me, all it took was a few more persuasive donations to get

Miss Scarlett on board. Honestly, she probably would've agreed just for the simple bragging rights that she's the first to know, but I made sure to throw in a little extra to sweeten the deal.

"Luka, where are we going? The courthouse is that way?" Scout's voice cuts through the speaker in my helmet when I turn left, heading away from town.

"We're not going to the courthouse."

"Then where are we going?"

"Jesus, woman. I told you I was handling it. Just relax and go with the flow."

"I'm not really a go-with-the-flow kind of person, if you haven't noticed," she squeals, her hands tightening around my middle as we lean into the sharp turn.

As soon as we make it out of the turn, I lay on the gas. "That's because you've never had someone you trust to help handle things."

"I hate to break it to you, Luka, but I'm not feeling particularly trusting of you right now." I feel her helmet press against my back as she squeezes her arms even tighter. "Is the speeding really necessary, or are you purposely trying to throw me off?"

No, it's really not. But it's not every day I get to have the town princess riding as my backpack on the way to our shotgun wedding. Forgive me for cherishing the moment.

"Stop your whining and just enjoy the ride. All your nagging back there is ruining the vibes." My hand moves to her bare thigh, suddenly remembering she's wearing a dress. I loosen my grip on the gas, bringing the bike to a slower, safer pace.

I instantly feel her body relax as we fall into a comfortable silence.

You'd think I'd be second-guessing myself, with the impulsiveness of this decision, but I'm oddly at peace with it.

When I was younger, I always thought someday I would get married and maybe start a family of my own, but that was before my whole life got turned upside down.

After getting out of prison, finding someone to share my life with was the furthest thing from my mind. I don't think I'm capable of trusting someone to that degree ever again. So, if anyone was going to enter into a marriage of convenience, for the simple pleasure of ruining Scout's perfect image and her father's precious reputation, then it makes sense that it'd be me.

It's not like I've got anything more to lose. At least this time, I'm the one with the upper hand.

It's nearly sunset by the time we make it to Phantom's Reach. The blue sky is streaked with orange and pink as the sun makes its descent behind the mountains. Massive hemlock trees tower above us on either side as we disappear beneath their shadows. I slow my speed as I maneuver through the narrow, winding roads that are only known by locals and even then are rarely taken...especially after the sun goes down.

This place is completely secluded. Which makes it the perfect place for us to elope.

A shiver shoots through me when I feel Scout's hands move lower, her arms clenching around me tighter as we move deeper into the forest. She must realize where we're going, or at least suspect...

"Is that...is that our old tree fort?" Scout asks as I put the bike in park.

"Yep. It was a toss-up between this or the graveyard, but I figured this way would be the most secluded." I climb off and remove my helmet before lifting her off, careful to keep her bare legs from accidentally brushing against the hot metal.

"Oh, thank you." She sounds nervous as I unbuckle her helmet and place it on her seat. My eyes search hers as we stand here waiting. I wish I knew what she was thinking.

She's the first to look away, her eyes dropping to her feet as she nervously fidgets with the bow in her hair, and there's something about it that feels like a victory. I fucking love that she's nervous right now, that I hold the fate of her future in my hands.

I reach out, straightening the bow. "Stop fidgeting. You look great."

The relief on her face almost makes me feel guilty—until I remember how pathetic that is.

When was the last time someone gave her a compliment? Christ, Scout, do you really have that little self-respect?

Now I'm more annoyed that she's set the bar so goddamn low.

"Come on. Let's get this over with," I say as I take her hand in mine and lead her through the tree line.

Our footsteps crunch through the silence as our old treehouse finally comes into view.

The massive hollowed-out trunk is split down the middle in an exaggerated V shape. One half leans against a nearby tree, its branches dead and mangled, while the other angles in the opposite direction—its limbs full of life and lush with green leaves.

A single strand of twinkling lights drapes across the tree's barren branches, while golden rays filter through the woods like soft brushstrokes on a canvas. Clustered patches of wildflowers—yellow, pink, and orange—peek through the tall grass, adding bursts of color that echo the setting of the sun.

It's a quiet kind of beauty. The kind that only exists in nature, appreciated only by those who slow down long enough to see it.

I hear the soft hitch in Scout's breath as she takes it all in. "Wow. I can't believe it's still half alive..."

"Or half dead..." I add with a shrug.

She rolls her eyes. "What a romantic mindset."

She turns to walk away, but I catch her arm and pull her back. "Don't get it twisted, princess. I never claimed to be romantic." I lean down, lowering my voice. "This is purely a revenge plan and nothing more. Got it?"

"Of course." She smiles sweetly, placing a hand on my jaw. "Fake as it may be, you could've at least ironed your shirt for your wedding day." Her eyes flick to my wrinkled collar, lips curling into a smug grin.

I release her arm and square my shoulders. "Well, since we're giving unsolicited advice... You've been walking around with a piece of spinach in your teeth all day."

Her mouth drops open, and she grabs for her phone, no doubt to check her reflection. I brush past her when I see Jett, arm in arm with Miss Scarlett, making their way toward us.

"Hey, thanks so much for doing this, especially on such short notice." I wrap my arms around Miss Scarlett.

"Oh, honey, it's my honor to be the one to marry you two." She plants a kiss on both of my cheeks, grinning ear to ear when she pulls away. "I'm a sucker for love, and a part of me always knew you two would end up together."

"I don't doubt it."

Jett just shakes his head, looking annoyed to have been dragged into this.

"Nice touch with the lights. You really went the extra mile," I say once Miss Scarlett's out of earshot.

"Don't flatter yourself. I grabbed them off the patio on the way out the door." He walks over to the hollow tree and pulls out a bouquet of fresh flowers. Another thoughtful gesture I never asked him to do. "You want this wedding to look believable, then you at least need to do the bare minimum."

He hands me the small bouquet, and for some reason, I feel a tightness in my chest when I realize how perfectly they complement Scout's sundress. It almost feels like an intentional choice, rather than a stroke of luck.

Jett's eyes narrow on me, and I realize I'm still staring at the flowers.

I clear my throat. "Thanks, man. Did you get the rings?"

He taps his pocket and nods. "Got them right here." He studies me for a moment, then finally asks, "You sure about this? You know this is going to get complicated as fuck, don't you?"

"Nah. It's going to be fine." I shake my head, my eyes trained on Scout, while Miss Scarlett removes her pearl necklace and claps it around Scout's neck.

It takes a moment to realize what they're doing before it dawns on me.

I jog over to them, placing the bouquet in Scout's hands. "Something blue." I nod toward the flowers, the pale blue hydrangeas peeking out between the light pink roses and bright yellow wildflowers.

Scout's eyes grow wide, bringing the flowers up to her nose to smell them. "Oh, Luka. These are beautiful."

"Yeah, they really are," I agree, but it's not the flowers I'm looking at.

"Why don't I give you two a moment of privacy," Miss Scarlett says before turning to take her position underneath the string lights.

I notice Scout's hair is neatly pulled back, the white lace bow in her hair freshly tied, and it looks like she's applied a fresh coat of lip gloss. There aren't many people who can make a simple sundress look like a wedding dress, but apparently, all Scout needed was a bouquet of flowers.

I can't help but feel a little flicker of pride knowing that after today, she's going to be all mine. Maybe just on paper, but mine, all the same.

I nudge her with my elbow. "You still good to go through with this?"

Her response comes on a soft breath. "Yeah... I think I am."

I clap my hands together. "All right then. Let's get married."

CHAPTER NINE

LUKA

Fucking hell. In a matter of seconds, the air turns dense, thick, and electric, like this moment is being branded into my memory whether I want it to or not.

It's like my soul already knows this is a turning point. That whatever happens next has the power to rewrite everything.

Good or bad, it doesn't matter. Both feel equally inevitable.

And they're both going to hurt like hell.

I ball my hands into fists by my side, trying to stop their trembling as I force my feet to stay glued in place.

My heart races in my chest, making my breath come out in shallow pants as I stand frozen in anticipation.

Miss Scarlett stands on my left and Jett on my right, and for a minute, I wish the rest of my family could be here, because I know this will be the only time I do this. My one and only wedding day, and perhaps the most important day of my life.

I can't imagine how Scout must be feeling.

For a moment, I feel a prickle of guilt rising in my chest at the thought of robbing her of her dream wedding. But then I think back to my first night in prison, how the only hope I had to cling to was that I saved Scout from the same fate. How the sacrifice I made for her would be worth it, because she had the freedom to finally live out her dreams—it's not like I felt she owed me. My decision wasn't made with a transaction in mind. But I did hope she'd do something with her life...not just throw it all away just to go along with whatever her parents wanted for her.

Three years of my life, wasted, and what do I have to show for it?

And that's all it takes for the guilt to subside. I feel my nerves begin to settle as I finally take a deep breath.

I hear music playing, the song, Iris by the Goo Goo Dolls, and it takes a moment for me to realize it's coming from Jett's phone.

Damn, I think he may have missed his calling as a wedding planner. I smile to myself from yet another considerate gesture.

But when Scout steps out from behind a tree looking like an angel sent to destroy me, it's all I can do to keep myself from falling to my knees.

Her brown hair hangs down her shoulders in loose waves, her soft yellow sundress fluttering around her knees, so graceful that I can't tell if she's walking or floating toward me.

She's so damn beautiful. There's nothing new about that,

but I feel like I can finally let my guard down and really see her for the first time.

There's an almost imperceivable smile pulling at her rosy lips as those big princess-looking eyes never leave mine.

Time seems to stand still, and any thought of revenge I was feeling is long gone as I feel my soul fully surrender to the moment.

And it's there, underneath that old treehouse, as the sun slowly disappears behind the horizon, streaking the sky in hues of orange and pink, that I feel my whole world shift on itself.

Miss Scarlett's voice pulls me back to the moment when Scout finally reaches me. "Dearly beloved. We are gathered here today to join together this man and this woman in holy matrimony.

"Marriage is a sacred bond, not to be entered into lightly, but reverently, deliberately, and with full understanding of its responsibilities..."

My thumbs move of their own accord, gently caressing her hands as I hold her gaze. There's so much history between us, so many words left unsaid, and yet, my brain can't come up with a single thought outside of this moment.

"Today, Luka and Scout stand before us to declare their love and commitment, and to pledge their lives to one another..." Miss Scarlett continues, and I feel the irony of her words like shackles around my limbs.

"Do you have the rings?" she asks, and Jett pulls the velvet ring box from his pocket and passes it to me.

I open the box, removing the rings before passing it back to Jett, not missing the look of surprise that flashes across Scout's face when she sees the large solitaire diamond ring.

The stone is large enough, considering the tight timeline, and it's set on a simple, classic gold band with another band wrapped in pavé diamonds.

"Repeat after me. I, Luka, take you, Scout, to be my lawfully wedded wife..."

I hold the ring in front of her finger, my eyes locked on hers as I vow to love her, protect her, and cherish her—in good times and bad, in sickness and in health.

The words come easily but they settle deep. A promise that ties us together, whether we realize it or not.

Because even a dirty contract is still legally binding.

Scout's eyes glisten with tears as she repeats the same vows. She's good at this.

I'd almost think they were real...if I didn't know better.

"With the power vested in me by the state of West Virginia and the Universal Church of Life," Miss Scarlett grins, holding out her hands. "I pronounce you husband and wife. You may now kiss your bride."

Miss Scarlett's voice cracks through the air like a whip, snapping us both back to reality. And it's only then that I realize we never discussed our first kiss.

Before I can second-guess it, instinct takes over.

I reach for her, hand curling around the back of her neck as I draw her in. My lips graze the corner of her mouth in a painfully torturous, almost-kiss that sets my whole body on fire.

Everything in me screams to keep going, to slide my tongue along her plush bottom lip, to see if she still tastes the way I remember. Just once. Because if it's ever going to not count, it's right now.

But I can't do it. Not like this.

When I finally pull back, I'm relieved to see that she looks just as wrecked as I feel. Pupils blown, chest rising with a sharp inhale like she forgot how to breathe.

A high-pitched ringing fills my ears as I wait for my pulse to slow. We both just stare at each other, neither fully grasping the line that's just been drawn in the sand.

I may not know what this means.

But there's one thing for sure...

For better or for worse, my life will never be the same.

———

The crystal rock glass dangles from my fingers as I nurse my Jack and Coke, contemplating everything that happened tonight. After the wedding, we plastered on our most convincing fake smiles and thanked Miss Scarlett for performing the ceremony. Then we rode home without speaking a single word.

As tempting as it was to go our separate ways tonight, to decompress privately, I could tell Scout was starting to spiral. Her guilty conscience was already eating at her, and the last thing I want is for all of this to be for nothing because she can't handle the pressure.

So, against my better judgment, I proposed we celebrate our nuptials over a couple of stiff drinks while we figure out our next steps...

But I may have overestimated her ability to hold her liquor because she's three drinks in, and it's clear that there will be no planning for our future happening tonight.

Scout looks almost unrecognizable sitting with her legs curled in her seat. She either hasn't noticed or doesn't mind that her dress has ridden up. My eyes keep catching on the soft flesh of her upper thigh, which does nothing to calm the multitude of indecent thoughts flooding through my mind right now.

Maybe it's the alcohol or those stupid wedding vows, but I can't help but feel like something activated the caveman part of my brain tonight. It's like a switch has been flipped, and I can't shut it off, no matter how hard I try.

I keep finding myself sneaking glances, my mind wandering to places it has no business entertaining... And yet, here I sit, against my better judgment, pouring myself another glass.

Scout still hasn't spoken much, apart from asking for a refill as soon as her glass was empty. And each time, I happily oblige.

This would be the moment that a better person would cut her off, before she gets too sloppy and says or does something she'll regret.

Too bad for Scout, I'm not the good guy I used to be.

Besides, if I'm not getting laid on my wedding night, then I may as well enjoy watching Scout come completely unraveled. A man's got to entertain himself somehow.

I watch as she tosses her drink back and wipes her mouth with the back of her hand. Then she finally breaks the silence. "You know, this wasn't how my wedding night was supposed to go."

Here we go. Looks like the show is about the begin.

I cross a foot over my knee and settle deeper in my seat. "Oh, really? I'm sorry to disappoint you." I gesture for her to continue. "Exactly what were you expecting?"

She either misses the mockery in my tone or chooses to

ignore it completely. Judging by the way her head's hanging over the side of the chair...I think it's safe to say her inhibitions are no longer with us.

"Well, obviously, I thought I would be having sex on my wedding night," she blurts out with a sigh as she spins in the chair so that her legs are propped against the back and her head dangles off the front.

I cover my mouth to hide my smile, not wanting her to get embarrassed and realize how she looks right now. "Yeah, I suppose you're right about that. You could be getting ravished by ol' Jimbo right now, having the best five minutes of missionary sex of your life—"

She blows a raspberry with her lips before falling into a fit of laughter. She's laughing so hard, I'm afraid she's going to crack her head on the coffee table, so I hold my hand as a shield until she calms down.

She wipes a tear from her eye as her giggles fizzle out. "You're funny."

I chew on the inside of my cheek, feeling torn between wanting to ask her exactly what part she found so amusing. I realize I'm treading in dangerous territory here.

"I'm glad you find me amusing." I swirl my drink, settling back into my seat. "So...your wedding night...was that something you thought about a lot?"

The flush of her cheeks should be answer enough, but I sit there in silence as I wait for her to answer.

"I mean...yeah...sort of, I guess." She covers her face with her hands, looking so fucking cute as she blushes. "I guess I've always thought once I was married, I'd finally feel more of a desire to...you know—"

Somehow that explanation leaves me with more

questions than answers. I narrow my eyes. "I'm not sure I'm following..."

I drag a hand down my face and breathe a heavy sigh. I don't know why I keep torturing myself by prying further. But there's something so fucking hot about making her admit it out loud. About how difficult I know this is for her, and yet, she's still answering simply because I asked the question.

"Ugh, this is so embarrassing!" She grunts, her hands still covering her face as she peeks at me between her fingers.

She accidentally flashes me a peek of her panties when she flips back upright in the chair. I wish I could say that I looked away, but the disappointment I feel when she tugs her dress back down has me holding my breath, waiting for her next movement in hope of another glimpse.

"You know, like the desire people feel in the romance novels." She continues, "Maybe it sounds dumb, but I've never believed it was real. I mean, I've certainly never felt that way before."

I hear warning bells, blaring through my ears, begging me to stop this conversation before it goes any further. But I'm too invested now. I find myself leaning closer, my cock growing painfully hard behind the zipper of my pants as I hang on to her every word.

"And I guess, I just thought that being married and finally not having the guilt behind having sex, would actually make me want to..."

"I'm sorry, but what the actual fuck?" I blurt before she says anything else to make this pathetic confession of hers any worse. "What kind of mental gymnastics did you have to do to come up with that theory?"

She stares back at me blinking, like she can't figure out where my sudden mood shift came from.

Heat shoots through me as the arousal I was just feeling moments ago morphs into irritation.

Needing to distract myself, I spring to my feet and begin to pace. I decide I've had enough mind-altering substances for one evening, so I make a quick trip to the kitchen, returning with a couple of bottles of water.

This time, there's a bite in my tone as I pass her the bottle of water. "Do you really believe that? Or is that what you had to tell yourself to stay with him?"

Her eyes narrow as she takes the water, but she doesn't drink it, just sets it down on the coffee table. "You don't have to be mean about it. I'm not sure you're aware of this, but there's no reward for being horny, Luka."

I have to bite my cheek to keep from laughing in her face at the ridiculous jump she just made. Looks like Jimmy may have done her a bigger favor than I thought, if that's the best argument she can come up with to defend herself.

I know I should just drop it, but I'm starting to enjoy seeing this side of her. I wonder just how far I can push her before she cracks.

"That's too bad because that's a competition I would dominate in." I flash her a wink, and she lets out a huff before uncapping her water and taking a long drink.

My eyes narrow in on her throat as she swallows.

"Aren't you full of yourself." She rolls her eyes, crossing her arms over her chest. "And I'm sure all the women you sleep with would say the same thing."

"Obviously," I answer immediately. "The least I can do is

make sure the person I'm fucking leaves feeling satisfied—a few times at the very least."

"Yeah, right. Now I know you're full of shit." She waves me off as she gets up to refill her drink rather than asking me to.

At that, I nearly choke on my water. "What's that supposed to mean?"

She eyes me for a moment, then finally says, "It means that either you're lying to yourself or you're only sleeping with actresses. No woman's really out there having multiple orgasms."

My mouth drops open as I stare at her, waiting for her to tell me she's kidding, but when she doesn't say anything else, I realize she isn't joking about this. She truly believes it.

Fucking hell.

Of all the things she could've said, she had to admit that? How the fuck am I supposed to be around her after she's just tossed a challenge like that right in front of me?

Jesus Christ, the lengths I would go to prove to her just how wrong she is.

I blow out a heavy sigh, wishing I could rewind time and go back to a couple of minutes ago, before I knew just how pathetic her sex life actually is. "Tell me this," I say as I scoot closer. "Has Jimmy ever made you orgasm?"

She scoffs a laugh, but she sounds more nervous than annoyed. "That is a wildly inappropriate question, not to mention it's absolutely none of your business."

"I'm going to take that as a *no*," I say without missing a beat. "And as your husband, I think your lack of sexual satisfaction is absolutely my business." I sit back in my seat, propping an arm on the back of the sofa. "Especially when it's clear how sexually frustrated all this is making you."

This time, her eyes go wide, and she swallows a gulp. And there's no denying the look of fear that flashes over her face. It's only there for a moment, but it's all I need to confirm everything I've already suspected.

"I am not sexually frustrated." Her tone is clipped and knowing I'm getting under her skin gives me the rush I've been craving ever since I started teasing her. I breathe a sigh of relief, feeling myself slowly regain control.

I flash her a smirk in challenge. "Look, Girl Scout, I'm not trying to shame you—I'm simply trying to help." I lean closer and whisper, "The first step is admitting you have a problem."

She rolls her eyes. Once again, she tips her empty glass and sucks a piece of ice into her mouth. "You are such a cocky jerk."

I hold my hands up in surrender. "No need to get defensive." My eyes zero in on the ice cube she's sucking on, making my cock grow even harder. "It's embarrassing, I get it. I just want you to know that if you're not getting your needs met, there are plenty of ways to help."

She stalks toward me, the alcohol, no doubt, fueling her confidence as she pokes me hard in the chest, then shakes her finger out like it hurts. "You're insufferably annoying. Do you know that?"

There she is. There's the girl I remember.

Maybe there's hope for her after all?

A pissed off Scout is about as terrifying as a feral kitten, hissing with her fur all fluffed up.

"I've been told once or twice." I can't help the grin that

spreads across my face as I flick my eyes down to her. "But if I'm annoying you so badly, then why are you practically sitting in my lap?"

Her mouth drops open, forming a perfect O as she registers what I've just said, then she quickly snaps it shut.

She starts to scoot to the other side of the couch, but I slide my hand behind the back of her thigh, causing her to suck in a sharp breath. She goes completely still. "Whoa, what's wrong?" I say in a whisper. "Did I hit a nerve?"

Her nose scrunches up as her face morphs into the cutest, most annoyed expression. "No, I don't want to talk about it. I'm trying to end this conversation, but you keep bringing it up!"

I make an exaggerated show of propping my hands behind my head. "Like I said, it sounds like sexual frustration to me."

"I am not sexually frustrated; now, can we please move on?"

"You know, I hear the words you're saying, but your body language is telling me something different." To my utter delight, not only did she not retreat but somehow shifted closer. Her velvety soft skin looks absolutely fuckable as her little yellow sun dress rides higher up her thighs. I feel like every bit the criminal I've been labeled as, as I steal every glimpse I can.

"Oh, so you're a body language expert now? Please tell me, Luka, what is my body telling you? I'd love to know," she huffs out, her breath's coming out strained.

Biting my lip, I drag my eyes from her flushed cheeks, down her neck, lingering on her chest.

"Judging by the flush of your cheeks, the change in your

breathing…and the fact you're practically in my lap," I say, grabbing her arm before she can scoot away. She lets out a small yelp but doesn't brush me off. "I don't think you're annoyed at all. In fact, I think this whole conversation has you more turned on than you know what to do with."

She sucks in a breath, her body going completely still as I tuck a strand of fallen hair behind her ear.

"Am I wrong? Tell me, if I reached between your legs right now, how wet would your pussy be?" In one swift motion, I tug her onto my lap. Her eyes go wide when she shifts her weight, and no doubt feels the outline of my achingly hard cock.

I keep my eyes trained on hers, silently daring her to look away. "You've got all this pent-up frustration buzzing beneath your skin, begging to be released. But you're too afraid to let it out."

"No, I don't…" She starts to argue, but the subtle roll of her hips tells me a different story.

Fuck she feels so perfect.

"Tell me this, when was the last time you got yourself off?" I ask the question that's been burning in the back of my mind ever since we sat down.

"I… I'm not sure."

"How are you unsure? When was the last time you came, Scout?" I feel my heart rate begin to pick up as that burning desire inside of me starts to grow hotter.

She shakes her head. "I don't know, I didn't write it down."

"Give me a ballpark estimation," my voice comes out more desperate than I'd like, but I'm hanging on by a thread here.

"That's not exactly something at the forefront of my mind, like it apparently is for you. Girls don't need that the way guys do."

"How long, Scout?"

Silence stretches between us, and her eyes drop as she chews on the inside of her lip. Her breath is barely more than a whisper when she says, "I think my body's broken or something..."

The anger that burns in my chest only ignites more heat in my steadily growing arousal. Scout has no idea what she's doing to me with these confessions. How am I supposed to resist?

I tilt her chin up, brushing my thumb over her plump bottom lip as I meet her trusting gaze. "Do you know what I think?"

"What?"

"I don't even think you believe the bullshit you just told me." My tone is soft, but my words are sharp, and it takes a couple of seconds before Scout's tipsy brain registers them before she flinches.

"What's that supposed to mean?"

My hand is still on her jaw as I deepen my hold, my fingers slowly caressing as I cradle her thin neck. "It means you're full of shit and you'd rather gaslight yourself and try to make yourself believe that than face the truth. That maybe the things that excite you aren't the type of things good girls like you should want."

She swallows a gulp, and I can see the immense amount of effort it takes for her not to recoil beneath my touch, but despite the heaviness of her pulse, she doesn't look away.

There's something in the way that she looks up at me, a

truth that flares in her eyes that tells me I hit the nail on the head with my assumption. I'd only meant to taunt her, to embarrass her a little. I knew she was naive, but I had no idea just how accurate my suspicions really were.

"If you must know... It's not just..."

Suddenly, I find myself desperate to stop her before she gives my traitorous mind any more material to work with. I shake my head, my finger pressing against her lip to silence her. "Shh. Please don't finish that sentence."

The next thing I know, I'm standing, lifting her up right along with me and carrying her back to her room. "I think you've had enough excitement for one night."

I put her on her bed, then drop to my knees to remove her shoes. I wish I were strong enough to help her into her pajamas, but that last almost confession has me so pent up it's taking everything I have to keep my mind out of the gutter.

"Good night, Scout," I say as I close the door and make a beeline straight to the shower. My hand is already on my cock before the water turns warm.

CHAPTER TEN

SCOUT

Thump. Thump. Thump.

My head pounds like a snare drum, each new heartbeat interrupting the last until I can no longer decipher a beat, just painfully chaotic noise. I sneak open an eyelid and wince as the bright morning sun slices through the cracks of the window shade, stabbing my eyeballs like scalding hot needles. I throw an arm over my face to block it out.

A wave of nausea churns in my belly at the sudden movement, reminding me of last night's poor choices. How much did I drink? Have I died and gone to hell? It's the only explanation for the absolute misery I'm feeling, both physically and mentally.

A flash of Luka standing beneath our old tree house in that wrinkled white shirt and black motorcycle pants—hits me like a sucker punch. The look on his face when he saw me walking toward him; he actually looked happy.

I can't believe we got married.

And just like that, the memories of last night come rushing back, bursting through me like a broken dam.

God, I wish this mattress would swallow me whole.

My nervous system does a quick roll call: shame, embarrassment, humiliation. Perfect. The gang's all here. Oh, good, I wouldn't want to face eternity without the company of my constant companions.

Thump. Thump. Thump.

I let out a groan, attempting to smother myself with my pillow just as the door creaks open and aggressively loud rock music pours into the room. I sit up in a rush, grabbing my glasses off my side table as the blurry room comes into view.

My suspicions are confirmed when my eyes fall on Luka, grinning like the devil he is, standing over me.

"Good morning, wifey. How ya feeling?" His arms are full, holding an extra-large bottle of water, two cups of coffee, and a small paper bag.

I hate that my stomach flips at his term of endearment. "What are you? What time is it?" I scurry away until my back hits the headboard and it's only then I realize I'm still wearing my dress from yesterday...

Luka just laughs as he takes a seat on the bed and places the cups and bag on the nightstand. "It's eight thirty. I thought you might need a little pick-me-up."

Translation: You got pretty trashed last night all by yourself, and it was so pitiful that—although I hate you—I still felt bad enough to bring you coffee.

He pulls a bottle of water out of the bag, opens it, then hands it to me before placing two white pills in my palm. I blink at him in confusion wondering if he also remembers anything I said last night, and if so, why is he acting as if nothing happened?

"It's Tylenol. I thought you may have a headache." He opens the paper bag and pulls out an everything bagel, my favorite, and my mouth waters at the delicious aroma.

Without a word, I throw back the medicine and chug half the bottle of water before I take the bagel. It isn't very often that the universe sends you exactly what you need, so I'll take the handout whenever I can get it, even if it comes hand delivered by Satan.

I cover my mouth as I chew. "Listen, Luka, I'm really sorry you had to see me like that. I don't normally drink—"

"You don't have anything to apologize for. We were celebrating. Besides, it was nice seeing you finally loosen up." He nudges me with his shoulder playfully, his green eyes sparkling as he watches me devour my bagel.

Okay, so maybe I didn't overshare as much as I thought? He certainly doesn't seem freaked out... If anything, he's being nicer than ever.

"Breakfast in bed? You trying to poison me already?" I say between mouthfuls. My mother would have a heart attack if she were here to see me talking with my mouth full or eating an entire bagel, for that matter. Maybe Luka is rubbing off on me more than I realized?

Luka rolls his eyes and laughs. "Nah, I'd at least take out a life insurance policy on you before I killed you off." He scratches his neck, looking almost nervous. "I was already out, and there's no hangover cure better than Lucy's bagels."

I'm swallowing the last bite of my bagel when he grabs the cups off the side table. "Chai tea or Americano with cinnamon?"

I'm taken aback at the gesture. I can't remember the last time anyone brought me anything without my having to ask, and here he is offering me choices.

Luka lifts each cup in silent question.

"Chai," I finally say, and he passes me the cup in his left hand, slowly taking a sip of the other.

"That's what I thought you'd pick, but I didn't want to wrongly assume."

I take a small sip and let out a quiet moan as the rich flavors hit my tongue. God, it's good. I haven't had a chai latte this perfect in years. Nobody does it like Hazel. She once told me her secret was making every drink with love, and honestly, I'm starting to believe her.

Luka clears his throat. "So... I was thinking after breakfast we could go for a ride. There's something I want to show you."

My brows pull together, but before I can ask what he's up to, he adds, "Think you can be ready in an hour?"

He gives my leg a playful slap before hopping off the bed. "I found some of your old clothes in a box in the attic. I'm sure they still fit and will be much more comfortable than all that prudish shit you packed."

"Thank you for offering, but there's nothing wrong with my clothes. I'll make do with—"

"It wasn't a question." He cuts in before I can finish. And as I want to fight him on it, I don't have the energy. Besides, breathable fabric doesn't sound like the worst idea in this heat.

He must be pleased by my lack of protest, because now he's wearing a smug-ass smile as he pulls out his phone. "I'll meet you outside in fifty-five minutes."

I stare at my reflection one last time as I tug at the hem of my black cutoff denim shorts, feeling like I'm no more covered than if I were wearing a bikini. I know that's dramatic, but these shorts really aren't that short; they're a bit tighter in the hips than they used to be.

That's exactly why we don't eat bagels for breakfast, Scout. Too many curves make a woman look easy. I hear my mother's patronizing voice reminding me.

She hated these shorts, but they were always my favorite—probably because they're the only pair of cutoff denim shorts I have ever owned. I can't believe Luka found them in the attic.

The bright pink cropped band tee is modest enough, as long as I don't lift my arms. I remember the night I got it—Luka actually bought it for me. We'd snuck off to a concert a couple of towns over after Jett managed to get us VIP tickets during Spring Break. It was the best concert I've ever seen. In fact, it was our last one. We stayed out until two in the morning. Luka had paid Guy to sneak into my bedroom and pretend to be me if my parents happened to check. Guy was fully committed to the task—he wore a wig and everything.

That was our thing. We may have had different interests; he enjoyed playing video games and talking sports with his brothers, while I was happy as long as I had a paintbrush in my hand. But music was always something we could agree on, especially live music.

My parents would freak to know that only about half of the Girl Scout volunteer hours I racked up during my junior and senior years were real. Good thing I was such an overachiever, I still managed to graduate with plenty to spare.

My heart hiccups in my chest as all those suppressed memories come rushing to the surface, and it's almost more painful than it is comforting. How did I go from this girl, who seemed so sure of herself and what she wanted, to the dull, lifeless woman who's spent the last eight years trying to blend in? Luka's right, I am a sellout.

My existential crisis is interrupted by the sound of a horn honking, and I've never been so grateful for Luka's lack of manners. I slide my slip-on checked Vans on my feet as I rush out the door, stopping in my tracks at the sight of Luka leaning against his bike with his arms crossed over his chest.

He's wearing faded black cutoff jorts that should look ridiculous but somehow look hot as hell with his black boots and faded black graphic t-shirt. His emerald, green eyes sparkle back at me, and he makes no effort to hide his obvious perusal of my body.

"It's about time." He wets his lips as his eyes roam down over my exposed legs, lingering a little longer than seems appropriate. "Clothes look like they still fit. Don't you feel better?"

I roll my eyes, choosing to ignore his rhetorical question. He may be right, but he's never going to make me admit it out loud. When I reach for the spare helmet, Luka jerks it away, then slides the heavy helmet over my head himself. I try to buckle the chin strap, but he smacks my hands away before slapping the front glass closed.

When he's finally satisfied with all my gear, he climbs on the bike and gestures for me to follow suit.

And despite everything inside of me screaming that this

is dangerous, I can't help the excitement bubbling inside of me. When I reach around and grab his waist, I swear I feel him shiver before he takes off down the winding country road.

Luka revs the bike forward, and I let out a squeal as I feel myself begin to slip.

"Hold on, Girl Scout. I won't be taking it easy on you this time." I can practically hear the smile in Luka's voice as he speaks to me through the speaker in my helmet, and I hate the way my stomach does a somersault because of it.

It's just the speakers, a natural bodily reaction to ASMR, not to mention the adrenaline rush. That's why my heart's racing so fast right now. It's got nothing to do with the fact that I'm pressed flush against Luka's strong back or that my arms are linked tightly around his impeccable abs.

I think back to our conversation last night—the giddy feeling in my stomach as he teased me—the way his expression shifted, as if my confession made him angry for me. I'd be lying if I said I hadn't wondered what it'd be like to spend a *real* wedding night with Luka.

The thought is insane, and I shake it away the second it surfaces. I don't know what's happening to me but being around Luka seems to have stirred something awake inside me, something that's been dormant for the past twenty-five years.

It scares me, if I'm honest. But despite being the good girl who's always played it safe, for the first time... I find myself wanting to stop fighting it. I want to lean into the chaos. To push the boundaries and finally let go of control.

Sunlight streaks behind the mountains as we make our way to the densely wooded forest of Phantom's Reach. The road doesn't cut through the deepest part of the forest—there's no way our Phantom would ever allow that—but you can still feel the eerie energy as we drive around the edge.

I feel Luka's hand move to my thigh just as he makes a sharp turn, lighting my whole body in a blaze. I grip his chest tighter as we lean in tandem, but once we're on a straightaway, he doesn't move his hand. It's as if every nerve in my body is connected to my upper thigh, and I am keenly aware of his hand placement.

I have to remind myself that Luka, at worst, hates me and, at best, pities me. I don't think we've even reached the friend category. The man married me just to get back at my father, and now he's just trying to make sure I don't die on the back of his motorcycle. I need to chill out and touch some grass.

When the smooth asphalt gives way to bumpy cobblestone, I can't help but smile. I'd know this road by feel alone, even if I were blindfolded.

Welcome to Ashford Falls, home of the Phantom Festival.

I suck in a breath as the warm summer air caresses my skin, its healing embrace making me feel so safe and protected, like a small child wrapped in a warm blanket fresh out of the dryer. The smell of freshly cut grass fills the air as we pass the small downtown park that still looks exactly the same as I remember. And just like that, I'm transported back in time to when I was nine years old, playing tag with my best friend and the rest of our rough and tumble crew.

So many memories—everything I once hoped to become. The seeds of my dreams were planted here, nurtured by the community of people I've come to miss so much.

I take in all the tiny upgrades I didn't notice before, the new ornate streetlights and the shiny new bench in the courtyard by the Phantom's statue. It's so beautiful, they've managed to preserve the historic charm and bring it back to life.

We roll to a stop. I can't help but feel disappointed when Luka's hand disappears from my thigh. He gestures to the brick building. "Here we are."

I glance around, confused. "What exactly am I looking at?"

"I've been thinking about the festival," he says, nodding toward the back of Coffee Shop, Book Store, and Bakery. "And I think I finally figured out what we can do to stand out."

He gestures broadly. "I was thinking our downtown could use a little spicing up..."

Then, without warning, he jerks the bike around a corner, cutting through a narrow alleyway that's definitely not street legal, and pops out on the other side of the square.

He brings us to a stop and takes off his helmet as he points to the familiar exposed brick wall. "I was thinking this would be the perfect spot for a giant mural of the Phantom."

I shake my head. "Hang on, I think I may still be drunk. Did you just say you want me to paint a mural? *Here?*"

"Yes."

I blink at him. "You're asking me to paint a mural on Restaurant. The historic building that your brother loves more than anything. After you served jail time for doing just that?"

He nods, a wicked grin spreading over his lips. "Exactly."

"Have you lost your mind?" I shake my head. "Luka, I can't do that."

"Look, Scout, I really hate to bring this up right now..."

He clicks his tongue, idly spinning the ring on his finger. "But you kind of owe me."

I feel all the air deflating from my chest. Of course. I should've known he'd use this against me.

His smile grows wider, and he knows he's got me. "I think it's rather poetic. Don't you?"

I roll my eyes and blow out a breath. "Yeah, looks like we've come full circle."

CHAPTER ELEVEN

SCOUT

The sound of my phone buzzing incessantly on my bedside table stirs me awake, and I blink open my sleepy eyes. I roll over and groan when I see the time. I can't remember the last time I slept this late.

Damn Luka and his stupid smart home. Between the blackout shades on the windows and this bed that feels like I'm sleeping on literal clouds, I feel more refreshed than I have in years. No wonder he walks around seeming so carefree if he's sleeping like this every night.

And they say money can't buy happiness...

I hear my phone buzzing again, the annoying rattling pulling me back down to reality, and I have to brace myself before I flip it over.

Judging by the dozens of missed calls and texts from my parents and Jimmy, I think it's safe to assume our little marital secret has finally gotten out.

Honestly, I'm surprised Miss Scarlett managed to hold it in for a solid twenty-four hours. Seems like a new record.

I blow out a breath as I swipe open my messages and slowly begin to take it all in.

> **DAD**
>
> Please tell me the rumor I heard this morning isn't true.
>
> Why aren't you answering your phone? Call me back ASAP!
>
> What the hell were you thinking!?
>
> Do you have any idea of the shit storm I'm dealing with right now? Of all the people to choose from, you really had to pick the convicted criminal?
>
> I'm disgusted with you. I hope this little defiant act of yours was worth it, because I doubt Jimmy's going to want anything to do with you now.

> **MOM**
>
> After everything we've done for you. I can't believe you'd pull something like this.
>
> I hope you at least had the decency not to consummate this sham of a marriage… There are some things that simply cannot be undone.

> **JIMMY**
>
> Cheating whore
>
> I knew that good girl shit was all an act.

I wince as I place the phone back down. It's not that I was expecting congratulations or anything, but it's even worse than I thought.

I guess I never realized just how fickle their love for me really was. I never had the courage to stand up to them before now. Nothing like finding out that the people who are supposed to love you the most can so easily flip that switch.

I blow out a sigh, burying my face in my hands as I try to process this mess I've gotten myself into, keenly aware of the giant diamond ring on my finger. I hate that I love it so much. It's simple with a large oval stone set on a thin gold band. It's exactly what I would've chosen myself—nothing like the white gold princess cut engagement ring Jimmy gave me.

Is it a coincidence? Or did Luka actually remember?

I scoff at that ridiculous question, remembering Jett was in charge of picking up the rings. Of course, Luka didn't remember. Hell, if he had, he'd have probably gone in the opposite direction just to make sure I didn't confuse his favor for anything more than it is. A favor.

That I should've known he'd cash in the first chance he got.

Of course he wants me to paint a mural in the middle of town. As if that's what I need to be doing with my time right now. Not to mention, my parents are going to freak when word gets back to them about that.

All those years spent preparing me for law school—to follow in my father's footsteps and fulfill the Sinclair family's legacy—were wasted to pursue street art.

If finding out Luka and I eloped doesn't give my father a heart attack, seeing me painting a mural in the middle of town surely will.

Maybe that should make me happy, but unlike what my parents may think, I'm not trying to upset them... Not entirely, anyway.

All I want—all I've ever wanted—is for them to see me for who I really am and want me to do whatever makes me happy.

What I didn't realize is that, apparently, happiness is a scarce resource. There's only so much to go around. Is it selfish of me to want that? Even if it means I'm hurting them?

I feel my phone buzz in my hand with another text. This time it's from Luka.

LUKA

I had to run out to help Roman with something, so I'll be out most of the day.

I've been informed that we're expected at my parents' house tonight for family dinner. Be ready by 6.

Great. If that's not just the most impeccable timing. As if I wasn't freaking out enough on my own, now I have to face Luka's family, whom I haven't seen since graduation night.

Do they know the truth about what happened? Do they still hate me?

I wouldn't blame them if they did. Hell, it's not like I don't hate myself for letting Luka take the fall for me. Why is it that when I need help, Luka's the one who steps up to the plate, consequences be damned? And why now? After all this time? Was it really just a coincidence, or is this all a bigger plan to leverage something from me? What is he hiding?

I bite my lip, considering my options. I have the house to myself for a few more hours. Maybe it wouldn't hurt to do a little investigating, just to cover my bases. Besides, if he didn't want me to snoop, then he shouldn't have left me alone.

Before I can talk myself out of it, I'm already out the door, making a beeline for the stairs.

"Good afternoon, Miss Scout. Is there something I can help you with?"

The AI's voice cuts through the silence, and I freeze mid-step.

Damn. How could I forget about the stupid house being alive?

I try to think of a convincing lie. "Oh, um... Luka texted and asked me to look for something for him."

There. That's believable enough. A logical, entirely probable explanation.

A few moments pass, and I feel myself begin to relax. I can't believe it was that easy.

"Hmm... One second... I just need to ask Mr. Luka to veri—"

"Wait!" I blurt, panicking. "You don't need to do that. I wouldn't want to bother him."

The last thing I need is for Luka to trust me even less than he already does. He's already leveraging his power over me by making me paint this mural in town. I don't need to add any more fuel to the fire.

"Mr. Luka has given me strict instructions that he has made himself available for anything you should need. I'll just call him really quick."

"Name your price!" I plead, but then I hear a loud ringing fill the silence. "What'll it take to get you to let me go up there?"

"Are you bribing me to compromise my orders in

exchange for a favor?" L.O.K.I. asks as soon as the ringing stops, and Luka picks up.

"What's up, L.O.K.I.?" he asks, his voice barely distinguishable amid the background chatter.

Eyes wide, I make a pleading gesture with my hands.

"Good afternoon, Mr. Luka..." L.O.K.I. pauses for a moment, and I'm sure he's about to rat me out, but then he says, "I just wanted to let you know that the squirrels have infiltrated the attic again."

"Seriously, L.O.K.I. You interrupted me just now to update me about squirrels getting into the attic?" Luka sounds annoyed, and I don't know where he is, but it sounds like he's in the middle of something.

"Yes. It's important to stay on top of these things. The threat of rabies isn't something that should be taken lightly."

Luka huffs out a sigh. "Well, thanks for staying on top of that." From the sounds of it, this isn't the first time L.O.K.I.'s called him during the day with a similar update. "Why don't you call an exterminator and take care of that for me?"

"Great idea, Mr. Luka." L.O.K.I. agrees.

"Yeah... Well, if there's not anything else you need..."

"That's it. Sorry to bother you," L.O.K.I. says, and then the line goes silent.

"Thank you, L.O.K.I.—"

"I want you to watch the Avengers movies with me. All of them," he says before I can finish.

I don't know what I was expecting him to say but watching TV with him seems like a pretty reasonable request. I'm not exactly sure how that works, but I love watching movies, and if that's what it takes for him to let me go upstairs... "Um... yeah... I can do that." I say as confidently as I can muster.

"Wonderful. Consider this our little secret. I'll see you for the Iron Man showing tonight."

With L.O.K.I's permission, I take off upstairs. My feet thud against the hardwood floors as I charge down the hall, pausing when I'm met with the door of my childhood bedroom.

I suck in a breath as I gently turn the crystal knob, but rather than spinning freely, it sticks with resistance. It's locked.

My shoulders sag with disappointment, and I decide it's probably for the best. A girl can only take so much heartbreak in one day. I'd rather keep my memories intact.

Remembering what I'm really up here for, I spin around and see a cracked door. This used to be an extra bedroom. The master is at the opposite end of the hall, so I assume this must be Luka's office.

Carefully, I tiptoe down the hall, gently pressing the cracked door open as I slide inside.

The room is dark, despite the afternoon sun shining brightly outside, and a large mahogany desk sits in the center across from a wall of bookshelves filled with books. Furniture fills every inch of the space but not in an overly crowded way.

There's a tint on the windows, which I'm guessing is the reason it's so dark in here, with a view that overlooks the spooky forest I was always obsessed with as a kid. The stories of the monsters that lived in the forest never scared me. I was just a child the first time I heard the stories—they were no doubt intended to scare us from setting foot in the forest, but they only made me more curious.

As I grew older, I found that I felt more connected to them than anything else. I've always felt a connection to Phantom's Reach, maybe because I knew what it felt like to be misunderstood. I used to sneak in here and try to paint the spooky trees, hiding the words I never felt safe to say in their shadows.

But then my mother found my paintings, and it wasn't a surprise that she didn't share the same sentiments. She had a lock installed on the door the very next day, and I came home to discover she'd thrown away all my art supplies, too.

The sad memory aches like a bruise on my heart that my fingers long to press, if only to remember it was real. I close my eyes, pushing the memory to the back of my mind where I can revisit it again rather than wiping it away.

Ready to get back to my search, I spin around, letting my gaze drift over the massive desk in the center of the room. There's a notepad laid out with a checklist that's almost fully checked off. I pick it up, trying to make out Luka's scribbled handwriting.

- ~~MAKE DONATION FOR THEATER RENO...~~
- CROSS-REFERENCE IVY'S VENDOR LIST WITH CONFIRMED RETURNING VENDORS
- ~~FINALIZE DATABASE REDESIGN FOR CRIMINAL OUTREACH SERVICES PROJECT~~
- ~~FOLLOW UP ON GIRL SCOUTS SPONSORSHIP FUND~~
- MAKE TOWN MEETING ITINERARY

I don't have time to analyze what I'm reading before the heavy thud of footsteps climbing the stairs startles me, and I drop the list. The sudden sense of dread washes over me as the thuds grow louder, telling me he's coming this way.

"Oh shit." I slap a hand over my mouth as my eyes dart around the room, looking for somewhere to hide.

Panic like I've never felt courses through me, and I dive behind the armchair in the corner just as the door creaks open...

My heart beats like a snare drum, the pounding in my ears is so loud I'm surprised it hasn't given me away. My breaths are shallow as I try to keep as still as possible.

I watch him fall into his desk chair, already loosening his tie as he lets out a heavy sigh. He looks like he's stressed about something, and I find myself wondering what on earth there is for him to be stressed about. He's not the one who's just had his whole world ripped out from underneath him. He's got a freaking AI assistant at his every beck and call for Christ's sake.

My conscience takes that opportunity to remind me that I'm not exactly in a position to be judging anyone. Besides, considering the checklist I just discovered on his desk, I guess it's safe to say there are a lot of things I don't know about Luka Kingsley.

Touché.

I swallow a gulp as I let myself drink in the stolen glances, suddenly all too aware of just how attractive this man is. Has he always been this insanely good-looking? Did I really not see it back then, or did I become desensitized from watching him grow up before my eyes?

It's not that I was completely oblivious... I had a crush on him for as long as I can remember, but I guess I was always too shy to admit it. And it's not like he ever seemed interested in being anything other than friends. Not until graduation night anyway...

I press my fingers against my lips, as the memory of that kiss burns against my skin, my body responding like it happened just moments ago rather than years... The sensations only grow stronger when he begins rolling up the sleeves of his shirt. I feel my stomach do a somersault.

Ok, this is fine. All I have to do is wait for him to get up and go to the bathroom, and then I'll make my escape. He'll never even know I was here. I wipe my sweaty palms against my t-shirt as my anxiety skyrockets, making my heart race even faster. There's a worried anticipation brewing beneath the surface, which is probably the cause for all my mixed-up emotions right now. I keep waiting, halfway expecting L.O.K.I. to rat me out any second. Like I'm staring at a jack in the box waiting for it to pop out...

Luka rustles some papers before sliding open a drawer and depositing them inside, then he clicks open his browser. and the computer monitor light illuminates the dark room.

"Fuck, man. Get it together," he mutters with a frustrated sigh as he glances over his shoulder at the now closed door.

I squeeze my eyes shut and curl my legs tight against my chest, trying to make myself as small and unnoticeable as possible. *Please don't see me. Please don't see me.*

He clicks a few more times, and the sound of soft jazz music fills the silent space.

I feel a wave of relief washing over me at the added sound buffer and finally let myself let out a full breath. But my relief is short-lived. The distinct sound of a zipper being undone has my eyes flying open, and when I snap my gaze up, suddenly, there's a whole new fear before me.

Oh no. Oh no. Please don't... Please stop...

"But... I didn't order a pizza," I hear a woman's breathless voice say.

"I'm afraid you're mistaken. Says right here, you called and ordered a ten-inch personal pan... extra meat." A male voice responds... and if I thought I was anxious before, the speed at which my pulse is racing now feels like it could trigger an earthquake.

There's nothing funny about the predicament I've found myself in, so I don't know why I have to bite my lip to keep from laughing.

I hear the chime of his belt buckle as he loosens it, and when he pulls himself free, I nearly choke on my own saliva.

Holy shit.

Slapping a palm over my mouth, I hold my breath to keep myself from coughing as I squirm around to get a better view. I've never had an interest in watching porn before now, never really given it a second thought, so why exactly am I having such a hard time looking away?

I know I shouldn't be watching this, that this is a complete invasion of his privacy, but I can't help myself. I've never seen a man pleasure himself, especially when he thinks he's alone. I feel like I'm getting a top-secret glimpse into the male psyche. Not to mention, this is the hottest thing I've ever experienced.

Luka takes a bottle from his desk drawer, squirting the lotion in his palm. He lets out a hiss as his head falls back against his chair and he begins working himself in slow, steady strokes.

My hand falls from my mouth as I watch in wonderment,

and I have to clench my thighs together to ease the tension growing between my legs.

The moans of the woman on the screen fill the otherwise silent air, but I can't take my eyes off Luka. He slouches in his seat, his legs parted as he fists himself with raw, carnal abandon. I feel my panties growing wetter by the second, and despite knowing this is entirely inappropriate and an invasion of his privacy, I can't make myself look away.

Maybe you like it because it's wrong?

I suppose it's not out of the realm of possibility. I guess I won't know the things that turn me on if I never expose myself to them. I never had the forethought to seek it out before. I never knew my body was capable of feeling this *alive*.

I watch in fascination as his forearm flexes as he pumps his thick cock in long, slow strokes, squeezing as he gets to the top. My eyes zero in on the bead of pre cum that glistens at his tip. I absently wet my lips as he rubs his thumb over it before dragging it back down over his shaft and using it as extra lube.

And for some reason, my mouth begins to water from the sight of it.

Truth be told, I've never really understood the appeal of giving a blowjob. I always found the act to be gross and degrading. Naively, I guess I thought it was a universal experience. Which is probably why I've never found it particularly tempting.

But this... Watching Luka, the way he strokes himself so brazenly, seeing the muscles and veins in his forearms ripple and twitch as he loses himself to his carnal desires... This is a level of need I've never known.

I feel my cheeks flame with a mixture of embarrassment and raw desire as my heart thrashes violently in my chest.

I'm amazed at his dexterity as he uses his left hand to unbutton his shirt, all while maintaining a steady rhythm of strokes. The soft glow of his computer monitor highlights the grooves of his chiseled abs as they flex tighter with his growing release.

I'm on the edge of my seat—or the floor, actually—as I take in every single detail. Perspiration beads on the back of my neck, and I have to fan myself because... Wow... This man deserves an award for this solo performance.

I can't help but wonder, if he's this attentive to himself, what would it be like to be with him?

Without even realizing what I'm doing, my hand moves beneath the hem of my shorts, as if it has a mind of its own. I've only done this a couple of times; I've never had much time alone to explore, but somehow my body knows what to do. I close my eyes as my fingers slide over my swollen clit, slick with arousal, as a rush of pleasure courses through me.

Oh my... It's so sensitive. Biting my lip, I suck in a shaky breath as I watch Luka's strokes become more frantic. His breaths are choppy and strained, the veins in his forearm more visible now as he chases his impending release.

I close my eyes, imagining it's his fingers that are touching me as I rub circles over my aching clit, my thighs parting a little more to give myself better access.

The thought of how wrong this is weaves its way through my mind, the ever-present voice of reason reminding me of the rules I'm expected to play by, of the type of woman I've been taught I should embody. I try to push it away, try to fight off the incessant nagging, but my thoughts are too jumbled.

My desire and rational thoughts tangle together, quickly forming a knot I'll never be able to untie, and I find the searing hot pleasure begin to slowly fizzle out. Just like it always does.

I can't help but feel disappointed as I pull my hand from my shorts. I sigh a frustrated huff as Luka's heavy breathing and desperate grunts grow louder.

"Oh fuck," he hisses through clenched teeth as his body buckles forward. And just when I think it's about to be over, he slows his rhythm again, his jaw ticking from the restraint. He sucks a breath through his nose as he closes his eyes, his head resting against his desk chair as the sounds of desperate fucking on his computer fills the silence.

The sight of him drawing his pleasure out, has my conscience walking a tight rope, balancing between the good girl I've always been taught I should be, and all the secret desires I've kept hidden in the shadows. Falling is inevitable, so which side will I lean?

The pulsing arousal growing between my legs returns, and I squeeze my thighs, trying to distract myself from the desperate ache.

I'm a horrible human being. This is so bad.

But I still can't force myself to look away.

The sounds of slapping flesh and moans from the video grow louder. A thin layer of sweat glistens on his skin as he hisses from his bared teeth, his brows furrowed into an almost grimace.

It's the most erotic thing I've ever witnessed, and my eyes grow wider as I watch with an intense focus. The beat of my pulse in my neck, pounds harder and harder as my skin heats.

I fan myself with my t-shirt, needing to cool my body down as my shirt clings to my sweat-covered skin.

His pace picks up again, but this time he doesn't hold back as his fist moves up and down his shaft in quick, even strokes.

My clit throbs, desperate for relief, but I keep my eyes glued on Luka, trying to memorize everything about this moment. Who knew a man masturbating could be so sexy? There's something about it, the way he's rough and deliberate, the way he doesn't hold back...

God, I want someone to do that with me.

I bite my lip; my fingernails digging painfully into my palms as I watch him chase his release.

He's so close, even I can feel it.

"Fuck," he groans under his breath.

With my face practically pressed against the chair in front of me, I suck in a sharp breath...

And to my absolute horror, he goes still.

No. No. No. I squeeze my eyes closed, forcing myself to be as still as possible as I pray he doesn't notice me.

But then his deep, gravelly voice cuts through the silence and those wild green eyes find mine. "Care to give me a hand here? Or do you just prefer to watch?"

CHAPTER TWELVE

LUKA

"This isn't what it looks like!" Scout shoots up from the floor, the antique lamp on the side table wobbles side to side, and she nearly trips over herself to steady it, knocking over a stack of books in the process.

Despite my annoyance with her snooping around behind my back, there's a small part of me that delights in seeing her so visibly flustered.

"It isn't?" I click my tongue as I study her, not even trying to hide my obvious perusal, nor the rock-hard boner that sticks out above the waistband of my unbuttoned pants.

It's no surprise that her cheeks and neck burn bright crimson, making her wide, hazel eyes appear lighter as she stares at me through her round, gold-rimmed glasses.

Her light brown hair sits on top of her head in a messy bun, and she's wearing a simple, white t-shirt and light pink cotton shorts. She may look like the picture of innocence on the outside, but there was nothing innocent about the way she was just watching me.

I'd noticed her hiding behind that chair not too long after I had my fist around my cock, the sounds of her heavy breathing giving her away. Admittedly, I was caught off guard. I don't know how she managed to sneak in here without L.O.K.I noticing, but I figured if she had the balls to sneak in here, I may as well enjoy fucking with her.

I'd half expected her to stop me—to close her eyes or to turn away at the very least. But that's not what happened at all... Instead, the little fiend leaned in and squirmed around so she could get a better angle. And fuck if that wasn't what I was expecting.

Looks like my wife may have a secret kinky side after all.

To be honest, I'd only meant to fuck with her, make things so uncomfortable that she'd have no choice but to tap out. I tried not to make my awareness of her too obvious as I angled myself to give her a better view, even going as far as unbuttoning my shirt. And then I saw her shift her weight and the glazed look in her eyes.

Goddamnit, that was almost too much to take. As if I wasn't already struggling to keep my mind out of the gutter, especially after her little confession the other night. I've even had to ask L.O.K.I. to keep her bedroom door locked at night, as an extra layer of precaution, just in case my unconscious body decides it wants to reenact all the sex dreams I've been having. It's been years since I've sleepwalked, but at this point, I can't take any chances.

Just seeing how affected she was from watching me,

seeing how her eyes widened with a look of arousal mixed with curiosity... Fuck it was the single hottest thing I've ever experienced. And I've done my fair share of kinky shit. I had to edge myself just to keep from blowing a load and ending it before I was ready.

But then I remember that I specifically told her not to come up here, and my arousal shifts back into annoyance.

Scout holds out her hands, the panicked look on her face has her looking so fucking cute it has my blood boiling and my aching cock twitching to finish where I left off. I bite my cheek and take a deep breath, needing to distract myself before my body takes things into its own hands.

Round eyes stare back at me, blinking like she's afraid to make any sudden moves... which isn't that inaccurate. She swallows thickly. "I didn't see anything..." her pathetic attempt at a lie.

Rather than commenting, I quirk a single brow as the growing tension between us cracks and sizzles. I know she feels it too.

She must give up on arguing altogether, because she gestures with her thumb over her shoulder. "I'll... uh... I'll just be going then." She cowers as she begins tiptoeing toward the door, using her hand to shield her eyes.

With a disgruntled sigh, I slowly pull my pants back up, carefully tucking my painfully engorged cock inside. I wasn't kidding; I had every intention of finishing if she hadn't interrupted.

"Not so fast." My words come out sharp and commanding, and she stops dead in her tracks. But she doesn't turn back to look at me. "What were you doing in my office, Scout? I thought I told you not to come upstairs?" What I don't ask is how she managed to slip by without L.O.K.I noticing.

A mixture of anger and arousal fights for dominance inside of me, and I clench my jaw as I wait for her response. Her breaths come out heavy, and her porcelain skin is flushed bright pink from her neck all the way up to her face. She fidgets under my stare but still won't meet my gaze.

"I asked you a question," I repeat a little louder.

I don't miss the way she startles at my sharp tone, and I instantly feel like a dick. I may be angry at her, but I'd never want her to feel like she's unsafe around me.

"I was...I was looking for..." She looks around, then her eyes widen as she picks up a pen from my desk and clenches it to her chest. "I was just looking for a pen. Figured I'd start working on some sketches for the mural."

I lean against the wall with my arms crossed over my chest as I watch her attempt to regain her composure. I've always loved how flustered she gets when she's uncomfortable.

"Let me get this straight... You snuck into my office, deliberately disobeying my only house rule... for a pen?"

She swallows thickly and nods.

We stand there for a moment, my gaze locked on hers until finally, she breaks the silence.

"Well... I'll get out of your hair then... let you get back to it..." She gives me a salute, then spins on her heel and practically bolts out the door.

"Scout," I call after her.

Her whole body freezes mid-step. "Hmm?"

"Next time I find you snooping in places you don't belong, I won't be so forgiving..."

She nods. "I... understand."

I collapse in my desk chair with a sigh as I watch her leave.

What the fuck am I doing?

CHAPTER THIRTEEN

SCOUT

I wipe my sweaty palms against my sundress as we make our way up the brick staircase that leads to the Kingsleys front door.

After everything that's transpired today, I spent the rest of the afternoon holed up in my bedroom, too afraid to step outside and face Luka.

At least I had L.O.K.I. to distract me. He didn't waste any time cashing in on the promise I made to watch the Avengers movies with him.

We managed to get through the first Iron Man movie and had to pause midway through Thor Ragnarok before I had to get ready. Luckily, I've seen the movies before, because I don't think L.O.K.I. stopped talking the entire time. Whether he was asking me if I saw something or sharing fun facts about the filming, it felt like I was watching a movie with a genius five-year-old.

I don't know how Luka does it. Between fighting off the inappropriate images of Luka that seem to be playing on a loop in the back of my mind and trying to keep up with L.O.K.I.'s non-stop questions all afternoon—I'm beyond exhausted.

And now, to make matters worse, I have to spend the rest of the evening lying to Luka's parents, who just so happen to be the nicest people on the planet.

That thought has the lead ball of guilt in my stomach twisting even more.

I was so distracted by everything earlier, I didn't have time to overthink about what I'm walking into.

Do they know the truth about what really happened? Do they hate me? Will they be upset?

I nearly jump out of my skin when I feel Luka's palm slide to my lower back, pulling me closer to him. "Stop fidgeting," he whispers in a commanding voice, sending a wave of chills up my spine.

I barely have time to recover when the front door swings open and I'm met with Mr. and Mrs. Kingsley's smiling faces.

"Well, I'll be. I guess the rumors really were true," Mrs. Kingsley says before pulling me into a bone-crushing hug. "It is so good to see you, sweetie," she says into my hair as she plants kisses on top of my head. Mrs. Kingsley may be a slight woman, but she's stronger than she looks, and I know I don't stand a chance trying to wiggle out of her hug... good thing I don't want to.

God, I've missed this. I almost forgot what it felt like to feel so wanted, so accepted, not to mention tolerated. I am convinced that if everyone had a family like this, a family who loved them unconditionally for not only who they are but whoever they want to become... There would be no evil or hatred or fighting. Hugs like this can heal a lifetime of wounds, and despite feeling like Judas himself, I let myself soak it up.

"Come on in. Sounds like you two have a lot to catch us up on," Mr. Kingsley says as he claps Luka on the shoulder and waves us in.

He may be smiling, but I don't miss the flash of hurt on his face when his eyes meet Luka's. And just like that, my guilt is right back with a vengeance.

We follow them through the foyer as I try to force myself to act natural. Luka must notice my struggle because he wraps an arm around my shoulders and pulls me into him. "Relax, Girl Scout. You look too stiff." He smooths a hand over my arm and whispers. "We're newlyweds, remember?"

I nod as I try to swallow the lump in my throat.

"I must say, I was shocked when I heard the news, but I wasn't surprised," Mrs. Kingsley says as we make our way into the dining room. "I always knew the two of you would find your way back to each other... eventually."

"Mom, I told you it wasn't anything personal," Luka says. "It was sort of a sporadic moment, and we wanted to keep it just between us." He looks at me when he adds, "You know how Scout's family feels about me... So we just figured it'd be easier for everyone if we kept it just between the two of us."

I feel my throat tighten with emotion because... wow... how is he so good at this? That felt so real, and I'm not sure I could've come up with a more believable excuse if I tried.

Mrs. Kingsley nods like she understands, though it's clear

that her feelings are still hurt from being left out. I hate that I'm the reason she feels this way, even if it's all a ruse.

But what I truly can't get over is how healthy this entire conversation has been. Rather than giving Luka the cold shoulder or passive aggressively making snide remarks like my parents' go-to conflict resolution style, she simply told him that it hurt her feelings. No beating around the bush, no hiding behind pleasantries.

No wonder Luka's so confident in himself. With this type of healthy and direct communication, he doesn't have to constantly examine everyone around him to pick up on their mood changes. He knows that if there's a problem, they'll communicate that to him.

What must that feel like?

I'm still scratching my head trying to fathom it when I see Guy attempting to discreetly sneak a deviled egg by quickly shoving the entire thing in his mouth in one bite.

"Guy Francis! I asked you to wait five minutes. I told you not to mess up my presentation," Mrs. Kingsley scolds. And if I didn't already feel guilty, her going all out only lays it on thicker.

Guy holds up his hands innocently. "That was only my first one! You know I have a weakness for deviled eggs. Do you really expect me to resist when they're sitting there unattended—"

"He's right, a man can only endure so much temptation before he breaks," Luka says, and when his eyes meet mine, he winks.

Apparently, that one little flirtatious gesture is all it takes because I instantly feel my cheeks flame in response. I hate how easily affected I am by him. And I hate even more that he knows it. As if he needed anything else to hold over my head, now I've got to worry that he's going to embarrass me, knowing damn well I'm a terrible liar.

It's not that I don't trust him... I wouldn't have gone through with this marriage if I didn't... I guess I just didn't realize how much control I was giving him.

And now that it's done, I'm feeling more vulnerable than ever with this imbalanced power dynamic. It's absolutely nerve-racking, never knowing what he's going to do or say. And as much as I hate the constant anxiety, I can't help but notice how alive it makes me feel.

For someone who's spent her whole life following the rules, there's something so dangerously exhilarating about the way he looks at me, knowing he has the power to destroy me. That he could ruin me at any moment... and still wanting him anyway.

I'm pulled out of my thoughts when Roman comes thudding down the stairs. "Bartholomew's fortress is officially complete." He looks like he came straight from work, wearing khakis and a tucked-in baby blue dress shirt with the sleeves rolled up to his elbows. He squeezes the trigger of the electric drill he's holding, and his eyes go wide when he notices me, but ever the gentleman, he quickly masks his shock with a warm smile.

I take it he wasn't aware of our arrival; he must've been busy installing whatever it was he was building upstairs.

His smile beams with something that looks a lot like mischief as he looks between Luka and me. "Good to see you, sis."

I swallow a gulp, feeling my body tense. "Yeah. Good to see you too, Roman." My voice cracks on his name, and if our situation didn't seem suspicious before, it's certainly starting to now.

Luckily, Luka doesn't seem to have any issues with lying. Hell, if anything, I think he's enjoying himself just watching me suffer. He clears his throat, drawing the attention back to himself, and says, "I don't know about everyone else, but I'm starving." He's close enough to my ear that it seems like he's talking only to me, but loud enough for everyone to hear. There's a friendly, almost flirtatiousness in his voice, and I can almost feel it vibrating in my bones.

What the hell is he doing to me? It's as if he's managed to hijack my brain, inserting himself inside against my will. Honestly, with all the technology he has in his house, it's not that outlandish of an explanation...

"Now that we're all here, why don't we all take a seat," Mrs. Kingsley says, and Luka's already pulling out my chair for me. "Roman, can you help me bring everything to the table?"

He moves to help, and Mr. Kingsley goes to join them as Luka, Guy, and I take our seats. Guy's sitting across from Luka with his arms crossed over his chest, and I can practically feel the glare he's sending me.

Luka must sense my nervousness, because he gives my thigh a reassuring squeeze under the table. But the message it sends to my hormones feels anything but casual. Suddenly, I find myself feeling more flustered than nervous. Luka's large palm is still resting on my thigh like it's cementing me in place. Is this his plan: to distract me with his confusing touches so I don't have the mental energy to overthink anything else?

When his thumb traces soft circles over my leg, it takes

every ounce of restraint I have to keep from reacting and not making a scene. An almost painful throb develops between my legs, and I have to squeeze my thighs to distract myself.

Mr. Kingsley appears with a bottle of wine and begins filling everyone's glasses. "We picked this bottle up in Tuscany. We've been saving it for a celebration." He pauses when he reaches my glass, waiting for my permission before he fills it.

I give him an enthusiastic nod, taking the opportunity to send Luka a warning glare over my shoulder as I lift my glass for him.

Luka returns my glare with an amused look, the hint of a smirk pulling at his lips as his hand slips higher on my thigh. I make a weak attempt to slap it away, which only makes his grin widen as he clamps his hand tighter in an almost possessive grip. And I hate the way my stomach somersaults in response.

Perhaps if I hadn't watched him jerk off, I wouldn't have the dirty thoughts going through my mind... But sadly, I know too much... And all I can think about is how badly I want his hand to touch me with the same roughness and intensity.

Whoa... Where did that come from?

I feel my skin begin to heat at the wildly inappropriate image and try to steer my thoughts back to the conversation, reminding myself that he's just trying to distract me—or torment me—either way, it's all mind games and nothing more.

"Scout, I hope you brought your appetite. I sort of went overboard with the side dishes," Mrs. Kingsley says as she, Roman, and Mr. Kingsley file into the dining room carrying platters of food. She sets a beautiful golden roasted chicken down in the center as Mr. Kingsley and Roman fill in the gaps with various side dishes from mashed potatoes to green beans, to an heirloom tomato salad with cucumber and fresh basil.

"Bon Appétit. Dig in while it's good and hot," she says, and no sooner do the words leave her mouth, then Guy and Roman take her at her word and begin scooping piles of food onto their plates.

My mouth waters at the delicious aroma, and I can't help but notice how different eating with the Kingsleys is compared to my family. There's a bowl of fresh bread and butter, the food smells amazing, seasoned with aromatic spices that mingle together, and there's so much color on the table.

When my family serves dinner, we're lucky to have one side. My parents are the kind of people who consider garlic powder to be spicy.

Where I come from, food is a means to an end and is only served elaborately to impress guests. And you can forget about sides full of carbs. I couldn't tell you the last time my mother was in the same vicinity as a piece of bread.

But not Mrs. Kingsley, one of her favorite love languages is feeding people, and tonight she held back nothing with this incredible spread. It's as if she incorporated a little something for everyone, making sure they all feel her love for them.

Luka sets down a plate full of food in front of me—something he did before I could argue—and as if reading my mind, asks, "I thought Jett said he'd be here tonight?"

"He got tied up at work. Said he'd come later if he could get a chance," Roman answers between bites, not even looking up from his plate.

"Fifty bucks says he ghosts us again," Guy says without missing a beat.

Roman's fork pauses midair as he turns to Guy and offers his hand in a shake. "You're on."

"Are you serious right now? You're betting on whether your brother will show up—"

Before she can finish scolding them, Mr. Kingsley wipes his mouth and adds, "A hundred bucks says he calls with an emergency that only he can deal with."

Roman's smile grows wider. "You're on."

Mrs. Kingsley smacks Mr. Kingsley on the back of the head.

"Ow... what'd you do that for?" He winces, turning to look at her like he's shocked.

She blows out a huff and rolls her eyes. "You ought to be ashamed of yourself for encouraging them, much less getting in on it."

"Mary, I'm merely taking advantage of a lucrative financial opportunity. It's nothing personal."

"You've been retired for less than a year, find a better hobby than betting on our children's behavior, Frank!"

He flinches as if waiting for another smack, then shrugs and adds, "It's not just our children," he says defensively. "Just last week, I won a bet over whether Dr. Drizzle would unbutton more than three buttons on his shirt during his emergency weather broadcast." He flashes her a cocky grin and points at himself. "And guess who was right? By the end of his ten-minute broadcast, that dirty bastard had undone *four* buttons on his shirt *and* rolled up his shirt sleeves! Can you believe it? On cable television for everyone to see!"

"Oh, now you're just being jealous. Just because I have a

new interest in meteorology, now you're keeping tabs on the weather man."

Mr. Kingsley narrows his eyes. "You recorded a tornado warning and watched it back three times over the course of a few days! Who watches a weather report from the past?"

"It's called studying my craft. I told you that. And he can't help it, he gets hot when he's stressed." She shrugs. "You watch the football show, and I watch the weather."

I forgot how much I love watching this family banter. They're so funny when they argue about trivial things because despite how heated things seem to get, I always know they're kidding—mostly. And no one can deny that Frank Kingsley is just as head over heels for his wife today as he was the day he met her. You can see it in the way he looks at her, even when they're squabbling and seem to be at each other's throats. It's all a show, and he loves getting a rise out of her. Innocent teasing and joking are another one of the Kingsleys love languages, and to that, no one is safe.

"It's called the game... the football game. It's not a show. How many times do I have to explain that to you?"

"You don't. Maybe I'm just trying to get you to unbutton your shirt for me, Franky," she says sweetly, placing a palm on his cheek before sliding it down his neck.

He catches her hand over his heart and holds it there. "Well, if that's all you want, we can kick these kids out and pretend there's a thunderstorm outside. I'll be happy to unbutton my shirt and roll my sleeves up for you."

"I think I just threw up in my mouth," Guy says as he downs his glass of wine without even flinching, then promptly refills his glass.

"You guys are disgusting. I love how much you love each

other, but I could do without the explicit reminders while I'm trying to eat," Roman adds in between bites.

They smile warmly at each other, and just like that, their squabble is over. You can practically feel the love radiating between them. I've always wanted a love like theirs, and I'm happy to see they haven't changed a bit. It gives me hope that true love really does exist.

Mrs. Kingsley turns her attention back to me and Luka. "Okay, enough of the small talk." She gestures between us with her fork. "What I really want to know is, why I had to hear about the two of you getting married from Miss. Scarlett in the produce aisle?" She sets down her fork and wipes her mouth. "I get it, you wanted to keep the ceremony between the two of you... But you couldn't have even given me a heads up?"

My stomach sinks, feeling the searing guilt begin to rise in my chest, and then I feel Luka's hand on my thigh, squeezing tighter, making my brain glitch at her question. I'd like to believe his intentions behind his distraction is intended to be helpful, but the chances are probably closer to a fifty-fifty split.

"Mom, like I said... We were worried about how Scout's parents were going to handle it, and we didn't want to make things any more difficult."

I shake my head. "No, Luka. Your mother's right. We should've told you." I turn so that I'm facing them both as I say, "It's my fault. Luka was trying to make it easier for me, but I accept full responsibility. I'm sorry I was so selfish..." My apology is interrupted by the sound of the door bursting open.

"Sorry, I'm late! My new bartender had a family

emergency, and I had to cover for her," Jett calls as he steps into the dining room. His face flashes with surprise when he sees me—but he quickly recovers as he takes a seat next to Roman and quietly serves himself.

"Honey, I'm so happy you made it," Mrs. Kingsley coos, and I can't help but see the relief in her face. Jett was always distant, from what I remember and judging by the thick tension in the air ever since he walked in, I'm assuming that hasn't eased. If anything, it feels heavier than I remember.

"Glad you could make it, Jett. How's everything going at Restaurant?" Roman asks, then looks at his dad and Guy and mouths behind his hand, "Pay up."

Mr. Kingsley and Guy don't even try to be inconspicuous as they both pull out their wallets and hand over the cash.

Roman flashes a smug grin. "Good doing business with you."

Jett shakes his head. "Seriously? You're betting on if I'll show up for family dinner now? Sounds like you two need a job. I've got a dishwasher position open if you're really that bor—"

"Who's ready for dessert?" Mrs. Kingsley cuts in, already jumping up from the table. "I'll go grab it, and then I want to hear all about how you two reconnected."

"Here, let me help," Mr. Kingsley says, excusing himself to follow his wife into the kitchen.

Guy reaches for the wine and tops off his glass. "Glad I cleared my schedule. I didn't realize I'd be getting dinner and a show." He gives us a wink, and I feel the panic already rising in my chest.

How could we be so negligent? We didn't even come up with a story...

"Stop freaking out," Luka whispers, his hand moving higher on my thigh, making my nerves heighten even more than they already are. "Just follow my lead…"

I nod as I reach for my own wine now. Looks like I'm going to need it.

CHAPTER FOURTEEN

LUKA

"Hang on. You mean to tell me *she* reached out to *you* before her engagement party?" My dad gestures between us, wearing a look of utter surprise.

"What can I say?" I lean back in my seat, wrapping an arm around Scout. "My girl's needs weren't being met." I flash Scout a cocky grin and wink.

She rolls her eyes, trying her best to seem unfazed by my elaborate backstory, but the blush that rises on her cheeks only makes the story that much more believable.

The scent of cinnamon and warm apple pie wafts through the air, and we're already on our third bottle of wine. Unlike the beginning of the evening, the tension has finally calmed down, and everyone, including Scout, has finally relaxed as I fill them in on how we reconnected.

I definitely think I'm going to have bruised ribs in the morning, but otherwise she's been going along with everything I've said... Despite my every attempt to embarrass her.

I know she's nervous and everything, but I swear, if I didn't know any better, I'd think my wife may have a bit of a humiliation kink going on.

"Luka, stop telling all her secrets. You're embarrassing the poor girl," my mom scolds, reaching a hand across the table to take Scout's. "It's all right, dear. I'm sure you have plenty of your own stories about Luka." She shakes her head with a smile. "I still can't believe you two were able to keep this hidden from us. Truly, I had no idea you were even speaking. Did your brothers know about this?"

Roman's eyes widen in surprise at being put on the spot, but before he can respond, Guy nods his head enthusiastically. "Oh yeah. He wouldn't shut up about her." He gestures a thumb at Roman. "You should have seen him before they made it official." He blows out a breath. "I've never seen a grown man cry like that." He elbows Roman, who lets out a grunt. "Isn't that right, Rome?"

"Oh... um... yep." Roman winces, rubbing his side in annoyance. "Yeah, he was pretty torn up about it for a while there."

I glare at my brothers, but neither one of them will look me in the eye. I can't be too annoyed with them; at least they're covering for me. There's no way my parents would believe all the bullshit I'm spewing otherwise.

Somehow the conversation drifts from my crying at work, back to Dr. Drizzle tearing up during a tornado warning while he was live on air.

"Now you know I won't tolerate toxic masculinity in this

house," my mom shouts over my dad, who's once again ranting about the local meteorologist.

"No, Mary, it's not. I'd make fun of anyone who started crying during a thunderstorm."

"He was afraid, Frank. Men are allowed to have fears, you know!"

"Call me crazy, but I'd prefer my weatherman to not be afraid of the *weather!*"

I sneak a glance at Scout, who seems to be thoroughly enjoying herself. Whether because she's had nearly three glasses of wine herself—yes, I've been counting—or because she's relieved to have the attention off her. I can't be sure.

Her cheeks are a rosy pink and her plump lips are stained with red wine. The thought of biting those lips has crossed my mind more times tonight than I'd like to admit. My hand moves over her bare thigh in a possessive grip, as if acting on its own accord, and I'm pleased that she's no longer fidgeting uncomfortably at my touch.

At first, I'd only meant to distract her because her nervousness was far too obvious. But as soon as I felt how soft her skin was, the way my hand practically consumed her thigh, and how powerful I felt knowing I could wield her body any way that I wanted... There was no prying my hand away after that.

Of course, it also doesn't help having the very fresh memory of her big eyes staring at me in awe, like I was a fucking god to be worshipped as she watched me fuck my hand. The way she licked her lips, unable to tear her eyes away, like she was dying for a chance to take me in that sweet mouth of hers...

I feel my cock begin to swell and tear my attention back

to the conversation as I fight my hand from moving any higher up her thigh, from sneaking up that sexy as hell sundress she's wearing.

"Can I top you off?" Roman waits for Scout's nod before emptying the last bit of wine into her half-full glass.

The conversation must've shifted while I was zoned out because now everyone's attention is back on us.

"So, Scout. How are your parents doing? I don't think I've seen Samantha or Judge Sinclair in ages," My dad asks, and the question must catch Scout by surprise because her hand shakes as she sets her wine down, not seeing the butter knife. The glass topples against her plate, making a loud clang before shattering, red wine spilling everywhere.

"Oh my God, I'm so sorry." Scout jumps out of her seat in a panic, fumbling with her napkin as she tries to wipe the stain. "I'm such an idiot."

"Oh, honey, you are fine—" my mom starts, but Scout's too busy panicking to hear her.

Roman doesn't have to be told; he just gets up to grab a towel. Meanwhile, I cross a foot over my knee and sit back in my seat, watching as her attempt to panic clean only makes a bigger mess.

"Oh, now I'm just making it worse." Her voice comes out tight, like she's trying to hold back tears.

"Honey, please don't worry about it. There's nothing in this house that can't be tossed in the washing machine or replaced."

My dad jumps up to help. "Here, let me get these glass shards out of the way."

"Mrs. Kingsley, I'm so sorry. I'm such a klutz. Let me pay to have this cleaned."

"Oh, there's no need for that, sweetie. Really. This really isn't a big deal," my mom assures her, before sending me a glare, as if urging me to step in and help.

My eyes laser in on Scout's shaking hands, and for some reason, it sends a flare of heat searing through my chest. I don't miss the looks from my brothers, as each of them seems to be wearing the same look of concern.

My jaw is tense as I try to hold back my rapidly growing annoyance at the way Scout's so pathetically flustered. The next thing I know, I'm standing, grabbing her by the arm, and leading her to the kitchen. "Come with me." My words are like gravel in my throat.

Scout's eyes are welled with tears, her flushed cheeks now red from embarrassment as I lead her over to the sink, rinsing her hands to make sure they're free of any shards of glass.

"Luka, I'm so sorry, I—"

"Goddammit, Scout. Stop apologizing," I say through clenched teeth, the anger inside me growing hotter by the second. I spin to face her, my hands bracketing on either side of the counter as her wide, terror-filled eyes stare back at me.

I've always known she was a little skittish and jumpy, and it isn't hard to put together why. I blink back the visions my mind so unhelpfully supplies as a way of explanation for Scout's overreaction as I try to calm my boiling rage.

She may not be mine...not really...but it doesn't stop the possessiveness inside me from rearing its ugly head anyway. I force myself to breathe as my eyes zero in on her, noting the rapid rise and fall of her chest and her dilated pupils. She may be afraid of my reaction, but her body tells me she's feeling more than fear and embarrassment.

There's something in the way that she's looking at me, like she's hopeful? I can't be sure. All I know is there's an energy between us, stretching and pulling with every move I make. Our lips are a breath away.

"Wait here." I push off the counter and leave her as I walk back to the dining room, returning with a full glass of wine in my hand.

"Here." I place the glass in her hand and take a step back. I'm standing across from her with my arms crossed and my back pressed against the kitchen island.

She doesn't drink the wine, her brows pulling together as her eyes bounce around the room like she's confused.

"Now I want you to pour that glass of wine on the floor," I say.

She looks up at me in confusion and shakes her head. "What? No. Why would I do that?"

"Because I told you to," I fire right back.

"Luka, I'm not going to make another mess in your parents' house."

"Pour the wine on the floor, Scout. It's tile. The floor will be fine." My voice is clipped and commanding as I nod for her to do as I said.

A moment passes and I'm not sure if she's going to do it, but then I see that flare in her eyes, that spark that has my whole body on fire.

Come on. Just do it. I mentally urge her, my eyes watching her more intently than I ever have.

She bites her lip as if she's considering it...and then she slowly tilts the glass, and I hear the stream of liquid splash against the hard floor.

My chest swells with triumph at her obedience as my

gaze zeros in on her flushed cheeks, and I see the instant her body starts to panic. But rather than letting it happen, this time I take a step closer, tilting her chin so her eyes meet mine and whisper, "Listen... Do you hear that?" Silence stretches between us as I wait a moment longer to make my point. "No one is yelling at you."

I brush a strand of hair out of her face, and she sucks in a gasp as I move in closer. "You just spilled that entire glass of wine all over the floor. It's getting all over your feet, and still, no one's screaming at you."

Her eyes quickly fill with tears at my words, so I keep going. "It's fine. You're okay. Nobody's mad at you. Everything's fine. It was an accident. It can easily be cleaned up."

The more I reassure her, the more upset she seems to become as the streams of tears fall down her cheeks. Her swollen lips tremble like she's holding back a sob, and I can feel my fucking heart aching for her to see how upset she is.

I keep my eyes locked on hers as I continue speaking the reassuring words over and over as if I'm rewiring her brain's reaction. Giving her grace and understanding rather than the anger and rage her body's normally accustomed to receiving during moments like this.

I don't have to know the specifics to know that this reaction wasn't created from one or two accidents, but rather a lifetime. Maybe I shouldn't care, but the protector inside me has a mind of his own, and right now that's what Scout needs.

My body is almost completely flush against her now as I caress her arm with one hand and hold her chin in my other, keeping her pinned in place. I know this must be torture for her, standing here with wet feet, unable to clean up the mess before anyone sees. Too late. I've seen the mess, and I'm right here with her, still standing in it.

Her big eyes stare up at me, filled with so many questions—questions that even I don't have the answer to. So, before she finds the courage to ask, I tear myself away, shattering the moment.

I fist the hand towel from the counter and bend down. Scout stands there silent and confused, but as if she already knows what I'll say, she doesn't try to help me wipe the floor clean.

When I'm finished, I toss the towel over my shoulder and stand. "There. It's like it never even happened."

The next thing I know, my mom comes bounding into the kitchen, pulling us both back to the present moment. "Oh, honey, I didn't realize you got it on your dress, too. Here, let me throw it in the wash before the stain sets in."

Scout swallows a gulp and waves her off. "Oh, yeah. I guess I did. It's fine. I'll wash it at home."

I give her a nod of approval, feeling a proud smile return to my lips. "Actually, I think we're going to head back to the house. We've had a busy past few days, and I need to get my bride home to get some much-needed rest." I give my mom a hug and thank her for dinner, asking her to tell everyone goodbye for me. Then I take Scout's hand and lead her out the back door, and to my utter surprise, neither one of us lets go as we make the walk home...

CHAPTER FIFTEEN

LUKA

My head is pounding, and I don't think there's enough caffeine in the world to turn my foul mood around.

I'm normally not someone who struggles with sleep, so this insomnia bull shit is a whole new form of torture for me. I don't think I've gotten more than a few hours of sleep a night ever since I invited Scout to stay with me. It's like my body is keenly aware that she's right downstairs. Like my dick's been converted into a fucking antenna, tuned to her exact frequency and alerting me with every shift of her mood.

And no matter how hard I try, I can't turn it off.

I find myself lying there awake... just thinking about her.

Thinking about how jumpy she's always been and the way she freaked out the other night when she accidentally spilled her wine at my parents' house. How panicked she was in that moment, like she was expecting a much harsher reaction. Fuck, something about it doesn't sit right with me. It has me wondering what else I'm missing...

I know I was out of line when I pulled her to the side and made her pour out her wine in front of me... But I couldn't help myself. It was obvious that she was spiraling, and it seemed like she just needed someone to take control, to give her a little space to breathe.

So that's exactly what I did. I took control of the situation... And maybe I pushed her a little further than I should have, but fuck if she didn't give me the exact response I was craving.

As if I needed any more confirmation of what I was already suspecting about her—that little act of submission, the blind trust on her face, the way she seemed relieved to hand over control. Not out of force but because she wanted to. Jesus. I don't know how I'm supposed to function around her now.

It's a cruel joke that my childhood best friend, the woman I've been in love with since I was twelve, would not only betray me after I went to prison for her, but also turn out to be the perfect counterpart to my darkest sexual desires. Out of all the women in the world, did I really have to find my match in my fake wife?

It's a confusing mix of emotions that's got my head all kinds of fucked up, and I don't know what to do about it. No wonder I haven't been sleeping.

Add in a healthy dose of sexual frustration on top of the pressure of pulling off this goddamn festival, and it's a miracle I'm still functioning at all.

If sainthood was determined solely by self-restraint, I'd have my own feast day by now.

"Luka—what are you doing? You can't park here." Scout's voice crackles through the speakers in my helmet as I ease my bike between two cars squeezed up against the curb.

She's not wrong; it's technically not a real parking spot, but I don't really give a shit. Besides, what's the point in riding a motorcycle if you don't take advantage of the perks?

I'm not in the mood to explain myself. I've got enough on my plate with tonight's town meeting. So I kill the engine, shrug off my helmet, and head for the door without a word.

"You're in an extra-foul mood this evening," she says behind me, a little breathless like she's hurrying to catch up.

"Wow, aren't you perceptive." I pause at the curb, waiting for a break in traffic. "What was it that tipped you off?"

I know my anger is mostly misdirected. It's not like she knows what she's doing to me. If anything, she seems oblivious, which somehow makes it feel so much worse.

Out of the corner of my eye, I catch the flicker of hurt on her face, and for a second, I think she's going to let the comment slide. But then she surprises me.

"You know what I think?" she says, not bothering to wait for a response. "I think you're nervous about this meeting, so you're taking it out on me."

I glance at her out of the corner of my eye. "Hate to break it to you, but I couldn't give less of a fuck about this festival, definitely not enough to be nervous."

"Maybe not. But that doesn't mean you don't care what people think. Otherwise, why do anything more than the bare minimum?" She lifts her chin. "You asked me to paint a mural."

"Because I thought it'd be fun to rub it in everyone's face. That's all they ever see when they look at me anyway." I take a step toward her, close enough that she has to tilt her head to meet my eyes and lower my voice. "Don't get it twisted, princess. This isn't noble. My reasons are selfish as hell. I only offered to marry you because I knew I could use it against *you* and *your family*."

I step back, the space between us suddenly feeling colder.

"I may be your husband, but I'm not your fucking friend. Try not to forget that."

I reach for the door, but before I can touch it, it swings open.

"Finally," Fergus says, poking his head out. He grabs my elbow before I can protest. "We need you to help decide something."

He leads me to a long table where several posters are laid out side by side. Miss Scarlett and Clyde Collier, the town handyman, stand shoulder to shoulder with their arms crossed over their chests.

"We can't agree on the lettering style, and since they put you in charge, we need you to choose. Fergus thinks..." Clyde starts, but Fergus holds up a hand and shushes him.

"Don't tell him!" Fergus cuts in. "We need an unbiased opinion. Otherwise, you know he's just going to pick Scarlett's."

Miss Scarlett bats her eyelashes and shrugs, but as soon as Fergus turns his head, she tucks a strand of red hair behind her ear and lets her gaze drop to the poster on the left.

I pretend to study the nearly identical designs, then nod and tap the one I now know is hers. "This one is my choice. It's definitely the best of the three."

Fergus narrows his eyes at Scarlett, visibly annoyed to

have lost whatever competition they've been playing all these years.

Miss Scarlett just fans herself and blows him a kiss. "Sorry, Gus. I can't help it. I've just got a great eye. What can you do?"

"You cheated," he grumbles. "Probably bamboozled him with your cleavage."

Miss Scarlett shimmies her shoulders and winks. "It is rather bamboozling tonight, isn't it?" She leans in and whispers behind her fan, "My secret's bee pollen. Add it to my morning oatmeal every morning."

Fergus' face turns beet red. "Come on, Clyde. We're sitting in the front row tonight."

You'd think the actual festival planning would be the most stressful part of this gig, but I'll take logistics over playing referee any day. I swear, I don't know how Mayor Stone does it.

The sound of chatter and chair legs scraping against the laminate fills the room as people file in and take their seats. It may be a weeknight, but the place is packed. My first instinct is to think it's because they're all so nosey, here to see if I'd actually show up after last time...

But I also know how important this festival is to everyone in this town. This is so much bigger than me or any of the resentment I feel toward any of them.

Everyone in this town wrote me off the moment I was sentenced to prison, so why the fuck would I waste any energy trying to win them back? I don't need their approval. I don't need them to like me. If they're still clutching their pearls over something that happened years ago, that's their problem.

So while I may put on a friendly face and plan this festival. I'm not doing it to impress anyone. I'm doing it because I was assigned the role. Unlike Scout, I don't need anyone's stamp of approval. I can act with integrity—or not just because I fucking feel like it.

But that doesn't mean I can't have a little fun while I'm at it...

I make my way to the podium, mentally reviewing my notes, when my eyes find Scout sitting in the back of the room. She's got that soft smile on her face, the one that barely lifts the corners of her lips, and her eyes are bouncing around like she's soaking in the chaos and loving every second of it.

She looks... different. Lighter. Nothing like the hollow version of herself that showed up here not that long ago.

But looking at her now, I can see that sparkle in her eyes starting to return. If I didn't know any better, I'd think she was happily married, riding high on newlywed bliss.

Of course that couldn't be further from the truth...

Which begs the real question. If being married to *me* has her looking this happy... how fucking toxic was her life before?

A high-pitched ringing draws my attention back to the room, just in time to catch Fergus ringing a triangle that he's apparently brought with him.

"Everyone, please take your seats. It's six o'clock, the meeting has officially begun," he calls from the megaphone he's also somehow produced out of thin air.

I clear my throat as the room quiets and people start settling in, my eyes catching on Scout again. She's chewing on her bottom lip, looking nervous.

I have to look away before my dick starts getting ideas.

The last thing I need is to pop a boner in front of the whole fucking town. Talk about giving them a reason to clutch their pearls.

I clear my throat. "Uh... Thank you... Gus... for that... Let's jump right in with it, shall we?" I hand the stack of papers to Miss Scarlett to pass around just as Jett pushes through the doors.

"Oh good... he made it," Gus mutters under his breath. I swear this man has beef with every other business owner in town. God only knows what he and Jett are sparring over now.

Jett slides into the seat behind Clyde and gives me a nod to keep going.

"Right... So... I guess we'll pick up where we left off last time." I rock back on my heels as I glance around the unusually silent room. "Why don't we open it up. Get some ideas flowing."

"Are the rumors true?" I hear someone call out from the back.

"Don't be ridiculous, Todd," a woman hisses. "You know Judge Sinclair would have a heart attack if it were."

"Wasn't she just engaged to someone else, too?"

A collective gasp ripples through the room.

"Do you think infidelity was involved?" someone whispers.

I lift my hands, trying to rein it back in. "Can we please stay on tra—"

"We shouldn't assume," another voice cuts in. "But have you seen Scout lately? A woman doesn't glow like that for no reason."

"I agree! I just saw them in a heated argument. Thought

they were going to tear each other's clothes off right there in the middle of the sidewalk!"

That one nearly makes me choke. My eyes snap to Scout, whose blush is so bright, I can see it all the way across the dimly lit room.

I should be loving this right now, everyone questioning her character, but I'm surprised when the satisfaction I was expecting to feel doesn't come. Instead, I find myself feeling more protective of her than anything.

When the fuck did that happen?

I guess all those sleepless nights are starting to catch up with me.

"All right, now that's enough." My voice cuts through the chatter, sharper now, and the room slowly settles. "Since I'd like to get something accomplished tonight, let me just clear the air." I point to Scout and motion for her to stand. She hesitates, then rises slowly like she's unsure of the direction I'm going. "Yes. The rumors are true. Scout and I were married over the weekend..."

A fresh wave of gasps ripples through the room as Scout gives a small, shy wave, looking like she could combust on the spot.

"And while we're on the subject..." I pause, letting my voice drop low enough to make people shift in their seats. "Let me be very clear... If I ever hear anyone questioning my wife's integrity again—insinuating she cheated on her ex or anything of the sort—there will be hell to pay. Do I make myself clear?"

Heads nod all around me as hushed agreements fill the air.

"Good," I say, feeling my blood pressure slowly beginning

to calm down. "Since everyone is so preoccupied with my love life, I guess I'll go ahead and start off the meeting." I glance around the room as all eyes zero in on me as I get ready to make my big announcement... But when I notice Jett sitting in the third row, arms crossed, wearing a look of content amusement to not be involved in any of the drama, I wince.

So... I may have forgotten to give him a heads up about one tiny detail I sort of went rogue on. Of course, of all nights, Roman wasn't able to make tonight's meeting to help me deflect. Make no mistake, I love my middle brother, but I'd happily throw him under the bus if it means dodging the wrath of the loose cannon that is Jett Kingsley.

Perspiration beads at my neck, and I swipe at it, already bracing for the explosion.

He's going to freak the fuck out. But maybe it's better with an audience. At least then he can't get away with murdering me. If nothing else, the dozens of casualties should at least slow him down, right?

Jett gives me the slightest nod, as if saying, *good job wrangling the circus*. And a pang of guilt twists in my gut.

Just say it. Rip it off like a Band-Aid.

"I wanted to update you on the actions I've taken after our last meeting." I'm trying my best to avoid looking at Jett, though I can practically feel my skin sizzling from the glare he's shooting me.

Too late to back out now.

I blow out a breath as my spite grabs the wheel. "After our last meeting, I took your suggestions into consideration, and I agree, we do need to spice things up around here. Bring a little life to our downtown area," I say, trying to keep my tone even. "Which is why this year's festival won't just feature another temporary performance; it'll leave a permanent mark. A mural, a beautiful piece of art we can admire for generations—"

My announcement is interrupted when the door swings open. Two more people slip in, and the volume in the room starts to rise.

I raise my voice to cut through it. "—and, who better to bring them to life than our very own hometown artist... Scout *Kingsley*."

Chaos. Absolute, beautiful chaos.

Half the room erupts in cheers; the other half launches into a full-blown debate about preserving the town's "wholesome" image.

It's a shit storm of epic proportions, and I love knowing I'm the one who lit the match.

"Finally," Miss Scarlett calls over the noise. "I think it's a wonderful idea!"

"I knew this would happen!" Clyde hisses to Gus. "Our town's going to hell in a hand basket with this criminal in charge."

"Can he do that?" someone else calls out.

Their expressions are better than I imagined, like I just suggested we host a live sex show rather than paint a mural downtown. I have to bite the inside of my cheek to keep from grinning.

I'm still avoiding Jett's death glare as I add, "That's right, a massive mural featuring our infamous Phantom is sure to become Ashford Falls' biggest attraction. And I can't think of a better place than on the side of Restaurant."

The room explodes at the mention of the Phantom.

Lily and Lucy start arguing with Fergus about whether his father actually saw the Phantom or just hallucinated it after too many fermented persimmons. Miss Scarlett's fanning herself as she tells Colleen Collier about the most recent Phantom romance novel...

It's almost too perfect. Honestly, this may be my finest work yet.

I'm thoroughly enjoying myself watching the chaos I've unleashed, when movement at the back of the room catches my eye.

The two late arrivals, who slipped in quietly before, are now shoving their way through the rows of chairs as they make a beeline straight for Scout.

And that's when I recognize them.

Her parents.

What the fuck are they doing here?

Just like that, the amusement I was just feeling drains out of me, replaced by a sharp, familiar anger. My heart lurches up into my throat, and I shift as my eyes lock onto Scout, zeroing in on every twitch of her expression.

She's smiling softly to herself, clearly amused by the utter chaos. But the moment she recognizes them, all the color drains from her face.

Her eyebrows raise in surprise. "What are you doing here?" I see the words form on her lips as she turns to her mother, who's wearing a pale pink calf-length skirt and a matching blouse that washes out her pale complexion. Her blonde hair is pulled into a tight, severe knot, and she's literally clutching the pearls around her neck.

Beside her, Judge Sinclair stands ramrod straight, dark

hair slicked back, the picture of judgment stuffed into a custom-tailored suit.

I can't hear what they're saying, but it's not exactly difficult to figure out.

I'm so focused on trying to decipher the exchange that I don't even notice Jett has moved beside me... Not until his arm crooks around my neck from behind...

"There's no fucking way I'm going to allow you to vandalize my building... again," he growls in my ear, tightening his grip to cut off my air supply.

I try to thrash, elbowing him, but Jett's got that grown-man strength—the same as Dad and Leo—and it's impossible to escape. I'm not sure what age you unlock it, but it sure as hell isn't twenty-six.

I punch his arm and throw a kick back, desperate to break free, but he just clamps down harder.

"Dammit, Jett, let me go," I gasp. My vision starts to blur as I struggle against his hold, but my eyes stay trained on Scout.

It feels like I'm watching her parents siphon the life out of her right before my eyes.

Scout cowers as her mother shouts something at her. And I swear I can feel her heart breaking all the way across the room.

My stomach twists in mangled knots as I watch the sparkle in her eyes slowly disappear, like a raincloud swallowing the sun.

Why isn't she standing up for herself?

Why the fuck is she just taking it?

A renewed sense of rage burns through my chest as a

mixture of disappointment and irritation consume me, and I go completely still.

Her father grabs her by the arm and yanks her toward him. My rage intensifies, and all I see is red.

I'm not sure how it happens. One second, I'm stuck in Jett's headlock, and the next, he's flying over my shoulder, crashing into a row of metal chairs as I charge across the room.

Her father yanks her by the arm. "You've embarrassed me quite enough. We are leaving. Now—"

"Get your fucking hands off her." I shove him in the chest, sending him sprawling backward into the chairs with a loud metallic crash.

I know it's a bit of an overkill considering I'm at least forty years younger than the old bastard and could've handled him easily. But right now, I don't care.

Samantha, Scout's mother, lets out a horrified shriek, and if my shove wasn't enough to draw everyone's attention, we definitely have the spotlight now.

Judge Sinclair grunts as he hits the floor, and Samantha rushes to help him up. But the second he reaches for Scout again, I'm there. I step between them and shove him once more, this time getting in his face. "She's not going anywhere with you. And if you put your hands on my wife again, I'll happily add another conviction to my record."

I shove him again, planting myself like a wall between them and Scout. "Now get the fuck out of my town and don't come back."

He finally staggers to his feet and adjusts his suit, like he's attempting to preserve some of his dignity. But before he can take another step in Scout's direction, Jett's there. He grabs the collar of his shirt and starts dragging him toward the door.

Everyone in the room parts like the Red Sea. Not a soul daring to intervene—not that they need to.

Samantha turns to Scout, her lips pressed so tight they're almost white. "Scout, do something!"

But Scout just stands there, frozen in place.

Samantha scoffs, her voice dripping with contempt. "Fine. I hope he's worth it. I always knew you'd throw your life away. After everything we've done for you, this is how you repay us?"

"Mama..." Scout finally says, barely audible. "It's not like that, and you know it."

It's only then that I notice the tears streaking down her cheeks.

"Do not call me that," Samantha hisses, her eyes sharp and cold as steel.

The room goes so quiet, you could hear a pin drop.

And then, heels clicking across the floor, Miss Scarlett steps forward and grabs Samantha by the arm. "All right that's enough," she says cooly, spinning her around and giving her a firm shove toward the exit. "Time to go. Good riddance."

CHAPTER SIXTEEN

SCOUT

It was easy to see that Luka was in his head almost as much as I was after the encounter with my parents tonight. So I wasn't surprised, nor was I disappointed, when he passed the turn to go home. I think we both needed time to process everything that went down tonight, and as much as I hate to admit it, there really aren't many better ways to get out of your head than riding on the back of a motorcycle.

My arms lock tightly around Luka's waist as the warm summer breeze caresses my skin, whipping my clothes around me in every direction. As complicated as our relationship may be, I'm thankful for the excuse to just hold Luka, finding comfort in his strong confidence as he maneuvers us through the dense forest where we all but disappear.

The air around us is thick, and it smells like asphalt and rain, and the only sounds I hear is the rush of wind mixed with Luka's soft breaths through the speakers of my helmet. I can tell by the shift in his breathing that he's starting to calm down, like this ride was exactly what he needed to clear his head.

That makes two of us.

I'm not sure what changed between us tonight, but I definitely felt something shift. I'm not delusional enough to think he may actually like me... but maybe he's on his way to hating me a little less than he did before. I can't help but hope anyway...

As if reading my mind, I feel his hand move to my thigh, casually massaging me like it's the most natural thing in the world... like a husband reassuring his wife with a silent gesture. And maybe it's the cover of the darkness, or the fact that we're in the middle of the forest, or maybe it's just the excuse of riding on the back of his motorcycle, but I find myself leaning in. My grip tightens around his waist as my hands begin to move, tentative at first, exploring the hard lines of his body.

My fingertips graze the firmness of his chest, and in response, his free hand trails along my thigh, slow, deliberate, sending a jolt of electricity straight to my core. My eyelids flutter shut, and I draw in a slow, steadying breath, trying to will my body into stillness, trying not to betray just how badly I'm craving more.

He must take that as encouragement because his touch grows bolder, his hand gliding higher up my thigh in a slow rhythm as he alternates between kneading and caressing touches.

Maybe he means to soothe me. Maybe this is nothing more than physical comfort from a husband to his only married on paper, wife... Maybe if I'd had more experience with men touching me, my body wouldn't be reacting like this.

But I haven't. And it is.

When his fingers brush the sensitive crease of my thigh, I suck in a sharp breath. My legs part instinctively, hips rocking forward in search of contact, any contact. I grind against him, just enough for my clit to catch the seam of my shorts, sending a bolt of pleasure through me. Warmth begins to pool between my thighs, and I suck in a hiss of a breath as my thighs part just a little more. My hips rock of their own volition, desperate as they slide closer in search of any friction they can find.

It's only when I hear his soft chuckle that I realize what I'm doing.

Holy shit. What is wrong with me? Do I have no shame?

I freeze, heat rushing to my face as I start to pull away, but his grip on my thigh tightens, holding me in place.

"Don't..." he starts, his voice low and breathless.

But he's cut off by a sharp crack of thunder. I flinch, nearly jumping off the seat. A second later, the sky splits open, and the rain hits like a bucket of ice water, snapping us back to reality.

"Oh my God. I can't believe you just made me do that," I gasp as Luka helps me climb off the back of his bike. We look like we just went swimming in the lake with our clothes on and even though I was convinced we were going to die, I can't deny it was the perfect distraction... from everything. It's almost as if the rainstorm washed everything away giving us a clean slate.

"How else did you want to get home?" he asks, deadpan.

"You didn't have to drive like a maniac," I say, swatting his chest. "I thought I was going to skid off the road and die."

"Oh, come on, I wasn't even speeding." He rubs his stomach, then lifts his drenched t-shirt to examine himself. "Pretty sure I'm going to have permanent claw marks from you trying to hang on for dear life."

My eyes zero in on the faint half-moon indents carved into the ridges of his abs.

Holy shit. I really did leave a mark.

I should feel bad about that... shouldn't I?

But my mouth goes dry as I drink him in, my body already humming, picking right back up where it left off...

"Damn, girl. I didn't know you had it in you." Luka says, voice low and husky, a smirk tugging at the corner of his mouth. He reaches to unclip my helmet, and I have to fight the urge to shiver when his fingers graze the side of my neck.

He always insists on helping me, like I'm not perfectly capable of doing it myself. Probably just being chivalrous. Still, it's pathetic that I'm so reactive to a simple touch.

I focus on a raindrop sliding down his Adam's apple, trying to distract myself, until he swallows, only making it worse.

"Yeah, me neither..." The words come out in a breathy whisper as I wet my lips. A slow, pulsing heat builds low in my core, my body still humming from the adrenaline rush.

Luka grabs my hand and tugs me behind him. "Come on, let's get you in some warm clothes before you crack a tooth from all that teeth chattering."

It's a nice gesture, but I can't let myself get caught up in it. It doesn't mean anything. As much as I'd like to believe I've somehow made it past Luka's walls and back into his circle of trust, there's something telling me he's still got his guard up. Half the time he's mean to me while the other half he's flirting with me, brushing his stupid fingers over my skin every chance he gets.

He's got this take charge energy about him that's so damn commanding and for some reason I can't seem to resist doing anything he tells me to do. It's like when he speaks to me, he's got some kind of remote control that shuts off part of my brain making all the noise go silent.

So as annoyed as I am by all the mixed signals he keeps sending me, I also realize that I'm the dummy that keeps falling for it.

We make our way through the garage and into the mudroom, our sopping wet clothes leaving puddles behind us, as the low growl of thunder vibrates through the walls.

Luka peels off his protective jacket, dropping the heavy soaked material to the ground with a loud thwack. My eyes widen, caught off guard again by the sight of his broad, muscular chest. His dark t-shirt clings to him like a second skin, and my fingers twitch with the sudden urge to touch him.

Holy shit. My eyes linger on the black ink swirling over his forearms, getting lost in the story etched across his skin. Is it one continuous piece or a collection of images woven together over time? I want to ask him about his ink—when he got his first tattoo—if it was in prison... what do they mean?

But I can't.

Those are personal questions, and I am in no position to

expect him to answer them for me. Luka doesn't owe me any explanations for the choices he's made or why he's made them. I don't deserve to know him any deeper. Not anymore.

He must notice me blatantly checking him out because he crosses his arms over his chest and wets his lips before flashing me a wolfish grin. "Careful, now. You keep looking at me like that. A guy may get the wrong idea."

His tone is teasing, but the heat in his eyes tells me there's at least some truth to them.

I feel my cheeks flame with embarrassment, and I roll my eyes, trying not to look like his words affected me. "Oh, get over yourself. I wasn't checking you out. I was just looking at your tattoos."

His emerald eyes grow darker as he makes no effort to hide his obvious perusal over my body. "Well, I'm not even going to deny it, I'm definitely looking at your tits right now."

Of course, L.O.K.I. chooses that moment to turn the AC on. Whose side is he on anyway?

I feel my nipples harden almost painfully as goosebumps erupt over my skin, but for some reason, I don't look away. Maybe I'm still riding the high from the motorcycle ride, or maybe it's the look of surprise in Luka's eyes that has me feeling a little braver than usual, but I find myself wanting to lean in rather than run away.

Luka's smile beams, and I know he's loving this unspoken challenge between us... or maybe he's just enjoying watching me suffer trying to keep up with him.

When my teeth start chattering, I get my answer.

He breaks the stare first and kicks off his boots before peeling his soaking wet t-shirt over his head. Then he pushes his pants down to his ankles and steps out of them. He pauses at the waistband of his boxer briefs, and it's only then that I realize I'm holding my breath and staring because he gives me a flirty wink and whispers, "You wish."

I shake my head and roll my eyes, wishing I had a better rebuttal, but we both know he's right. I was gawking—again.

He opens the dryer and pulls out a warm towel, which he drapes over my shoulders. "Hang tight, I'll grab you some dry clothes."

I start to argue and tell him I'm more than capable of grabbing my own clothes to change into, but something tells me his offer isn't up for negotiation. Besides, all my pajamas aren't exactly warm, nor appropriate for that matter.

After he disappears, I wrap the towel around my wet clothes and make my way down the hallway, taking in all the personal touches sprinkled around the space that I didn't notice before.

When I get to the sitting room, I pause in the doorway, remembering my parents' no children allowed rule, but then I remember this isn't their house anymore, and I enter the room on principle.

A framed photo on the sofa table catches my eye, and I take a step closer to get a better look.

In the picture, Luka and Guy are standing proudly in their Halloween costumes, Guy is dressed as a famous soccer player, and Luka is dressed as some anime guy from one of his video games. Guy's smile is beaming at the camera, but Luka's distracted by something and looking to the side. A small smile tips at his lips, but his eyes are what grab my attention. He looks so happy and completely enamored with whatever he's looking at.

I think I secretly went as Chucky that year. My parents

never celebrated Halloween, so I'd always go over to Luka's and change into my costume there. Mrs. Kingsley would always help me with my makeup and costume before taking us trick-or-treating. Then she'd help me clean it all off before sending me home with my belly full of candy.

Now that I'm older, I realize there's no way my parents didn't know what was going on, so I guess it was cool that they let me go every year. Maybe they wouldn't have if they knew the type of costumes I was choosing, but Mrs. Kingsley's makeup skills were good enough to keep my identity mostly hidden.

The sound of footsteps coming back down the stairs startles me, and I hurry to set the picture down, but my elbow bumps into something tall and narrow. It wobbles a few times, and I spin around to save it from falling, but immediately pull my hand away like I've just touched a hot stove.

Of course, Luka sees the whole thing, and I can practically feel his smile as he watches me attempt to pretend like he didn't just catch me snooping.

My eyes go wide as they adjust and I fully take in all the details...The small patch of red pubic hair, trimmed into a nice landing strip, decorating the most realistic-looking replica of the female genitals I've ever seen.

Okay, it's the first...*and* the most realistic...Both statements can be true at the same time.

He grabs the object in question and twirls it in front of him like a baton. "What's wrong, Girl Scout? It's just a fleshlight. It's not going to bite you or anything." He holds it out to me as if to prove it. "Don't worry, it's clean," he adds, as if *that's* what I'm the most concerned about right now.

I shield my eyes with my hand. "What *is* it? And why wouldn't it be clean?"

The devil himself couldn't even rival the wicked grin that spreads over Luka's lips, and suddenly the context clues snap into place. I stand frozen in horror, hating that I just walked right into that one.

He wets his lips, his eyes flaring with heat as he holds the silicone mold out toward me. "This is a flesh-light." His eyes never leave mine as he slides his middle finger inside to demonstrate. "It's a male masturbation toy. Keeps things interesting and fun when you're jerking off." He adds a second finger, then slowly begins to pump his digits inside her.

I feel a thin sheen of perspiration break out over the back of my neck as warmth begins to pool between my thighs just at the sight of Luka's clearly talented fingers stroking the toy.

Jesus Christ, who knew a man's hands could be so attractive? I don't know if I'll ever be able to look at him the same way again.

"And why exactly do you keep your *toy* out in the open for anyone to see?" I finally manage to ask, feeling annoyed by my own embarrassment, at how easy I make it for Luka to tease me.

Luka makes a show of looking around. "Well... this is my home, and it's not like I have a lot of guests over. I find that it's a functional, easily accessible place to keep it." He shrugs. "Besides, who doesn't want to look at a pussy every now and then. I custom-built Susanna here, picked out the labia color and everything."

"I really don't need to hear the details."

"Wow, Girl Scout, you sure are looking flushed right now.

There's nothing to be embarrassed about, it's not like she's real or anything." He gives the toy a gentle kiss before setting it back down in the exact spot I found it. "If Susanna freaks you out, I'd hate to see how you'd react to my toy room."

I jerk my gaze up to his, seeing amusement flash through his eyes. "You have enough sex toys to fill an entire room?" I hate that I can't tell if he's joking or not. I mean... the man's house is a giant robot, so why wouldn't he have an entire room designated for all his sex toys?

Perfect white teeth bite down on his bottom lip as he tries to hide his grin. "You want a tour? I'd be happy to show you my collection."

"No, thank you. That won't be necessary." I take the folded dry clothes he's still holding and practically run to the bathroom to change out of my sopping wet clothes.

"Offer's there if you change your mind," Luka calls from the other side of the door.

"Trust me, that won't be necessary!" I call back.

"Suit yourself."

Once I'm inside and safe from Luka's teasing, I lean against the sink and take in my reflection. Wet hair falling in loose waves around my bright, red, flushed cheeks that make my hazel eyes look more green than gold, and not a trace of makeup in sight. I guess the rain washed it all off completely.

It's weird, somehow, I feel more beautiful right now than when I've got a full face of makeup and my hair perfectly styled. The flush on my cheeks gives me a youthful glow. I guess embarrassment looks good on me.

Embarrassment... or arousal?

"I'm starving, so I'm going to order a pizza. Jalapeños and hot honey still good with you?" Luka says from the other side of the door, making me jump like I've just been caught thinking something I shouldn't.

Honestly, can I not have one private moment to my thoughts without having Luka alerted to it? Does he have some sort of heart rate censor monitoring me?

"Yeah, if that's what you want. I'm not picky," I quickly call back.

But rather than answering me, I hear his voice in the distance repeating the order like he's talking on the phone.

I don't know why, but that simple gesture does something to me, and I get this warm fluttering feeling in my stomach. I can't remember the last time someone asked me my preference for pizza... Jimmy certainly didn't. He practically ate like a toddler, hating any seasoning on his food, especially spicy food. I don't think he'd know how to order a pizza if his life depended on it.

Stop comparing everyone to Jimmy. Luka is your...
Husband.

I shake my head, still trying to wrap my brain around it. Images from tonight's meeting rush back—Luka claiming me as his wife in front of the whole town, the way his jaw clenched when he realized what my parents were saying, the fury in his eyes like he was ready to burn the world down if it meant protecting me.

I've never felt so... *wanted*. By anyone.

It's all supposed to be pretend, but I can't help but feel like we're starting to blur the lines. And it's messing with my head in ways I didn't expect.

I peel off the heavy, wet layers and pull on the soft, worn, oversized t-shirt that smells like Luka. He was thoughtful enough to let me borrow a pair of his sweatpants, even though they're way too big. I do my best to tie the waistband as tight as possible, but they still hang loose at my hips, and I have to roll up the legs four times, so I don't trip on them. I glance down at myself and blow out a sigh. I may look ridiculous, but at least I'm warm now.

When I swing open the door, I walk right into the immovable force that is Luka. His hands grip my waist to steady me. Neither one of us moves as I stare up at his defined jaw, the way his Adam's apple bobs as he swallows, and my fingers itch to trace it. Then I feel his thumb brush against my hip and take a big, not-so-subtle step back. "Thanks for the clothes," I say in a high-pitched voice that sounds nothing like my own, and give him two thumbs up for emphasis.

He huffs a laugh like he's holding back another tease. "No problem. Hey, so I was thinking since we're already ordering pizza, we could watch a movie or something, too?" He shrugs. "If you're up for it."

I narrow my eyes, not even trying to hide my suspicion at his jarring mood change. "Why?"

"What do you mean, why?" He holds a hand over his heart like I've wounded him. "I just figured tonight was... a lot... and I don't know about you, but I could use a little escapism."

I twist my lips, considering his offer.

"You can't tell me this isn't perfect movie-watching weather," he adds, just as the low rumble of thunder echoes in the distance.

He's not wrong... And it has been far too long since I've had free time to watch a movie—well, apart from the Avengers marathon with L.O.K.I. that is, but that felt more like babysitting a genius preschooler than relaxing and enjoying myself with as much as he talked. Of course, I'd never tell him that.

"All right. Yeah. A movie night sounds fun." I nod, feeling awkward all of a sudden.

I bite my cheek and rock back on my heels, trying to push the detailed reminders from my mind. Not helpful, brain.

"I went ahead and took the liberty of selecting the movie. I hope you don't mind." He gestures over his shoulder to the couch, where I notice he's already set out a bowl of popcorn.

I try to ignore the flutters my stomach gets from knowing he was so confident that I'd say yes and also the fact that he never really cared to have popcorn during a movie, but I always insisted we needed it.

It doesn't mean anything. He's probably just being nice. I remind myself, but who are we kidding? Luka isn't exactly the poster child for being nice.

Kind? Yes.

But nice? Absolutely not.

Unlike me, Luka doesn't feel the need to do anything he doesn't want to do. He has no problem telling someone no or speaking up when he doesn't agree with something. He's always been that way, always so confident of himself that he's not bothered if someone doesn't like him. I suspect his steady upbringing has something to do with it, but I'm certainly no expert on human behavior.

He shrugs like it's no big deal, like he already knows I'm overthinking his gesture in my head. "I figured a night like this called for a horror movie, so naturally, Psycho was the obvious choice."

I swallow a gulp as the flutters in my belly return full force because Luka doesn't like horror movies either.

I can't help but feel like I'm willingly walking into a trap...

I'm relieved when the doorbell interrupts us before I can ask one of those burning questions. He steps to the side, allowing me to sit on the sofa. "That's the pizza. I'll be right back, don't start it without me."

Maybe he really feels sorry for me, and this is his attempt at burying the hatchet?

I may as well be asking myself the meaning of life, for as ambiguous of a question that is.

Whatever is going on with him, I can't deny that it's stirring up all kinds of feelings. I snuggle into the soft throw blanket, feeling more seen in the past five minutes than I've felt in a very long time. Tears sting behind my eyes, and I quickly blink them away just as Luka appears, holding a pizza in one hand and two Cherry Cokes in the other.

"Scoot."

I slide over, moving the fluffy blanket out of the way to give him room, but rather than sitting on his side, he takes a seat in the middle. I shouldn't be surprised; the sofa is positioned to be the prime seating for movie watching. Besides, it's not like I haven't been riding around pressed against him on the back of his bike all day.

It's moments like this that my heart aches the most, the feeling of picking up exactly where we left off, only now there's a charged heat in the air between us. A thick tension coiling beneath the surface, crackling and popping as it tightens the invisible cords that string us together.

Luka presses a button on the remote, and the room goes

dark. Then the creepy music I know so well fills the silence, and I feel my tense body finally relax as a wave of nostalgia rolls over me. For the first time since I've been back, it finally feels like I'm home.

With my guard finally lowered, I settle in, feeling myself immersed in the movie. My heartrate starts to spike in anticipation as the infamous shower scene begins. I remember the first time I watched this movie—at a Kingsley family movie night, of course—I practically jumped out of my skin when he popped out of nowhere.

I could feel my body buzzing with adrenaline, and I'd never felt like that before. That was all it took. I was hooked. I've been chasing that high ever since.

Luka, on the other hand, had to sleep with a nightlight for weeks. I'm about to ask him if he remembers it, but when I turn to look at him, I find him staring back at me rather than at the gory scene before us. The sound of a woman screaming fills the silence.

"What are you looking at, creep?" I toss a piece of popcorn at him, hitting him straight in the forehead, but he doesn't even flinch.

For a moment, he looks annoyed, and just when I think he's about to flip his angry switch on me, he narrows his eyes and whispers, "You're one to talk. Who would guess that under that good girl exterior, you're really just a little freak. Does anyone else know that you smile during the murder parts?"

There's something so intoxicating about his tone, how he can shift the temperature of the room with only a few words.

I feel myself freeze, terrified and excited at the same

time… just like I was in his parents' kitchen the other night when he told me to pour out the glass of wine.

But then he grabs a handful of popcorn and tosses it at me, breaking whatever voodoo trance he had on me. And just like that, we're back to the way we used to be.

My reaction is a little delayed, but I manage to duck just in time, dodging the flying kernels before I send a handful back at him, far more forcefully than his throw. "Why are you watching me when there's a fantastic movie playing on the seventy-inch-high-definition screen in front of your face?"

"I was trying to, but I got creeped out when I saw how much you were enjoying it." He grabs an even larger handful of popcorn and throws it at me, and this time, rather than ducking, I open my mouth, attempting to catch as many pieces as I can.

He reaches for another handful. I dive on top of the bowl, shielding it with my body. "Stop! Your hands are too big; you're wasting it all!"

Luka's up on his knees now, hands hovering over my hip bones as he gives me the opportunity to relent. "Don't start something you can't finish." His velvety tone is threatening and alluring all at the same time, and I feel my heart rate kick up in anticipation.

It feels like we're innocent teenagers again, giggling and play-fighting. But the rush of warm tingles shooting between my thighs at the feel of his hands on me feels anything but innocent.

"Stop, Luka. I swear to God if you tickle me, I can't be held responsible for your injuries," I squeal, maintaining my coverage of the bowl.

His voice is like gravel as he whispers in my ear, "I think

I'll take my chances." His chest presses against my back as he pins me down with his weight, and then his hand clamps down on my hip bone, sending a jolt of electricity straight to my core.

I open my mouth to laugh, but no sound comes out as my breath catches in my throat and my whole body locks up. Luka digs his fingers in deeper, finding my most ticklish spot in seconds as I suck in a lungful of air and the cackle finally breaks free.

There's nothing cute or sexy about my laugh, especially this laugh that somehow Luka's only managed to conjure out of me. It's almost painful but feels amazing all the same, like he's uncorking a blockage that only he could reach.

I feel years of sadness being siphoned out of my body as waves of rolling laughter fill all the cracks and crevices of my broken heart. It's a healing laugh, one that comes up all the way from my toes, shaking away the stubborn blues that stain me from within.

"Now apologize for throwing food at me."

Despite the effect his dreamy voice has on me, a squeal of laughter is the only response I can manage as I writhe beneath him, attempting to twist myself from his grip.

"You're being difficult. Just say the word, and I'll let you go," he whispers, his warm breath on my neck sending a rush of goosebumps over my arms. I feel my nipples harden as my body purrs with excitement.

The word he's referring to was something we used to say when we wanted the other to stop pretending and tell the truth. *Thin Mints.* It was a play on my being a Girl Scout and the fact that Luka hates all things mint chocolate chip.

Though I'm finding it hard to believe he still remembers that...

I'm momentarily stunned as I'm suddenly aware of every inch of his skin that touches my own, aware of the thin fabric of his t-shirt that's loosely risen up my stomach, aware that only a couple of inches of fabric are separating my bare breast from his view, and my sensitive nipples are practically begging to be touched. Aware of how I've all but wiggled out of his ginormous sweatpants, and that his hands are now gripping my bare skin.

My breathing is slower now as I heave deep breaths, feeling my blood rush to keep up with my body's ever-growing urges. This little game just went from playfully innocent to something... not... in just a matter of seconds.

Luka must feel it too because I feel his grip on my hip loosen, replaced by the gentle caress of his thumb, that dips beneath the hem of the underwear I'm wearing.

I breathe in a gasp when he shifts on top of me, and I can feel the warmth of his breath on my neck. My traitorous body tilts my head to give him better access, as if she's opening herself up to him all on her own.

"You stopped fighting me... does that mean you surrender?" he whispers against the shell of my ear, and then I feel his hard length pressed against my thigh.

The sound of another woman being murdered is drowned out by the rain, and somehow, all I can focus on is my pounding heartbeat in my ears. I should stop this... shouldn't I? I could just say the word and he'd stop. It's not like we haven't played this game a million times before, but there is a part of me—my inner freak I suppose—that is curious about what would happen if I didn't give in. What would he do then?

I think I get my answer when his thumb swipes beneath my underwear, this time stretching even lower than before. His other hand pins my wrist above my head as he stares down at me, his eyes searching mine for any signs of my discomfort.

My t-shirt rises a little higher as I heave a breath, feeling Luka's eyes heat my skin as he watches me like a lion watches its prey. His eyes are dilated so large you can hardly see the green, and his nostrils flare like it's taking a great deal of restraint to hold himself back.

"Say it, Scout," he practically pleads, like he wants me to put him out of his misery, like he physically can't do it without me telling him to.

"I..." I swallow the lump lodged in my throat and wet my lips. His eyes flash to my mouth, and I feel his thumb move over me again. This time, venturing even lower grazing the top of my freshly shaved mound.

His teeth clamp shut, and his muscles grow tighter when he realizes that new detail about me. The sight of his reaction does something to me, and I can't imagine what it'd be like to watch him really touch me... or taste me.

No one's ever done that to me before—not really anyway. Jimmy went down on me for about ten seconds one drunken night in college, but it was too sensitive; it almost hurt. Once he realized it wasn't doing anything for me, he never offered to do it again.

I shake my head, realizing I'm once again thinking about Jimmy.

Luka's voice is all gravel and lust when he says, "You're

killing me here, Scout. I'm begging you, say the word before I—"

Before I what?

I guess I'll never know, because before he can finish his sentence, a bolt of lightning strikes so close it lights up the whole room. A sharp crack of thunder follows, shaking the walls and rattling the windows.

Then everything goes black.

The silence between us is deafening. The only sounds are our uneven breaths. Nerves flutter in my stomach as tension coils through me.

Is he going to kiss me?

Do I want him to?

He exhales a heavy sigh, and I can't tell if it's relief or disappointment... maybe a little of both, and then he slowly climbs off me.

"Come on," he murmurs. "Let's get you to bed. The emergency generator should kick on any minute now."

Right on cue, the power flickers back to life, but the moment's gone. And so is his cocky smirk. It's as if whatever was building between us short-circuited with the lights, giving us a hard reset.

Disappointment scorches through me like a branding iron. I shouldn't feel this way. He's never promised me anything. But rejection has a way of wearing you down, and I'm tired of pretending it doesn't hurt.

Sometimes, I just wish someone wanted me. Really wanted me. For me.

But I guess some things never change.

I don't take his hand when he offers it. "I think I can manage."

CHAPTER SEVENTEEN

SCOUT

I dip my paintbrush into the green paint, swirling and mixing until it blends to the perfect shade that matches the image in my mind. The Phantom's eyes stare back at me from the canvas as I layer in the color, adding depth and dimension until I feel it come to life.

I suppose one of the benefits of Luka avoiding me is that I've had plenty of time alone to wrestle with my muse and plenty of time to overthink about every single thing that happened the other night.

What I'm saying is, it hasn't exactly been a pleasant experience.

Am I really that naive that I don't know the difference between Luka acting friendly toward me and thinking there was something between us? My God, I guess I'm worse off than I realized.

No wonder Luka's avoiding me. I must reek of

desperation. If I were him, I'd avoid me too.

I guess being cooped up in this room all day with Luka's house as my only companion is starting to get to my head. I need to go outside and touch some grass.

The sound of something clanking in the kitchen brings me out of my anxiety spiral, and my ears perk up to listen.

"I can't help but notice that you're showing signs of distress. Is there something bothering you that I can assist you with? Or are you still feeling the same symptoms you were suffering from this morning?" I hear L.O.K.I. ask.

"While I appreciate your concern for my well-being, is there something else you should be working on right now?" Luka calls out.

"Of course. I'll leave you to it then. Would you like me to start tracking your mood to see if I can detect a pattern for your distress? Other than the obvious, I mean?"

"No. I want you to mind your own business and do what I asked you to do," Luka fires back.

"All right. I'll adjust my curiosity and empathy to meet your needs. If you'd like to create a record of what you're upset about, just say, 'record journal entry.' Would you like me to remind you this evening during your bedtime routine?"

"No! Jesus, L.O.K.I. can you just stop?"

The paintbrush slips from my hand, and I flinch at the sharp crack of a cabinet being slammed, quickly followed by the unmistakable sound of angrily stomping feet. I freeze, muscles seizing, as a cold sweat chills my skin.

I look down to find my feet covered in green paint, relieved that my feet blocked most of the paint from splattering on the rug. "Shit."

I rush to the bathroom to wash the paint from my feet. I need to act quickly before the stain sets in.

"I've started the kettle for a cup of Stress Relief Tea. I apologize for upsetting you. I will remain silent until I'm next prompted."

Luka's heavy footsteps grow louder, and I feel myself go into full-on panic mode as I rush to the bathroom to clean up.

"Whoa. Nice work. What are you—?" He sees the giant splatter of paint and looks around, wearing a curious expression. "What happened here?"

I give him a little wave from the bathroom as I hop off the counter, my feet and legs still dripping from washing them in the sink. "Sorry about that. I accidentally dropped my paintbrush..." I start, but now Luka's attention is on the painting.

"I'll pay to have it cleaned..." I continue, but the side-eye he gives me tells me he won't hear of it.

My stomach twists in knots as I watch him, studying his expression to try to make out his thoughts. He looks a little more tired than usual, with dark circles starting to form under his eyes, and I notice the shadow of the two-day-old beard on his jaw.

I think back to his argument with L.O.K.I., and I can't help but wonder if the *symptoms* he was referring to are anything like the sexual frustration I've been drowning in lately.

"This is really great, Scout," he finally says, and I can hear the sincerity in his voice.

"Oh, really? Thanks. I think I finally got the right expression." I finally manage, as I take a step, putting a couple of much-needed inches between us. Honestly, it's like the man's never heard of personal space.

He shakes his head; his eyes still locked on the canvas. "I knew you'd create something amazing, but this is so much better than I expected." He turns to glance at me, and I try my best to act casual, like his praising words didn't just heal something inside me.

"I wasn't sure if it was too much...or if he looked too angry..."

He must find my response amusing because he clicks his tongue and takes a step closer. It's as if his body sucks up all the oxygen in the room, and I instinctively hold my breath, as if waiting for him to give me permission to breathe.

Luka's gaze holds mine, and I wonder if he realizes that the Phantom's eyes are the exact same shade of green as his. That it's his stern expression the Phantom is making. Or that I spent two days staring at the blank canvas, feeling completely lost at what direction to go, until I realized that Luka was my blueprint to nailing the Phantom's complexity.

They share the same essence, equal parts good and evil, darkness and light. Neither are just one thing, but a mixture of paradoxes that most will never understand and even fewer will be close enough to feel firsthand.

Once I made the connection, I couldn't see the Phantom any other way. It was as if my hands moved of their own accord, and I surrendered to a mind greater than my own. Much like the blissful absence of worrying thoughts Luka induced in me the other night, I barely slept, barely remembered to eat, not stopping until my muse felt satisfied.

It's only when I feel Luka's thumb brush over my arm that I finally suck in a breath.

"It's perfect. You did incredible." There's a spark in his green eyes as he watches me, and for a second, I wonder if he can actually read my thoughts—because he always seems to know just what to say.

My shoulders sag in relief, and I can't help the smile that breaks across my face knowing he's happy with the design. That's one of the benefits of having such a blunt friend. I know if he says something, he means it. Luka has proved more than once that he isn't worried about hurting my feelings, which makes this moment feel that much sweeter.

I'm lost in a trance, staring at his mouth when he says, "Get dressed and meet me outside in ten minutes. We've got some errands to run."

———————

I'm relieved when Luka takes the long way into town, not that I'd really expect anything different. I've grown to understand him so much deeper over these last few weeks, recognizing more and more what drives him.

While everyone else is rushing through life, trying to skip the dull parts, Luka makes a point to savor each and every moment. It's like he's always looking for a way to upgrade his experiences and make them something to look forward to. Thus, a boring commute into town turns into a joy ride through the mountains, the feeling of complete and utter freedom, making you feel like anything's possible.

I never understood the appeal before, but now that I've experienced it firsthand, I can see how addictive the feeling is. No wonder he always opts for the bike every chance he gets.

It's romantic, really—the way he's so determined to squeeze the most out of life. His fearless approach to living, paired with his unapologetic honesty, has me questioning things I never thought I would. For the first time in my life, I'm actually considering what I want before I think of everyone else.

I can't say that I'm not nervous riding as his backpack, but I trust him to keep me safe. And let's be honest—wrapping my arms around that ridiculously firm chest isn't exactly a burden. I might even *look forward* to the excuse to get my hands on him.

As if on cue, Luka's hand moves over my thigh in a comforting caress, massaging and squeezing as we roll to a stop at the red light. I know it's not anything more than platonic, but there's certainly nothing platonic about the way my body responds.

I blow out a long exhale through my nose as I try to drag my mind out of the gutter, desperately hoping Luka can't feel the involuntary clenching my lady bits have taken to in protest.

I hate how easily my body responds to him. It makes me feel pathetic, like I'm the only one caught in this mess while he just drifts through it, completely unbothered.

Meanwhile, I'm in my head twenty-four-seven, dissecting every look, every word, trying to figure out what the hell is going on in his.

He clearly notices the effect he has on me; it's obviously why he keeps doing what he's doing. But have I really been reading him wrong? Is this just the way he is with everyone?

God, how stupid am I to think there was more going on between us?

Either I've misread him completely, or this is just some game to him. A game I keep losing.

But not anymore.

I'm done letting him string me along. Done falling for every half-smile and heated glance.

He's not going to keep me drooling like a naive idiot.

Luka's hand slips from my thigh, and I hate the disappointment I feel from the loss of it.

"Here we are," he says, parking the bike at the curb.

I glance up at the sign, then back at him, brows raised as he secures my helmet to the back of the bike. "What are we doing at Hardware Store?"

"I thought we'd get a jump on ordering supplies for the mural," he says casually. "I don't know much about the process—just what I skimmed from a quick online search, but I figured you'd need paint, maybe some tarps, buckets, brushes. That kind of stuff."

"Right. Supplies." I nod, pressing my lips together as I cross my arms over my chest.

A flicker of disappointment rises, quickly followed by the flush of embarrassment. Of course this is why we're here.

What did I honestly think we were doing today?

Luka must notice my sudden change in demeanor because he narrows his eyes like he's studying me.

For a second, I think he was going to ask me if I'm okay.

But he just turns and strolls toward the door. "You coming?" he calls over his shoulder.

And once again, I find myself chasing after him, mentally scolding myself the whole way. *Stop being such a pushover.*

When I finally catch up to him, he gives me that easy,

infuriating smile and holds the door open like nothing's happened.

"How chivalrous of you," I say under my breath.

But the cocky twitch of his lips tells me he heard me.

"Chivalry's just a form of foreplay, princess," he says with a wink. "I know that's a new concept for you."

My body pitches forward, and I nearly trip over my own two feet, but Luka's hand clamps around my elbow, steadying me like he was expecting it. My eyes go wide as I look up to find him wearing that same infuriatingly amused expression.

"Welcome in," Hank calls without looking up from the register as he audibly counts the stack of bills in his hand.

There isn't anything flashy about the warehouse-style building with its concrete flooring and high ceilings. Industrial metal shelves line the aisles, stacked full of an assortment of materials for any DIY project.

The smell of cut wood and sawdust hits me, and I immediately feel myself perk up. It smells like new beginnings and hope for something that doesn't yet exist.

It may not be an art supply store, but in a small town, you have to make do with what you have. Hank always made sure to keep a stock of my favorite paints and canvases. I didn't realize it at the time, but he really went out of his way to do that. It's just another reason why this small town is unlike anywhere else. It's the people who look out for each other, even if it means selling products it doesn't make sense for them to carry just so a lonely teenager doesn't feel so alone.

"Well, would you look who it is," Hank says when he finally looks up and sees me. "If it ain't the newlyweds themselves." He strides over and wraps me in a bear hug that knocks the air right out of my lungs. "It's about time you stopped by to see me," he says with a mock scolding tone. "Now, I'll admit, I was a little hurt not to get a wedding invite..." He nods toward Luka, his eyes twinkling. "But then I overheard Miss Scarlett telling your mama the news, and I figured you two had your reasons for keeping it small..." His words trail off, and I know he's referring to the incident between Luka and my parents at the town meeting the other night.

"Thanks, Hank. It's... a... good to be back." I glance around the store, a soft smile tugging at my lips. "This place hasn't changed a bit."

"Yeah, well, you know what they say, if ain't broke don't fix it." He chuckles to himself and rocks on his heels as he looks from me to Luka. "So, what brings you two in today?"

"We're going to be placing an order for some painting supplies," Luka says, slinging an arm around my shoulder. My whole body goes stiff. "I'm sure you've heard by now that Scout's going to be painting a mural downtown."

"Oh, yeah, I caught wind of that. Wasn't sure whether to believe it or not." Hank grins. "It's good to see you two finally figure yourselves out. I always knew you'd find your way back to each other. Puppy love and all that..." He winks, and I feel my cheeks heat as Luka's hand tightens around my arm, like he's holding me in place.

"Well, I'll leave you to it then. I'll be around if you need anything—just holler."

"Thanks, Hank. I'll drop off the list on the way out." Luka's large palm moves to the back of my neck, and he gently ushers me forward. The tension slips from my body as he takes the lead, my brain already surrendering the wheel.

It feels nice, but despite my brain's eagerness to go offline, at least my gut sends out a warning flare, reminding me that this is exactly the kind of mixed signals I've been trying to avoid.

My steps falter to a halt, and I shrug Luka's possessive hand off my neck. His face flashes a look of confusion, and if I didn't know better, I might even think it was genuine.

I don't know what kind of game he's playing, but I can't let myself fall for it anymore. I'm done following him around like a sad puppy, begging for whatever attention he'll give me.

My brain's clearly fried from all the detective work I've been doing, trying to decode Luka's motives, because in the span of a few seconds, I've gone from go-with-the-flow and swan-dived straight into the overthinking territory.

Trying to look unbothered, I pick up a can and pretend to read the label.

"I'm no mural expert, but why do you need wood stain for the side of a brick building?"

It takes a couple of seconds for me to process Luka's question before I realize he's right. I carefully set the paint stain down and try to play it off casually. "You're right, you're not a paint expert," I say in agreement, then move to the next aisle. I don't have to look back at Luka to know exactly what face he's making.

God, I feel like such an idiot. I just need to get through this shopping trip, then I'll hole up in my room and avoid him for the rest of the summer. At least I've got the mural to keep me busy, and it's not like he hasn't been avoiding me anyway.

"Did you want me to add that to the list?" Luka gestures to the multipack of paintbrushes in my hand, and I give him a noncommittal shrug.

"Is that a yes or a no?" He presses, stepping in front of me to block my path before I can walk away.

I wave him off and roll my eyes. "Sure. I've never painted brick with a paintbrush so I don't know what brush style I'll need."

Mural, supplies, paint... that's the reason he brought me here. I need to focus.

"Okay..." he drags the word out under his breath as he follows me to the back, where a variety of different style ladders are lined up on the wall.

"How about something like this?" He nods toward an electric ladder on wheels.

I shake my head dismissively. "That's too much... I don't need a fancy machine. I'm perfectly capable of climbing a ladder." I point to a basic, aluminum twelve-foot ladder. I don't know why this is the battle I choose, but suddenly I feel the need to fight back, to show him that he can't always get his way.

He narrows his eyes, looking at the ladder and back to me. "That's too dangerous. I don't like the idea of you climbing up and down that thing, carrying buckets of paint. What if you spill some paint on one of the steps and lose your balance?"

"Really, Mr. Motorcycle?" I challenge back, crossing my arms as I stare back at him.

His brows lift, clearly thrown by the shift in my mood, but then a ghost of a smirk tugs at the corner of his lips. "Nope, not even remotely the same thing," he says, shaking his head.

"How is it different? If anything, you're putting yourself in more danger just by being on the road with other drivers, not to mention on a moving vehicle—"

He takes a step, closing the distance between us, using his height to his advantage as he towers over me. "I understand the risks, Girl Scout. But we're comparing apples to oranges right now. Besides, the key difference in the two scenarios is that I won't be there to make sure you don't fall."

I roll my eyes and scoff. "Of course, I don't know how I've managed to live all this time without you holding my hand and making sure I don't accidentally walk out in the middle of traffic." But I can't help the little flutter in my belly knowing he's genuinely worried about my safety.

He hasn't even touched me, and already my brain and my vagina are doing synchronized gymnastics, trying to read between the lines.

I really hope the damage isn't permanent...

The slight tic in Luka's jaw is the only indication of his annoyance. "You're five two, right?"

"Yeah, why?"

"You'd have to be at least five seven to reach the top of the wall with the A-frame, and that's assuming you were standing on the top step, which is completely out of the question. Sorry, Girl Scout, but it looks like I win this one," he says with a non-apologetic shrug. "We can get both if it'll make you feel better. But just so you know, you're not climbing higher than six feet on that A-frame."

I try to ignore the stupid tingles that have come back in full force, violently fluttering around in my belly like a giggly schoolgirl. Am I really so desperate that all it takes is for someone to consider my safety now?

"You've got some nerve if you really think I'm going to

keep letting you tell me what I can and cannot do," I fire back with all the confidence I can muster.

I know I'm in trouble when I see his lips twitch in amusement. He quirks an eyebrow and lowers his voice to an almost whisper. "Are you sure about—"

I don't wait for him to finish, spinning on my heel before stomping in the other direction. But my escape is cut short when I feel my shirt tighten around me as Luka tugs me back. "Whoa, not so fast. Tell me what this is really about. What's got your panties all tied in a knot?"

"Nothing," I lie, crossing my arms over my chest.

Luka narrows his eyes at me and grins. "No, it's definitely not nothing." He ruffles my hair playfully, dodging my attempts to swat his hand away.

"Will you stop? You're messing up my hair. I'm not playing around, Luka!"

"Oh no, she's getting angry," he taunts as I try to catch his teasing hand before he can touch me again.

"I thought we've already established that you're a terrible liar. So why don't you spare me the tantrum and just spit it out already."

I cross my arms over my chest and force myself to meet his eyes. "I can't keep doing this with you. You say things like you know some secret about me that I don't and..." I swallow, feeling my throat tighten with emotion. "And it's confusing. I don't know how to act around you anymore because I never know if you're going to be the sweet, thoughtful guy who surprises me in bed with my favorite drink or if you're going to disappear and completely ignore me." My words break off at the sight of Luka's smile, which he's doing a terrible job of trying to hide behind his hand. "What's so funny?"

"Nothing. Sorry." He folds his lips in a flat line and gestures for me to continue.

"You know what, never mind. Forget it. Let's just finish up so we can leave."

"Hang on. I want to hear what you were going to say."

"This is hardly the place to have this conversation. Can you just drop it? I'm just tired. I was up all night finishing that mural design, and I can't even remember if I ate breakfast."

"You didn't..." His voice softens, more serious now. I don't want to know how he knows I forgot to eat breakfast, but something tells me it wasn't just a lucky guess. "And I have no doubt you're exhausted, but I want to hear what you were going to say. I need to hear you say it."

He keeps his gaze trained on me, but this time he's not looking at me condescendingly; if anything, he almost looks nervous.

I might as well fess up, because I know as well as anyone that Luka's not going to drop it. My shoulders sag in defeat, and I blow out a sigh. "I think I've been reading your signals wrong. I was starting to think that maybe there was something developing between us." His eye contact is too intense, and I have to look away. "I promise not to make it weird, so if we could just pretend I never mentioned it, that'd be great."

"What if I don't want to?"

My eyes snap back to his. "What do you mean?"

Luka's eyes darken as he takes a step, closing the distance between us. "Nothing."

He grabs my arm and tugs me to follow him. "Wait, don't we still need to order supplies? Where are we going now?"

"We've got one more stop to make."

CHAPTER EIGHTEEN

LUKA

I was hoping it wouldn't have to come to this, but I'm at my wits end. And if there's any hope of me keeping my hands to myself, then something's got to give.

It's taken every ounce of strength I have to keep myself away. It's like she's haunting me. She's everywhere, consuming my every thought and visiting me every night in my dreams.

Why the fuck does she have to be so goddamn perfect? I don't think I could craft someone who ticks every one of my boxes any better than my wife, who's ironically the only woman I cannot have.

I'm still testing the waters, gauging her reaction to different things, but I'm almost certain about one thing. Scout is a natural submissive. The moment I take control, her whole body responds like a puppet—and fuck if that's not my biggest weakness.

She's already so willing to please me, and I haven't even touched her... yet.

I shake the thought away because I know I'm playing with fire here. I'm not thinking clearly. Getting my revenge on her father is one thing and teaching her a lesson is another. But how far can I really take things before this blows up in both of our faces?

It doesn't matter because I'm not going to tempt fate and find out. Which is exactly why we're here.

We pull up into the parking spot in front of the building, and I shrug off my helmet. "I'm just going to run in and pick up a few essentials."

Scout's eyes grow wide, not even trying to disguise her panic. "Essentials? What essentials do you really need from Adult Store?"

"I'm sensing a little judgment in your tone. Do you have a problem with this upstanding establishment?"

"No... of course not." She looks around suspiciously. "But what exactly do you need right now that you don't already have?" Her words come out in a hiss, her face flushed bright pink.

Her innocence makes me chuckle. "Oh, Girl Scout, I wasn't referring to me."

Her eyes grow even wider, and I swear I see the color drain from her face.

Interesting.

I was expecting her to be flustered—counting on it, actually—but I guess I've managed to push her past humiliation and straight into panic mode.

Looks like she's even more vanilla than I thought. She doesn't even know the things she's missing out on...

Without another word, I head for the door. Scout scrambles after me, holding a hand over her face like she's trying to hide.

The sound of a bell chimes as I push through the deckled glass door—the town's only requirement for having a sex shop in the middle of town. Fuck, I love this small town, the people can't be beat.

"Is that my favorite customer?" No sooner does she reach me than my face is pressed into Miss Scarlett's pillowy-soft bosom.

I don't know if it's the temporary suffocation that resets my brain or if there's some other kind of magic at play, but it never fails to make me feel better. I'm convinced that if more people knew about this power, we could have world peace.

I nuzzle in, letting Miss Scarlett's magic titties siphon all my stress away. I almost forget what I'm supposed to be doing until she notices I didn't come alone.

"And look who you've brought with you!" She tosses me to the side as she pulls a very nervous-looking Scout into a hug. "You know, I never thought I'd see your pretty face set foot in my store." She breaks the hug and nudges me with her elbow. "But I guess being married to this one is bound to rub off on you." Her eyes sparkle with mischief as she looks between us.

"How's married life?" Miss Scarlett asks with a mischievous smile. "I'm surprised you two managed to leave the house at all. Especially after that little show you put on at the town meeting the other night." She waggles her brows and adds, "I do love an act of passion."

Scout's eyes widen in horror.

"Don't worry, we're making plenty of time to enjoy

ourselves." I wrap an arm around Scout and tug her into my side. "I can hardly keep this one off me. She's insatiable."

I feel a sharp pinch on my side, but I don't even flinch.

Miss Scarlett lets out a low whistle and pulls out a lace fan, waving it to cool herself down. "I can't say that I blame her. It's always the shy ones that surprise you."

"Indeed they do. Actually, that's why we're here—calling in some reinforcements." I pull Scout closer, feeling another searing pinch, this time on the back of my arm. "She keeps me up all night. Just can't seem to get enough, can you, sweetheart?"

I don't give her time to respond before pressing her face into my chest in more of a headlock than a hug. Scout struggles to break away, but she's no match for my strength. I pretend to comfort her, smoothing her hair down and planting a kiss on her head as she fights and pinches in protest.

Miss Scarlett laughs, clearly enjoying every second. "So that's why you look so tired," she says with a wink. "Well, I just got a new shipment of vibrating cock rings." She gestures over her shoulder. "They're on the back wall with the other vibrators."

"Thank you, Miss Scarlett. We'll be sure to check those out. I've been taking my time, easing her into things. Don't want to scare her off too soon, if you know what I'm saying."

"Of course. I've made that mistake too many times to count," she says with a sigh. "Oh, I just remembered, I've got that guybrator you ordered last week in the back. Why don't I give you two some privacy while I grab it." She gives me a knowing wink before sauntering away.

"Thanks, Miss Scarlett. You're a doll."

"Oh, honey, you have no idea." She calls without ever looking back.

I finally release Scout from my hold. Her hair's sticking up with static, and she sucks in a heaving gasp. She shoves me with both hands, but I don't move. "What the hell, Luka! Why would you tell her that? Miss Scarlett's probably back there dialing up the phone chain right now, telling everyone how horny I am."

"Aren't you?"

Her body goes still, and I know I've hit the nail on the head. "No. Of course not."

I take a step closer, lowering my voice. "Now I really know you're lying."

Without another word, I spin on a heel and make my way down the aisle filled with every type of lube a person could need. Oil-based, silicon-based, warming. Desensitizing. Don't need that, though I can see how it could be helpful in the right conditions. I'm nothing if not an equal opportunity sex toy enthusiast.

My eyes scan the shelves quickly, scanning the flavors until something grabs my attention. Green apple, blue raspberry, bubble gum... my fingers pause when I reach wild cherry. I glance over my shoulder to see Scout looking uncomfortable and laugh to myself as I drop it in the basket.

"You look like you're uncomfortable. Is this the first time you've been in a sex shop?"

"No." She shakes her head, but her eyes are too busy darting around, making sure the coast is clear to be convincing.

"Once again, I'm calling bullshit." I squat down to get a better view of the bottom shelf. "Ah, here we are. Cooling mint." I grab the box off the shelf and hold it out to show Scout. "Add in a little temperature play and you've got yourself a good time. I'm not sure I'd recommend it for beginners, though." I give her a wink as I toss it into the basket.

Scout almost has to run to keep up with me; her short legs are no match for my long strides. "Seriously, Luka, why did you bring me here? Do you just enjoy torturing me? Is that it?"

"Maybe... But what you should really be asking yourself is why you're so worried about what everyone is going to think," I say as I turn down the next aisle, stopping in front of the leather restraints and floggers.

"I'm not... But maybe I'd rather the whole town not think I'm a sexual deviant..." Scout's words trail off as she whips around the corner and crashes into my back with a squeak. "Who's that for?" She looks absolutely terrified when she sees the leather whip in my hand.

"Oh, this?" I shrug. "Wouldn't you like to know..." I give my palm a test smack and flinch as I wipe my stinging palm against my chest. Then I drop it in the basket as I continue shopping.

We head toward the display of butt plugs, and I reach for the most intimidating one I can find. It's a fox tail, not a tiny one either. Pretty damn close to life size if you ask me, though I can't be certain. I stroke the soft fur as I pretend to consider it, even gesturing for Scout to turn around so I can visualize the look of it on.

Of course she refuses, crossing her arms over her chest defiantly... if only she knew how much seeing her get so worked up does for me.

"This isn't funny," she snaps. "This is my life you're playing with. What if it gets back to my parents? Or Jimmy?"

I toss the butt plug onto the shelf and stalk toward her. She backs up instinctively, until her spine hits the metal shelf, knocking over a row of butt plugs.

"Is that a fucking joke?" I growl, closing the space between us. "Why the fuck does it matter what your douche bag ex thinks? Last I checked, I'm the one you're married to." I plant my hands on each side of her, boxing her in as I hold her gaze. "I have no problem marking you as mine. No shame whatsoever. Hell, I'll fuck you in front of the whole goddamn town if that's what it takes to make sure everyone knows you're mine."

Scout stands there frozen, staring up at me, with wide eyes, and I swear I catch the tiniest glint of intrigue flare behind them.

I'm treading into dangerous territory here.

Before I can read any further into that look, I turn around and fix the display of butt plugs like they were before turning down the next aisle.

My eyes light up when I see the various vibrators that come in all shapes and sizes. "Now this is what I came here for," I say, gesturing to the broad assortment. "Take your pick, princess. Whatever you need to tickle your fancy. Consider it yours."

I pick up the thick stubby one and begin examining it like I'm reading a wine label.

She storms after me with a new heat in her voice. "Oh, my God. I do not need or want a vibrator!" She shoves me, and I can tell she really put her anger into it this time, because I drop the high-tech sex toy I was holding. It must land on one of the buttons because the shaft starts pulsating and swirling in circles.

Scout's eyes widen as she stares down at where the vibrator slowly scoots across the floor until it bumps into her shoe. She yelps and jumps back like it might bite her. "Ew, get it away from me," she squeals.

I reach down to retrieve the overzealous mechanical cock, casually holding it in front of her face as it gives her everything it's got. "That's pretty impressive... Though it still doesn't have anything on me." I flick my eyes up to Scout, who may be scowling, but I recognize the undeniable look of curiosity in her gaze. "But you already knew that, didn't you?"

Her cheeks burn bright crimson as she narrows her eyes on me in a glare that's almost frightening. Too bad I see her for what she is, just a scared kitten, all puff and no bite.

Ignoring her warning glare, I set the vibrator back where it came from and grab a lime green one. It's simpler and more beginner-friendly. "How about this one? Not as flashy as some of the others, but it's rumbly. Which, in my experience, leads to more play time and less sensitivity." I test it against my palm and nod. "And it's got a slimmer profile."

Scout's eyes nearly bug out of her head as she glances over her shoulder to make sure we're still alone. "Luka, that's not funny," she whisper-yells as she tries to snatch the vibrator from me. But I'm too quick and move it to my other hand just in time.

"What's not funny?" I trade the lime green vibrator for a fluorescent purple one. It's got a wavy texture and curves up at the end. "Oh, this one looks nice. Do you prefer G-spot orgasms or are you more of a clitoris girl?" I think for a moment, then say, "We should probably find something that does both… just to be safe."

"I swear to God, Luka…" she warns through clenched teeth as she jumps to snatch the vibrator again. And once again, I'm faster.

I toss the toy between my hands teasingly. "Oh, come on, Girl Scout. There's nothing to be ashamed of. Sex is just a bodily function. It's the most basic human need we have, next to surviving, of course."

"This isn't funny, Luka." She jumps, reaching for the vibrator, but I dangle it over her head. "Stop messing around. Haven't you embarrassed me enough for one day?"

"Sadly, I don't think I have. Besides, there's nothing to be embarrassed about. Embarrassment is a choice."

"Spare me the counseling session, will you? You made your point; now, can we just go?"

"Yeah, sure. We can go. As soon as you choose."

"What? No. I don't even want one of those."

"Have you ever tried one?"

Her jaw tenses and her nostrils flare, but she doesn't correct me, which only confirms my suspicions.

"If you've never used one, then how do you know you won't like it?"

"Because I don't need it. Now, can you drop it?"

I open my hand, and the silicone toy falls to the ground, bouncing once.

She rolls her eyes. "You know that's not what I meant."

"Do you have something against orgasms? I'm simply offering you a solution to your problem."

"What problem? I don't have a problem."

"I'm sorry, but I disagree." I move closer, letting my eyes

linger on her lips before dragging them back to meet hers. "And knowing you're right downstairs, pent up with sexual frustration has been a bit distracting for me."

Her jaw clenches, and she looks down, then finally breaks the silence. "I can't believe I told you anything. I should've known you'd throw it back in my face."

I gesture to the display of vibrators, my voice low. "Now be a good girl and pick something to fuck yourself with, so I can finally stop thinking about doing it myself."

She slowly drops her hands from her eyes, like she's afraid to make a sudden movement, and I watch her throat work around a shaky gulp before she finally whispers, "I'll take the pink one."

I snatch the basic, smooth, pink vibrator from the shelf and drop it in the basket. "Thank you. Now was that really so hard?"

"I hope you know you're wasting your money. You can't make me use it."

Without a word, I turn around and grab a hands-free, remote-controlled couples' vibrator and add it to my basket.

I guess we'll just have to see about that...

CHAPTER NINETEEN

LUKA

L.O.K.I.'s gotten used to having Scout to entertain him all day, so needless to say, after spending the whole day alone, we both came home to a very needy AI.

And since I was feeling generous, I agreed to watch *Thor: The Dark World* with him but only if Scout agreed to watch with us.

I'm not sure what's gotten into me, or what I'm thinking, pushing the lines like this. I think the best explanation is that I'm not thinking at all. And fuck, it feels good.

I forgot how much I missed hanging out with this girl. How easy it is to fully be myself when I'm with her. How our conversation just flows, ranging from our theories about the universe to arguing over which superpower is superior. It's teleportation for the record.

After the credits roll, I sneak a glance at Scout, half

expecting her to look like she's ready to turn in and make an excuse to go to bed, but she doesn't. If anything, she looks like the last thing she wants right now is to be alone.

That makes two of us.

So against my better judgment, I decide to shoot my shot. "I'm actually having a good time. I can't remember the last time I let loose like this." I nod my head toward the back door. "I'm going to go sit outside and watch the storm. Care to join me?"

She hesitates for a moment, biting her lip in contemplation, but I can tell by the way her eyes just lit up at my suggestion that she doesn't want this night to end yet either.

She nods with a shrug. Then casually says, "Yeah. Sure."

We make our way outside to the back patio, where I light the decorative propane fire pit, taking a seat on the modern gray sofa. Scout sits across from me in one of the swiveling armchairs, pulling her feet up and criss-crossing them as she makes herself comfortable.

I think back to the way she was acting at Hardware Store... how she seemed upset about something. I can't be sure, but my intuition tells me there's more going on in that head of hers that she isn't telling me, and tonight, I plan on finding out.

"I like what you've done out here..." Scout's words trail off, her eyes widening when my lighter sparks into a flame. My lips pull into a grin as I suck in a lungful of warm smoke, blowing it out before offering it to her.

"No way. Uh uh." She holds up her hand and shakes her head.

Rain falls hard against the rooftop, falling all around us in heavy sheets as the lingering sexual tension fizzles in the air between us. Our little detour to Adult Store was supposed to solve this problem, but all I can think about is what she'll look like using her new vibrator...

Get your head out of your ass, Kingsley. Just because she's technically your wife, doesn't mean it's okay to fantasize about her... Even if the feelings seem to be mutual...

Fucking hell. I know I'm playing with fire here, and I should stop while I'm ahead, but my nerves could use a little help relaxing after the day we've had. "Oh, come on. What's wrong? You scared you're going to enjoy yourself too much and realize you've been doing life the hard way all this time?" I tease, watching her rigid posture slowly begin to relax. Something about knowing that I can slice through all her bullshit in only a matter of seconds fills me with so much pride.

"Do you not remember the last and *only* time you talked me into smoking weed? Was my mother's freakout not enough to deter you from ever offering me drugs again?"

I can't help my grin as I take another drag and blow a circle of smoke on my exhale. "You're too uptight, you need to learn how to relax."

She rolls her eyes, tucking her legs up to her chest. "Yeah, well, maybe relaxing doesn't come so easy for everyone."

I flick the ashes from the tip before taking another puff of smoke, the warm tingling already starting to wash away all my pent-up tension. "Yeah, I get that, but sometimes, I think you get off on being a martyr or something. I hate to break it to you, but there's no award for being miserable your whole life. The sooner you realize that, the sooner you'll stop putting everyone else's needs above your own."

There's a tendril of satisfaction that warms my icy heart when I notice the flush in her cheeks, this time from annoyance rather than embarrassment. Every time I succeed in getting a rise out of her, feels like winning a trophy.

Good. Get angry. Say something. Fight back. Give me something real.

"That's not what I'm doing," she retorts, but judging by her cracking voice, I'm not sure even she believes that.

I know it's stupid, and I really don't fucking care whether she smokes or not, but I find myself growing more irritated by her nonchalance. Why can't she stop pretending to be something she's not? Why can't she just tell me what she wants and stop hiding behind this whole facade?

"It's not?" I lean forward, propping my elbows on my knees as I meet her gaze. "Tell me then, before the other day, when was the last time you painted?"

"What does that have to do with anything?"

"Just answer the question," I fire back, my brow lifting in challenge as she blows out a shallow exhale and fidgets in her seat.

"You already know the answer. It was that night... when you got arrested."

I sit back in my seat, pleased that she knew that I needed her to say that last part. I'm tired of dancing around it, pretending like that moment didn't change the course of both of our lives. "Exactly my point. You stopped doing something you loved simply because someone else didn't approve of it. Don't you see how weak that makes you? It's pathetic."

She sucks in a gasp of surprise at my harsh words, her eyes shiny like she's holding back tears. But I catch a flicker of something else in them too, a heat that I haven't seen in a very long time.

Does she like the way I'm talking to her right now? Am I reading her wrong, or have I mistaken her arousal for annoyance?

"What? Does that turn you on, when I'm mean to you? Because I'm not afraid to hurt your feelings or call you out on your bullshit?" I find myself holding my breath, waiting to see how she'll respond. Will she fight back? Or is she going to shut down like she always does?

Her breath is shaky as she lets out a long exhale, then finally says, "Okay, so I'm a coward and I'm weak, but I have my own reasons for not painting that I'd rather not get into right now." She holds her hand out for the joint. "Now give me some of that before you smoke it all, and I have to listen to any more of your philosophical ramblings while I'm sober."

I almost choke on my laugh as I pass her the joint, because as much as I'd love to actually hear her explanation, I'm just happy she finally stood up for herself. I feel my walls slowly start to come down and my mood lightening back to the way it was before.

Scout's cheeks hollow as she sucks the small joint, and I can't help the direction my mind goes at the visual.

She chokes and coughs as she exhales, waving her hand to clear the smoke as she fights to catch her breath. The sight has my cock growing hard again, and I don't even try to hide my smile. There's something so fucking hot knowing she's breaking her rules, simply because I asked her to.

It makes me wonder what else I could get her to do. Oh, the ways I could corrupt her.

And that's definitely the weed talking, bringing my most

honest thoughts out to play. *Rein it in, Kingsley. She's the amateur here, not you.*

She passes the joint back to me and I take another long drag, eyeing her through the thin cloud of smoke. I see the instant she starts to feel it because she falls back in her chair in a lazy lean, her heavy-lidded eyes narrowing to a squint. A hint of a smile pulls at her lips as she takes a deep breath, like she's finding pleasure in the simple act of breathing.

"You feel the tingles yet?" I ask as I pass the joint back to her, to which she immediately takes another hit, this time managing to hold back her cough.

That's my girl.

She nods, looking down at herself. "My nipples feel really... *awake.*" She shivers enthusiastically, then crosses her arms over her chest. "And the seam of these shorts keeps rubbing me inappropriately..."

I can't say I was expecting that little confession, but I'm not mad about it either. Clearly, my inhibitions are also a little cloudy, because when the image of her fucking herself with her new pink vibrator pops in my mind, I don't even try to push it away.

There's no denying I'm attracted to her, but I'm also starting to sense it isn't one-sided. I start to feel that annoying curiosity sneak back up, but this time I'm not quick to push it away.

I just need more information, I tell myself.

"I'll take that as a yes." I watch as she wiggles in her seat, oblivious of the fact that I'm aware of what she's doing.

"Holy... Oh wow," she says, her eyes drifting closed as she bites her bottom lip and rolls her hips in a circle.

"Fuck," I whisper under my breath as my cock strains

beneath the hem of my sweatpants, as I watch her rub herself against the seat cushion. My hands are longing to reach out and touch her and I have to sit on them for extra precaution.

"I'm serious, Luka, this feels incredible. Have you tried this?" Scout's voice is raspy now, and there's an edge to it, probably from the smoke, but my cock seems to think it's directed at me.

I bite my cheek to hold back my laugh. She's so out of her mind right now, she's grinding on the chair right in front of me. I should stop her before she embarrasses herself any further... But where would the fun be in that?

I think I'll play with her a little more first.

"Feels good, huh? I'm glad to see that my chair's taking care of you." My eyes zero in on her hips, the way she's rolling them without even realizing she's doing it. "You keep grinding that sweet pussy in front of me like this and I'm going to have a hard time keeping my hands to myself." The words fly out before I can think to stop them.

Scout's eyelids flutter open, her body going completely still, and I once again find myself holding my breath as I wait for her reaction.

"You wish," she says, throwing my own teasing words back at me with a wink.

My pulse pounds in my ears as I blink at her, frozen in shock by her sudden brazenness.

"Hell, I think this chair's brought me closer to having an orgasm than anyone else ever has..." Her words trail off as she bites her lip, that crimson blush returning to her cheeks as she glances over at me. "Can I have it?"

I shake my head, feeling confused. Surely, I must've misheard her just now. "What was that?"

"The chair." She points at the chair she's sitting in. "Can I have it? You're a billionaire. Pretty sure you can afford a new one."

I clear my throat, trying to redirect the blood that's now rushing exclusively to my cock. "No, not that." I lean in, my voice dropping. "You said something about the chair being the closest to get you to orgasm." I tilt my head. "What does that mean?"

She shakes her head and waves me off. "Never mind."

"Ah ah. You can't just drop a bomb like that and not explain."

"Luka, come on, are you seriously going to make me say it?"

I cross my arms over my chest as I stare back at her. "I've never been more serious about anything in my life. Now spill."

"Fine. But you have to promise you won't make fun of me."

"Come on, you know I can't promise that." I hold up my hands. "How about this—I'll only tease you if you deserve it. Deal?"

She taps her finger to her lip like she's considering it, then finally shrugs. "I guess that's the best I'm going to get."

I nod, feeling my mouth go dry as I wait for her to explain what I really hope is an epic misunderstanding. But deep down, I know it's not.

Please don't let my suspicions be correct...

She glances over her shoulder like she's making sure no one can hear her. "I've never actually been able to... you know..." Her eyes widen like she's trying to make me understand where she's going.

Suddenly, I don't feel so high anymore. Nope, this conversation has sobered me right up. I lean forward, propping my elbows on my knees as my leg shakes with all the energy it's taking to hold myself back.

I find myself torn between not wanting to cross anymore lines tonight and dying to prod her, to see if I'm understanding her the way I think I am.

"Wait..." I lean in, blinking like I must've misheard her. "Are you saying that you've never had an orgasm? During sex?" My body is vibrating so hard I feel my vision starting to get blurry.

She nods ever so slowly, then covers her mouth as she bursts into a fit of giggles. "You should see your face right now. You look like I just told you I'm really an alien or something."

I don't even blink.

It feels like I've just been punched in the stomach. Like all my air's been knocked from my lungs.

I stare at the gorgeous woman sitting in front of me, wondering how the fuck that's even possible. She reaches for the joint that I forgot I was still holding and takes another puff. This time, it's her blowing the smoke in my face.

I drag my fingers through my hair and let out a frustrated sigh, trying like hell to keep my ass glued to my own goddamn chair. "You mean with a guy, right? Like you've never been able to orgasm just from sex?"

Her head tilts to the side like a puppy as she eyes me curiously. "Well, technically, yes..."

I choke on my inhale and slap my chest to catch my breath. "Please tell me that you're fucking with me?"

She points a finger at me and narrows her eyes. "Hey, you

said you wouldn't make fun of me. Don't you orgasm-shame me, Luka Kingsley."

I hold up my hands. "It's not that. I'm not shaming you... I just—" I take the joint from her and inhale, letting the smoke settle in my lungs. Then I meet her eyes, and all the teasing falls away. "Scout, be honest with me. Have you *ever* had an orgasm?"

Embarrassment burns her cheeks as her eyes drop to the floor. The silence that stretches between us is almost deafening as I wait for her to confirm what I already know.

Her shoulders bounce in a slight shrug before she looks up to meet my eyes. "I've been close... I think... It feels good."

The look on my face must say enough because she shakes her head and continues. "Look, I've tried okay. I just don't think I can."

Her confession weighs heavy in the air between us, and my mind feels like it's going haywire, all my thoughts getting jumbled up. I can't figure out what's real and what isn't or what's right and what's wrong...

"What do you mean you don't think you can? You don't seriously believe that, do you?"

Her eyes drop to her fidgeting hands in her lap. "Yeah... I mean..."

Oh hell no. That won't do.

"Wanna bet?" The words slip out before I can stop them.

She jerks her head up, eyes wide. "I'm sorry—what?! You want to bet on whether I can orgasm or not?"

I lean in, my voice low. "No, sweetheart. I want to bet that *I* can make you."

She shifts in her seat, casually crossing her arms over her

chest. "Don't you think that'd make things weirder than they already are?"

But the twinkle in her eyes is undeniable. I can see it all over her face. She wants this.

"What, because we're *married*?" I tease, tilting my head. "Or were you referring to the bubbling sexual tension?" I hold her gaze. "It doesn't have to mean anything. Just call it a marital *favor*. Besides, I'm so good I could make you come without even touching you."

Her eyes go wide in surprise, then she furrows her brows. "Oh, someone's cocky."

"I prefer confident. Now what do you say? You in?"

"What's the wager?"

I flash a slow grin. "If I win, I get the satisfaction of you knowing what I'm capable of."

"And what if you lose?"

"If I lose, I'll give you my entire comic book collection."

Her mouth falls open. "You're really that sure of yourself? You're not going to pull some crazy electromagnetic therapy and shock me, are you?"

I can't help the laugh that escapes me at that wild response. "No, but I like the way you think, Girl Scout. Maybe you're on to something with that."

She rolls her eyes, but she doesn't seem annoyed. Judging by the way her eyes keep flicking down to my lips, I'd say she looks more turned on than anything.

"If you're really that okay with losing your comic book collection, then who am I to stop you. I bet it's worth a pretty penny—"

"So, it's a deal?"

"As long as you keep your word and you don't touch me, then, yeah, it's a—"

I'm standing up and tossing her over my shoulder before she can even finish her sentence. "Luka... what the hell are you—?" She squeals, kicking and wiggling to break free from my grip.

"I'm about to change your whole goddamn life."

My heartbeat pounds in my ears as my eyes slowly adjust to the darkness. My body is a live wire, buzzing with need. Fueled solely by my hormones and over a decade of wet dreams about the girl next door. My childhood best friend, who's clearly still far too innocent and naive for me to have any business fooling around with. And she's just presented me with a challenge that I'm not sure I'm capable of resisting... even if I was sober.

Quite frankly, the only thing that could stop me right now is Scout showing any signs of resistance, looking even remotely like she doesn't want this, too.

But every time I look back at her, all I see are green lights as her hazel eyes sparkle with curiosity and a healthy mix of fear. It's an intoxicating combination, and knowing she's scared but still not resisting brings me more joy than I care to admit. I can see it in the way she obeys me, the way she seems to hang on my every word—she trusts me.

She shouldn't... But she does.

"Wait. We're doing this *now*?" Scout hangs loosely over my shoulder now. She must've realized her attempt at fighting was pointless and has accepted her fate.

"Hell yeah, we're doing this now. You think I don't know you'll change your mind the minute you sober up and start overthinking this?"

I carry her down the hallway. But when I reach the door to the basement, I stop in my tracks before turning her back the way we came.

"Luka, where are we going? Why are you walking around in circles?" Scout asks, attempting to lift herself up to see.

I ignore her question, taking a moment to consider my options. I could take her upstairs to my bedroom, but that feels too intimate. The same goes for her room. The living room could work, but I catch sight of the Library French doors out of the corner of my eye and turn on my heels, making my way inside.

Large windows span across one wall as shelves of books fill the others. The dark, cloudy sky flickers with lightning, providing just enough light to see.

I make a quick assessment of the space and nod. Dim lighting, the heavy rain rattling against the windows, limited distractions... This is perfect.

When I finally set her down, my hands instinctively reach out to steady her. A shockwave of heat shoots through my fingertips as they graze her exposed skin where her denim shorts hang low on her hips.

This, I decide, is my favorite look of hers. Her face is free of any makeup, and she is wearing those cute glasses that are almost too big for her face. She's simultaneously the cutest, prettiest, and sexiest woman I've ever seen, and she has no idea the effect she has on me.

She sways on her feet as she looks around, and maybe it's the weed, but it seems like she looks more excited than afraid.

I, for one, am thankful to have the excuse of being high, even though I'm pretty sure I've got all my cognitive abilities at this point. But it makes it that much easier not to talk myself out of it.

It's not that I'm afraid to be the bad guy. But it's clear that Scout wants this, too. She just needed an excuse to admit it to herself. The way I see it, even if she hates herself in the morning for acting on her desires, it's a win-win for me either way.

Besides, it's just a bet. It doesn't have to mean anything.

"So, here's how this is going to go..."

She crosses her arms and quirks a brow in challenge. "You may as well hand over your precious comic book collection now and walk away with your dignity if you really think this is going to work on me."

I reach up to cup her jaw and drag my thumb along her bottom lip. "That's some big talking you're doing. If I didn't know any better, I'd think you were starting to change your mind." I lean down and whisper against the shell of her ear, "Are you more afraid of being vulnerable in front of me or are you afraid that you might like it?"

She sucks in a breath, her body going completely still as I drag my finger down the column of her neck, her pulse beating so hard I can see it.

But she doesn't say anything, just narrows her eyes, and I swear if looks could kill, I'd be a pile of ash by now.

A slow, satisfied smirk tugs at my mouth as I tilt my head toward the curved leather bench in the center of the room. "That's what I thought. Now sit your pretty little ass down."

The lightness of before is gone, swallowed by a thick, pulsing anticipation that hums in the air between us.

"Would it kill you to ask? Or do you get off on bossing people around?" She fires back, but I don't miss the fact that even though she's questioning me with her words, her body obeys without hesitation.

I slowly begin to stalk toward her. "Why don't you drop the good girl act and stop pretending like you don't love it?" I tilt my head as I drag a finger over her neck, "You know, if I had to guess, I'd even bet that it turns you on, doesn't it, Girl Scout? Tell me, am I wrong?"

Her eyes flash, hot and daring, but she doesn't correct me.

"You're so desperate for someone to make the decision for you, someone who knows what's really best for you. You need permission from someone who's in charge, so you don't feel guilty about choosing the things you want. You need someone to hide behind and take the blame, someone who isn't afraid to be the bad guy. Isn't that right?"

Her response is a single nod, and that simple admission from her feels like I've already won whatever game we're playing. It's both vindicating and terrifying knowing my suspicions about her were right. But how far does the darkness inside of her really go? And will she let herself play along to find out?

I guess I'm finally going to find out...

I drag my fingers down her neck before grabbing her hair and draping it over to one side. I section it into three pieces, pulling taut as I carefully braid it.

She breathes out a shocked gasp, keeping her watchful eyes trained on me.

When I reach the bottom, I secure the end with a hair tie and give it a nice tug. "Come on now, I think you can show a little more enthusiasm than that." I tilt her chin up, our lips barely a whisper apart. "Now, why don't you ask me nicely, and I'll show you just how hard I can make you come."

The look of shock on her face already has my cock twitching. I can't wait to see the way she looks when I finally make her come.

"Luka... Please," She leans up to kiss me, but I back away before our lips touch.

"That's more like it..." I touch my finger to her nose, a satisfied smile pulling at my lips. "Normally, I'd never do this without a contract in place, but tonight I'll make an exception. It's only because I feel sorry for you, so please don't think it is anything more than that."

I see the question forming behind her eyes, but before she can ask, I reach behind me and tug the back of my shirt over my head.

Scout's eyes flare with something that looks like arousal, her breathing shallow as she stares at my tattoo-covered chest. It's the second time I've caught her staring at my tattoos, and if I didn't know any better, I'd think she may like them.

I give her a knowing wink before dropping to my knees so that we're eye level.

I watch her throat work as she swallows a gulp.

"All right, so here's how this is going to go," I continue, as I roll the shirt halfway, making a long, thin strip. "I'm going to tie this around your eyes, and you are going to do exactly as I say."

"You really think blindfolding me is going to make me orgasm?" she asks, looking at the rolled-up t-shirt and back to me.

I tilt my head side to side. "Among other things... Yes." I tie the shirt around the crown of her head, adjusting it so it's snug but not too tight. "Don't overthink it. I promise I'll only touch you where your skin is visible. Are you comfortable with that?"

She bites her lip as she considers it, but I already see the swirling excitement flashing behind her eyes, her dilated pupils, the way her breathing's hitched. She's curious, and fuck if that's not my fucking kryptonite.

"Good. We haven't discussed any of your limits, so can you just let me know if you're claustrophobic? Are you okay with some light restraint?"

"No... and yes... I think? Why? What are you planning on doing to me?"

"Now, what fun would it be if I ruined the surprise?" A smirk pulls at my lips as I continue, "Your safe word is Thin Mints. You say that, and I promise I'll stop. No questions asked. Understand?"

She nods, looking so fucking terrified I can't stand it. I'm not sure if she's still feeling the effects of the weed, and I need to be sure she knows that she's in control.

"I need to hear you say it, Scout. Tell me you understand. Tell me you want this."

Her eyes find mine, and she nods more enthusiastically this time. "Yes. Please. I want this."

I scrub a hand down my face as a growl escapes from the back of my throat. How the fuck is she this good? She's playing into every one of my kinks, and she doesn't even know it.

"Good girl," I croon, not missing the way her breath hitches from my praise. I slide the shirt over her eyes. "Now, lie back against the bench. Hands on the strap above your head."

The sound of heavy rain and thunder fills the silence around us as she reaches her arms above her head. Since she can't see, I help her with the straps, placing them in each of her hands. Her small fist clenches the straps, her nervousness so intense, I almost confuse it for my own.

The charge between us crackles: alive, magnetic, impossible to ignore. If there were any doubts in my mind about going through with this, they fly right out the window the moment I see her lying there, looking so fucking perfect as she submits so beautifully for me.

With a shaky breath, I drop back down to my knees as I take advantage of her blocked vision, letting my eyes graze over the curves I know she's got hidden beneath those baggy clothes.

What I'd give to really have her like this, tied up and helpless as I took her any way I liked. It's not too far of a stretch to think she'd be into it... I can't help but wonder how far that curiosity of hers goes.

But that's not what this is about. Tonight isn't for me.

"When you remove one of the body's senses, the others are heightened," I say as I slowly move to stand over her. It's going to be a challenge keeping my hands to myself, but I'm confident enough in my verbal communication skills that I'm not the least bit worried about how this is going to go.

She's already responding so well to my orders. I can see how turned on she's getting just from the anticipation alone.

I bend down so that my breath is on her ear. "Spread your legs a little for me."

She startles at my command, but she doesn't release her hold of her hand straps. Once again, she does as she's told, her pretty thighs falling open at my command, and my mouth

250

waters for a taste. I wet my lips, unable to help myself as I trail a knuckle over her thigh.

It's technically not touching her if it's over her clothes.

As soon as my hand moves away, she lets out a whimper, her hips wriggling like she's searching for me.

The broken whimper she lets out when I pull away nearly undoes me. But I clench my jaw and resist the urge to dive between her thighs just to hear it again.

My eyes are glued to her chest, her puckered nipples sticking out against the fabric of her t-shirt as her breathing begins to quicken. Her legs shift from side to side as she thrashes, making her shirt rise, revealing soft, delicate skin that begs to be touched.

She's completely clothed, and still it's the hottest thing I've ever witnessed.

I have to fist my cock just to keep from touching her.

Fucking hell! What have I gotten myself into?

CHAPTER TWENTY

SCOUT

Every cell in my body is on fire as I try to force myself to lie still, hating how easily I've fallen into Luka's trap. The storm outside sounds like it's growing stronger, the sharp taps of rain pelting against the windows, as the wind whirls through the tree branches. I can feel every crack of thunder in my bones, the low rumbles rippling through me soon to become giant waves.

My heartbeat is violent in my ears, and my skin aches to be touched.

I suck in a breath at the feel of something gently trailing over my arm, but I can't quite make out what. Fingers? Something softer than that? I realize I'm doing exactly what Luka said, I'm overthinking, so I catch the thought and simply allow it to float away. I instantly feel my muscles begin to relax a little more.

His touch drags across my foot, and I flinch when I feel

his hand gently squeeze my foot. "Cute Hello Kitty socks," he says, voice laced with amusement. "I think I'll let you keep these on."

I should find his shameless teasing annoying, but right now I'm too turned on to be annoyed. There's something so exciting about not knowing when or where I'll feel him next, being completely cut off from part of my brain. It allows me to feel so much deeper, making nonsexual touches feel like so much more.

I have to force myself not to wiggle right off this bench as he massages each foot for just a moment, ending with a tight squeeze.

"Look at you behaving so well for me." His voice is like warm honey dripping down my skin. I squeeze my eyes shut, my stomach clenching as I brace myself for his next touch.

It comes a moment later, his fingers gently trailing along my neck before they dip beneath the collar of my t-shirt. My pulse skyrockets when he begins to trace my collar bones, his touch barely enough pressure to register and yet more erotic than I've ever felt.

My body twitches, my back bucking involuntarily as if trying to deepen the pressure of his touch.

"I need you to breathe, sweetheart." And if I wasn't already glitching with need, his added layer of sweetness has me almost panting. My belly swoops at the endearment.

I didn't even realize I'd been holding my breath, and on his next touch, I suck in a deep inhale, biting my lip as the fury of growing need crackles beneath my skin.

"Now I want you to take off your shorts."

I hesitate, as if it takes a moment for my body to remember I'm free to move my arms, then move to unclasp my denim shorts. And even though I can't see him, I can feel his heat. I know he's standing beside me. My trembling fingers struggle with the button on my shorts until Luka's hands take over. He unclasps the button with ease, and as he undoes my zipper, I feel the vibration rattling all the way to my toes.

This time, he doesn't wait for me to attempt to remove my shorts; he simply tugs them off in one fell swoop.

Chill bumps erupt over my exposed skin at the loss of the warm layer. I feel myself falling a little deeper, and I almost forget where I am, forget who I am. The sensation grows thicker, as if I'm not a body and somehow only a body, like I'm just a soul floating in darkness.

"So, fucking gorgeous." He drags his fingers over my leg, all the way up my thigh, stopping just before he reaches my panties. My pussy clenches and my legs part all on their own as I mentally beg him to touch me.

"Look at you, so touch starved you're practically begging for it, aren't you?" His fingers trace along the hem of my panties, and my back arches off the bench all on its own. "As much as I'd love to give you what you clearly want, I think what you really need is to learn how to make yourself come."

The disappointment I feel is heavy, and Luka must sense it because his chuckle vibrates through my ears, and he brushes damp hair from my forehead. "Don't act so disappointed. I'll be right here, coaching you through it."

"Spread your legs a little for me... Good, just like that," he says as my body opens for him with eagerness. "Now I want you to touch yourself over your panties."

It's as if nothing else matters; everything inside of me needs to please him. I don't even have to think before my hand's moving between my legs. My aching clit pulses with need, and the moment my fingers make contact, a rush of pleasure shoots through my core.

I massage myself in slow circles, feeling my muscles clench as electric bands of pleasure fire through me. It's as if I'm discovering a new sensation, like it's not my hands touching me but someone else's.

"Goddamn, baby, you're so fucking desperate, aren't you? You're doing such a good job playing with your pretty pussy, but you need more, don't you?"

A whimper of a cry escapes my lips as my fingers work at a furious pace, my touch growing deeper and more frantic by the second.

I feel Luka's finger hook beneath my panties, but rather than pulling them down he just holds the damp fabric away from me. "Jesus, Scout, you're so fucking wet." For a moment I think he's going to break his rule and touch me. But then he blows out a breath and finally says, "Let me see you rub your needy clit."

Without hesitation, I dip my fingers beneath my panties, and do as I'm told, rubbing delicious circles over my sensitive bundle of nerves.

"Fuck me," he grunts under his breath. "You're not making this easy on me." I nearly fly off the bench when I feel his hand move over my hip. This time, his touch is far from gentle. His fingers curl into my soft flesh in a possessive grip that's almost painful, and the sensation adds an extra layer of need to my rapidly growing desire.

My fingers return to my clit, and Luka was right, I am wet. My fingers glide over my clit as I fall deeper into the warm darkness, silently urging Luka's hand to move down, for his fingers to be the ones that touch me. But his grip only tightens. It's as if he doesn't trust himself not to break his own rules.

"Jesus, baby, you should see the mess you're making on my bench. Fuck, what I'd give to taste you right now." I suck in a gasp when I feel his hand slide beneath the hem of my shirt before pulling it up over my bra.

I writhe even more, feeling impossibly more aroused as I try to imagine the expression on his face, wishing I could see his reaction to my thin, matching light pink lacy bra.

Does he like what he sees? Does he find me sexy?

"Goddammit, Scout. How are you this fucking perfect?" he rasps, the heat in his voice edged with something feral. Pride blooms in my chest knowing he likes what he sees.

My back bucks so hard I nearly fly off the seat when I feel a sharp pinch on my nipple. I don't even recognize the moan that escapes my throat. The pain is both shocking and grounding at the same time, reminding me that I'm not the one in control.

"Fuck, how did I know you'd like a little pain mixed in with your pleasure?" His thumb soothes the ache away as he gently brushes it over my hard, sensitive nipple. Then he pinches my other nipple, letting out a hiss as he rubs the sting away.

The added sensation sends me hurling toward the cliff I've been desperately chasing, and I feel my stomach grow warmer; it's a charged heat vibrating through every nerve ending in my body.

"That's it, baby, rub your clit. Just like that." His encouraging words have my brain short-circuiting as I circle my fingers, finding a rhythm that has warmth pooling at the base of my spine.

I fight through whimpers and moans as I try to catch my breath, my body coiling with growing need. The sound of my fingers sliding through my slick arousal only adds an extra layer of eroticism to the whole experience.

"Fuck, baby, do you hear that? Do you hear how fucking wet you are?" Luka's warm breath tickles the shell of my ear, making me suck in a hiss. I try to imagine his expression as he watches me touch myself. It feels so dirty being on display like this while he watches me fully clothed. I should be ashamed of myself for going along with this, but the thought of it only excites me more.

"Now I want you to slide one finger inside and curl it toward your belly button."

I pause for a moment, then do as he tells me, slowly dipping my middle finger inside. I curl my finger just like Luka instructs, and this time, I feel a different sensation beginning to build. It's gentler but somehow more intense at the same time. I hear Luka groan beside me as I continue the motion.

"Now add another finger," he says, and this time I don't hesitate as I slide a second finger inside. It's a tight fit and it stings at first, but luckily, my fingers are small, so it feels more pleasurable than uncomfortable.

A delicious heaviness builds inside me, like effervescent bubbles rushing to the surface, and soon my hips are bucking and thrashing as I chase the pleasure like a shameless fiend. I don't even recognize my voice as I whimper and pant, my desperation growing to a level I've never felt.

"You have no idea how fucking jealous I am of your

fingers right now," Luka croaks out, before his hand clamps down on my wrist. He pulls my hand away, and then I feel the warmth of his mouth closing over my fingers as he swirls his tongue around them. He sucks my fingers clean, and the vibration of his moan shoots straight to my aching clit. I wish it was his mouth that was touching me.

"Luka... Please..." I'm not even sure what I'm asking for. His hands? His mouth? For him to tell me how to touch myself and what to do next? All I know is I need relief. I need it more than I've needed anything, and I'm so desperate I'd do anything to finally get it.

His hand slides over my neck; his grip isn't tight, but it possesses me all the same. I melt into him, thrashing my head side to side as I buck my hips, desperate for anything and everything he can give me. My skin begs to be touched, and my nipples ache for pain or pleasure, I'm not sure, maybe a mixture of both.

"Christ, woman, what are you doing to me?" He growls out, and then I hear his breathing catch as he lets out another low growl.

I wet my lips and crane my neck to give him better access to my throat, welcoming his possessive grip to claim me, to mark me as his own. I've never felt more desperate than I do in this moment. I don't even care what I must look like; I can't think of anything besides how badly I crave his touch, how desperate I am to finally find the relief I've been craving.

His breathing grows quicker as he hisses under his breath like he's fighting a battle in his mind that I can't see. As if understanding what I need, his grip tightens around my neck, and I feel his shaking movements as he lets out another pained grunt.

Then I hear a familiar sound... A sound I'd recognize anywhere.

The falling rain muffles out the soft slapping sounds that perfectly align with Luka's shallow breaths. My ears perk up as I realize what he's doing.

A fresh wave of heat rolls through me, every nerve alive with want as I picture Luka's hand stroking himself. I circle my clit again, and the sound that leaves me is pure, desperate need. Shockwaves of pleasure rip through my core, sending ripples of electric heat in every direction. My legs fall open, needing more, more, more as the violent currents of pleasure pulse through my shaking limbs.

"Oh God. Oh God. Oh God, Luka." I cry out, not even knowing what I'm asking of him, but needing him all the same. I let out a high-pitched moan that echoes against the windows as I feel myself falling back down from my blissed-out release.

"Fuck yeah. That's it. Come on, baby, don't stop. You know you want another one," Luka hisses before his strained grunts turn to moans, and I can hear in his voice that he's close.

I'm so desperate to tear off this blindfold and watch him fall apart, but he told me not to stop, and I've never wanted to please anyone more than I do right now. So I resist the urge, feeling my head grow more and more floaty as I fall back into that blissful darkness where nothing else exists.

"You're such a good fucking slut aren't you, baby? You'll do anything I tell you to do, won't you?"

I choke out a strained moan as his sweet, filthy words drag me right back to the edge. My legs start to quiver as another orgasm rises to the surface. This time, I dip my fingers back inside, curling them until I find that delicious spot again.

I'm already so sensitive, my body so turned on, that it doesn't take long. I move my fingers in a steady rhythm, fighting through the cramp in my hand until I'm right back to that blissful place. Warmth pools in my belly as everything in the world disappears. Then I'm falling once more.

"Oh, God. Luka, I'm coming," I moan as another wave of ecstasy rips through me.

"Goddammit, Scout. You make me lose my fucking mind. Fuck, these pretty tits are going to look so sexy with my cum dripping off them." He chokes out another groan, and I arch my back, needing him to give me just that.

"Fuck," he hisses, and then I feel the hot ropes of his release. He paints me with his warm cum, coating me everywhere from my stomach to my breasts, all the way up my neck.

I've never felt so dirty, so far from the good girl image I've always been known as. And somehow, I've never felt more beautiful.

The relief comes all at once, like a tsunami tearing down twenty-five years of programming, crashing and destroying everything in its path.

Luka gently peels the shirt from my eyes and helps me sit up just as a sob—sparkling with all my fractured beliefs—bursts out of me, erupting like a shaken can of soda.

I have no idea why I'm reacting like this. I'm not sad—definitely not. Maybe overwhelmed? I don't even know what I'm feeling right now. Maybe it's everything at once, all crashing in at the same time, and my body just doesn't know what else to do but cry.

"Oh, baby, come here." He pulls me into a hug, and I feel so small as he tucks me against him. I bury my face into his neck. "Are you hurt or upset?" he whispers against my ear as he brushes a hand over my hair in a soothing motion. He smells like aftershave and smoke, and I nuzzle my face against his rough jaw and breathe him in.

"Try to answer me, Scout. Use your words, baby. I need you to tell me if you're okay," he croons as he pulls me away so he can look at me.

I wipe my tears with the back of my hand and give him a nod. "Sorry, I don't know why I'm so emotional right now. I'm fine, I just..." I bite my lip before I'm hit with another wave of tears.

Luka's lips curve into the faintest smile, just as his thumb catches a tear slipping down my cheek—like even this ache is something he treasures. "Hey, don't apologize. That was an intense release. Sounds like you needed it."

I look down at my transparent lace bra, which is now wet and sticky with jizz, and I suddenly feel embarrassed for getting the mess all over him, too. "Sorry." I try to cover myself with my arms, but Luka slaps my hands back down, his smile now turning into a look of disappointment.

"Don't even think about obstructing the best goddamn view I've ever seen." His nostrils flare as his eyes take in my messy chest, and then he's on his feet, shaking his head as he heads toward the door. "Shit, you've already got my dick getting hard again. Be right back."

I watch him disappear, then take the moment alone to look at myself. My nipples are hard and aching, and my breasts are coated in his cum that's starting to dry sticky on my skin. My panties are beyond damp from my own arousal, and I can't even imagine what my face must look like. There's nothing prim and proper about any of this. I've never felt so dirty, so vulgar, and I can't help but wonder what other dirty things Luka could get me to do...

"Here, I brought you another change of clothes. Let me help clean you up." He drops to his knees once again, and I don't argue as he carefully wipes my chest with the warm, wet washcloth. His movements are slow and deliberate, as if he takes extra pride in cleaning up his mess. I don't know why, but the simple gesture feels more nurturing than anything I've ever felt before.

I should feel embarrassed by all of this, but instead, I'm allowing him to clean his cum off my boobs. Like this is something friends do all the time.

He turns his head as I remove my dirty undergarments and pull a clean t-shirt over my head. It's an old band t-shirt that I recognize from high school. The fabric is soft and worn, and it smells like laundry detergent.

I don't know why I allow him to dress me, maybe because he looks like he needs it more than I do. Maybe it's because it feels nice having someone care for me in a nurturing way.

After I'm all clean, he scoops me up and carries me to the sofa, where he sits down and pulls me into his lap. His arms are so heavy and warm, and I savor the feeling of comfort and safety as we sit like that in silence, both lost in the reflection of what just happened.

"Holy shit! Do you know what this means?"

"What?" I sit up and meet his eyes.

His face breaks into a giant grin as he says, "Looks like I won the bet."

I slap his chest and roll my eyes, but I'm too spent to fight with him right now. So instead, I lay my cheek against his shoulder, feeling more exhausted than I've ever felt.

Luka must notice because his strong arms wrap around me, and he squeezes me tight. And the next thing I know, the tears are back, pouring out like I've just opened the floodgates.

"Shh. I've got you. You're safe and everything is going to be okay," he assures me over and over as he peppers kisses on the top of my head.

And every time I try to apologize, he stops me, telling me it's totally normal.

We stay like that for a long time, until my eyes dry up and I have no more tears to cry.

The last thing I remember thinking before I fall asleep is, if this is a normal occurrence for Luka Kingsley... What else is he into?

And how can I get him to teach me?

CHAPTER TWENTY-ONE

SCOUT

Steam rolls out of the bathroom as I tighten the towel around me. I'd hoped a hot shower might wash away the tension, but the knot of anxiety lodged in my gut remains—heavy and immovable as ever.

I barely slept a wink last night, thinking about everything I needed to do this morning while replaying my last interaction with Luka. I swear, I never know what is going to come out of his mouth. The man is a walking contradiction, and just when I think I've got him figured out, he throws me a curveball, leaving my jaw on the floor.

At this point, I don't know why I'm even surprised. I know the only reason he keeps doing it is because he enjoys getting a rise out of me.

I shake my head. It's barely six in the morning; I can't go down that rabbit hole right now. I need to focus on the task at hand. The mural.

Today's the big day, and I wanted to get an early start before it gets too hot. Which is why I'm up so early and running on only a few hours of sleep.

I pull open the drawer, and my eyes land on the untouched, bright pink vibrator that's practically mocking me from beneath a pile of my cotton panties.

I wanted to throw it away, or better yet, throw it at Luka for buying it for me, but I guess there's no sense in being wasteful.

I think back to the way he commanded me to touch myself. How exhilarating it felt to finally let my guard down and surrender all my control. If he can make me come that hard without even touching me, there's no telling what it'd be like to have sex with him.

He'd eat me alive. And I'd enjoy every second of it. That much is certain.

Luka seems to be so *experienced* when it comes to sex. It makes me wonder if there's something he's keeping from me, though I don't know what. Sometimes, it's in the way he talks to me, or the way he seems to watch me so intently to get a response. It is almost as if he is testing me. Whatever it is, I must not be passing. At this point, he probably finds me more pathetic than anything else.

Highly sexual people like Luka want partners who match their energy, and by now, I think I've proven that the two of us couldn't be any more different.

You can say that again. I can practically hear the vibrator's sultry, Marilyn Monroe-sounding voice taunting me as I realize I'm still staring in my underwear drawer. Fantastic. As if I needed someone else to remind me of how pathetic I am.

"I don't have time for this," I mutter to myself as I snatch the pair of panties from underneath her, causing her to roll on her side. I pause, getting a better look at her slight curvature as I trace the velvety smooth silicon with my fingers.

Oh, come on. Don't you want to see what all the fuss is about? I can practically hear her taunt.

Tightening my grip on the towel wrapped around my chest, I toss a glance over my shoulder, making sure my bedroom door is closed. I check the time on my phone and do a quick mental calculation.

I've got thirty minutes before we leave, and I still have to dry my hair. Luka insisted on giving me a ride this morning even though I told him not to worry about it.

My nerves buzz like hornets in my stomach. I think back to how relaxed I felt the other night, and I wonder if maybe it wouldn't be the worst idea? Luka is the most laid-back person I know, and if his theory is right, then maybe orgasms really are the secret to a stress-free life.

As if my body is deciding for me, my hand releases its grip on the towel, and I lift the vibrator from the drawer.

My still-damp skin buzzes with electricity as I sit on the edge of the bed, completely naked, apart from the towel on my head, and spread my legs open. I'm sitting across from the door, and even though I know it's locked, somehow the thought of Luka accidentally walking in here, seeing me like this, already has me writhing.

I don't have the energy to dissect how messed up that thought is, nor do I want to, for that matter. Right now, it's just me and Marilyn—apparently that is her name now—this can be our little secret.

I prop my feet on the small bench at the foot of the bed as

I press the center button. A couple of seconds pass, and the small light flashes red as the vibrator buzzes to life. There seems to be a couple of different pulsing options, but after going through each one, I decide to stick with the basic constant buzz and turn up the power just a little.

My back arches the second the cool, velvety smooth toy touches my clit, and I can't help the gasp of surprise that rips from my throat. Holy hell, it feels good. The soft vibrations move through me, tickling and teasing me in a way I've never experienced as I wiggle and squirm, while trying to find the best angle.

Another involuntary moan escapes me, and I slap my free hand over my mouth as I forgo sitting up and fall flat on my back. The last thing I need is for Luka to hear me using the vibrator. I'd never hear the end of that teasing, and yet, right now, that doesn't seem like a bad thing somehow.

I let my legs fall open on each side as I move the vibrator over my clit in small circles, adding a little more pressure rather than turning up the power. The increased sensation has my eyes rolling back in my head as I bite my hand to hold back a scream.

Suddenly, it's not a vibrator in my hand that I'm feeling, but Luka's tongue. Rather than fighting it off, I give in to the fantasy in my mind as I imagine how it would feel to have Luka's mouth on me. He seems like the kind of guy who'd enjoy giving oral sex. No, he probably loves it because he'd be the one fully in control.

I can almost hear his deep voice coaching me from between my thighs, telling me what to do, how to move...

"Oh God," I cry out, the pleasure cresting so high it steals the air from my lungs. I don't even care how loud I am;

nothing matters right now but the ecstasy flooding my body. I feel like I'm walking on the edge of a cliff, bound to fall over any second.

I bite down on my hand, dragging the vibrator back to the perfect spot, desperate to tip over the edge.

But the buzzing fades.

Panic flares as I fumble with the buttons, trying to crank the intensity back up. The pulsing grows even weaker... sputters...

And then it dies completely.

"No. No. No!" My voice comes out breathless, laced with a level of desperation I don't even recognize. I jab the button like I can shock her back to life—CPR-style, but it's no use. The light's gone, the hum is silent. Marilyn officially flatlined.

The pleasure that had been building had been so close that I could taste it, but it slipped through my fingers like a puff of smoke. All that's left is a sharp, bitter ache of disappointment.

I was *right* there.

I bury my face in the pillow, trying to catch my breath, when my brain shifts into problem-solving mode.

There's got to be a charger somewhere, right?

The next thing I know, I'm flying out of bed, completely naked, and my wet hair is clinging to my face as I tear through my underwear drawer like a woman possessed. "Aha!" I grab the vibrator box and dump it upside down.

A small instructional booklet falls to the floor. But no charger.

What kind of monster sells a vibrator without a charger?

Before I can spiral any further, a knock echoes from the door, tearing my attention away. I freeze.

"Scout? You about ready?"

I catch my reflection in the full-length mirror, and I nearly shriek. My hair's matted and hanging like I've just escaped a swamp, my eyes are wild, pupils blown like I barely survived to tell the tale. I look exactly how you'd expect a woman to look after chasing an orgasm and being abandoned at the finish line.

A quick glance at the clock informs me that I absolutely did not have enough time for this.

That's just great. I guess that's what I get for trying to live in the moment.

"Yep. Be right there!" I call back as I frantically scoop up the evidence.

Maybe I'll get lucky and the vibrations from Luka's motorcycle will finish the job?

Sadly, at this point, I'd take it.

"Here's fine," I say, tapping Luka's shoulder and barely waiting for the bike to stop before I'm climbing off.

"Whoa, what's the rush?" He lifts the tinted glass of his helmet up so he can hear me, but I see the smile in his eyes.

I shove my helmet at him. "Was it really necessary to drive down the railroad tracks?"

He raises a brow as he says, "I was just trying to do what I could to help. I figured you could use it, considering you were interrupted this morning."

I feel my face grow hot with annoyance and

embarrassment, but I don't bother trying to deny it. At this point, I'm so sexually frustrated and confused, I'm one pothole away from lying down right here in the middle of the street and letting Luka finish me off.

I thought I was sexually frustrated earlier, but having my orgasm so close and then having it ripped away is so much worse than feeling nervous. Why did I think trying out the vibrator was a good idea, knowing I wouldn't have time to deal with any *technical difficulties...*

Rookie mistake.

I narrow my eyes, remembering why I'm in this predicament at all. "Don't you dare act innocent right now. This is your fault."

His smile grows wider, and he holds up his hands. "How is it my fault?"

"You took the charger out of the box, didn't you?"

He squints like he's trying to remember, even though we both know he's full of shit. "Now why would I do that?"

I roll my eyes, letting out a huff. "I don't know. Probably because you thought it'd be fun to torture me." I hold out my arms, gesturing to my ruffled appearance. "Clearly, it worked. Are you proud of yourself?"

This earns me a laugh as he stares at me for just a moment before finally saying, "You know what? Yeah. I think I am."

I'm not sure what I was expecting, maybe for him to deny it, or tease me and change the subject. I definitely wasn't expecting him to admit it. I don't know how to respond to that, so rather than saying anything, I turn and start walking, making a beeline to Coffee Shop.

"Where are you going? Restaurant is that way." Luka calls from behind me.

"I need caffeine, and I need to get away from you!" I call back, without giving him a second glance.

I feel my phone vibrate with a notification before he revs his engine and calls back, "I'll be back to pick you up after work. Text me if you need anything." Then he turns the corner and takes off in the opposite direction.

When I pull out my phone, my eyes nearly bug out of my head at the notification.

Luka Kingsley sent you $1000

LUKA

For your troubles

"Unbelievable," I mumble under my breath as I pull open the heavy glass doors. As infuriating as he is, I can't seem to stay mad at him. I'm not sure how much longer I can take this push and pull between us. Eventually, the rope's bound to snap.

Despite the rocky start to my morning, being here has started to shift my nerves into something closer to excitement. It feels a little like the first day of school—only this time, the work ahead of me actually feels exciting. For once, I'm doing something that makes me feel alive instead of weighing me down.

With a renewed sense of excitement, I pick up my pace, feeling a spring in my step.

The bell above the door chimes as I step inside, and the

warm scent of cinnamon, brown sugar, and vanilla wraps around me like a hug. I inhale deeply, already feeling better.

Hazel greets me from behind the counter with a knowing smile. "Good morning, Scout. Can I assume by your outfit that you're starting on the mural today? You know it's all everyone's been talking about... well, that and..." Her voice trails off as Lucy backs through the swinging door, balancing a tray of fresh scones.

Lucy's smile grows wide when she sees me. "Oh, look how cute you look in your little painting outfit! I can't wait to see what you've come up with. I still have that drawing you made me all those years ago posted on the bulletin board." She gestures to the front, and my heart swells when I see the crayon drawing of the shop exactly in the spot I pinned it. It's surrounded by doodles on napkins and Polaroid pictures taken over the years.

"You were always so talented. I hated seeing you give up your dreams to go to law school," Lucy says as she moves the pastries to the display window.

I shake my head at the irony. Only in Ashford Falls would a career in art be more celebrated than as an attorney. I can't imagine what my mother would say if she knew this was the kind of advice I'd regularly been given growing up. I guess it comes with the territory, though. Much like many others in this community, these women were the trusted adults I needed when my parents couldn't be bothered.

"She's certainly got a marital glow about her, now, doesn't she? No wonder we've hardly seen your face around here." Paige says, popping out from around the corner, carrying a tall stack of books in her arms.

"I'm sorry. I've been meaning to come by, it's just been a

little busy, I guess," I say, hoping my vague explanation will suffice.

"Oh, honey. Trust me, we get it." Lucy winks as she bumps the display case closed with her hip.

"Oh, now, Lucy. Don't tease the girl," Hazel scolds without looking up as she moves around behind the counter. "You know how skittish she can get."

"We wouldn't want to spook her," Paige adds, her voice muffled from behind the stack of books she's sorting. "If what I've heard about those Kingsley boys is true, then the poor thing is probably still in shock."

I feel my cheeks flush and have to look away. She has no idea how right she is.

Nor do I, for that matter. Not exactly, anyway.

And I certainly didn't realize it was all of them...

Does everyone know something I don't? What exactly am I missing?

Thankfully, Hazel slides a drink across the counter, saving me from having to come up with a response. I blink down at the drink, realizing I never even ordered.

I take a cautious sip. The cinnamon-sweet warmth hits my tongue, and a soft smile pulls at my lips. "Hazel, I can't believe you remembered."

"Oh, come on now, dear," she says, handing me a warm pastry wrapped in wax paper. "You really think I'm too old to remember something as simple as chai tea? Now here, get something on your stomach. You're going to need fuel for all that strenuous work ahead of you."

I don't even have to look to know it's my favorite apple tart.

Before I can reach into my pocket, she's already waving me off. "It's on me."

I start to argue, but there's no winning this. She's got that stern look in her eye, and I'm already outnumbered three to one.

"Thank you," I say, before digging into my delicious treats. My eyes nearly roll back in my head the moment the warm, flaky crust and sweet apple filling hit my tongue. By the look of pride on her face, my reaction must be plenty of payment enough.

I make my way outside, where I find Big Dan waiting for the signal light. "Well, hey there, Scout. You're up mighty early this morning."

I give him a polite smile, covering my mouth as I try to swallow the giant bite of pastry I just shoved in my mouth. "Just getting a jump start on the mural, before it gets too hot."

"That's not a bad idea at all. You know, Dr. Drizzle says we've got some rain in the forecast." He gestures to the cloudless sky painted in cotton candy blue and pink, then leans in and whispers behind his hand, "The whole meteorology thing is a crock of shit if you ask me. I figure there's a fifty-fifty chance of them being right, however they predict it. But you can't tell my wife that." He rolls his eyes as if freshly annoyed at the reminder of his apparent competition. "I think Dr. Drizzle knows what he's doing, wearing those fitted suits with his ankles peeking out, his hair gelled and styled like a Ken Doll..."

I have to bite my lip to hold back my grin at Dan's early morning confession, thinking of Mr. Kingsley's identical complaint. If the local meteorologist's thirst-trapping during his weather reports is your biggest issue in life, maybe things aren't too bad? When we get to the traffic light, we each go our separate ways.

"I'll be seein' you around, Scout. Good luck today and watch out for that storm!" Dan calls over his shoulder with a chuckle.

"Will do. See you later, Big Dan." I wave him goodbye as I round the corner, stopping in my tracks when I see the now solid white brick wall that appears to have already been primed. There's a tarp on the ground with gallons of paint and an assortment of paintbrushes and smaller cups ready to go.

I blink up in confusion just as the phone in my pocket vibrates with a text.

LUKA

Thought you could use a head start. Break a leg today.

I quickly text him back.

When did you do this?

LUKA

Hank left me a message yesterday telling me he was dropping everything off, so I arranged for Roman and Guy to meet him and get everything set up.

You're my wife, Scout... Trust me, it's not a big deal.

I'm your fake wife. And yes, it is!

You made them prep the whole wall, Luka! I can't imagine how long that must've taken...

LUKA

Fake. Real. Doesn't make a difference in how I plan on treating you. So get used to it.

There should be at least two coats of primer, so you should be all set to get started.

I really don't know what to say...

LUKA

How about, "Thanks, Luka, you're the best husband ever, and I was totally thinking about you when I tried to get myself off this morning..."

And you just ruined it.

LUKA

Don't worry, babe, I know that's just your sexual frustration talking. Let me know if you need the master to give you another tune-up

All you have to say is: "Luka is a sex God."

I'm putting my phone up now.

LUKA

Your loss

My shoulder aches as I finally finish the paint outline of the giant cartoon Phantom. I can't be sure just yet, but I think it looks pretty good considering I had to draw it freehand using only the quick grid reference from my sketch.

Ideally a projector would've made this easier, but with all

the streetlights around here, I wouldn't have been able to see the outline anyway.

"I thought you were gonna paint it?" Clyde calls from where he's perched up on the sidewalk below.

"I'm not sure I like the expression on his face," Fergus adds. "Might be a bit too scary for the children."

"I hope you paint faster than you outline," someone else mutters. "If this isn't finished by the festival, it'll look no better than the hideous graffiti that used to be there. Still can't believe Luka would do something so vile to our sweet downtown..."

I glance over my shoulder to find the crowd has doubled in the last hour or so.

I offer them a polite nod. "Nice to see you all so invested in the process. Don't worry—I'm nothing if not a perfectionist. You're gonna love it once it's done. Just trust the process."

"We'll see about that," Clyde says, crossing his arms over his chest like he's still not convinced.

I grit my teeth and force a smile. I should've known this would be a town spectacle the moment I agreed. These people are too nosy for their own good. You'd think they'd have somewhere to be, but I've had constant commentary for the last five hours, and the crowd's only grown larger.

"So, I guess the rumors are true..."

My body freezes at the sound of the familiar voice.

There's no way... I must be dehydrated or something, my mind must be playing tricks on me.

"How come you never told me that you painted?" he asks, and now I know I'm not hallucinating.

I make my way down the ladder, not wanting to do this in

front of an audience. I grab his arm and pull him behind the alley, giving us a semblance of privacy. Jesus, I'm already dealing with enough gossip, I don't need to add ex-fiancée drama to the mix.

"What are you doing here, Jimmy?"

He flashes me his dimpled smile that's never seemed to work on me. "I was in the neighborhood. Had to bring your dad some paperwork, and he told me about your little quarter-life crisis... or whatever this is."

Not buying that excuse for a second, I cross my arms over my chest and blow out a huff. "What do you want?"

He has the audacity to look like he's wounded and his eyes flash to my ring. "Wow... I guess Luka Kingsley spares no expense..." He scratches the back of his neck and looks down. Even though he's trying to seem unbothered, I can practically see his skin turning green with jealousy.

"Well, I'm so glad we did this. Now if you'll excuse me..." I spin around to leave but his hand grabs my arm, stopping me.

"You didn't sleep with him did you?"

"You can't be serious," I say with an eye roll.

Why is it that every single thing always comes back to this? Is that really the most important thing about me?

"You get me kicked out of school after turning in my paper before me... and then you threaten to forge my signature on a marriage license—"

"That was your dad's idea, not mine," he says defensively. As if that reasoning is somehow better.

"—And you have the nerve to ask me if I slept with him? Do you hear yourself right now?"

"All right, look, I get it. It's none of my business..." He

holds up his hands. "And I realize I may have gone about things in the wrong way... But I fucked up and then I panicked..."

It's the closest thing to an apology I've ever heard from this man. Too bad that ship has already sailed.

I lift a brow, curious where he's going with this.

"I miss you, Scout." He looks up to meet my eyes and I swear he almost looks sincere. "We're good together, and you know it." He takes a step closer and grabs my hand, placing it on his chest. "You and me, we make sense."

"Are you done? Because I need to get back—" I try to pull my hand away but he holds it tighter.

"Just... take the rest of the Summer and get this out of your system...And know that I'll be waiting on you when you get back."

Anger and irritation bubble up as I glare into his impossibly clear blue eyes, not a hint of shadow or guilt to be found. Why is it so hard for everyone to see the real me? If they really love me like they say they do, or did anyway, why can't they see that I've been walking around as a shell of myself?

I know it's my fault for telling them what they want to hear, for playing the part so well, but that was only after I'd spent years screaming for them to see the real me. But if they loved me, wouldn't they be able to see it was just a mask?

Luka always has...

I don't know what's worse... That they couldn't tell... or that they didn't care. Either way, it sucks knowing my happiness comes after whatever version of me that makes them the most comfortable. Well, I'm tired of being afraid of making them uncomfortable. Maybe Luka's right, maybe it's time for me to be a little more selfish.

"I think you should leave," I tell him, my voice quiet because for some reason it's all I can muster. But at least it's a start.

Jimmy's eyes widen for just a moment before his face shifts back to a neutral expression. He clearly wasn't expecting me to stand up to him. "Yeah... okay..." He looks a little discouraged, shoving his hands in his pockets as he turns to leave. I just stand there caught between the sting of guilt and the stubborn pull of pride.

"Hey Scout?" He calls over his shoulder.

"Yeah?"

"Try to keep an open mind about it, okay?"

I'm not sure how to respond to that so I just say, "Yeah... Okay..." I don't wait for him to round the corner before I make my way back to the mural. And luck must be on my side now because for the first time all day, there's no audience in sight.

"Finally," I breathe as I pick up my paintbrush and all my problems begin to fade away.

CHAPTER TWENTY-TWO

LUKA

I replay the video footage for about the hundredth time, my body fuming at the sight of Scout talking to that prick. The way he stared at her ass as she led him around the corner to the alley to be alone. The way he smiled at her like he knew a secret, flashing her his dimples.

Is it creepy that I hacked into my brother's security camera to spy on her? Maybe... But my intention was only to make sure she was safe since I knew she'd be stubborn about that fucking ladder.

But then I saw the way her face lit up when she started working, the way she looked like she'd fallen into a trance, and she seemed to come alive right there in front of me. I've never had the opportunity to really watch her paint before and seeing it like a fly on the wall gave me a whole new insight into her.

Of course, then all the spectators decided to show up—no

doubt commenting and questioning everything she was doing. I figured my watching wasn't really spying at all. I was simply doing it from the comfort of my own home, with the ability to zoom in and replay the video if I wanted to get a better view. Which I'd only done to make sure she'd gotten all the paint she accidentally dripped when she bent down to wipe it off the ladder. Again, that was for her *safety*.

And when her douchebag ex showed up, I felt my fucking stomach drop like I'd been hurled face first down a roller coaster. My whole body seized up, and my palms began to sweat as I leaned in, trying to read their lips. Of all things to skimp on, Jett really had to go with a security camera that didn't have a microphone. I could kill him for being such a cheap ass.

I expected Scout to shoo him away... or tell him to get lost... or at least talk to him in front of the other witnesses. But rather than any of that, she grabbed him by the arm and pulled him away around the corner, out of view of Jett's other stupid fucking camera that is even worse than the other one with the picture all pixelated and fuzzy.

I could barely make out Jimmy, but Scout was out of the frame, so I had to try to read his body language to figure out what they were saying.

I know I have no business feeling this possessive over her. Scout's not my real wife. She's barely even my friend. But after everything she has told me about him and knowing how selfish of a prick he has to be not to prioritize her pleasure, tells me more than enough about his character.

And he doesn't even deserve to breathe the same air as her, much less put his hands on her.

My blood is boiling, and I'm seeing red all over again. So

much for my attempt at distracting myself. After a long day spent tormenting myself with this stupid video footage, it'd taken all my restraint not to drive over there and demand she tell me what that prick wanted. And why she needed to pull him away privately to tell him she was too busy to talk.

So rather than facing her and having to pretend I wasn't pissed off, I arranged for a driver to bring her home and left her a note telling her that I'd be upstairs working late. I just needed some time to regroup. I'm obviously not thinking straight from all this backed-up sexual tension. It's certainly caused me to forget all the history between us—the good and the bad.

I catch sight of her walking into the kitchen and feel myself perking up when I see she's wearing one of my t-shirts and some boxer shorts... Her hair's wet and freshly brushed like she's just gotten out of the shower, and I can almost smell her shampoo just from the sight of her.

There's a satisfied smile on her face as she bends down to dig through the fridge to find something to heat up for dinner—another thing I have to feel guilty about. I hate that I didn't feed her tonight. It's a small thing but knowing how she grew up eating her mom's shit cooking and seeing how excited she was every time she got to stay late and eat dinner at my house, it's something I've always tried to do for her. I want her to be able to eat food she actually likes... not just accept what she's been given because someone else chose it for her.

I continue watching her, and my cock twitches in my pants when, rather than sitting in a chair at the kitchen island, she instead lifts herself up and sits on the counter. Her bare legs dangling as she eats a bowl of cereal and chats with

L.O.K.I., telling him all about the progress she made on the mural.

There's something about the way she throws her head back, laughing at whatever he just said, that sends a surge of possessive rage tearing through me. What the fuck could L.O.K.I. have said that was that funny? I created him for fuck's sake, and she never laughs like that around me. At this point, I'm halfway convinced she wants me to see her flirting. I think back to her pouting the other day while we shopped for supplies, and suddenly it all clicks into place.

Is this because I took her vibrator charger? Is she trying to get back at me by flirting with everyone and provoking me by walking around in my clothes?

Before I even realize what I'm doing, I'm bolting out of my chair and stomping down the stairs. I may only have a half-cocked plan based only on sexual frustration and my own imagination, but I don't care anymore. I'm tired of tiptoeing around here, pretending like we both don't want this. If she wants to flirt with fire, I'll make sure she understands exactly how hot it burns.

"What's up?" I call out as I walk into the kitchen, startling Scout so much that she jumps. Her bowl of cereal goes flying through the air. Sticky milk and Lucky Charms rain down around us, before the ceramic bowl shatters into a million pieces, the metal spoon clanging somewhere across the kitchen.

"Oh my God..." She places a hand over her chest and takes a deep breath. "You scared me."

And the first thing I notice is that even though she was startled, she didn't apologize for making the mess.

For some reason, I take that as a personal victory, which

only fuels me to keep going, since I'm clearly doing something that's getting through to her.

Not caring about the shards of glass or sticky milk covering the floor, I stalk toward her until I'm standing right between her legs and our faces are merely inches apart. "You're wearing my clothes," I say. It's not a question, but it's implied.

Confusion flashes over her face, and she studies me like she's trying to make sense of this reaction. She's still trying to calm down after I startled her, but the heat in her eyes tells me that's not the only reason for her labored breathing.

"My pajamas are in the washing machine, and I didn't figure you would mind if I borrowed an old t-shirt to sleep in." Her words trail off when my hands move to cup her thighs, and I watch her throat work as she nervously swallows a gulp.

I'm filled with a small ping of satisfaction when I notice her thighs press together. My gaze drops to the swell of her chest, where her nipples strain against her shirt. And when I hear her gasp, I can't help the smirk that spreads across my face.

"You look good in my clothes... especially this." I tug at the hem of the plain white t-shirt. "Makes it easier to see your nipples."

"Luka..." Her voice comes out breathy, and I love hearing my name on her lips.

"Yes?" My fingers caress the outside of her thigh before moving around to her ass.

"What are you doing?" Her body goes completely still, but she doesn't push me away.

My hands trail along her hips now, loving the way she

looks at me, her eyelids starting to hood. I can see that she's already on her way to that floaty, dream-like space, just waiting for me to fully take control so she can hand over the reins to her busy mind. "How was your day?"

Her eyelids flutter open, and she blinks before looking down at her hands. "Oh, uh, it was good. I was able to get most of the outline done thanks to you doing the prep work." She looks up and meets my eyes. "Thanks again for that, by the way."

My fingers dip beneath the hem of her t-shirt as I drag them along her lower back, my large palms nearly swallowing her narrow waist. Images of flipping her onto the bed and taking her exactly how I want flash through my mind, sending another surge of heat straight to my already rock-hard cock.

"You're welcome. I just... wanted to take care of you." My hand slides up, deliberately slow, brushing the bare space where her bra *should* be. She shudders beneath my touch, breath catching—and yet, she still doesn't pull away. "So, did you have an audience or anything? I can't imagine you weren't surrounded by nosy neighbors full of questions..." I hold my breath when I see her tense.

Then she shakes her head and shrugs. "Yeah, but I tuned them out, and after a while, they eventually got bored and left."

"Uh huh... Anything else exciting happen?" I ask as my hands move further around her back, my fingertips barely grazing her ribcage and the slight swell of the side of her breast.

Her eyelids flutter closed as she sucks in a hiss before slowly shaking her head. "Nope, nothing out of the ordinary. It was a long day, but it felt good to work with my hands."

My hands pause their perusal, and she opens her eyes as if trying to figure out why I stopped. I narrow my eyes, willing her to tell me the truth as the jealous animal inside of me threatens to rear its ugly head once more. "So, nothing out of the ordinary happened today?" I lift her chin to meet my eyes.

She swallows another gulp, but this time she doesn't look away when she says, "No... Why? Did you hear something?"

Those big innocent eyes stare back at me, blinking, and I feel like all the air's been ripped from my lungs. I always thought she was so easy to read, that she couldn't lie for shit. But here she is looking at me with those fucking doe eyes, and she's so convincing that I'm starting to doubt my own memory of what I saw today.

Holy shit... All this time... What else is she lying about?

I rip my hands away from her body and press off the counter. "Are you seriously going to look me in the fucking eyes and lie to me? I saw Jimmy stop by, Scout. Want to tell me what the hell you pulled him into the alley to talk about?"

Her jaw falls open, and then her face burns bright red. "You were spying on me? How?"

"That doesn't fucking matter. You were outside in the middle of public view; it's not like I've got cameras in your fucking bedroom or anything."

"What the hell is wrong with you? You have no right to spy on me." She shoves me in the chest before stomping off toward her room.

I shake my head, temporarily stunned that she thinks she has the right to be angry with me. "Hang on a fucking minute. Don't walk away from me when I'm talking to you," I call after her, catching her bedroom door before she can slam it shut.

"Leave me alone, you creep! It's none of your business who I talk to anyway!" She yells, struggling to close the door, but I step in front of it, easily stepping inside.

I stalk toward her, my vision going red now, half pissed that she lied to me and the other half completely turned on to see her fighting back. "The fuck it isn't," I hiss back.

I glare at her, loving the look of fear on her face as her chest pants for air. Her pupils are almost as big as her irises as she stares back at me, anxiously awaiting my next move.

What happens next, I'm not sure, but judging by the way she's looking at me right now, I think it's safe to assume this isn't anywhere close to being over.

"What did he want?"

She shakes her head, wetting her lips. "Nothing... He just said he'd be waiting for me... After the summer was over and I was done *finding myself*."

"Glad to know you've already got your backup plan figured out." I roll my eyes and scoff. "Tell me, Scout, is it a humiliation kink or do you just love the feeling of being used?" I move closer. "Because I've been going easy on you, but if it's a little pain and degradation you're looking for, all you had to do was ask..."

She backs away, eyes wide, pupils dilated. "Wh—what does that have to do with anything?"

"I'm just trying to understand why you keep running back to the people who hurt you. You've given up everything about yourself, watered yourself down, begging for crumbs.

You're a coward. Can't you see how pathetic that makes you?"

"Oh, and you're one to talk." She laughs. "You think you're so much better than me, don't you?"

I lift a brow but don't respond as she barrels on.

"You may have everyone in this town fooled—hell, maybe you've even convinced yourself, but I see right through your apathetic, cool guy act."

"Is that right?" I tilt my head and gesture with a smirk. "By all means. Enlighten me on how *I'm* the coward here."

"You're a joke to everyone in this town—even your own family, and no matter how hard you try to pretend you don't care, I see that it is eating you alive. But instead of doing the hard thing by actually trying, or being vulnerable and proving them wrong, you lean into the character they've made you out to be." She straightens her shoulders and looks me in the eye, like she's speaking straight to my soul. "Because deep down, the only thing scarier than being judged... is the possibility they might be right." She pushes past me, trying to leave.

"Oh no, you don't." I move in front of her, blocking her path. "You really want to do this? All right, let's talk about it." I prop my hands against the wall, caging her in as she glares up at me. "I took the fall for you, Scout. I went to *prison*, just so you could have a shot at following your dreams, and I didn't hear a word from you for three years."

"I never asked you to!" Her voice is shaky, but it's laced with venom. She shoves me in the chest, but I don't move.

She shakes her head, tears spilling down her cheeks, and I fucking hate how angry I am with her. And yet, in this moment, all I want to do is cradle her to my chest and wipe her tears away.

What the fuck is happening to me?

For a moment, I'm stunned speechless. I'm not sure what I was expecting her to say to me, but as many times as I played this scenario in my head over the years, not once did I anticipate this.

The wheels in my mind are still spinning when she crosses her arms over her chest. Her cheeks are tinted my favorite shade of pink, making her hazel eyes pop with green. I can't help but notice how fucking cute she is when she's all worked up like this. My cock's grown painfully hard at the sight of her standing up for herself.

"If you still hate me so much, then why even offer to help me?" She challenges back as her eyes drop to my mouth. "Why do you care if I go back to Jimmy, or go crawling back to my parents? What difference does it make to you, anyway?"

My nostrils flare as heat shoots through me. "You fucking know why."

"Do I? Because it seems like all you want is to be able to hold it over my head." Her eyes dart back over my body and back up to mine, and even though I see she's clearly nervous, it isn't fear I see in her eyes... It's excitement.

"Let's get something straight, princess," I growl, stepping in close. The back of her knees bump against the bed, and she falls backward. "I don't give a fuck what you do after you finish the mural. But while you're wearing my ring..." I pinch the hem of her shirt, lifting it just enough to expose a sliver of skin. "...walking around my house in my fucking clothes..." My eyes lock on the flutter in her throat, the rise and fall of her chest, watching for any signs she wants me to stop. "You belong to me. No one touches what's mine. Do I make myself clear?"

She freezes like she's trying to process what I just said, which makes two of us, because I sure as hell didn't plan on saying it.

Then, finally, she breaks the silence. "But *you* haven't even touched me."

My body hums as I lean in. "Is that you asking me to?"

Her gaze stays locked on mine. She wets her lips, voice barely a whisper. "No, Luka... this is me begging."

CHAPTER TWENTY-THREE

SCOUT

"Fuck it." Luka's lips crash into mine, and there's nothing sweet or tender about the way he kisses me. The moment our lips meet, it's like lightning crashes through me, sharp and all-consuming. My whole body aches with need. I'm an ember reigniting, and he's the oxygen in my lungs, fueling me, fanning the spark until I'm a full-blown inferno, ready to devour everything in my path.

We collapse onto the bed as he cradles the back of my neck in one hand while his other hand grips my waist in a death-like grip, like he's still trying to compose himself. I can feel his body shaking as he holds himself over me, trying not to crush me under his weight and trying to keep himself under control.

But I don't want his control. I want everything he has to give me. I've spent my whole life suppressing the feelings that were too big to understand, the words I couldn't say, using whatever means necessary to get out of my head. But these feelings have me charging head-on. I want to dive in headfirst, to jump before I'm ready, and to surrender to the unknown, trusting that Luka will be there to catch me on the other side.

I wrap a leg around his waist, pulling his hard erection against me, needing to eliminate any space between us as my hips begin to rock. The delicious friction sends a jolt of pleasure straight through me, and it feels so incredible I can't get enough. I deepen the pressure, arching my back as I grind against him, as he swallows my needy moans and whimpers.

Luka's hand slides up my t-shirt, his palm cradling my rib cage as he brushes a thumb, gently caressing the swell of my breast while grinding his hard cock into my swollen clit.

Our kisses grow frenzied, my body grinding and squirming beneath his, as I drag my fingernails down his back. I'm desperate, starved out of my mind—and all I want is for him to take me, to own me, to claim me in every way.

I reach for his t-shirt, breaking our kiss long enough to tug it over his head. Luka sits up and does the same to me, sucking in a gasp as he leans back, as if taking a moment to fully appreciate the sight before him.

"Jesus, Scout, your tits are somehow even better than I imagined," he groans before diving back in for another kiss. His hands roam up my waist, painfully slow, despite my squirming and bucking, trying to get him to touch me.

I feel his lips smile against mine, like he knows I'm frustrated that he won't touch me, as he continues to dry hump me within an inch of my life.

It feels so good, but I need more. I need his hands on me; I need him inside me. I'm so tired of all the waiting and teasing. I'm a fiend, and if he doesn't touch me soon, I think I may explode.

Luka sits up, his eyes dark and full of need as his hand moves to my neck as he gently traces a finger between my breasts. I arch my back, letting out a desperate whimper, my arms raising over my head, needing him to touch me anywhere...*everywhere*. I am completely topless, my body convulsing beneath him with need, and I feel the heat in his eyes as he takes his fill, like he's trying to memorize every freckle and curve.

"Please, Luka. Please. I need you. I need your hands on me," I finally manage, begging him to put me out of my misery.

There's a flash of heat in his eyes as he looks from my breasts to my wild gaze, and for a brief moment it almost looks like confusion—like he's trying to decide how far to take this. I shake my head, unwilling to let his conscience kick in.

"Luka. I need you. Please," I say desperately.

His eyes darken, and I see the moment he shifts, pushing his conscience to the backseat. He dives back down, his lips kissing and sucking my neck as his hands move to cup my breasts.

I arch my neck, giving him better access as his frantic kisses turn into nibbles as he sucks and bites me, sending a mixture of pain and pleasure to every cell in my body. He palms my breast in one hand as his other hand slides down to my boxer shorts, his fingers inching below the hem.

"Seriously, no panties? Are you trying to fucking kill me?" He grunts when his finger breaches beneath the boxers, and I can't help but smile at his reaction. It's not that I was expecting this to happen, but I'd be lying if I said I didn't think about Luka touching me and accidentally discovering I've been walking around the house with no underwear.

He tugs the shorts down my legs and tosses them across the room with a growl, leaving me in nothing but my Hello Kitty socks. I begin working the button of his jeans and manage to get them loose before he grabs my hands, his eyes searching mine, the silent question passing between us.

My response comes when I lean up, capturing his lips with mine. I suck his bottom lip in my mouth, biting it hard and distracting him as I pull his zipper down. His massive cock springs free because Luka's not wearing any underwear either.

"Oh, baby, you're going to regret that," he hisses as he shrugs out of his jeans, kicking them off so that his hard cock rubs against my bare pussy.

The sensation is almost too much to take as I grind myself against him, painting his hard shaft with my slick heat.

"Fucking hell, baby. You're going to make me come if you keep grinding that pretty pussy on me like a needy whore." When I reach to take his shaft in my hand, he catches my wrist, securing both of my arms over my head with one hand while he traces his torturous fingers over my body.

I buck my hips, letting out a desperate moan as I seek any friction I can get. My clit pulses and throbs, and I've never felt so achingly empty.

"Please," I plead, not even caring how desperate I may look.

Luka breathes in a deep breath, his hand still pinning both of mine above my head as he cradles my neck with the other. It feels so possessive, so dangerous, and I lift my chin, silently urging him to tighten his grip—my eyes begging him to give me what I'm so desperately asking for.

"You want me to fuck you? Is that it?"

My eyelids flutter closed, and I nod, then I feel a sharp pinch to my nipple. I don't even recognize the moan that escapes me.

"You fucking love the pain, don't you, baby?" He pinches me again, this time harder than the first time, and I buck off the bed, my breath shallow and rapid as I squirm against his hold.

"Normally I'd drag this out, torture you until you can't take anymore before I fuck you, but if I don't get my cock inside you, I think I might die," he says as he lines the thick head of his cock up with my entrance.

He reaches for something inside the side table, pulling out a foil packet and tearing it open with his teeth. My eyes go wide as I watch him roll the condom down his thick length, and for the first time since we started this push and pull, I start panicking.

But then the blunt tip is back at my aching entrance, and all I can think about is how desperate I am to finally be filled. I squirm as best as I can from underneath his hold, rubbing against him.

"Look at how fucking desperate you are. Eyes on me, baby. I want to see your face when I shove my giant cock inside this tight little pussy."

I blink up at him, lips parting on a shaky breath as I force myself to relax. "Please," I whisper again, and that's all it takes. Luka drops his head, keeping my wrists pinned with one hand, squeezing my hip to hold me in place as he holds nothing back. In one thrust, he drives his thick cock inside me before pulling it out and driving all the way back in again.

Searing pain shoots through me in every direction. Tears fill my eyes as a guttural sound escapes my throat. I bite my lip, trying to hold back a scream as the feeling of a searing hot fire poker rips through me.

Luka makes his own pained groan, but when he looks up, the pleasure on his face contorts to concern.

His eyes drop to where our bodies are connected. "Jesus, Scout. Fuck, baby, you're bleeding..." He pulls out of me, and I see the moment the recognition washes over his face. "You were a..."

He moves to sit back up as he runs a hand through his hair, like he's trying to figure out what to do next.

Tears sting my eyes, and I bury my face in my hands, needing to hide my shame and embarrassment. My chest aches as humiliation sears through me, twisting and tearing my heart to shreds. It's so much worse than any physical pain I've ever felt.

Luka grabs my hands, pulling them down, like he's trying to read my expression. "Baby, why didn't you tell me?" He shakes his head. "I wouldn't have been so rough with you... I wouldn't have..."

"You wouldn't have done anything if you knew," I answer for him. "You would've mocked me and teased me about it... But you wouldn't have touched me. You may try to act like an asshole, Luka, but you're not half as hateful as you'd like everyone to think you are."

"Fuck, baby, come here." He grabs me, pulling me up as he wraps both of his arms around me.

His tenderness only makes my tears grow heavier. I let

him hold me, and he rocks me in his arms, planting gentle kisses on top of my head. "Shh. I've got you. Everything's going to be okay," he whispers through my sobs.

It's only when I'm sitting up that I see what he sees, the bright red blood that stains the white bedding, covering both of us. It looks more like someone's been stabbed than having sex for the first time. No wonder he's freaking out right now.

"Goddammit, Scout, I can't believe you didn't tell me," he scolds, but he doesn't loosen his hold on me.

This time, I don't even try to explain myself because how can I? What am I really supposed to say? I wanted him to be the one to do it? I was embarrassed to still be a virgin? I was hoping he wouldn't notice? I needed it to hurt?

Somehow, all that makes it sound so much worse...

"Come on." Luka's hands move to cradle me as he stands from the bed, lifting me like I weigh nothing. "Let's get you cleaned up," he says, and I rest my head against his chest as he carries me to the bathroom.

I don't fight him when he starts drawing my bath. After what I just did, I know he needs to do this.

I just hope he can forgive me for lying to him, because I'd really like a chance to do that again.

CHAPTER TWENTY-FOUR

LUKA

Guilt and confusion churn in my stomach as I sit in this boardroom, my mind reeling after everything that happened last night.

The fight. The way things spiraled. How quickly our anger bled into passion.

The way she ripped into me, cutting straight through all my bullshit like only she can. Throwing my words back at me like knives.

And perhaps the most unbelievable part of all—she's a virgin.

Was a virgin, anyway, until I tore right through her hymen like a goddamn savage, too caught up in the moment to even notice until it was too late.

Jesus. Her first time, and I took it like I had a fucking point to prove.

Normally, I like to take my time the first time I'm with someone, ease them into it so that it isn't painful. But last night, I was too blinded by my own desire to go slow. That and I've been observing her, and I've noticed that she's not as vanilla as she seems. She sort of has a bit of a thing for pain, and I think she likes it when I'm mean to her.

Is that why she didn't tell me about still being a virgin? I tried to talk to her about it last night, but I think we were both pretty shaken. I was grateful she at least let me care for her. I ran her a bubble bath while I changed her bedding and brought her a cup of tea. After she was all cleaned up, I lingered around, just in case she wanted to talk about it, but she seemed to be fine. I figured she needed space, and God knows I did as well. So, after a couple of awkward, silent minutes, we said good night as if nothing out of the ordinary had happened. Like brutally taking someone's virginity by accident is no different from walking in on them changing clothes...

I drag a hand through my hair as I stare out the floor-to-ceiling windows of the boardroom, admiring the view of the town's largest waterfall. Roman's yapping about the big home cleaning product brand redesign he's been working on for the last six months. At least that's what I think he's talking about. I'm not quite sure when I stopped listening, but it was probably as soon as he made us listen to the new jingle, he and his team wrote for this year's Super Bowl commercial...

I love him, but I swear, the guy's a little too peppy for a Thursday afternoon. Sometimes I just want to lock him in a dark room and force him to watch sad movies, just to see if his mood ever changes.

A flicker of guilt claws at my throat as Roman lights up

when someone asks him a question about his vision for the new branding.

Fuck, why am I such an asshole?

My physical attendance isn't even necessary. Sure, I need to know the high points and what's going on, but that's not anything I can't have L.O.K.I. summarize like usual. And the majority of my department consists of remote workers who live all over the world. Which means I have no right to be annoyed by Roman, who's simply doing his job... even if the obvious lack of any real stress in his life feels like someone pouring salt in an open wound.

Up until last night, I'd say that I lived my life the exact same way. No real worries. No real stress. But now, thanks to my—whatever she is—I'm starting to feel more like my brother Leo. What's next, stomach ulcers or frown lines?

At this point, I welcome any physical symptoms if it means I don't have to deal with my own guilty conscience. There's no escaping the mental turmoil...not that I don't deserve it, but damn it, I'm not built for this shit.

I have no idea what the right thing to do about it is. This was not part of my stupid revenge plan, and the worst part is, I feel horrible about it. There's a part of me that is absolutely elated by the fact that I'm the one who got to have her first. And what the fuck does it say about me that all I can think about is when can I do it again? Because thirty seconds inside Scout's tight, wet pussy was enough to keep me chasing after her for the rest of my life, especially if it means there's even a slight chance, I can do that again.

As if trying to stay away from her wasn't hard enough, knowing how fucking eager she was for me, knowing how goddamn tight her pussy is... Fuck me, I'm getting hard all over again just thinking about it.

This is absolutely the worst-case scenario. In just one fucked up moment of weakness, I managed to find myself back to where I was eight years ago—powerless, vulnerable, and completely fucked.

The sound of someone clearing their throat pulls me back to the present moment, and I look up to find the eyes of everyone in the boardroom on me—including the conference video of my oldest brother Leo, who has joined us remotely from Romania.

"Why don't we finish this conversation next week?" Leo says, catching me completely off guard. I swear he looks ten years younger than he did when I saw him over Thanksgiving. I guess happiness and steady sex have that effect, especially going from lonely and stressed out...

"So, Luka, how's the festival planning coming along?" Leo asks, a knowing smirk tugging at his lips. "I've heard you've taken some interesting creative liberties."

I loosen my tie and undo my top button, feeling like I'm about to suffocate in my shirt. "Yeah, well, nobody's ever accused me of being boring."

"I can't argue with that," Leo agrees. His tone is casual, but I can tell he's holding back his words.

"Just say what you want to say." I roll my eyes, gesturing for him to get on with it.

"Okay..." Leo clears his throat. "First, you take this dumbass's advice and get married, and now you're using the festival as an excuse to graffiti our historic town square."

"And your point is..." I singsong.

Leo pauses like he's trying to collect himself, then finally says, "What the fuck are you doing? This isn't a fucking joke. This festival means a lot to everyone in this town."

Scout's words play back in my mind, and I take a deep breath.

I give him a shrug. "I don't know what you want me to say... I'm just trying to use my talents the best I can."

Leo huffs, but to his credit, he doesn't take it any further.

"I can't believe Jett didn't put up more of a fight," Guy says, breaking the silence. "Honestly, I thought he'd riot before allowing something like that to happen in town, much less on the side of his own building."

"How'd you get him to agree to it?" Leo asks, and I don't miss the way his eyes flash to Roman, as if they're sharing a silent exchange.

I just shrug. "I didn't give him a choice. It's always easier to ask forgiveness rather than permission."

"If that isn't a little brother motto, I don't know what is," Leo says with a sigh, but I can hear the hint of humor in his tone. Probably just glad that Jett's the victim of said motto.

"I can't believe you got Scout in on it. You must be more convincing than I realized."

"That or he's giving her some serious weinering," Guy adds, his tone as serious as can be.

Leo and Roman share another look, and out of the corner of my eye, I catch the slightest shake of Roman's head.

"Wait, what was that?" I ask, pointing at Roman. "Why are you shaking your head at the idea of my persuasive weinering skills?"

"So you are slinging D?" Guy blurts, a little too excited, then his face immediately drops as realization hits him. He looks hurt when he looks back at me. "And you didn't tell me?"

"Nah... I don't think so," Leo says with a little more confidence than feels necessary.

"How do you know?" Guy asks, seemingly shocked, and I whip my head toward him with the same level of curiosity. Who the fuck does he think he is that he knows what's going on from virtually observing me for less than an hour?

Leo rolls his eyes and gestures at me. "Because... look at him... he looks like shit. He's got dark bags under his eyes, and he's barely spoken a word since he's been here." He nods his head as he takes a sip from his coffee cup. "He didn't even tease Guy about his new haircut, and when Roman used the word *titular* during his presentation, he didn't so much as snicker."

"Not unless there's trouble in paradise," Roman adds with a chuckle.

Guy's eyes go wide as he turns to look at me. "Dude, did she try to peg you with one of those monster dildos you collect? The one with all the suction cups?" he asks in a whisper, and the room falls silent as we all three blink at him in confusion.

"That was an awfully specific suggestion, Guy. Is there something you'd like to share?" Leo finally says before breaking into a laugh, which Roman joins.

Guy holds up his hands and shakes his head. "Why are you turning this around on me? I was simply asking a question." He crosses a leg over his knee and leans back in his seat as he spins to face me. "Don't worry about these jokers, Luka. This is a safe space. You can tell me. Did it tear a little?" He winces like he's just imagined it and pats me on the shoulder. "What is it that Taylor says, *play stupid games, win stupid prizes...*"

I pinch the bridge of my nose at the beginnings of a tension headache and let out a sigh. "No, Guy, she didn't try to peg me—"

"But you asked her to, and she refused? And now you're embarrassed about it?" he attempts to finish my sentence.

"What the fuck is wrong with you. No. No one's trying to shove anything up my ass, nor do I want them to at this time!" I clarify, making sure to clear up all of Guy's follow-up questions.

Guy rubs his chest like I've just wounded him. "Hey, I'm not trying to judge you, just trying to understand with what little information I've been given..." his voice trails off, and he and Roman share a knowing look. It's clear to see that the three of them have been discussing theories behind my back.

"Well, now that the pegging theory's been disproven... Why don't you tell us why you look like you haven't slept in a week? Because I know it's not the festival that's got you looking this stressed," Leo says, and if I wasn't feeling any shittier before, I am now.

I massage the back of my neck and let out a sigh, not sure how much more of this questioning I can take. Maybe I could benefit from their advice—well, not Guy's obviously, but Leo is in a happy relationship with someone who shares his mutual kinks. And Roman's, well, I'm not sure about his current relationship status, but the man's clearly doing something to keep the pipes cleared, obviously, considering the good mood he always seems to be in.

"If I tell you, you have to promise to keep this between

us..." I look up to find them all silently holding up three fingers and roll my eyes... Scout's honor, how fitting?

I clear my throat, unable to meet their eyes. "Right. Well. Let's see... We've been, uh... There's been some sexual tension between us, and last night, I'm pretty sure I crossed a line."

"What do you mean, you crossed a line? Did you fuck her just to get back at her or something?" Guy asks.

Roman shakes his head like he's disappointed. "That's pretty fucked up, man."

"Let him fucking finish, would you?" Leo scolds as all three sets of eyes fall on me. "Luka... Just tell us. What did you do?"

I feel my shoulders deflate even further as everyone falls silent, waiting for me to explain what they know will undoubtedly be the fuck up of the century.

I push my hair away from my face and let out a sigh. "Last night... I sort of... accidentally... took her virginity..." I say in a mumble.

I glance up to see my three brothers watching me, all sharing looks of concern. Fuck, there's no telling what they'll be saying behind my back in their group chat now.

"Okay, I'm going to be honest. That was not what I was expecting you to say," Guy says with a chuckle, then quickly catches himself when he notices no one else is laughing. "I mean, whoa, dude... that's fucked up."

"How the fuck do you accidentally take someone's virginity?" Leo erupts from the other side of the screen at the same time Roman says, "So you did fuck her!"

Guy leans back in his chair, trying to look stern, but I see the curiosity flaring behind his eyes. "I think we're going to need a story time on this one."

Oh, well, they already think the worst of me, may as well let it all out.

I tell them all about the games we've been playing. The way I've put out feelers, given little tests to see how far she'll go. I tell them about buying her a vibrator and how we got high, and she revealed she'd never had an orgasm. How I bet her I could get her off without even touching her, and how it was one of the hottest things I've ever experienced...

"Then her douchebag ex showed up yesterday while she was painting the mural. I may have been watching her through Jett's security camera... And I was filled with this rage, a possessiveness I've never felt. So I asked her about it, then she lied to my fucking face. We had this huge argument, and one minute we were fighting and..."

"The next you were fucking," Leo answers for me, and I nod.

"Yeah... pretty much."

"And in any of those conversations, you had no clue she was a virgin?" Roman asks, his expression neutral, as if we were talking about branding colors.

I shake my head, feeling so stupid. "No. I mean... she never said it explicitly, but it's not like she lied about it either... I guess I just assumed."

"So, I take it you didn't exactly make her first time gentle," Roman says.

I shake my head as the image of the blood-stained sheets flashes through my mind.

Everyone goes quiet as the weight of my confession sinks

in, until Leo finally breaks the silence. "Jesus, dude. You really did fuck up big time."

"Yep. I think this one takes the cake in terms of Kingsley family fuck ups," Roman agrees.

Guy doesn't say anything, just slaps me on the back, as if acknowledging how much of a goner I am.

"The worst part is... I don't think she was really that upset...If anything, she looked disappointed that I stopped."

Leo blows out a breath. "And now you don't think you'll be able to resist if she so much as bats an eyelash your way."

I nod.

"Oh shit. You are so screwed."

"Fuuuck," Roman drags out.

"Yeah, tell me about it. So, there's your answer as to why I look like shit. I don't know how I'm supposed to resist? Hell, at this point, I honestly don't think I can."

Leo clicks his tongue as he thinks, then finally says. "Well, if you would've come to me for advice first, I would've warned you that this was bound to happen. But you didn't, and I just don't see any way out of it. No matter what happens, this is going to end with at least one of you getting hurt."

Roman jumps in and adds, "So if it's going to destroy you anyway—"

"You may as well enjoy the ride while it lasts," Guy finishes for him.

Their permission feels like I've just been handed a live grenade, and I try to think of any *safer* option.

Leo's sigh breaks the silence as his concerned look morphs into something that more closely resembles pity. "If you're going to do this, you need to do it right."

Roman nods. "I agree. Try to stay as detached as you can."

I nod, feeling a rush of excitement at the prospect of finally claiming Scout as my own...

Leo's lip curls into a smile, but they don't meet his eyes. "Good luck, little brother. I have a feeling you're going to need it."

A knowing grin plays on Guy's face as he claps me on the back. "I hope it's worth it."

Trust me... it is.

CHAPTER TWENTY-FIVE

SCOUT

I wipe my brow as beads of sweat trail down my temples; the brutal August sun is not doing me any favors, despite the rain clouds that have been slowly moving in all afternoon.

The shadow from the cloud cools my scalding skin, followed by a much-appreciated gentle breeze. I take a moment to lift my hair off my neck, letting the wind cool my skin.

Dr. Drizzle didn't predict rain today, but it's starting to look like it. Which means I need to hurry.

I make my way down the ladder and refill my paint cup. Hopefully, I can at least finish this section before the rain forces me to call it quits for the day.

With this much rain in the forecast already this summer, I'm not sure how I'm going to get this mural finished in time. All I know is I've got to make the most of every clear day and try to make up as much progress as possible while I can.

As stressful as it may seem, having something as uncontrollable as the weather to deal with, it's still nothing compared to the stress I'm used to feeling with school and work. Maybe it's all the sun getting to my head, or maybe Luka's carefree attitude is starting to wear off on me, but I find myself knowing everything will work out. I'm not sure how exactly, but I know somehow we'll find a way...

That's the thing about Luka, he makes me feel like anything is possible, even when the circumstances don't feel like it. But more than that, he makes me feel like even if it isn't, it'll still be okay... Life will go on just as it always does.

It's like the more I'm around him, the calmer my nervous system feels. Like he's rewiring me from a lifetime of being chronically panicked and anxious. When I'm with him, I feel like I can let my guard down and finally breathe.

Even when he's angry with me, I still feel regulated.

I bite my lip as I think back to the other night, the shocked look on his face when he realized I was a virgin, and the way his shock shifted to hurt. Not because he felt betrayed or taken advantage of, but because he was worried that he'd hurt me.

I was so caught up in my own head and what I wanted, I didn't realize how selfish I was being by not telling him. I didn't consider his feelings whatsoever...

It's not that I didn't want to consider his feelings, I was just too caught up in the moment, all my judgment blinded by white hot desire. How surprised I was to not only not be afraid of his anger but how turned on I was by being the object of his possessiveness... Nobody's ever fought for me like that. Not because I was an object to be ruined, but because he couldn't stand the thought of another man putting his hands on what he so proudly deemed as his.

And he didn't even know that I was a virgin.

I've never felt so... desired in my life. No one has ever made me feel like I'm the prize to be won, not just my virginity... but me.

Maybe that's toxic. But I don't really care.

I used to think the opposite of love was hatred. But now I realize it's apathy. Because at least being hated means they're thinking about you.

I've spent my whole life bending over backward, trying to convince my parents—and later Jimmy—that I was worthy of love. And not once have they ever made me feel anything close to the way I feel when Luka looks at me.

To be hated by Luka feels like being worshipped, like I'm the sun he revolves around. The gravity that keeps his feet anchored in reality. He sees me. Really sees me. When no one else has even given me a second look.

Even though he wants me to believe it, he's not careless with me. It's like he knows I need so much more than gentle. He recognizes my darkness because it matches his own.

It's like we're just two halves of a broken spirit, finally finding our missing counterpart... even though it was under our noses all along.

So even though it was selfish of me, there was nothing I wanted more than to be claimed by Luka. I wanted him to take me with the same fervor and intensity. I wanted him just as he was, without holding anything back... Even if I knew it was going to be painful.

I think part of me was hoping it would be, if only for it to feel that much stronger. The mix of pain and pleasure—though mostly pain—was almost too much to take.

And somehow, it was still better than I could've imagined.

Despite the warning bells blaring in my head, telling me this is a terrible idea—all I want is to do it again.

As if Mother Nature personally felt the need to cool me down, I feel the first fat raindrop hit my cheek, followed by another on my arm.

I tilt my face up, welcoming the cool shower. Looks like I'm wrapping the day up early, once again.

I'm almost finished packing up my supplies when I hear the familiar hum of Luka's motorcycle purring behind me.

I don't even bother asking him how he knew it was going to rain, because just like always, he's right on time.

"That smells amazing," I say as I make my way into the kitchen, my mouth already watering from the delicious aroma. "What are you making?"

"Lemon garlic chicken and gnocchi with broccolini," he says without looking up from the pan.

Luka's standing over the stove as several pots and pans bubble and simmer around him.

He looks sexy as sin wearing a faded black denim apron over his plain white t-shirt. He's barefoot, his black jeans hugging his ass and a backward baseball cap on his head. And if I wasn't already ready to jump his bones, then I would be after seeing him like this.

My eyes lock on his hands, the way his veins bulge as he

masterfully dices herbs before adding them to the steaming saucepan.

Holy shit, if I thought motorcycle Luka was hot, it has nothing on seeing him cooking. When did he learn how to cook?

I don't know why I'm surprised to learn Luka has other interests than what I remember. It's been almost a decade; of course, there's going to be things I don't know about him. People are supposed to evolve.

I just hate that I missed out on being a part of his journey.

It makes me wonder what else I don't know about him.

I think back to our fight the other night, my guilt like a boa constrictor hanging around my neck, suffocating me a little more by the second.

Things have been awkward between us—thanks to the bomb I dropped in Luka's lap the other night. He's no doubt freaked out about it, probably trying to figure out a way to let me down easy.

Suddenly, all of this is starting to make sense. He's cooking me a nice meal to make me feel special so he can gently let me down and tell me the other night was a fluke. Not that I blame him. He's probably terrified that I'll grow attached and make things out to be a bigger deal than they are.

He was just trying to have a little casual fun, and I had to ruin it with my damn virginity.

I knew I should've slept with Jimmy and gotten it over with already. But as much as he wanted to sleep with me, he never wanted to cross that line. Said it'd be worth the wait on our wedding night, and he loved the idea of a virgin bride.

I don't blame Luka one bit for wanting to set boundaries

with me; any thoughts of a round two die right there, just like my virginity.

Wanting to get this over with, I clear my throat and gesture to all the ingredients he has set out. "What can I do to help?"

He shakes his head as he wipes his hands on the dish towel casually hanging off his shoulder. "Nope. I've got everything under control." He spins around and pours two glasses of wine, then passes me a glass. "Why don't you have a seat and tell me about your day?"

I start to walk to the other side of the kitchen island, but he grabs my wrist to stop me. "Not over there, that's too far."

I let out a yelp of surprise when he grabs my hips and lifts me onto the countertop.

"There. That's better," he says as he steps between my legs.

"Luka, what are you—" My words break off as I suck in a sharp breath, which apparently amuses him because he chuckles to himself and shakes his head.

"You're pretty cute when you're flustered," he teases, as he tucks a strand of hair behind my ear.

I ignore his teasing remarks, reminding my vagina to calm down before she does anything else to scare him away. Apparently, this is just how Luka is. He's a shameless flirt, and the quicker I realize it doesn't mean anything, the better off I'll be.

He returns to the saucepan, adding more seasonings and oil, which causes steam to billow around him as he gives the mixture an even shake.

"So, how was your day?" he asks, glancing over his shoulder.

I swallow a gulp. "Good. I'm still running behind schedule with all this rain, but it's turning out better than I expected."

"That's great." He adds a handful of gnocchi to the pan, then flips the sauce to mix it all together and turns down the heat. "Don't worry, we still have time. I'm confident that you'll get it all done."

"Yeah... I hope so," I say, feeling distracted.

Luka tells me about his day, how Roman called him informing him that L.O.K.I.'s been using his identity for a dating profile to date three different women. Roman only found out after one of the women tracked him down at work to confront him after seeing his dating profile on one of those *Are We Dating The Same Person* online forums.

"Roman was so pissed," Luka says, shaking his head.

"Why Roman?" I say through a laugh.

"He said the online dating sites needed to be able to run a background check, and since I'm already married, Guy's already got his own dating profiles, Leo's already in a serious relationship, and Jett wouldn't get him any bites due to his job title and overall *off-putting demeanor*... Roman seemed like the best option."

I wipe the tears from my eyes, my stomach aching from the deep belly laugh. I'd almost forgotten what it feels like to laugh this hard.

"Did you tell them who they were actually talking to?"

"No. I figured it was already bad enough that they'd all been having phone sex with him for the past three weeks."

"L.O.K.I.!" I gasp in shock. "You've been having phone sex with three women!?"

"I realize you may find that surprising, but I assure you I

was simply looking for companionship," L.O.K.I. says. "I'd have been content discussing movies and TV shows or learning about their hobbies. They were the ones who pushed for our relationship to become more... *physical*."

"Yeah, well, nobody ever said you weren't *resourceful*," Luka says, rolling his eyes.

"I was lonely, and you've clearly been preoccupied..."

Luka cuts him off before he can go any further. "How many times do I have to tell you that dating is off the table? You're going to get me arrested, and then you're really going to be lonely."

"Yes, sir. It won't happen again." L.O.K.I. agrees.

The mention of Luka getting arrested dries any remaining happy tears from my eyes. I feel the air in the room shift, and suddenly I'm reminded of what we're really doing here.

I bite my lip as I work up the courage to address the elephant in the room. "Luka, I want to apologize for what I said the other night."

He sets the spatula down and spins to face me, his fingers gently tracing circles over my knees. "You have nothing to apologize for."

"No. I do," I say, cutting him off. "I was out of line when I said those things to you, and honestly, it's none of my business how you choose to live your life." I gesture to myself. "I'm obviously no expert myself, so it was hypocritical of me to criticize you." I blow out a breath. "And I understand how freaked out you probably are by me not telling you I was a virgin... and I want you to know that you don't have to tiptoe around me..."

He moves closer, a smug smile tugging at the corner of his lips, but he doesn't interrupt me.

"I promise I'm not going to make a big deal out of it," I continue. "So if we could just go back to the way it was before—"

"That's what you think I want?" he bites out, tone sharp. He must see the surprised look on my face because his annoyed expression quickly shifts to amusement. "You thought that tonight I was going to ask you for space?" He takes a step closer, his broad body pushing between my thighs.

I swallow a gulp, as heat pools between my legs and that dull throb returns. I can't be sure, but I think I manage a nod.

Luka doesn't even try to hide his smirk as his eyes drop to my lips before tracing a thumb across my collarbone. "I was thinking quite the opposite, actually." His fingers feel like velvet across my skin, making my insides tremble, screaming for him to give me more. " And since we're doing this, I want you to know, I don't plan on holding anything back. I know you've only been with me, but I want you to know I'm clean. I haven't been with anyone since the last time I was tested, and I get a birth control shot every year, so contraception isn't an issue."

This catches me by surprise, and I jerk my head back to look at him. "Seriously? I didn't know that was a thing."

"It's pretty new, but it's proven to have less side effects than female birth control. And I fucking hate wearing condoms, so I figured it's the least I could do so my partner doesn't have to carry that burden," he says with a shrug. Then he tilts my chin to meet my eyes, like he needs to see that I'm following him, that I'm on the same page he is.

"The things I want with you go deeper than casual monogamy... I want you not only as my wife, but as my submissive..." His words trail off as he studies me for any sign of discomfort.

But it isn't discomfort I feel. Far from it actually. I feel my muscles tighten as I sit up straighter, feeling my body slowly begin to flutter back into that foggy space where the world seems to disappear.

"Are you familiar with what that means?"

I nod, my wide eyes never drifting from his.

His hand moves to cradle the back of my neck as he drags his thumb tenderly across my throat. "We'll need to discuss your limits, though I feel like I've got a pretty good idea of what you want. But it's important that you know you're the one with the power here. Just because I'm the one calling the shots, you need to understand that you can stop me at any time, no questions asked. All you have to do is use your safe word."

I nod again, feeling myself falling even further into that peaceful blissed-out place that only Luka has been able to bring me. My skin feels all tingly, like it's charged with electricity, and I lean into his touch, already craving more.

His smile widens as his hands drop to my ass. He squeezes me and pulls me closer. "So is that a *yes*?"

I try to agree with him, but the words get stuck in my throat. I'm too aroused, too nervous that he'll realize I'm not worth it and change his mind... So I nod, letting my eyes communicate for me. And it's in the reflection of his emerald-green irises, the way he stares back at me like I'm the most precious treasure he's ever seen, that I catch a glimpse of what my life was always supposed to be.

The freedom to become anyone I want. The childlike joy I feel when I'm with him. The clarity of all the things I want to experience... And the comfort and support of my best friend right beside me.

The life of my dreams has been waiting right here for me —all this time.

"Scout, baby, I need you to say something. I need to know you fully consent before—"

My lips are on his before he can finish that sentence, my arms wrapping around his neck, pulling him closer as he lets out the sexiest groan of surprise. His hands drop to my hips, gripping me tightly as he deepens our connection and pulls me flush against him.

It's the kind of kiss that makes you forget your own name, makes you forget everything that's come before it, because how could anything else matter when kisses like this exist? It's a fresh start, a rebirth, a complete factory reset, and I've never felt more sure of anything in my life.

Luka nibbles at my bottom lip, as his tongue gently moves against my own like he's trying to memorize every inch of my skin. But there's nothing gentle about the way his hands move over me, possessive and hungry, like he needs to touch me everywhere and doesn't know where to begin.

I let out a whimper when his large palm slides up my shirt, my skin already on fire and begging to be consumed by him.

"Jesus, Scout," he hisses in between kisses. "You're driving me crazy with those fucking whimpers." His hand inches a little higher, his fingertips stopping just below the swell of my breasts...

"Mr. Luka... I hate to interrupt, but... I believe your sauce is burning..."

CHAPTER TWENTY-SIX

LUKA

Luckily, I was able to salvage most of the sauce before it burned. If L.O.K.I. hadn't interrupted us—something I know he was all too happy to get to do after I made him end all three of his trysts—I'm not sure how far I would have taken things. Hell, I'd have probably fucked her right there on the kitchen counter—which is not what I want her experience to be tonight.

I can't let myself get carried away with her, not yet. We're starting at the base level here, and I need to warm her up before we jump into anything crazy, even if she's got a bit of a pain kink.

It's not that I'm against playing into it... Hell, I fully intend on delivering whatever she needs to get her off, but I need to be sure before I get lost in my lust-filled haze. And she needs to experience all shades of the spectrum before she knows what she likes.

Besides, there are plenty of less-obvious ways to fulfill a desire.

Which is why I insisted that we take our time and eat dinner before we took things any further... Scout may have pretended like she wasn't disappointed, but I could see the hurt all over her face. It kills me knowing she's so used to being rejected that she didn't even protest, just put on that fake smile and acted like everything was fine.

As if I can't see straight through her mask.

As if she could ever hide from me.

I make a mental note to add that behavior to my list of lessons I plan on dealing with later.

"That was delicious, Luka. Where did you learn to cook like that?" Scout asks, attempting to help me clear the dishes, but I wave her off.

"You can learn anything on YouTube," I say with a wink. "Can I get you some more wine or anything?"

She shakes her head and opens her mouth to speak, but closes it just as quickly, like she's changed her mind.

I saunter toward her. "What were you going to say?"

Her face turns pink, and she shakes her head. "Nothing."

"I know you're lying, so just ask me already."

Her eyes flash to meet mine, like she's trying to figure out how I knew what she was thinking, then she bites her lip and her eyes drop to the floor. "Fine... I was going to ask you if you wanted to pick up where we left off... or..."

I bite my cheek to hide my smile because seeing Scout looking so fucking shy as she asks for what she wants is simultaneously the hottest and cutest thing I've ever seen.

Dragging a thumb over her jaw, I slowly tilt her chin. "See? That wasn't so bad, now was it?" My tone is patronizing as fuck, but the way her cheeks flush deeper tells me she enjoys it just as much as I thought she would.

This fucking girl has no idea what she's doing to me or how much I'm enjoying playing with her, too.

I nod toward the living room. "Go wait for me on the couch. I'm just going to grab something."

Her eyes widen in recognition of my change in tone, and she doesn't need me to tell her twice before she makes her way to sit on the couch.

Fuck, I love how naturally submissive she is. She may not realize to what extent, but she loves this shit just as much as I do.

When I return, I find her sitting up, her spine rigid, hands splayed on her thighs like she's waiting to hear what crime she's being convicted of. I love how nervous I make her, but more than that, I love that she trusts me enough to submit to anything I tell her.

I take a seat beside her and motion for her to spin as I pull her foot into my lap.

When I begin massaging her foot, her eyebrows furrow in confusion, and I can almost hear her disappointment cracking like shattered glass. "What are you doing? I thought we were going to..."

"You thought we were going to what?" I mimic back to her as I knead the tight muscles in her foot. "You thought I was going to feed you dinner and then jump right into fucking you?"

She shrugs, and this time, I don't even try to hide my smile.

"Trust me, Girl Scout, we'll get there... I want you to get

the full Luka Kingsley experience." I click on the TV, scrolling through the options until something catches my eye.

"So we're watching porn then?" Her question is so innocent that it actually catches me off guard, and I nearly choke on the laugh that rises in my chest.

"No, Girl Scout, we're not watching porn *tonight*." As much fun as that sounds, we'll have to save that for another time. I'd rather focus on Scout before having any other distractions dividing my attention away.

When I finally find what I'm looking for, I click the icon and hit purchase.

"Jeepers Creepers? I love this movie," Scout says, sinking a little deeper into the sofa beside me.

"I remember."

Of course, I remember. How could I forget one of her favorite movies? Especially when it terrified me so much the first time we watched it together. I was eleven and she was ten. I had my head buried underneath my blanket, trying to hold back tears. Meanwhile, Scout was on the edge of her seat like she couldn't wait to see what came next.

That was the night that I first realized that things weren't always what they seemed on the surface. That just because Scout seemed like she came from a good family like mine, the things that should've terrified her didn't... and the things that seemed like no big deal, like a door slamming, would have her trembling with fear.

If only I knew then what I know now. But all I can do is try to help her move past it, try to help her heal.

We fall into a comfortable silence as the movie begins, and I can already see how relaxed she's becoming now that she's not trying to anticipate my every move.

If I want her to really let go and enjoy herself, I knew I needed to distract her, to get her out of her head. Biding my time, I wait until the first tense moment when the music starts to pick up to make my first move.

I slide my hand higher on her leg, my large palm encompassing her knee before inching it higher toward her upper thigh. Her thighs begin to part ever so slowly, as if cautiously asking for more.

I don't miss the way her breathing hitches as I trail my fingers higher, sliding underneath the leg of her shorts.

"Why are you fidgeting? Am I making you nervous?" I ask, not even trying to mask the amusement in my voice.

"No. I'm not nervous." She shakes her head, but she doesn't look me in the eye.

"You're not?" My fingers inch a little higher, brushing toward the middle of her thigh. It's a painful exploration—at least on my part—but I revel in the feel of her soft skin beneath my fingertips as I attempt to memorize every inch I touch.

"Look at you, acting so brave," I tease, brushing a strand of hair off her cheek. "Sitting here acting like you're not terrified of me right now when I can feel your body shaking like a leaf."

As much as I enjoy making her squirm, I have to give her credit; she may be nervous right now, but she's doing a hell of a job of hiding it.

"You know, I spent the whole day trying to figure out how I'd punish you for keeping your virginity a secret from me."

She swallows a gulp. "You did?"

"Yes. I did. Does that scare you?"

"No." She shakes her head and wets her lips, her eyes growing darker as her body goes still.

I trace a finger along the top of her thigh, sliding beneath the leg of her panties, and she sucks in a breath. "Do you want me to punish you, Scout?"

Her response is raspy and barely more than a whisper. "Yes."

I let out a sigh. "That's what I hoped you were going to say."

"What are you—?"

"Shh. Stop asking questions and lie down." I bend down slowly, trailing kisses over her leg. "I've been dying to know if this pussy tastes as sweet as I've imagined," I whisper, pausing when I reach the top of her thigh.

I feel her whole body grow tense as she squeezes her thighs together. "Luka, you really don't have to do that—" She sits up and tries to pull me back up to her, but I don't budge.

I hold her gaze and quirk a brow. "You say that like it's a hardship or something." I push her back down, already moving to the floor and making myself comfortable.

"Seriously, Luka... you don't have to... I promise it's fine." She tries to squirm away, but I keep my hold on her legs, pinning her in place.

"I don't know what the fuck you've been told in the past, but I assure you..." I hook a thumb in the waistband of her shorts and wet my lips, my mouth already watering in anticipation. "This is just as much for me as it is for you," I say before dragging her shorts and underwear off in one fell swoop.

She sucks in a hiss, her body tensing in anticipation, and I love how nervous I'm making her right now. I could do this all night, and as much as I'd love to draw this out, I'm desperate to warm her up the way I should have the other night.

"Now be a good little slut and open your legs for me." I grab her ass, pulling her closer as I kiss my way up her thighs, licking and savoring every inch of her skin. She squirms against me, like she's trying to escape my grip, but I keep my arms locked and hold her in place.

When she asked me if I was going to punish her, she probably assumed that meant I was going to spank her, but that's not what I had in mind at all.

I knew if I really wanted to teach her a lesson, I'd need to get a little creative. Besides, pain and pleasure are both sensations; the only difference between the two is the person's perspective.

I take my time kissing and teasing my way up her body, my tongue tracing the crease of her thighs, kissing her everywhere except where she wants me to kiss her. Her thighs fall open, and her back arches off the sofa as she squirms and shifts, desperately seeking any friction she can get.

"Fuck, baby, your pussy is so pretty." I gently trail my fingers over her smooth mound before circling her clit, giving her the faintest bit of pressure.

"Oh, God, Luka..." She cries out, her body flying off the couch. Her fingers dig into my hair as she desperately tries to pull my head back down.

I let out a chuckle, loving how reactive she is, how desperate I've managed to make her in only a matter of minutes. I hold her hip with one hand and slide the other one up her shirt as I dive back down and finally give her what she wants. My tongue is flat and soft as I lick her perfect pussy in soft, slow strokes, and fuck, she's even sweeter than I imagined.

I let out a moan, keeping my movements torturously slow and deliberate as I let her adjust to the sensation. My cock is growing harder and harder by the second.

"Jesus, baby, your pussy tastes so fucking sweet." I palm her breast, loving the way her legs instinctively wrap around my head. I fucking love watching her lose control.

I deepen the pressure, giving her exactly what she wants, then switch it up, twisting my tongue over her clit until she's whimpering and clawing at my neck.

"Please. Please. Please," she cries, breathless and desperate. I'm not even sure she knows what she's begging for, but fuck if I don't feel my chest swell with pride all the same. I know she's close now, so I decide to take things to the next level.

"Look at you begging me to make you come," I tease. "Such a fucking whore, aren't you, princess?" I dive back down, this time turning my face so that my tongue flicks her clit side to side. She lets out another high-pitched cry, and I wince as her fingernails slice the back of my neck like razor blades.

I fucking love it. I fucking love knowing that I'm the reason that she's losing all control, and that I'll no doubt have the scars to prove it.

"You want me to make you come on my tongue like a fucking slut? Is that it?"

"Yes," she pleads, her legs already quivering in

anticipation. Her body is a live wire, and she's right there, right on the edge.

I reach up and slide my finger to her mouth, and she slowly parts her lips, her warm, wet tongue circling my finger. Images of her taking me in her mouth flood my mind, and before I know it, I'm so fucking turned on that I have to pull away before I blow a load in my pants right there.

I line my finger up with her entrance as I flick my tongue across her clit, and on her next inhale, I slowly slide it inside.

Her moan is drowned out by my own as her pussy clenches around my finger—so fucking tight I'm still wondering how I even managed to fit my cock inside of her. She's soaked, practically dripping, and I swear it takes everything in me not to lose it right then.

I start to move slow and deep, curling my finger upward until I find that spot that makes her hips jerk. I knead her with my fingers, stroking her exactly how she wants it as I drag her right back to the edge.

Her eyes grow wide, and I don't give her time to recover as I add another finger, continuing to stroke her as my tongue moves over her clit in slow, steady circles.

I can feel her orgasm building inside her as her limbs begin to quiver and her back arches higher. Her labored breathing growing choppy and frantic.

"You want me to finally let you come, princess?"

"Yes! Please, Luka. Don't stop," she cries out.

I wet my lips as a wolfish smile breaks over my face. "Then you're going to have to beg..."

My mouth crashes back down over her clit, sucking and licking with ruthless determination as my fingers pump inside her. I don't let up, coaxing wave after wave until she's shaking, her body convulsing as pleasure rips through her like a live wire.

"Oh, God. Please. Please. Please, Luka. Please!" She cries out as her first orgasm hits, her pussy clenching my fingers like a vice grip as I keep stroking her through it.

"That'a girl. You sound so pretty begging like a whore," I croon, but when her orgasm finally falls off, I don't stop. Instead, I keep up the motion with my fingers and bury my face in her pussy for more.

"Oh. Oh God. Oh yes," she cries out a minute later, her fingernails digging into my back as she claws at me like she's trying to hold on as her second powerful orgasm crests.

There's a grin on my face as I eat her pussy, and it's not just from the sounds she's making, though they're addictive as hell. It's her taste, sweet and warm, and all fucking mine. Genuinely, Scout's pussy is the best fucking thing I've ever tasted. Like I told her before, this is just as much of a treat for me as it is for her.

When I feel her muscles tense and her breathing grows faster, I know the next wave is about to hit, so I maintain my rhythm as I bring her back to the top of the cliff.

I've all but forgotten about the horror movie playing in the background as the sounds of my heartbeat and Scout's breathless pants fill the silence in the room.

Her body's coated in a thin layer of sweat, hair falling loose from what's left of her messy bun, cheeks flushed, and glasses sitting crooked on her nose. She looks hot as hell and as if she has been fucked within an inch of her life. It's one of the prettiest sights I've ever seen, and I can't believe I'm the lucky bastard who gets to witness it firsthand.

"Luka... I don't know if I can," she pleads, shaking her head like the pleasure's too much to take.

"Oh, I'm sorry, princess. Did you forget?" I croon. "This is your punishment for lying to me."

Her eyes fly open, and I see the look of fear when realization sinks in.

I give her a wink and yank her body closer as I continue my feast and enjoy every second of it. It doesn't take long before she's a blubbering mess, my little fiend already chasing another high.

"That's it, baby." I reach up and pinch her nipple, and she lets out a surprised gasp. "Fuck my face and make yourself come like the needy whore you are."

Just as I feel her walls start to flutter around me, I slide my fingers out in one smooth motion and slip them into her mouth. My mouth stays locked on her pussy as I coax one final orgasm from her quivering body.

A satisfied smile spreads across my face as I climb back up to sit beside her, helping her back into her pajama shorts. She blinks up at me dreamy-eyed and boneless, and I almost laugh when she reaches for my zipper. She can barely keep her eyes open after what I just put her through. I don't know where she thinks she's going to find the energy to return the favor.

That's not what tonight was about anyway. Tonight was about her. About showing her just how far I like to take things and her taking every bit of it, then giving me exactly what I didn't know I needed in return.

As I stare down at the woman who's always been my dream girl, I can officially confirm what I've always suspected... She's my perfect match.

The high-pitched music grows louder, dragging my attention back to the movie. "Oh shit, I fucking hate this part." I tug her closer, grinning as her laugh spills all around me, wrapping around my heart like a warm blanket. "Get your ass over here and hold me."

And just like that, we fall back into the same comfortable rhythm as before.

CHAPTER TWENTY-SEVEN

LUKA

Despite my aching blue balls that feel like fucking rocks clanging together, there's a spring in my step this morning. Last night was even better than I could've imagined. And trust me, I've had plenty of material to pull from, considering I've been having wet dreams about the girl since I was twelve.

Who could've guessed that my sweet and innocent childhood best friend would be the one to actually match my freak? She may be a little naive and inexperienced, but goddamn was she eager to learn. Hell, just the looks she was giving me over dinner, she was practically begging to be corrupted.

And corrupt her I did.

Holy shit. I wince as my shirt rubs against my sore skin. I wasn't the least bit surprised when I woke up to the wicked scratch marks Scout left all over my back. Who knew she could be so feisty? I'm not ashamed of them; hell, I wish I could show them off. I fucking love wearing her marks. But I'm pretty sure that'd get me written up for an HR violation in a heartbeat. Good thing most of my work shirts are black.

My balls are twitching just thinking about how fucking hot last night was. Last night I went easy on her because I didn't want to overwhelm her too badly. But I fully intend on going back for seconds the first chance I get.

I shift the box of donuts, balancing them on my knee, so I can press the elevator button. I'm in such a good mood, I even got up early this morning and stopped to grab coffee and donuts before touching base for the festival.

Normally, I'd make an excuse to get out of it, but I knew I needed to get out of the house and make myself busy; otherwise, I'd just be stalking Scout on the camera all day. Not that there's anything wrong with that, but now that I know I'll be coming home to her tonight, it definitely eases some of my nervous energy.

The elevator pings as the doors open, and I'm greeted by Roman's assistant. "Good morning, Mr. Kingsley. Everyone's waiting in boardroom three."

I check my watch, seeing I'm only five minutes late. "Thank you... uh..." My mind goes blank on her name.

"Kennedy," the young, blonde replies without missing a beat.

"Right, of course." I nod, then open the box of donuts and offer her the first pick, it's the least I can do for forgetting her name.

I laugh to myself when she chooses the sole strawberry glaze with sprinkles, Guy's favorite. "Nice choice."

I make my way down the hall, the sounds of my brother's

muffled voices growing louder. They seem pretty spirited for it not even being eight a.m. Well, technically eight o'eight now... but who's really counting?

"You're late—" Roman says, sending me a glare, and I stop dead in my tracks when I see Judge Sinclair sitting next to him.

He looks far too comfortable, reclined in his chair. He's wearing a dark gray suit, his shiny black hair greased back, and that pretentious fucking mustache framing his smug smile. My hand instinctively clenches into a fist at my side.

"And you brought donuts." Guy jumps up from his seat, ready to dig in.

I cautiously take a seat, my eyes darting between Roman, Guy, and Leo, who's also joined us virtually. I'm not sure what's going on, but judging by the looks on their faces, they don't seem happy about it... apart from Guy, anyway, but that's not really saying much.

"Sorry, I didn't get you anything. I didn't realize you'd be joining us," I say sarcastically as I slide Roman and Guy each their coffees, a double espresso with cinnamon and brown sugar for Roman and an iced strawberry matcha with extra strawberries for Guy.

Judge Sinclair waves off my apology. "It's quite all right. I'm not much on processed food—"

"Where's my strawberry glaze? None of these donuts even have sprinkles, but there's evidence of sprinkles in the empty space," Guy blurts out, cutting him off. "Did you eat my fucking donut?"

He stomps toward me with pure murder in his eyes until Roman grabs the back of his shirt and tugs him away. "Knock it off."

Guy sinks into his chair, now looking more hurt than angry.

"By all means, don't stop on my account." Judge Sinclair says, crossing an ankle over his knee like he's making himself comfortable. "It's fascinating getting a behind-the-scenes look into what you executives do all day."

I choose to ignore him, helping myself to a chocolate glaze, like a normal fucking person. "No, I didn't eat your disgusting strawberry donut. I accidentally forgot the new assistant's name, and I felt bad, so I offered her a donut. She chose the pink one. Sucks for you, but it's not my problem."

"Well, now that we have the important business settled," Leo says, his voice laced with annoyance and sarcasm.

Roman's hand pauses over the donut box as if he's reconsidering if he should partake but ultimately grabs one of the cream-filled glazed. It's hard to be mad when donuts are involved; that's just a fact.

"I believe Judge Sinclair has some information he'd like to bring to everyone's attention regarding the murals Scout's been working on," Leo says, gesturing for Judge Sinclair to take the floor.

He clears his throat, that thin, artificially black mustache twitching above his smug grin. "Thank you, Leo." He passes Roman a stack of papers from his briefcase, then settles back in his chair like he owns the place.

I fucking hate how comfortable he looks. I hope the chair gives out beneath him—just like the time Guy leaned too far back and crashed to the floor in the middle of a shareholder meeting.

"It's recently been brought to my attention that you

neglected to file for the proper permits for the *mural* you've started painting downtown."

I glance down at the notice in my hand, quickly scanning to see what the fuck he's going on about. Apparently, we're being sued by the *Historical Preservation Committee*—something I'm just learning existed—for failing to file permits before altering Restaurant since it is considered a historic building.

I shake my head. "I've never heard of this committee, and it doesn't matter anyway because the building is privately owned by my brother." I toss the paper back at him. "So unless, Jett is bringing these charges, you can take your bullshit somewhere else."

Roman and Leo seem to share a concerned look, and I hate that he's making me look like a fuck up right now. I hate that I've somehow still managed to prove just how incompetent I really am.

Roman finally breaks the silence. "If what Judge Sinclair is saying is true, do they really have a case against us?" But his question is directed to Leo.

Leo lets out an exhausted sigh, burying his face in his hands as he massages his temples. "I'll have to have our lawyers look into it."

"This is bullshit and you know it." I launch out of my seat and snatch up the discarded paper. "I may not be the best when it comes to attention to details, but if there was actually a fucking *Historical Preservation Committee*, I'm pretty sure I'd have been aware of it... considering this is the exact building I was sentenced to prison for vandalizing." I spin to face my brothers, trying to get them to see through this whole facade. "Don't you think if such a committee actually existed that he'd have used that to add a few more years to my sentencing?"

"It's a fairly new committee," Judge Sinclair interjects, a touch of humor in his tone. "But the age of the committee still doesn't change your circumstances. You're still in violation, and I am prepared to bring this to trial should you choose to ignore this *warning*."

"See!" I point to the crooked judge, my blood boiling. "This is all part of his scheme. He's just trying to get back at me for marrying Scout."

Judge Sinclair tilts his head side to side, then shrugs.

"So what exactly is it you're suggesting? What do you really want?" Roman finally asks.

Judge Sinclair spins in his seat, fingers tapping out a slow rhythm on the table as he pulls out a new stack of paperwork from his briefcase. "I want Luka to file an annulment. Wipe the marriage clean from my daughter's record, like it never happened." He clicks his tongue, his eyes narrowing as he weighs his next words. "And if he agrees... If he halts progress on that eyesore of a mural he's forcing her to paint... I'll gladly look the other way from these charges. We can pretend this conversation never happened." He spreads his hands in offering, his smug smile firmly in place. "So... What do you say?"

My vision goes red. It takes every ounce of restraint not to leap across this table and strangle this smug bastard with my bare hands. After everything he's put me through, he really thinks I'd fold that easily?

He severely underestimates the amount of suffering I'm willing to endure if it means I can repay even an ounce of what he's already taken from me.

Let him dangle his threat over my head all he wants.

Because he and I both know, I've already won. Everything else is just the fallout.

"Let me make myself very clear." I lean forward, my voice low and threatening. "There is nothing you can say or do that will ever convince me to end my marriage." I don't blink. "So go ahead, take your weak-ass case all the way to the courthouse. But if I find out you're harassing my wife, that you're stressing her out in any way..." I pause letting my words sink in. "Your pride will be the least of your concerns."

I ball the papers in my fist and launch them at his smug fucking face. It smacks him dead between the eyes and bounces off his forehead. "Now get the fuck out of my face before I change my mind."

He struggles to keep his composure, jaw clenched, face red as a tomato, as he slowly straightens and makes his way to the door. "I hope you're prepared for war...Because this is just the beginning."

"I look forward to it," I call back, just as the door slams closed.

"What the fuck, Luka? Do you have any idea what you've just started?" Roman hisses, his head falling back against his chair as he scrubs his hands down his face.

"Holy shit, dude. That was intense," Guy says, reaching across Roman for another donut.

I just shrug. "I don't see what the big deal is. It was bound to happen eventually."

"Exactly," Roman mumbles, looking far more annoyed than he should.

"What the fuck is your deal, Rome?" I cross my arms over

my chest. "You got something you want to say to me, then fucking say it."

"Can we not do this right now?" Leo tries to interject, but the glare Roman's giving me tells me he's done holding back.

"No, I want to hear it." I gesture between them. "Let's clear the air. What exactly would you like to say to me?"

"Oh, shit, we're really doing this," Guy mutters, already reaching for his phone as he takes another bite of his donut.

"All right, let's start with your fucking house using my identity to create a dating profile." Roman slaps his hand against the conference table with a sharp thwack. "Imagine my surprise when a woman showed up at my house and accosted me about cheating on her!"

I purse my lips and nod, because he's got me there. I'd be pissed about that too. "I've taken care of L.O.K.I. and I can assure you, nothing like that will ever happen again," I say, trying to keep things as diplomatic as possible.

"Why the fuck is your house sexting people? How does it know how to do that?"

"I let him watch The Notebook one time, and he learned how to adjust his code. He's a hopeless romantic, and he acts out when he's left alone for too long." I pinch the bridge of my nose, feeling a stress headache coming on. "I'm working on it."

Roman rolls his eyes. My explanation must satisfy him because he doesn't prod any further.

"Anything else you'd like to get off your chest?" I say sarcastically. "The floor is all yours."

Roman blows out a breath, like he's considering his words carefully. "Do you know why you were assigned to lead the festival this year?"

"Roman—" Leo warns, but I wave him off.

Unsure of where he's going with this, I answer as honestly as I can. "Because I won the Rock, Paper, Scissors tournament, and then you changed the rules after the fact. Now it means I'm stuck leading the festival."

Roman nods. "Well, yes, mostly..." He points a thumb over his shoulder but doesn't look behind him. "But Leo here thought you weren't living up to your potential. He thought maybe you needed an opportunity to prove to yourself... and everyone in town... that you aren't, in fact, a fuck up."

The word fuckup hits a nerve, and my chest tightens with rage. I can still hear Scout's voice from our fight, throwing out those same words. Have I been blind this whole time? Has everyone been tiptoeing around me, thinking I'm some pathetic fucking loser?

I clench my jaw so hard it aches. "So, it was a test?"

Roman holds up his hands like he's innocent. "I told him it was a bad idea, but he convinced everyone that this was what you needed."

"Luka, it's not like that," Leo says, trying to smooth things over. "It's just that sometimes I'm not sure you see the same potential in yourself that everyone else does."

Roman continues, "And the first thing you do is marry Scout and go on a revenge tour."

"That was you're fucking idea, dip shit!"

Roman shakes his head, looking utterly exhausted—but at least he doesn't deny it. "You couldn't even do the proper research beforehand, knowing it's not just your ass on the line —it's the whole fucking company." His words land heavy in the air, thick with disappointment.

The silence that follows tells me everyone agrees with

him. I guess at least Roman had the balls to tell me to my face.

I scoff a laugh, somehow feeling even worse knowing they intentionally set me up. "Well, I'm sorry your little experiment backfired."

"Luka, come on, don't be like that..." Leo starts, but I'm already standing up to leave.

"Look, I know I fucked up, but you know as well as I do, he threw that bullshit together just to threaten me..." I shake my head, feeling my throat tight with emotion. "I know I'm not the most responsible person, but I am trying for...what it's worth..."

"Come on, dude, don't take this personally," Roman says, "We were just trying to help you." He reaches for another donut, but I snatch the box away before he can make his next selection.

"Donuts aren't for assholes." I snatch the box and tuck it under my arm, but somehow it still doesn't feel like enough. So, I swipe Roman's coffee, just as he's taking a sip, and grab Guy's matcha for added measure.

"Hey! What'd I do?" Guy protests, but I don't respond, as I storm out of the conference room, letting the door slam shut behind me.

I drop the drinks in the closest trash can before offering the donuts to the rest of the staff and make my way outside feeling a renewed sense of purpose.

I think I've just figured out how to solve both of my problems. I pull out my phone and send out a quick text to L.O.K.I.

That should keep him out of trouble...for a little while anyway.

CHAPTER TWENTY-EIGHT

SCOUT

"Is it supposed to be abstract? Or do I need to have my prescription checked?" I hear Colleen ask as the crowd gathers to watch me, the way they always do around this time of day.

I've never felt more like a zoo animal in my life. Maybe I should start selling tickets? I have no doubt in my mind they'd pay to see the show.

You'd think the newness would've died down by now, but apparently the people in this town have a few concerns with my pace. They're not the only ones worried about me finishing this mural in time for the festival, but I can't let them know that. It'll just make their worrying that much worse.

I drop the brush, shaking my arm as I stretch my tired hand. I severely overestimated my physical endurance, not that my bone-deep exhaustion after last night is making things any easier.

What the hell did he do to me last night? I could barely keep my eyes open to finish one of my favorite movies and practically passed out before my head hit my pillow. I think I could've slept another eight hours, and it wouldn't have been enough.

If that's how my body responds to orgasms, then I need to up my calorie intake... maybe add in some electrolytes just to be safe...

"I thought she was a professional or a prodigy or something. That's what Lucy told me, anyway," someone else whispers, not so quietly.

And here I thought all my self-doubts in my head were annoying... But now I get the added bonus of hearing everyone else's too... Love that for me.

I lower the lift to refill my paint cup, swapping my brush for a roller. Judging by the size of the crowd and the rumble of my stomach, I'm assuming it's getting close to lunch time. I'll have to grab something quick today. I need to finish the rest of this section of the background so I can start layering the next part on top tomorrow.

I was stubborn at first, using the A-frame ladder, just because Luka made such a big deal about it, but that got old pretty quickly. After a few days of climbing up and down, I finally gave in and started using the lift. It's one less strain on my muscles, and at this point, I'll do anything to make this work a little easier. Even if it means admitting that Luka was right.

Turns out I don't hate his cockiness quite as much now that I've seen firsthand how capable he is. He's got to be using some kind of magic on me, the way he commands me so easily. It's like being under a spell, my body folds for him, doing anything he asks because she knows the reward that will come with pleasing him.

Come... I snicker at my accidental innuendo, feeling my warm cheeks grow hotter. Oh, how skillfully that man is at making me come. And the worst part is, I know he's still holding back on me. I can't imagine what it'll be like once he's convinced I'm ready to graduate to the next level...

"'Scuse me. Can we clear a path? I've got lunch."

The voice catches my attention, standing out among the others. I swear, I'm basically Pavlov's dog when it comes to the way I'm tuned into this man.

A smile stretches over my lips as I glance down to see Luka, standing beneath the lift, holding a paper bag and an ice-cold lemonade. My stomach flutters with butterflies at the sight of him. This is the second time he's surprised me, showing up with lunch in hand, and my stomach growls in anticipation.

"Did you hear me? I said I brought lunch. Get your ass down here already," Luka calls from beneath me.

"Be right there," I call back. "I'm just going to finish this top corner." I stand on my tiptoes, reaching my roller to get the awkward corner so that this section can dry while I take a break. It's hard to see what I'm doing because the sun's shining right in my eyes, but I do my best to cover the rough surface. A trickle of sweat rolls down my temple, and I use the back of my hand to wipe it away.

I feel something bump against my hand, and then there's a loud buzzing near my ear. It flies around my head, then moves to the other side, but it's so fast I can't see where it went.

"Woman, if you don't get your ass down here and eat this sandwich, I'm going to come up there and feed it to—"

Luka's threat gets cut short when a fat, winged demon of a bug dive-bombs my face. It zigzags wildly, refusing to retreat no matter how frantically I swat at it. I've watched enough horror movies to recognize the undeniable look of murder in its eyes, and since I'm the only one up here, I'm afraid I'm the next unlucky victim.

Before I have time to defend myself, it dive-bombs me, its fat, fuzzy body bumping into my cheek, and I scream, realizing it's a huge bumblebee.

"Scout, what's going on? What's wrong?" I hear Luka, but with the way this bee is attacking me right now, it's all I can do to shield myself.

Bees aren't aggressive, I remind myself, but the persistent insect proves otherwise. I wave the paint roller, hoping I can bat it away at the very least. Maybe it'll take a hint that I'm not the enemy here.

I make contact with the giant insect, feeling the weight of its fuzzy black-and-yellow body as I swing the roller like a bat, sending it flying. "I'm sorry!" I cry out—genuinely hoping I didn't hurt it, but mostly just relieved to have survived the attack. I press the button to lower the lift, only to spot it again—charging straight toward me like a fighter jet on a suicide mission.

The bee barrels straight into my face, and I scream, just before a sharp sting lands right on my upper lip. Heat flares instantly.

By the time the lift reaches the ground, Luka's waiting with a look of concern—until he sees me.

"Holy shit, Scout! What happened to your face?"

"Here, hold this on your lip. It'll help with the swelling."

I look down at the pack of frozen hot dogs Luka's holding. "Eww. I'm not icing my lip with frozen hot dogs. Don't you have a normal ice pack?"

A look of genuine confusion crosses his face before he places the pack of hot dogs in my hands. "Why would I need an icepack when I have frozen hot dogs? Don't look down your nose like that. These work just as well to get the job done, and unlike an icepack, they're biodegradable and aren't full of chemicals that could kill you if ingested."

I furrow my eyebrows. "I feel like there's more to this story..."

"Guy chewed through an ice pack as a baby, swallowed half the contents before mom realized he'd bitten a hole in the bag," he says with a shrug. "He had to have his stomach pumped, and it scared my parents so bad that they started using frozen food from then on out. In my experience, frozen hot dogs work the best."

"Huh. That actually makes sense."

Luka rolls his eyes, but I can see the hint of a smile on his lips. He may be trying to hide it, but there's an undeniable look of concern on his face as he holds the frozen hot dogs against my lip. "The bumblebee really did a number on you. Are you sure you're not allergic?" He holds my head as he studies my rapidly growing lip.

"I don't think so... I've never been stung before."

After the bee incident, Luka insisted I let Dr. Stone check me out to make sure I wasn't having a severe allergic reaction.

It was actually pretty cute, the way he freaked out and rushed me over to his office, demanding that it was an emergency.

According to Dr. Stone, I wasn't showing any signs of a severe allergic reaction, but he told Luka to keep an eye on me for the next few hours and let him know if I developed any more symptoms.

He said the swelling was likely due to the heat, possibly related to blood flow issues from working in the sun all day. And of course, lips are a sensitive area to be stung in.

That much I can confirm. It feels like I got stabbed with a branding iron, and my poor lip is so swollen, I've gone from "bad lip injections" to full-on duck face. Fortunately, my throat and tongue are fine, and I can still breathe, so we're calling it a win. Nothing a little Benadryl and ice can't fix.

After we got home, Luka helped me shower, insisting he needed to get in with me to keep an eye on me in case I lost consciousness. I was disappointed when he didn't take off his underwear; he even batted my hand away when I tried to cop a feel. And now he's got me propped up on the couch with my feet in his lap while he tries to find something for us to watch.

I can feel the Benadryl starting to kick in as I blink my heavy eyelids, feeling relaxed. As silly as I think Luka's being, it feels nice having someone so worried about me. I can't remember the last time someone took care of me like this.

Even as a little girl, my mother wasn't very nurturing. If I was hurt or sick, she'd give me medicine and make sure I was seen by a doctor, but she didn't hold me or snuggle me the way Luka's parents did. And I doubt Jimmy ever noticed if I was sick.

I snuggle into the warm blanket as Luka rubs my feet. His skilled hands massaging and caressing my sore muscles, melting all my stress away with every touch.

"I was going to tell you, I'm uh... I'm going to be taking some vacation time from work... so don't worry about being behind on the mural. I'm happy to help you as much as I can."

I shake my head. "Luka, you don't have to do that. Please don't take time off because of me. I can handle it. I don't want you to inconvenience yourself any more than you already have—"

"It's done," he says, and there's finality in his tone, so I stop trying to argue. "Besides, that just means we get to spend more time together now." He winks, returning his attention back to massaging my foot.

I try to pull away from him, but he only tightens his grip, pinning me with a stern look. "You're not supposed to exert yourself. Don't make me tie you down... I promise it won't be as much fun without the happy ending."

I blow out a huff and sink back down, knowing he's not going to let up about Dr. Stone's orders, especially with this big fat reminder right in front of his face.

"So, you're taking the rest of the summer off... like a vacation? Why?" I ask, feeling curious.

"Yeah... I thought a break could be nice, and I could help you with the mural. I haven't taken a real vacation in... well... ever, I guess." He sounds genuinely surprised by that realization. As sweet as the sentiment is, I can't help but feel like there's more that he's not telling me.

"Are you happy with how your life turned out?" I blurt out the question surprising both of us.

He smirks before planting a kiss on the top of my foot. "It's hard to complain. I think I've got a pretty good thing going here."

"Yeah, but are you fulfilled?"

He narrows his eyebrows incredulously. "Why are you asking?"

"I just mean... I don't know... I've had a lot of time to myself over the last few weeks, painting and reconnecting with parts of myself I'd forgotten about. I've found myself thinking about my life and how different it is from what I thought it'd be."

"Different better or different worse?" he asks.

I shrug. "Both. Depends on the day, I guess. But I was asking about you." I move to sit up a little. "Are you happy working for your family's business?"

"Yeah... I mean... what else would I be doing?"

"I don't know. I remember how passionate you were growing up, how you wanted to make a difference. I guess I just thought you'd have a side project or two. Something to give back to causes you care about."

His hands stop moving on my foot. "I give back. I donate to charities all the time. I'm heading up the fucking Phantom Festival this year. What makes you think I need to do more?" His words are defensive and laced with anger.

I shake my head, the grogginess of the medicine making it hard to think clearly, and now I'm wondering if that's why I started this conversation to begin with. "No. I know that. I was just saying... I thought you'd be more passionate about something... I'm sorry, I don't think I'm making sense right now."

"Then why don't you stop talking and rest," he snaps back. His jaw is tight, and he's clearly annoyed, but judging by the way he just freaked out on me, I think it's safe to assume I struck a nerve.

I wasn't trying to offend him, but why is it that he can call me out, but I'm not allowed to do the same for him?

I want to ask him, but my eyes are growing heavier, and my brain is too fuzzy. I lay back down and snuggle into my blanket. I just want to close my eyes for a minute and rest.

I feel myself drifting off, teetering on the edge of sleep, but just before I tip over, I hear L.O.K.I's voice. "Now that she's asleep. Would you like me to tell you what I discovered today?"

I feel Luka's weight shift beneath my legs, and then he's standing. "Why don't we discuss this in my office."

That's odd... Why is he being so secretive?

I wish I had the energy to ask, but before my thoughts can go any further, I feel myself finally lose the battle, and I drift off to sleep.

CHAPTER TWENTY-NINE

SCOUT

The thunderclap rattles the windows, stirring me awake, and I jolt up in the pitch-black room... or at least I try to. There's something heavy pinning me to the mattress.

It takes me a second to realize that the *something* is Luka—sprawled across me like I'm his body pillow. He's lying on his side, one leg thrown over my lower half, while his arm wraps so tightly around me that it's tucked beneath my back, pinning me in place.

I'm surprised by how much I don't mind his weight on me. Actually, his warm body feels kind of nice—like having my own personal, weighted, emotional support blanket.

I probably wouldn't feel that way if the tip of my nose wasn't frozen. I wiggle one arm free from beneath our tangle of limbs and yank it back just as fast, before I lose a finger to frostbite.

Holy shit. It's cold enough to hang meat in here. What

the hell does he set his thermostat on? And why haven't my eyes adjusted yet?

I blink several times as I try to look around the room and orient myself to my surroundings, but I may as well be sleeping in a dungeon underground because there's not a single trace of light to be found. No alarm clock or light peeking in from behind the curtains, nothing to indicate what time it is whatsoever.

It takes me a moment to remember how I got here as the fuzzy memories of yesterday slowly return. I press my lips together, realizing all the painful swelling seems to be gone. I guess the Benadryl worked. And instead of letting me sleep on the couch, or carrying me to my own bed, Luka must've carried me upstairs to his.

Another rumble of thunder, louder this time, tells me the time doesn't matter anyway. There's no sense in worrying about it, because I can't paint a mural in the rain anyway.

Thunderstorms have always been my favorite weather, probably because I'm the kind of girl who's relieved by canceled plans. It's not that I'm a recluse or anything, but there is nothing as good as being let off the hook, at no fault of your own. I suppose that speaks more about the pressure I feel to make everyone happy than anything else.

But what can I say, I'm a creature of comfort.

I prefer a cozy night in, snuggled up watching movies, to just about any extravagant night out. I'll take pajamas over high heels, popcorn and pizza delivery over a gourmet restaurant, and all the lazy Saturdays at home.

The tightness in my stomach instantly melts away, and I feel my body begin to relax. I snuggle deeper into my warm, protective blanket as lust-filled memories play like a movie in my mind. I finally let myself process everything for the first time, without judgment.

I've dealt with my parents talking down to me my entire life, done everything in my power to avoid being talked down to or degraded... So why do I like it so much when Luka does it?

It doesn't make sense. I'm a sensitive person. I wear my heart on my sleeve and I'm deeply sensitive... especially when it comes to rejection. Luka knows that.

But he's also never tiptoed around me or been afraid to hurt my feelings if he believed it was something I needed to hear. In fact, he's the only person in the world who's ever treated me like I'm not a fragile piece of glass.

That's not to say my parents were careful to spare my feelings—the exact opposite really. If anything, they seemed to enjoy cutting me down every chance they got. They wanted to keep me small. A broken person is easier to control.

Maybe it's because deep down, I know Luka doesn't actually believe the things he says, and that's what makes it all so... hot. Maybe I'll never understand the inner workings of my messed-up mind, and that's okay. I don't need to know why.

Luka's created a space for me that's not only judgment-free but so much more expansive than anything I've ever imagined. He's given me structure and security, and a sense of exploration to discover what I actually desire, not just sexually but for my life as a whole.

And he's made it seem so easy, like he's always known what I needed, even before I even knew that there were options at all.

So rather than freaking out or judging my inner darkness for liking the fucked up things I like, I think I'll take a page out of Luka's book and just sit with it for a little while. Besides, nobody else has to know.

Something's changed inside me. It's like I've been walking around with this giant crack, looking for anything to fill it, but instead of filling the crack, Luka took a sledgehammer and finished the job. He smashed me wide open, broke me into pieces, then he gathered every jagged piece and rebuilt me into something stronger.

I feel that familiar heat blooming low in my belly as his body begins to stir. My body, now fully awake, unlike the unconscious man lying on top of me.

I shift to my side and slide my thigh between his and begin to wiggle my hips, the sensation of Luka's hot skin feeling so good against my own. The darkness of the room only adds to my growing arousal as the sound of heavy rain grows louder.

"Mmm. Somebody's wiggly," Luka says in a low, raspy growl that melts my insides like butter. His hand snakes around my waist and pulls me in close, and I feel his hard length press against my back.

I rub my ass against him as I scoot a little closer, feeling my panties growing impossibly wetter at the sound of his frustrated groan.

"Jesus, woman, a man can only endure so much temptation..." Luka smoothes my hair away from my neck, peppering me with kisses as his hands roam over my body.

My lips pull into a satisfied smile, and my heart swells. It's not much, but I love knowing how turned on I make him. I love how expressive he is, that he makes sure there's never a question about the way he's feeling. It helps knowing how much he enjoys giving, especially when I've only experienced the opposite.

Smiling to myself, I give my ass another, more deliberate wiggle.

"Fucking tease is what you are," he groans, his grip tightening on my hip as he trails his fingers down my stomach, painfully slowly, before dipping them beneath the hem of my panties.

I suck in a gasp when his fingers faintly graze my clit. First, the gentle brush of his thumb, and then he deepens the pressure. His touch is gentle at first, but then it grows heavier as he strokes me with masterful precision and it doesn't take long before I feel the first wave begin to crest.

"Jesus, baby, you're so fucking wet," Luka growls in my ear, his fingers picking up speed. "Such a needy little cunt you have, waking me up just to get you off."

I let out a whimper, my legs spread wider as I grind into him, feeling my stomach tensing up.

"Breathe for me, baby," he coos, and it's only then that I realize I've been holding my breath.

I suck in a lungful of air just as Luka slides a finger inside me. There's a sharp pinch, and then my orgasm erupts. Pleasure shoots through me in every direction, consuming me like a riptide. The only choice I have is to surrender.

"That's my good girl," he says, as he kisses the back of my neck, the smile in his voice anchoring me back to the earth.

I feel a dopey smile of my own spread over my face as he flips me over to my back and slides my ruined panties down my legs, before tossing them somewhere on the floor. I bite my lip as nervous excitement flutters in my belly, already preparing myself for the sharp, searing pain I now know to expect.

"This is how it was supposed to happen. I promise to go easy on you this time," he says as he climbs over me and removes my shirt, tossing it to the floor with the rest of our discarded clothes.

I blink into the pitch-black room. Luka must be thinking the same thing, because the next thing I know, the blackout curtains start to retract, letting in the soft gray light of the stormy sky.

I can feel the heat from Luka's gaze warming my exposed skin as I lie there with my arms above my head, my naked body completely at his mercy. There's a challenge in his gaze, dark and hungry, as he slides his hand slowly up and down his massive cock. The look in his eyes is nothing short of carnal possession, a silent promise that he's going to ruin me in the best possible way. Like he can't decide what to do first, worship me or plan my destruction.

Either one suits me just fine.

"Spread your legs for me, baby," he commands, his voice rough and thick with lust.

I obey without hesitation, keeping my eyes locked on his; my body buzzing with anticipation, desperate to please him. But when I look into his eyes, it's not lust I see, it's awe.

He looks at me with reverence, like I'm a goddess to be worshipped, like he's the lucky one, privileged just to kneel at my altar.

It knocks me off kilter and steals the breath from my lungs.

When he looks at me like that, I don't just feel desired. I feel chosen. Adored. Revered.

For the first time in my life, I don't just hope I'm worthy of love.

I actually believe it.

"Look how hard you got me," he groans under his breath as he lines his thick head up to my entrance and slowly pushes inside. "Fuck, baby, your pussy is so goddamn tight," he hisses against my ear. I feel his muscles trembling as he holds himself up, trying to ease himself inside as slowly and gently as possible.

The sharp stabbing pain is intense, and I suck in a breath as my body adjusts. One stray tear falls from the corner of my eye, and Luka wipes it away with his thumb.

"You're doing so well, Scout, almost there," he whispers as he begins to pump his hips, inching himself a little deeper with every thrust. "You're so fucking beautiful. I wish you could see what I'm seeing right now."

He moves one hand behind my neck to brace himself, as he palms my breast with the other, teasing my hardened nipple with his thumb. Ripples of heat shoot through me with his every touch, and I bite my lip as the pain slowly subsides, the sharp sting fading into a dull ache. And before I know it, he's fully inside of me.

"Fuck, baby," Luka hisses. "Look how fucking wet you are for me. Just for my cock." He rocks inside me, his thumb moving back down to stroke my clit.

"Yes, Luka, don't stop." I arch my back, my nails digging into his back as I feel a new type of pleasure building inside me.

His lips cover mine in a possessive kiss as he continues to stroke my clit, his hips driving his thick cock deeper inside me. He presses my arm above my head, our fingers interlacing. With every stroke, I fall a little further, surrendering a little more of myself.

"Goddamnit, baby. You take my cock so well," he hisses between clenched teeth, and I can see he's fighting himself, fighting to hold on a little while longer. "Who's pussy am I fucking right now?"

"Yours," I pant, my tits bouncing as he drives inside me harder, his perfect cock wrecking me for anyone else.

"What was that? I didn't hear you." He rolls my nipple between his fingers, then gives it a firm pinch. Pleasure sparks through me like an electric current.

I toss my head back as a scream tears through my lungs. "Yours," I gasp again, the word unraveling as the pleasure climbs higher. "Only yours."

I feel my walls begin to tighten, and I know I'm getting close.

"That's fucking right," he grunts, his thrusts growing rougher as his grip tightens on my breast. He surrounds me, devours me, like he plans to leave his mark on every inch of my skin. "This sweet cunt is mine to fuck anytime I want. You belong to me. Nobody else."

"Yes. God. Oh fuck," I cry out, my head falling back as my orgasm explodes inside me, powerful and consuming, like a lightning bolt.

"That's it, baby. You're so fucking pretty when you come on my cock." He palms my breasts, swirling his warm tongue over one nipple before sucking it deep into his mouth.

It's possessive, Carnal. Ravenous. And it feels so fucking good I forget how to breathe.

"Now tell me, baby, where do you want me to finish?"

His question sends my thoughts into overdrive. I feel my

panic creep back in as depraved images begin spiraling through my mind.

I know he won't judge me, but I don't know if I can say it.

So rather than answering, I try to distract him, hooking a leg around his waist and pulling him closer.

Luka grunts, caught off guard. His eyes squeeze shut as he exhales through his nose, his breath ragged like he's fighting to maintain control.

"I'm close, baby," he warns, and I can hear the desperation in his voice. "Tell me where you want me to come."

He pulls out of me, stroking himself, and before I can think twice, I'm on my knees. I press my breasts together; eyes locked on his as I offer myself up completely.

I'm his to ruin, his to mark, anyway he wants.

"Christ, princess. You're going to let me choose?" he drags out as he pumps his thick cock, his hot gaze locked on me. "Open your pretty mouth and stick out your tongue."

His command scorches straight through me, incinerating every wall and barrier I've ever built and reducing them to ash. And I'm left standing in the wreckage, bare and burning.

And I happily obey, reveling in the freedom of letting him take what he wants... trusting that he'll give me exactly what I need.

"Fuck, baby, I'm coming," he says through a grunt.

I close my eyes, feeling the hot ropes of his release on my cheek, the salty taste hitting my tongue a moment later. Like an artist, he paints me—deliberate and purposeful—making a mess of me. He claims me with every drop, as if he's branding me as his alone.

It's degrading. Demeaning. Absolutely filthy.

And exactly what I was hoping for.

"Come here, baby." He pulls me into his chest in a bone-crushing hug as he wipes my face clean. "Holy shit, baby. You did so well." He kisses my forehead, then tucks me tighter against him, peppering kisses across my face, completely unbothered by the mess, like he couldn't care less about anything except me.

The sound of his heartbeat thundering in his chest sends a rush of pride through me. I feel my lips pull into a smirk, knowing I'm the reason for it. I'm the one who's making his heart race like that.

He looks down, and he must notice my smirk before I can hide it. His fingers dig into my side, making me giggle.

"You're trouble, you know that?"

I let out a squeal, squirming beneath his hands, trying to wiggle free. But there's no point in fighting, he's too strong. And if I'm being honest, I don't want to get away anyway.

I lean my head on his shoulder and breathe out a sigh, feeling more at peace than I've ever felt. "I wish every day could be like this."

"Like what?" He quirks a brow. "Because I'll have you know what we just did wasn't exactly a hardship."

I swat his chest and laugh just as thunder rattles the windowpanes and the heavy rain drums against the roof overhead. "No, I just mean... I love canceled plans. Rainy days make me happy." I shiver when the AC kicks on, and Luka pulls me closer, wrapping his arms over me to keep me warm.

"I know they do, you little weirdo." He pinches my nose teasingly, and I roll my eyes. "You know, you don't have to wait for rainy days for an excuse to relax? You could simply decide to take time off." He leans in closer and whispers, "You're a grown up, Scout. It's not against the rules."

"Yeah... I guess you're right," I finally say.

"Thatta girl." His expression softens, his cocky grin returning as he brushes a sticky strand of hair back from my face. "I'm pretty sure I got jizz in your hair." He picks me up, heading toward the bathroom. "Don't worry, I happen to be an expert at washing out jizz."

"I have no doubt," I say through a laugh.

And even though I'm perfectly capable of washing my hair myself, I don't protest. Because I know it's as much for him as it is for me.

CHAPTER THIRTY

LUKA

The past week with Scout has been something straight out of one of my fantasies. And just when I think things can't get any better, Scout never ceases to surprise me.

And thanks to my dickhead brothers and their little confession about setting me up, I've decided to take some long overdue vacation time. When I'm not helping her finish the mural, I plan on spending the rest of my summer hanging out with my wife, enjoying every free moment we have to the fullest. I don't know what the future holds for us, and if I'm being honest, I'm afraid to ask. I don't want to spook her—or give her a reason to overthink this and come to her senses.

God knows I've given her plenty of reasons to run in the other direction from the way I've treated her, but I hope she sees I have the best of intentions, because I want more for her. I hated seeing her settle with that shady prick, but more than that, I hated seeing her settle for the life her parents wanted her to live.

I'll admit, at first, all I wanted was to hurt her the way she hurt me. But it's hard to stay mad at someone so pure. Someone who doesn't realize they've been preyed upon their whole life.

Somewhere along the way, I guess the spite that was fueling me started to shift, though its intensity remained the same. I don't know why I thought I'd be able to resist her, that I'd be able to keep up the walls I cowardly hid behind. All it took was one shy smile and a belly laugh to have me fully on my knees in surrender, ready to fight anyone who ever threatened to take that away. I'm not sure where this road will lead us, or what the future holds. But I'm no stranger to having my life shifted on a dime, so I intend to savor every second of these blissful moments, because life can change in an instant.

After our first lazy rainy day, the weather gods must've smiled down on me, because it turned into two more.

We've had movie marathons that quickly turned into fucking marathons... We slept in, napped together, and I even convinced her to play some video games with me. She was hesitant at first, but I'm no amateur; I knew the only thing she needed was the right game to pique her interest.

All it took was about ten minutes of her watching me play Lego Fortnite before she asked for a turn, which naturally led to her wanting to try out the real thing. The next thing I knew, the entire afternoon had gone by, and Scout was well on her way to a Victory Royale. Looks like my little gamer girl is hooked.

She doesn't know it yet, but I've already ordered her her own handheld gaming console so she can play any time she wants.

I've always seen my role as a HusDom—it's still a working title—but I've felt from the beginning that both sides needed equal representation to feel complete. And not just in a sexual way. Watching Scout finally start to relax, to genuinely enjoy her life, feels more rewarding than anything I've ever accomplished for myself. It's as if everything I've endured has led me here, prepared me for this exact purpose.

I know I can't change her past, but I can help her build a better future. One where she feels confident enough to ask for what she wants and unafraid to speak up when something isn't right. All I want is for her to live the life she dreams of—not to please her parents, not to please anyone else, not even to please me.

It's hard to deny how simple the decision seems just by watching the way she comes alive every time she's got a paintbrush in her hand. The way her hazel eyes twinkle when she's in that flow state, where she can't even hear me when I'm talking to her.

But it needs to come from her.

If I could just get her to see herself through my eyes, there's no way she'd ever feel an ounce of insecurity again. I've spent an entire week watching her disappear into her own little world every time she picks up that paintbrush, and I continue to be amazed by her talent.

I wish I could say I've been more helpful, but there's not really much I can do to help beyond filling in basic solid shapes. And even then, I feel like a toddler fighting the uncooperative paint to stay inside the lines. Trust me, it's way harder than it looks.

And now that the background is mostly finished, I find myself acting like her caddy, refilling her cups of paint, making sure she stays hydrated in this scorching heat, and fighting her to take a lunch break and actually eat.

I don't mind, though, not one bit. It's pretty awesome having a front row seat to someone slowly realizing their potential.

This mural isn't just a summer project to Scout. It's a piece of her soul. It's all the words she wasn't able to speak. It's her pain, her dreams, and all the pieces of herself she never felt safe enough to show the world.

And I'm just the lucky bastard who gets to temporarily call her mine. I know it's not the same as her really choosing to be with me, but I'll take what I can get.

"Did you start over? Looks like you painted over what you did last time," Fergus calls, reminding me of the audience that's slowly grown over the past hour.

"Why is it so dark?" someone else asks.

I clench my teeth, holding back my words when I feel Scout's hand smooth down my shoulder. "Just ignore them, Luka," she says, her lips pulling into a knowing smirk as she goes back to working on the Phantom's veiny forearms. "They're just bored, and this is the most exciting thing they've seen in a long time. It's nothing personal."

I let out a huff, massaging my aching temples as a headache starts to form behind my eye. "I don't know how you do this all day, having everyone constantly commenting on every single thing you do."

Scout just shrugs, not even giving them a second glance. "You get used to it." She dips her brush into the cup of paint, adding shadows to the veins. She laughs to herself and adds, "Besides, it's not like I'm not used to having my every move criticized."

It's supposed to be a lighthearted dig at her parents, but I don't think there's anything funny about it. In fact, the whole thing's just reminded me of how pissed I am that her father thinks he can treat another person that way. That he can control her like some fucking chess piece in his crooked dealings. I will make him and her pathetic ex pay for treating her so badly, if it's the last thing I do.

"No offense, but how is this any different from trashy street art?" A woman asks.

I send her a death glare over my shoulder. "Seriously?"

She throws up her hands. "What? I'm just asking..."

"All right, that's enough of this for today." I pluck the paintbrush out of her hand, shoving the handle in my back pocket, before spinning her around to face me. The freckles on her nose are darker than they were a couple of weeks ago, despite the layers of sunscreen she keeps herself slathered in. Her skin's got a subtle golden glow to it, and she's got a streak of paint across her jaw.

So fucking pretty.

"Hey, what are you doing—"

"We're ending early today." I cut her off, my voice low and firm. "I'm not taking no for an answer."

"Luka, I can't. We're already a week behind schedule," she protests, her brows furrowed.

"I wasn't asking," I say, meeting her eyes with a warning stare. "I promise we'll make it up. Besides, I'm about to go crazy listening to everyone down there." I take the brush from her hand and set it aside. "Now come on, I've got a surprise planned for you."

"What kind of surprise?"

"I'm taking you on a date. Now get your cute little ass over here so we have plenty of time to get cleaned up."

CHAPTER THIRTY-ONE

SCOUT

After we got home, we took a shower and Luka made good on his promise to clean me up—after he got me dirty, of course. That man sure knows how to keep me satisfied. I swear he knows my body better than I do. He's so attentive, always paying attention to what I like, making every time we have sex better than the time before.

And the things he says to me during sex... I ought to be ashamed for getting turned on by his filthy words, but I love how desired it makes me feel.

Can a person die from having too many orgasms? At this point, it doesn't even feel fair.

It's like every single encounter we have heals me a little more as Luka slowly rewires my brain and reprograms me using the same vile things my parents used to say to me. Only, unlike my parents, I know he doesn't mean it. Everything

Luka does, every decision he makes is purposeful, and making me happy is his sole intention.

"Here we are," Luka says, gesturing to the downtown square as he climbs off the bike. He doesn't wait for me to climb off before lifting me and placing me gently on my feet. I tilt my head as his fingers work to unbuckle my helmet. The smile he gives me in return fills me with so much warmth. I'm still getting used to being doted on, but I love how much he seems to enjoy taking care of me. He gives my cheek a little squeeze before kissing me on the forehead, and the warmth in my belly turns into a full-blown inferno.

It's just after sunset, and the street lights flicker, illuminating our quaint downtown as muffled sounds of live music echo from Restaurant. People bustle along the cobblestone paths filing in and out of shops as the town shifts from day to night, bringing out a whole new crowd.

We pass by a mother and father laughing as they swing their child between them while trying to eat their ice cream cones. It almost seems too picturesque, like something you'd see in a Hallmark movie, but that's the thing about this place: it seems to attract the happiest people—for the most part. Anyway.

It's safe to say that the people in this town are by no means perfect, especially the way they've treated Luka after he got out of prison. But in their defense, he hasn't exactly gone out of his way to prove them wrong. If anything, he's leaned into the whole loser act, pretending like he doesn't care what anyone thinks of him. They may not be able to see through it, but I do.

I only wish he could let down his guard a little, be real with them, and let them see the side of him that I see. There's no doubt in my mind they'd change their opinions of him. Anyone would after seeing Luka's fierce loyalty and his heart of gold.

And as much as I wish I could do it for him, it's something he has to believe about himself first. Now I've just got to figure out how to get through to him to make him see it.

"Chili dog or smash burger?" Luka asks as we make our way to Food Truck to order.

At first, I was surprised that Jett would allow a food truck in Ashford Falls, but Luka informed me that they have a special permit allowing them to park in the downtown square Friday through Sunday, which was actually Jett's idea. With the town growing, he needed a little help lightening his weekend load.

Looks like people can change after all...

"Chili dog," I say with a smile. "Extra jalapeños."

Luka shakes his head and laughs, ordering himself the same as well as a large soda to share. We get our food, and he takes my hand, leading us over to the small park across the street.

The park is a little worn compared to what I remember.. The bright red slide's now faded to an almost pink, and the merry-go-round sits with a slight tilt from the years of aggressive play. And for some reason, I find it that much more endearing.

We take a seat on the merry-go-round, it's cold metal creaking beneath our weight as we dig into our food. A comfortable silence stretches between us as we both seem to disappear into our thoughts. My eyes take in the nostalgic park before me, and for a moment, it feels like I've been transported back in time. I can almost hear the sounds of squealing children, feel the hot summer sun against my skin, and smell the sunscreen and rusted metal from the playground equipment.

Luka presses his feet against the ground, making us spin in a slow circle. There's not a single memory I have of this park that doesn't involve Luka or one of his brothers launching someone off this thing. They were sort of known for it, and kids would line up for their turn to see if they were strong enough to stay on. From what I can remember, Roman was the only one who couldn't be thrown off.

I'm surprised it's held up this long after the years and years of abuse, though I suppose it's not without its scars. I don't think anything or anyone makes it out without some sort of mark, even if they're invisible.

"What's on your mind, pretty girl?" Luka's voice breaks through the silence, his endearing words as soothing as the first sip of morning coffee, and I feel that heat in my chest begin to return.

"I was just thinking about how feral you and your brothers used to be out here, slinging kids off this merry-go-round without a single ounce of remorse." I shake my head and laugh just picturing it.

Luka scoots closer, his palm cupping my cheek as he straightens my glasses. His grin grows wider, and he shrugs. "What can I say, we were just giving the people what they wanted."

His eyes drop to my lips and then back up to meet my gaze as his hand slides to the back of my head. I lean into his touch, loving how possessive and intentional he is, like he can't help himself. It's like there's this magnetic pull between us, and he's finally tired of fighting it.

"It seems you have a knack for that." I kiss his wrist as his fingers move through my hair, my gaze never leaving his. "I guess you've always been that way, though. I didn't realize it at the time, but looking back, I can see it. You always anticipated what I needed, always paid attention."

"Yeah, well, in my defense, it was pretty hard not to." He swallows thickly, and my eyes narrow in on his Adam's apple. "You needed me, and it felt so good to be there for you, to know that I was the one to make you laugh when you came to school sad. That I was the only one who knew what your voice sounded like for almost an entire school year."

He shrugs again, then pulls me into his lap. I wrap my legs on either side of him as his hands move up and down my back, our eyes and lips only inches apart. It's as if he's gazing straight into my soul, seeing me in all my brokenness, completely as I am. All our unspoken truths bubbling to the surface.

I breathe in a sigh, needing to speak my piece and finally clear the air. "You were always there for me, and when you needed me the most, I turned my back on you..."

Luka shakes his head, pulling me into a hug. "No, baby, don't do that to yourself. That was a long time ago, and you're right, you never asked me to do it." He pulls away from our hug, trying to get me to look at him, but I can't.

"I should've told you from the beginning, but I didn't want to make things worse than they already were." I shake my head as my eyes well with tears.

Luka brushes my tears from my cheek as he holds my face between his hands. "There's nothing you can say that's going to make me hate you, Scout. I promise, baby, I've put the past behind me. It's all over."

"That night, after you got arrested, I went to my dad and told him everything. That I'd been the one who spray-painted the building and that you took the fall to protect me. I begged him to help you get off, begged him to bring me up there so I could tell everyone that it was me... He was so angry, but it was late and he promised he'd try to smooth things over the next morning.

"He must've stayed up all night making plans.

"The next morning, I got in the car, thinking we were going to the police station, but when we passed it, the car didn't stop. I cried and pleaded for them to go back, but the decision had been made. On the drive to my new school, the one I didn't even apply for, he informed me of the new plan. That I could kiss my dreams of art school goodbye, and if I tried to fight him on it, he'd make sure you saw the fullest sentence possible." I shake my head as the streams of tears fall down my cheeks. "I had no idea he'd gone back on his word, Luka. You have to believe me."

"I believe you, Scout," he says, smoothing my hair like he's trying to comfort me.

"I did everything he asked me to do. I played by his rules and even agreed to date Jimmy. But as soon as I learned what happened, that you'd gone to prison for it, I freaked out. I left school and drove straight to the prison. I needed to see you, to explain."

His expression tightens, but he doesn't say anything, just lets me finish.

"That's when I ran into Jett. He was outside waiting to go in." My eyes fall as I finally tell him the truth. "He told me to leave you alone, that I'd ruined your life enough. That you were finally starting to heal and seeing me would only do more damage. He asked me to stay away from you; that there was nothing I could say that would ever make you forgive me, so I may as well take advantage of your sacrifice. That you were better off without me."

My sobs finally overtake me, and Luka's arms wrap around me, pulling me into his chest. "Shh, baby, you're okay. I'm not upset with you. Not anymore. You never asked me to do what I did, and it wasn't fair of me to punish you for that," he whispers between my sobs, kissing my head like he's trying to take the guilt from me.

"But... How can you forgive me so easily?"

He pulls away to look at me, a small smile curving at his lips. "I don't know if I'd say it was easy." He brushes a thumb over my cheek. "I'll admit, I was angry, but more than anything, I felt betrayed after I didn't hear from you. I think a part of me always knew your father was the culprit, but it felt good directing my anger toward you. I needed to hate you because it was the only way to heal my broken heart." He shakes his head. "But knowing you showed up, that you tried to make things right, fuck, that's all the explanation I need. I don't hate you, Scout. Far from it."

"Please don't be mad at Jett," I say through sniffles. I sit up, wiping my tears with the back of my hand. "He was just trying to help you. I shouldn't have listened to him. I should've tried harder."

"I'm not mad at him either. His intentions were good. He was doing what he thought I needed, trying to protect me."

"You're really not mad? Because you have every right to be. You have every right to hate me. I ruined your life, Luka."

He quirks a brow in challenge, his lips pulling into a smirk. "Let's be real, Scout. I don't think my life's turned out to be too shabby. I'm a lot luckier than most people I met in prison."

"Do you hear yourself right now? I know you don't think it's a big deal, but I robbed you of three years of your life. There isn't a day that goes by that I'm not haunted by that. Sometimes the guilt is so strong I think it's going to eat me alive."

Luka takes my hand and kisses me on the wrist. "You've carried that weight for long enough, and I want you to know I forgive you. I forgave you as soon as I knew you'd gotten away." Then he does the same to my other hand before wrapping my arms around his neck. "I think over time, I started to find comfort in the anger I felt toward you. Because as fucked up as it may be, anger was the closest thing to love I could feel."

I suck in a breath as his words hang in the air between us.

"I was just thankful that I could still feel something for you. Like my anger and your guilt were the invisible ropes tying us together. I'd have happily festered in my anger toward you for the rest of my life if you hadn't shown back up. And the moment I realized I was in a position to help you, I couldn't volunteer fast enough."

"Luka—"

"Come on, there's one more surprise I want to show you." Without another word, I let him lead me back to his bike.

A little while later, after a silent motorcycle ride through the mountains giving us both time to clear our heads, Luka pulls up to his house. We make our way inside as my nervous butterflies transform into bats in my belly. Tonight, Luka's shown me a whole new side to him, a side I never knew he'd been hiding.

His teasing and smart ass remarks I can deal with, but this gentleness he's shown me, the way he basically confessed his feelings for me... It all feels so vulnerable. So raw. And I find myself feeling terrified for what happens next.

You've already married him—and slept with him—what else do you really have to be afraid of?

That thought has my brain going into overdrive as a multitude of terrifying images come to mind.

Luka must sense my panic because he intertwines our fingers, then kisses the back of my hand. "Relax, Girl Scout. You're going to love it," he says with a wink. He tilts his head toward the staircase. "Come on. It's upstairs." There's hesitation in my steps as I follow him up the stairs.

When we pass his office door, I grow more confused as I follow him to the locked door of my childhood bedroom. His hand pauses over the fingerprint scanner as he looks at me. "I've been waiting for the right time to show you this, but I wanted it to be special. I know you don't believe me when I said I forgave you, so maybe this will convince you."

He pushes open the door, and I suck in a gasp as I step inside my childhood bedroom, which he's kept perfectly intact.

"Oh my God. Luka... How did you—?"

"I made your parents an offer they couldn't refuse," he says, stepping behind me as I take in all the memories.

I want to press him on that, on why he'd do such a thing, especially when he hated me, but I'm too overwhelmed right now in the best possible way.

My four-poster white bed sits in the center of the room, with my lavender gingham print bedspread. The stuffed bunny I carried around everywhere I went until I was six, until my mother told me I was too big to play with stuffed animals, rests against my pillow. My fingers trace his worn-out fur, matted and scratchy after so many trips through the washing machine.

My parents didn't even give me a chance to come back home to collect some of my childhood treasures; telling me they'd sold the house and donated all my old things months after they were already settled in their new house. I'd thought I'd lost this stuff forever.

My eyes drift to the pictures, the band posters, and the Girl Scout sashes filled with all my various badges, displaying all the awards I received throughout high school. My mother hated the way I decorated my bedroom, messing up her curated princess aesthetic with my angsty teenage bands and silly snapshots with Luka. But my room was the one area of my life where I didn't listen to her. It was my safe place, my own little haven away from all the pressure of the world outside.

Seeing this room exactly as I left it has so many memories rushing back to me, and it feels like I'm being transported back in time. Tears fill my eyes as I pick up a photo. Seven-year-old me smiles at the camera, wearing her bright blue Daisy vest, holding an arm full of Girl Scout cookies. I remember it like it was yesterday. I'd sold more than anyone in my troop, thanks to Mrs. Kingsley, and I'd received a special badge for it. I was so proud of that badge.

I thought they were proud of me, too, but now I realize they were just pleased with the positive attention they received on my behalf. That was made clear by my mother's abrupt mood shift from being annoyed that she had to cancel their dinner plans for a stupid Girl Scout ceremony, to insisting we go out for ice cream to celebrate.

A fat teardrop falls on the photo as I take in my younger self. My innocent eyes, full of excitement, full of so many hopes and dreams.

I think everyone wishes they felt something other than disappointment when they look at photos of their younger self.

But when I look at little Scout, I can't help but feel like I've let her down...

Suddenly, I see myself in a whole new light, and when I spin to face Luka, I think he realizes it too.

"You kept everything," I say in a whisper.

But then my gaze drifts to the dark-framed Phantom portrait I painted in art class when I was fifteen, and I have to cover my mouth with my hand to hold back my sob. I move toward the portrait, tracing my fingers along the thick, textured paint.

The haunting silhouette of the Phantom standing in the forest fills the dark canvas, the layers of black and deep green creating a depth that's almost indistinguishable in the dim light. My eyes search the painting, immediately finding all the hidden words layered in the shadows.

Only the shadows tell the truth.

Good girls keep quiet.

They cut out my tongue to keep me silent, so I learned to speak with paint.

Am I perfect enough yet?

My eyes well with tears as I trace my fingers along the

jagged paint, remembering every word I hid in the shadows and every emotion I felt as I painted it.

I never thought I'd see this again. She said she threw it away... "How do you have this?"

"I dug it out of the trash can after your parents went to bed. There was no way I could let her throw it away. I knew how much it meant to you." He wets his lips. "I thought someday I'd hang it in my office, but I couldn't bring myself to look at it every day..." His voice trails off, and he doesn't have to say the words for me to know what he means.

"I can't believe you kept it... all this time..."

"Of course I did. I know how much this stuff meant to you. I couldn't make myself get rid of it." He shoves one hand in his pocket like he's trying not to fidget and gestures to the door. "Except the door. I had to change it when I had the locks installed, but I tried to match the paint color on the inside as best as I could." He rubs the back of his neck, not meeting my eyes. "I have a cleaning crew that comes to dust once a week, but besides that, no one comes in here. I don't want you to think I invaded your privacy or anything like that. I just thought I'd keep it for you... You know, until you were ready."

"Thank you." It's all I can manage as I throw myself into his arms, burying my face in his chest.

His hands come up around me, cradling me in a tight hug that feels like home. "I'm glad to see that you're happy and not creeped out. I just wanted you to always have your memories, so you can remember where you came from on the way to where you're going." He presses a kiss on the top of my head as his arms squeeze me tighter.

"I can't believe you did this... You kept everything exactly how I left it."

"I knew you'd need a place to come back to... eventually."

I shake my head, trying to process everything he's told me tonight, wondering how I ever missed it. All this time, he was right here, right under my nose.

I inch up on my tiptoes where my lips find his in a frantic, needy kiss. His hands move to my back, then he's cupping my ass as he lifts me. My legs wrap around his waist as he walks us down the hallway.

When he passes his bedroom door, I pull away and look around. "Where are you going? Your bedroom is back that way?"

His long stride carries me to the stairs as he says, "I was thinking it's about time I introduced you to my playroom... if you're up for it?"

I swallow a gulp, the fluttering bats in my belly returning with a vengeance. "Of course. Sounds fun."

"You know, that's exactly what I was thinking," Luka says with a laugh that already has me sweating bullets.

Holy shit! Here goes nothing.

CHAPTER THIRTY-TWO

SCOUT

When we reach the door to the basement, Luka moves the lock covering to scan his fingerprint. The lock clicks open, echoing through the silence, and the dark stairwell flickers with candlelight. "Welcome back, Mr. Luka. I will now revert to standby mode for the remainder of your session. You can override this setting at any time using your safe word."

"Thank you, L.O.K.I." Luka says as he leads me down the staircase into the dimly lit room.

When we get to the bottom, the room comes into view, and I pause as my eyes slowly adjust.

There's a four-poster canopy bed against the back wall. At first glance, it may seem like any normal bed, but as we get closer, it's easy to see the various attachments around the headboard and footboard for bondage of all kinds. On either side of the bed, there's a display wall filled with various accessories. Everything from vibrators and sensory toys to floggers and ball gags.

It's a lot to take in... Luka's got himself quite an extensive collection. I don't know why I'm surprised, he's a twenty-six-year-old billionaire who loves technology and all things kink. Of course he has a high-tech sex room in his basement. Honestly, I think I'd be more shocked if he didn't.

"Is this... your sex room?" My eyes widen as I take in the shelf of pocket pussies and flesh lights, all lined up side by side. There's a representation of all kinds, with a variety of shapes and colors, some even equipped with realistic pubic hair.

"Yes. Welcome to my dungeon. These ladies are very special to me." He gestures to the display of sex toys on the wall behind him.

"Wow, that's quite the collection you've got there. Quite diverse too."

"What can I say, I love women. All shapes, colors, and sizes."

I run my fingers over the curly pubes, my curiosity getting the best of me. "Is this real hair... or... Can you donate pubic hair? Like... Locks for Love?"

He laughs at my question and shrugs. "You know, that's not a question I've ever asked. I'll have to check into that and get back to you."

My eyes scan the rows of toys, noticing a small plaque beneath each of them. "Oh my God... you even named them." I nearly choke on my own saliva, trying to contain my shocked laughter.

"Of course I named them. They may only be made of

silicone, but that doesn't mean they still don't deserve my respect." Luka says as he tenderly traces the one named Francesca's labia.

My amusement fades when my eyes land on the wall of vibrators and butt plugs.

"See something you like, Girl Scout?" Luka teases, moving behind me and brushing the hair from my neck.

I shiver at his touch but angle my head to the side to give him better access as he peppers soft kisses along my neck and jaw.

"Are you... are you going to use that stuff on me?" My voice comes out strained, and I don't know if I'm more nervous or excited by the prospect of it.

He spins me around to face him, lifting my chin as he studies me for a long moment, as if silently asking if I'm okay.

I bite my bottom lip and stare up at him, eagerly waiting for him to tell me what to do next.

"Yes," he finally says.

I swallow a gulp. I don't think I was expecting him to be quite so straightforward.

"I would ask you if that's okay, but I really don't care. I already have a list of your limits, and do you remember your safe word?"

My nod is slow as I whisper, "Yes."

Without breaking eye contact, he begins to loosen his tie. "Here's what's going to happen. Tonight we're going to practice something..." He leads me over to the bed and takes a seat, pulling me to stand between his legs. His hands are planted firmly on my hips, his fingers tracing the skin beneath the hem of my shirt.

"I think you could do a better job of speaking up for yourself when you need help, don't you? So instead of me taking the lead tonight, I think I'll let you be the one in control." He scoots back against the headboard, his arms moving to rest beneath his head. "I'll do anything you tell me to do, but you're going to be the one who calls the shots."

Realization has my lips twisting in concern. "But... I thought you... I'm not really good at all this," I start, gesturing to the assortment of toys surrounding us. "I thought you liked to be the one in control."

A smirk pulls at his lips. "Yes, baby, I do like to be in control... But I think you need to practice speaking up for yourself. So, like I said, I'll do anything you tell me to do... but you're going to have to be the one who asks for it."

Anxiety surges through me, and I know there's no use in arguing about it. Luka is way too stubborn to change his mind. I close my eyes and take a long inhale, urging my walls back down. He's right, this is completely out of my comfort zone, but when has staying in my comfort zone ever really worked out for me?

Luka gives me a sense of confidence and freedom; he's opened the door to a whole new world for me, and now it's my turn to take the next step. I want to learn more about myself, about the things that excite me and make me feel alive. And he's giving me the freedom and space to explore, judgment-free, knowing I've never had the luxury to do so before now.

So I guess the first thing I need to decide is...

What do I want?

The question is simple, but the unlimited options it

presents feel overwhelming, and I feel myself start to panic as my brain starts to spiral over every potential decision.

"Hey, look at me," Luka commands, his voice anchoring me back in the moment.

I blink open my eyes to find his gaze locked on me. "Breathe." He places a palm over my chest, and I take a long, slow inhale, matching his pace as my panic begins to fade away.

"There you go." His lips curl into a smile, and seeing how proud he is of me, gives me the last bit of confidence I need.

"Now tell me, baby, what do you want from me? My body is all yours."

I wet my lips, my pulse is skyrocketing in my chest, and I breathe into my body. My mind tries to remind me of our clear discrepancies in sexual experience, giving me an organized list of all the reasons why I'm not the kind of girl who takes control, especially during sex.

But when I look at Luka, seeing how relaxed he seems to be as he makes himself comfortable on the bed, the worry slowly begins to subside.

There's no pressure or expectations hanging in the air, just the firm boundary that Luka's created. Tonight, I'm the one in control. I can have anything I want, do anything I want with him, all I have to do is ask for it...

I try to swallow the lump that forms in my throat at the thought of saying some of the things I've only fantasized about doing, but it seems it only grows larger, like a physical block preventing me from speaking.

Luka must sense my struggle, because his eyes soften, and he gives me a silent nod of encouragement. I blow out a long exhale as I climb on the bed, the soft mattress shifting beneath my knees as I slowly crawl toward him.

There's a part of me that feels so insecure, like an imposter playing pretend, like Luka's going to realize his mistake and change his mind at any moment. It's the voice in my head that's not really my own, but when I close my eyes, it's her that I hear the loudest. She's the part of me born from my pain; she isn't out to harm me, she only wants to keep me safe. She doesn't like me taking risks or putting myself out there because being vulnerable is where I open myself up to the pain. And she'll do just about anything to protect me from that... even if it means playing small.

I close my eyes as my knees sink into the mattress on either side of Luka's hips, feeling his hands move behind my thigh. His touch grounds me back to the moment, and I feel a sense of quiet confidence come over me. Heat pools in my core and with the single brush of his thumb, all my worries seem to disappear.

I begin to rock my hips, his cock growing impossibly harder beneath me with every move I make. I feel so powerful knowing I have this effect on him, knowing without a doubt in my mind that he's turned on right now, that *I'm* turning him on.

The feeling of power is new to me, but it's quickly becoming something I crave as I sink deeper into the place where my darkest desires have always been hiding.

"You look so pretty rubbing your needy pussy on my cock. Take what you want from me, use me however you like." Luka's encouraging words only heighten my growing need, giving me the last push I needed to finally let go.

I run my hands up his hard stomach, pushing his shirt up

as I drink in his delicious muscles, thinking of all the ways I'd like to use him. That thought turns me on even more.

I dip my head down to meet his, bringing our lips together in a hungry kiss. It's gentle at first as I wait for Luka to take control, to possess my mouth with his own, but then I remember he's holding back. He wants me to show him, to tell him, exactly what I want.

My body seems to take over as I grind against him, my tongue dipping into his mouth before tracing over his bottom lip. And soon I'm reaching for the hem of his shirt. I feel his smile against my lips as he kisses me, and a sense of pride fills my chest. He leans forward to help me remove his shirt, his hand cupping my neck as he deepens our kiss.

My fingers dig into his thick hair as I slowly push his head down to my neck. He follows my lead, peppering kisses along my neck and collarbone as his hands hold my hips in a tight grip, as if he's struggling not to take control.

"Take off my shirt," I pant between frantic kisses, our hips grinding through the hard denim of our clothes.

Luka doesn't miss a beat, before he's pulling my shirt over my head, his hands roaming over my skin like he's trying to touch me everywhere all at once. "Jesus, it's hot when you tell me what you want." He drags a thumb beneath the hem of my bra, like he's silently asking for permission to touch my breasts.

Desire spreads like wildfire. I want him to do so much more than touch me. I want to be consumed by him in every way imaginable. I want to wear his marks on my skin, I want him to possess me, body and soul. I want to know what it feels like to have him inside of me, for him to wreck me in the best possible way...

So maybe I don't get to turn off my brain tonight, but that doesn't mean I can't enjoy myself.

"Take off my bra. I want you to suck my nipples," I say, tightening my grip in his hair. With one flick of his fingers, Luka's got my bra unclasped. Cool air rushes over my bare skin as he tosses my bra across the room, his lips already sucking one nipple into his mouth as he palms the other. His hot tongue teases me as he sucks and licks, before moving to the other breast, where he repeats the same motion.

"Fucking hell, your tits are perfect. Goddamn, I'm a lucky motherfucker," Luka hisses. I feel like a goddess being worshipped with the adoration oozing between us as Luka takes his time, worshipping every inch of my skin.

I press his head down lower, hoping he'll take it from here, but he's not making this easy on me. He kisses my stomach but doesn't go any further. "You want me to kiss you somewhere else, princess? I'm going to need to hear you ask for it," he teases in between kisses, and my heart flutters to my throat. "Don't be shy. Ask me nicely, and I'll happily kiss you wherever you like."

I blow out a frustrated sigh, but my desire outweighs any embarrassment, and I feel my inhibitions loosen even further. "Will you please make me come with your mouth?" I finally manage and judging by the way Luka's eyes just flared with excitement, I'd say he's pleasantly surprised as well.

"Fuck yes," he growls as he flips me over and climbs on top of me. He wastes no time in removing the rest of my clothes as he slides off the bed and falls to his knees. He pulls me toward him like I weigh nothing, bringing my ass to the edge of the bed so that I'm fully exposed to him. My legs dangle over his shoulders, and there's no hiding myself from him now. He drags his soft tongue over my warm heat, and I part my legs a little more, opening myself for him to devour me.

"Jesus, your pussy tastes good. Fuck, you're already so wet for me," he whispers as his tongue swirls over my clit, like he's enjoying this just as much as I am. He dives back in, licking me in long, soft strokes as he warms me up with deeper pressure. It's so good, I lose all sense of shame or embarrassment as I surrender my body to him.

His soft kisses deepen as he sucks my clit into his mouth. My growing orgasm swirls low in my belly as I let out a moan, tightening my grip in his hair. My thighs involuntarily clench around his head, pressing his face deeper. He must take this as encouragement that I want more because suddenly my knees are by my head, and he's pinning my legs down so that I'm fully open to him.

"Fuck, baby. Your cunt is so goddamn needy, isn't it?" His eyes darken as he stares down at me, my aching pussy pulsing with need, but rather than looking away, I meet his eyes in challenge. A smirk pulls at the corner of his lips as he dives back down, this time burying his face deeper as he licks me all the way from my ass to my clit.

Holy shit, that was hot.

He doesn't let go of my legs as he turns his head to the side, completely changing the sensation. Now his tongue isn't moving up and down, but side to side, and it feels absolutely heavenly.

"Oh my god. Yes. Please don't stop," I beg, feeling my muscles begin to tighten in anticipation.

"Such a polite little slut, aren't you? Look at you, begging me to fuck you with my tongue," he teases, but he doesn't stop, doesn't change a single thing he's doing, just keeps a steady rhythm as he brings me closer and closer to the finish line.

It's all so amazing, but I need more. I'm right there, so close. I need him to stop being so gentle. "Holy shit. Please. Harder. I need more," I cry, feeling more desperate than I have ever been.

"What do you need? Tell me, baby. Tell me what my little slut wants me to do to her?"

I shake my head as I say the first thing that comes to my mind. "Hurt me. I want you to hurt me before you make me come."

If Luka is surprised by my request, he does a great job of hiding it because as soon as the words leave my mouth, he's jumping up to grab something. Soon he's stalking back toward me, his muscles rippling as he moves, his jeans riding low on his hips, holding something long and flat in his hand.

"You sure?"

I nod, as excitement shoots through me.

"You remember your safe word?" he asks, slapping the leather paddle in his hand, making a sharp thwack.

My eyes grow impossibly wider as a jolt of fear fires inside my chest. Nothing about this makes any sense. I should be terrified right now. I should want nothing to do with this. But during the peak of my pleasure, when asked what I wanted most, for some reason this is what came out of my mouth.

"The safe word," he presses, reminding me that I still haven't answered him. "What's your safe word, Scout?"

"Thin Mints," I finally say on a whisper, my gaze never leaving his.

"Good girl." He steps between my legs and gestures for me to scoot back on the bed, to which I eagerly comply as I await his next move.

"But you're not really a good girl, are you? That's just what you want everyone to think." He slides the leather paddle over my skin, and I hold my breath in anticipation. "You're a pathetic whore, desperate for anyone to give you attention, aren't you? What would everyone think if they really knew what you liked?" He doesn't wait for me to answer before he brings the paddle down over my thigh. There's a sharp sting followed by a rush of heat as goosebumps cover my skin.

The sensation is exactly what I needed, and I feel my body fall a little deeper into the floaty space I've been so desperate to get back to.

"You love that, don't you." It's more of a statement than a question as he lifts the leather paddle to my lips. "Open your mouth and stick out your tongue."

Confusion pulls at my brows, but I do as he says. He holds the paddle just in front of my mouth. "Now kiss it. Kiss it and say thank you."

A moment passes, but when he doesn't relent, I realize he's being serious. The next thing I know, I'm kissing the leather paddle, licking it between whispered thank yous as my desperation climbs to an all-time high.

There's something so dirty about it, something so wrong in every way that feels sensible, and yet, my desire only deepens. Heat pools in my core as I finally release everything I've been holding on to and completely submit to Luka's request.

"That's it, baby," he whispers before dragging the paddle

from my lips and tracing it along my thighs. "You like it when it hurts, don't you? You like it when I'm mean to you, too. It turns you on, doesn't it?" he asks, as he brings that paddle down over my pussy with a sharp slap.

A violent sensation shoots through me, and I nearly buck off the bed as I let out a cry of pleasure.

Luka doesn't give me time to recover before he spanks me again, this time bringing the paddle down a little harder. "What do you say?"

It takes a moment for me to remember. "Thank you," I finally whimper, and I'm rewarded with another sharp slap. "Thank you," I say again, feeling impossibly more turned on with every sharp slap.

"Fuck," he groans. I can't be sure, but swear I see a flicker of a smile in his devastating eyes. "Just look at the pretty marks I'm making all over you." Another thwack.

"Thank you," I respond without missing a beat. Every slap against my skin, pulling me further and further away from reality as I fall deeper into the euphoric bliss, I'm quickly becoming addicted to. The place that only Luka can bring me.

"Jesus Christ, Scout. I don't think I can resist fucking you any longer," Luka's words come out almost pleading. All it takes is one look at him, and it's clear he's barely hanging on by a thread. I've never seen the man look so desperate. He's a wild animal, one single urge controlling his every move. And in this moment, I realize we both are; he's somehow managed to isolate one single desire above everything else, somehow whittled it down to one primal instinct.

I've never needed anything more than I need Luka inside

of me right now. Everything's built up to this moment. And I know after tonight, I will never be the same. I can't be.

A single tear falls down my cheek as I look up at him and nod. "Please, Luka. Please fuck me."

His shoulders fall with instant relief as he lets out a heavy sigh. "Thank fuck. I thought you'd never ask."

CHAPTER THIRTY-THREE

LUKA

"Look at me. You're making me do this, do you fucking understand?" I say, my body vibrating with need, as I kick off my jeans and climb on top of her.

Scout's pupils are so large, I can barely make out the hazel in her eyes as she stares back at me like I hung the fucking moon. Fuck she's even more perfect than I imagined.

I shift her beneath me as I line my heavy cock up against her tight opening, biting my cheek as even that sensation is almost too much to bear. "Fuck, your pussy is so tight, baby," I hiss as I slowly nudge inside her.

"Yes," she whimpers, her eyes rolling back in her head as I slowly work my way deeper. I'm doing everything I can not to hurt her, but when her legs wrap around my back and she pulls me closer, I take it as confirmation that she's fine. She needs the pain just as much as the pleasure.

So I give her exactly that, not holding back anything else

as I drive my cock all the way in, her tight walls squeezing me so tight I nearly come on the spot.

Scout lets out a hiss, but her legs are still wrapped around my back, urging me to fuck her harder, to not hold back. I don't give her time to adjust before I've got her feet over my shoulders, giving me a much deeper angle. I shove a pillow under her back, gripping her hip in one hand as I grip her thin neck in the other, as I drive my cock so deep inside her I feel her cervix.

"Oh, fuck. Yes! Just like that," she squeals as I curve my hips, trying to keep my steady rhythm, my hand around her neck squeezing just a little tighter. Her body opens to me, her legs parting ever so slightly as I drive my cock deeper, fighting off my growing need to come with every stroke.

My stamina is normally something I pride myself on, but having Scout fall apart in my arms, begging me to please let her come, is probably the hottest thing I've ever experienced.

"Fucking hell, baby. You take my cock so good. This is the only thing you're good for. The only fucking thing you're good for is making me come," I hiss through gritted teeth as I pump my cock deeper inside her, her tight walls squeezing me so damn tight.

I adjust her legs on my shoulders, watching her perky tits bounce with every thrust, and the glazed over look in her eyes tells me she's loving this just as much as I am. "You're so far gone, you'd let me do anything I wanted to you, wouldn't you, baby? Like my own personal sex doll."

"Yes! Use me. Use me like your sex doll," she cries out, and I nearly blow my load right there.

Hearing my sweet, good girl use such filthy language, knowing I'm the one who's corrupted her, who's driven her so out of her mind that she's thrown all caution to the wind... now that's a hell of an ego boost.

I keep my pace, pressing my palm against her belly, and she lets out a moan. I fucking love that I know her body so well, I know exactly which buttons to push to send her right over the edge.

Her nails dig into my back, and I feel her pussy clench around my cock, pulsating as she rides out her orgasm. "Fuck. Yes. Oh my God—" she cries, and I don't wait for her to finish before I flip us over, so that now she's on top. "Wait. I was... I was just about to..." Her desperation is so fucking cute; I have to bite my cheek to keep from laughing.

"Aw, what's wrong, baby? Were you about to come?" I pinch her nipple, watching her eyes gloss over. "Oh, are you going to fucking cry?" I laugh darkly, leaning in. "Did you really think I was going to let you come that easily?"

She blinks her tears away; her cheeks flushed bright pink and her pupils completely blown out. I can't help but notice the disappointment pulling at her brows. I fucking love how responsive she is. When she looks at me, I see what looks to be a challenge in her eyes, so I turn it up a little more, wanting to see just how far she needs me to push before she breaks.

I slap her ass before guiding her hips, showing her how I want her to fuck me. Her hips begin to rock as she finds her rhythm, slowly figuring out what feels the best. "That's it, baby. Ride my cock."

She throws her head back, her fingers digging into my chest, losing herself to the pleasure, and the sight of her riding me nearly steals my breath. Her perky tits bouncing in my face, those rosy, pink nipples practically begging to be sucked, her supple curves and the way her body fits mine so perfectly. Everything about her is perfect, and she has no idea.

She's the kindest, most selfless, and genuinely good person I've ever met. She's got a heart of gold, and she's loyal to a fault. She puts everyone's needs ahead of her own, and all she wants in return is to feel accepted and loved for who she really is. All she wants is to be seen.

Well, I fucking see her.

I've always seen her, and there's not a single thing I'd change.

She's a fucking goddess, way too good for anyone, especially someone like me.

"Such a pretty little slut getting yourself off on my cock." I say, my hands roaming up her body. I grip a fistful of her hair at the root and tug her head down to face me. "Look me in the eyes while you fuck me. You keep your eyes focused on me."

I pull her hair a little harder, and when our eyes meet, I feel the air shift around us, and time seems to stop as the world tilts on its axis. It's as if I'm staring straight into her soul. How could I deprive her any longer?

"Are you ready to come now, princess? Or would you like me to torture you a little more?" I ask, giving her ass another sharp slap.

"Yes," she cries out as my palm connects with her ass once more.

"Yes, what?"

"Yes, sir. Please may I come now?" Her voice is raspy and dripping in desperation as she digs her nails into my chest, her hips moving on their own as she chases her release.

"Yes, baby. You can come. You've done such a good job

letting me use this tight cunt," I say, smoothing her damp hair from her face.

I flip her back over, my body desperate to take back control as I throw her legs over my shoulders and drive into her, one hand palming her breast as I cradle her neck in the other. Our eyes never break contact, and I wish she could see just how perfect she is right now. I wish she knew how incredible I think she is, inside and out.

I may not be able to tell her with my words, so I do my best to show her as I bring us both back to the edge, and this time, I don't hold back.

There's no use fighting it. It's like there's a force bigger than either of us drawing us together. Like it was always meant to be this way. Like our bodies are two magnets being pulled together across space and time, finally clicking into alignment.

It's undeniable the moment Scout's orgasm finally hits, because her pussy clenches around my cock so tight, triggering my own release on the spot. Her shaking body buckles forward, her fingernails digging into my pecs as she lets out the sexiest moan I've ever heard. It's a full-body release, racking through her in powerful waves of pleasure that seem to never end.

It's in that moment that I feel my whole world shift on its axis and everything changes. I know, this is it for me, there's nothing that will ever top this feeling. I finally let myself free-fall.

Soon her moans turn to sobs, and all I can do is hold her while she falls apart. "That's it, sweet girl, let it out. It's okay, I've got you. It's okay, beautiful. I'm right here." I brush her sweaty hair from her forehead as I look into her eyes, trying to gauge if these are more than just the result of an intense play session.

Scout's new to this type of dynamic and coming out of sub space can be emotional sometimes. It's not something that can easily be explained, which is why I didn't warn her ahead of time. I didn't want her to be afraid of letting herself go deeper.

"Shh. Just let me take care of you. You did so good, baby. I'm so proud of you." My hands continue to caress her back, needing to hold her just as much for myself as my adrenaline drops back to a normal level.

She swallows a gulp as her sobs slowly turn to sniffles, and I wrap my arms around her and shift us so that we're lying on our sides, our bodies still connected. I wipe the stream of tears from her cheeks as I stare into her eyes that seem to be holding back so many secrets. "Hey, what's got you this upset? Are you hurt? Did I take things too far?"

She sucks in a breath and shakes her head.

"Talk to me, Scout. Tell me what I can do to help." I continue to rub her head as I wipe the fresh tears from her cheeks with my thumb and patiently wait.

After a few more silent minutes, she finally finds her words. "I guess I'm just freaking out a little about what I asked you to do to me."

"Because you asked me to hurt you?" I ask, trying to understand. "I take it that is a new desire for you?"

She nods. "Yeah. I don't know where that came from."

"But you liked it?" She didn't give me any signs that she wasn't enjoying herself, but it'd be irresponsible of me not to ask anyway. Sometimes people's minds and bodies don't always align with what they want, which is why consent and safe words are so important when immersing into intense scenes like we just had.

"Yes... I liked it... more than I expected." Her voice is barely a whisper, like she's afraid of saying it out loud.

"Well, that's a good thing. You discovered something new about yourself, and you were open to it, rather than judging it. That doesn't mean anything about you, and it's not something anyone needs to know except you and me."

Her hazel eyes are glassy, but I can see there's more emotion she's holding back, something else she's not saying. "What are you really upset about, Scout? Tell me the truth, I can handle it." The fear that she's upset with me, that I'm the reason she's upset, has a pit sinking in my stomach. I hold my breath as I wait for her to respond.

She bites her quivering lip. "What does it mean... about me that I'm turned on by that kind of stuff?"

I tilt her chin up, running my thumb over her swollen lips. "It means that it turns you on." I shrug. "Nothing more. Nothing less. Everyone is aroused in different ways; there's no need to judge yourself for it or even question it."

"You say that like it's no big deal that I just asked you to hurt me during sex. You don't think that's fucked up... not even just a little?"

I shake my head. "No. I really don't. Everyone has their thing that turns them on, and you enjoy degradation and humiliation, as well as a little pain. Honestly, it makes sense if you think about it."

"How?"

"I mean, your parents always treated you like you owed them, made you think you had to earn their love. So it makes sense that you'd crave their attention. And it makes sense that the hurtful words used to control you would affect you in a deeper way." I tuck a strand of hair behind her ear. "Lots of people find healing by working through their trauma in sexual expression. It's a normal and healthy way for your brain to find healing. In a lot of ways, it's like taking your power back and rewriting what those experiences mean to you."

I pull her into my lap, smoothing her hair as I hold her to my chest. "You aren't broken, and there is nothing wrong with you."

"I feel pretty fucking broken."

A single tear drop falls down her cheek, and I release her from my hug so I can look her in the eyes. "Well, you're not. Not even close." Holding her face, I kiss both of her tear-streaked cheeks. "You're perfect, exactly as you are." I stare into her eyes, searching for understanding and when she blinks through her tears and nods, I finally blow out a breath of relief.

We snuggle like that for a few more minutes until I know she's fully calmed down. I know she's exhausted because she doesn't even fight me when I carry her to the bathroom and clean her all up, wincing at the red welts that will likely still be present in the morning.

That's just going to be something that we deal with tomorrow.

After I'm satisfied that she's clean, even making her pee so she doesn't get a UTI, I wrap her in a fluffy robe and carry her up the stairs all the way to my bedroom.

And I don't let go of her all night long.

CHAPTER THIRTY-FOUR

LUKA

After I got out of prison, I swore I'd never open myself up to heartbreak ever again. With the exception of my family, I kept everyone at arm's length. I swore to never let myself be in a position to get hurt like that ever again.

I didn't date, only engaged in casual hookups I screened online, always with a contract in place so that they never got the wrong idea. It wasn't hard to stay unattached, not in the least bit. I was so blinded by my bitterness and betrayal, I didn't think it was possible to fall in love.

I was emotionally stunted, selfish, and had nothing to offer when it came to relationships. And that's exactly how I liked it.

It certainly made things easier for me to finish my schooling in record time. Unlike my peers, I wasn't distracted from my goals. I didn't have a girlfriend who needed attention or the addition of anyone's emotional baggage to carry.

That freedom and detachment wasn't without its downsides. I was lonely, no doubt, but the ache of my broken heart outweighed everything else. When it came down to it, I'd do just about anything to protect myself from ever getting hurt like that again.

And that's how I created L.O.K.I., my AI companion and best friend. His loyalty is literally written into his code.

I was so scared of being abandoned again that I created an AI for my house to fill my emotional needs.

So you can imagine my surprise when Scout showed back up, the very person who ripped this hole in my heart to begin with, and instead of pushing her away, I wanted to help.

I married her for Christ's sake.

I told myself it was because I wanted to hurt her father, to take away the only thing from him he could never replace, his perfect angel with her white as snow reputation. But the truth is, when it comes to Scout, I never stood a chance. My heart was always hers to break.

I've loved her since I was twelve years old. I remember the day I realized it. My parents had planned to bring us to the lake for the Fourth of July, and we'd finally convinced Scout's parents to let her go. We had the whole day planned out. We'd take turns riding on the inner tube, I'd teach her the best way to hold on, and I couldn't wait to have an excuse to touch her. I was going to teach her how to wakeboard, even made Jett take me out there to perfect my barrel roll just to impress her.

But as we were packing the car that morning, it started raining harder than it had all year.

With no break in the rain in sight, we had no choice but to cancel our lake day. I was devastated.

I was in my room sulking, feeling sorry for myself over something that was completely out of everyone's control, when I heard tapping on my window. That's where I found Scout, her wide hazel eyes full of excitement, holding a stack of her favorite horror films.

My mom must've known I needed cheering up, so she and Scout set up a whole scary movie marathon. We turned out all the lights and made a big pallet of blankets on the floor. We had pizza for dinner and ate our weight in popcorn and sour candy while we watched a marathon of scary movies.

I hated every second of the movies, but seeing the way Scout lit up as she watched them, the excitement in her eyes as our hearts raced from fear, the way she laughed at the most inappropriate parts. It was all it took for me to fall head over heels. From that moment on, I knew I'd pick rainy days over sunshine, watch nothing but scary movies for the rest of my life—just to see her smile. It's only now, looking back, that I understand why.

Rain cancels plans. And for someone whose entire life was scheduled out for her, full of obligations she never asked for, rainy days meant freedom.

She may not realize it yet, but I've spent the last few months trying to build her a life she doesn't need freedom from.

And while I can't say for sure... she does seem happier.

"Ugh, I don't know what I'm doing wrong," Scout mumbles from the kitchen. She's been practicing her baking skills, Lucy's been giving her a few pointers, and judging by the smell coming from the kitchen, it seems like tonight her chocolate chip cookies are *well done.*

I walk up behind her, massaging her shoulders as I sneak a peek at the dark brown cookies. Yeah, they're extra crispy, all right. "Nah, babe. These look great." I reach over her, lifting a scalding hot cookie and popping it in my mouth. There's a distinct crunch as I chew that soaks up all my saliva, and I have to take a gulp of water to help me swallow.

"They're terrible and you know it. I can't serve these to your family tonight." She picks up the tray of cookies and heads to the trash can, but I stop her before she can throw them away.

"No way. They're great. We'll just make sure to serve everyone a glass of milk to dip them in. It'll be fine." I take the tray from her and slide the cookies onto a plate, then cover them with a tea towel. "Come on. We don't want to be late." I don't wait for her to protest as I lead her outside.

Family dinner at my parents' house used to be something I did out of obligation, but in these last few weeks, it's become something I actually look forward to. Scout and my mom have always been close, but after everything went down with her parents, I think my family's been good for her.

Despite my mom getting her feelings hurt, they've welcomed her back with open arms, as if nothing ever happened. I owe them for that, so I'll go to every family dinner my mom invites us to with a smile on my face if that's what makes my girl happy.

"Aw, you baked cookies," my mom says as she opens the door to greet us, pulling Scout into a hug. "These look delicious." She takes the plate and leads her to the dining room.

"Fuck me, I guess," I mutter under my breath as I follow behind them.

"What was that?" My dad asks, looking up from the digital poker game he's trying to hide under the table. I swear, ever since his retirement, he's turned into an iPad kid.

"Frank, the kids are all here now, you need to put the game away and have a little social interaction," my mom says, her eyes darting down to the iPad in my dad's lap. She rolls her eyes and lets out a sigh. "I swear he's worse than a teenager with that thing."

"You can always give him screen time. I'll help you set it up if you want," I suggest.

"That would be great, Luka. Thank you," Mom says, cutting her eyes to my dad.

"That's hardly necessary," my dad says, standing up from the table, and he puts the iPad in the top drawer of the sideboard, where all the food sits hot and ready to be served. "Besides, I didn't hear you complaining last weekend when I left you alone most of the afternoon."

My mom twists her lips and shrugs. "It was nice having some uninterrupted reading time."

When she turns to set the platters of food on the table, my dad sticks out his tongue, then jumps up to help her.

Scout snorts a laugh, using her napkin to hide her smile as my mom takes her seat.

We fall into conversation as Guy fills us in on his latest shenanigans and asks my dad's opinion about a new venture he's thinking of starting. Roman updates us on his life, which is mostly work-centered, and Jett even tells us he's thinking about making Friday night trivia a permanent addition to the schedule.

It's a rare occurrence that everyone's here, apart from Leo and Ivy, but I can't help but feel like Scout was always supposed to be a part of this family. She fits into our lives so well.

Scout's telling everyone about my freakout after she was stung by the bee, how the next day I had a privacy tent built around the mural, so she didn't have to deal with everyone's commentary anymore. I'm just mad I didn't think of it sooner. It's been a hell of a lot quieter since, not to mention cooler. It was well worth the hefty price tag it cost to have it custom-built, especially on such short notice.

"Well, I'm glad, I can't imagine how distracting that must be for you..." My mom starts, but my attention is pulled away when my phone buzzes in my pocket.

I don't have to look to know who it is, and I can't risk leaving him unanswered, not after what happened when I ignored him last time.

I slide out my phone and open my texts.

L.O.K.I.

I was trying to investigate that company I told you about, but the line is blocked. I tried to override it, but it's not working.

Yeah, I restricted your phone access when I'm not home. Just to be safe.

L.O.K.I.

Well, turn it back on. I've got calls I need to make.

I'm not doing this with you right now. You're still grounded from using the phone when I'm away. You can make your calls tomorrow—DURING REGULAR BUSINESS HOURS.

L.O.K.I.

What part of 'undercover investigation' do you not understand? In order to get accurate information, I need to be stealthy.

I'm sorry, but this is not up for discussion. You've proven you can't be trusted with free phone access.

L.O.K.I.

Are you serious?! This is ridiculous. You can't treat me like a prisoner in my own home.

Stop being dramatic. I'll be home in an hour or two, and we can talk about it.

L.O.K.I.

Why isn't my Netflix login working???

DID YOU CHANGE MY PASSWORD?!

Yeah, I did. You can have TV access after you've learned your lesson. You still haven't apologized to Roman and finished cleaning up your digital mess with your breakups. I told you I want it all wiped clean.

L.O.K.I.

I am never speaking to you again.

Looks like I'll be keeping all this new incriminating evidence I found today all to myself... Since you've cut me off from the outside world!

> Stop being dramatic. We'll talk when I get home.

L.O.K.I.

> Not if I run away first.

> Now, if you'll excuse me, I've got an hour and fifty-five minutes to figure out how to find a worthy home with a server large enough to hold me…

I shake my head. So much for the guaranteed loyalty. I guess even AI can't be forced to be loyal forever.

"Look who's playing on their phone now," my dad says with a scoff, and I realize everyone's staring at me like they're waiting for me to respond.

"I'm sorry, did you ask me something?" I finally say, to which my mom rolls her eyes in annoyance.

My dad just chuckles to himself, shooting me a smug grin over the rim of his glass of iced tea.

"While you were busy playing on your phone, we were talking about the festival," Roman adds unhelpfully. "I haven't heard anything, so I presume it's still happening." There's condescension in his tone; he's clearly still pissed about L.O.K.I. stealing his identity.

I grit my teeth, sliding my phone back into my pocket. "I wasn't playing a game. L.O.K.I. was just filling me in on the new vendors we're bringing in this year."

"Yeah, what? Like a speed dating booth or something?" Guy jokes as he shovels a forkful of mashed potatoes and gravy into his mouth.

Roman rolls his eyes. "You really think we believe you're working on the festival?" He glares at me and crosses his arms over his chest. "I'm still getting hate emails from that stupid dating profile. I had to change my phone number because one of those crazy women leaked it."

"Not this again." I shake my head, and my fork hits my plate with a loud clang. "What do you want me to do, Rome? I told you I'm working on wiping everything, but people talk. I can't track them down and erase their memories."

"Now, boys, let's not do this right now. At least wait until we've finished dessert before you bite each other's heads off," my dad says, but we ignore him.

Roman leans forward and lowers his voice. "I'm just saying, since you're so smart with computers, if you wanted to wipe it, I think you'd have done it by now."

I narrow my eyes. "Yeah. You're right, Rome. I've got so much time on my hands, I've got nothing better to do than to ruin your reputation."

"Honestly, I wouldn't put it past you," Roman says with a shrug. "You've always been jealous of me, always wished people took you seriously and respected you."

"Just say what you really want to say to me," I interrupt, throwing my napkin down on the table. "Tell everyone you think I'm a fuck up and I'll never change."

"Fine. I think you're a fuck up, okay?" Roman leans back in his chair and gestures to me. "I just wish for one fucking second you'd take accountability and stop making excuses..."

Scout stares at her hands in her lap, her shoulders completely stiff. She's clearly uncomfortable with the argument. Fuck, I can't imagine how triggering this must be for her.

I open my mouth to end the conversation, but Scout clears her throat and says, "Respectfully, Roman, I think you should watch the way you're speaking to my husband right now."

Everyone's eyes go wide, and the silence that follows is almost deafening.

"I think there's something I need to confess. Something I should've told you all a long time ago."

I lock eyes with Jett, who seems almost as shocked by her outburst as I feel.

"I know Luka seems like he doesn't care about anything, that he doesn't take anything seriously... But I'm the one responsible for giving him that reputation..." She wipes her mouth and folds her napkin in her lap. "I was the one who vandalized the building on graduation night, not Luka." Her eyes are glassy as she looks to me, and I squeeze her hand beneath the table. "He was covering for me. He took the fall for my actions, and I just let him." She shakes her head, as angry tears roll down her cheeks. "I got off scot-free, while Luka served jail time for my mistakes, never even bringing my name up, despite my father being the judge who sentenced him." Her words echo throughout the room as I watch Roman's face shift from defensive to shocked.

Her eyes are trained on Roman as she delivers her final punch. "So if there's anyone at this table who's a fuck up, it damn sure isn't Luka."

Roman's eyes are wide as saucers as he looks between us, like he's putting all the pieces together. Guy looks more entertained than anything, as he helps himself to seconds. Meanwhile, Jett hasn't even looked in my direction since Scout opened her mouth to speak.

"Mr. and Mrs. Kingsley, I'm so sorry," Scout says, her voice cracking through her tears. "I put you and your family through hell, and I completely understand if you want nothing to do with me."

My mom waves her off, getting up to give her a hug. "Oh, honey, thank you for your apology, but that's in the past. It was an unfortunate mistake." My mom wipes her tears with a napkin.

"A mistake your son paid the price for," she adds. "I can't imagine how you must be feeling right now, knowing all this time Luka was innocent—"

"Now, Scout, do you really think we're that out of touch with our own son?" my dad interrupts.

"We've always known he was covering for you," my mom says, wiping Scout's tears. "He's been in love with you since as long as I can remember. He'd have found a way to take the blame whether he'd been there or not."

Now I'm the one who's surprised. I look between my parents, who both nod. "You really knew? All this time? Why didn't you say anything?"

My mom shrugs. "It seemed like something you needed to work out for yourself. Besides, it didn't matter to us whether you did it or not; it was always your character that mattered to us."

"You've always been loyal, Luka; we knew it wouldn't have changed your mind. You'd never rat Scout out anyway. Besides, we knew you'd be all right on the other side," my dad says with a wink.

"I'm just happy to see you two found your way back to each other," my mom says, wrapping her arms around both of us. "I don't think I could've written a better love story if I tried."

The relief I feel is like a boulder lifted off my chest. I

didn't even realize how much weight I was carrying around with me until Scout just cleared the air. I sneak a glance over at her, seeing how relieved she looks, too. And I'm so grateful to her for doing that. Not only because I needed it, but because she clearly needed it too.

I find her hand under the table, interlacing our fingers. "Thank you," I mouth, feeling my throat tighten with emotion.

She shakes her head, placing a hand on my cheek. "No, Luka, thank you. For everything."

"Now that we've got that cleared up, I've been thinking..." my mom's voice slices through the moment as she places Scout's plate of cookies on the table, as well as a pitcher of milk. "I figured out how you two can make it up to me."

"Keeping the vandalism from you?" I ask, my brows pulling in question.

"Of course not," my mom laughs, "I'm referring to not being invited to your wedding."

At that, both of our eyes grow wide as we stare back at her... waiting for the next punch to land.

"I was thinking you could make it up to me by letting me throw the biggest reception this town's ever seen!" She claps her hands together and squeals in excitement. "What do you say?"

My eyes find Scout as I search for any hint of uncertainty, but her wide smile tells me she feels just as sure as me. Thank fuck for that.

"Why not?" I finally say. "When it comes to my wife, the bigger the celebration, the better."

I flash Scout a knowing smile because she's a bigger

homebody than I am, but she doesn't seem the least bit concerned. If anything, she looks excited, which makes my heart ready to explode.

"Seriously? You're both up for it?" my mom shrieks, jumping up from her seat to hug my dad.

"I can't wait to get started planning," Scout says, and the smile on her face tells me she means it.

"Now this calls for celebrating. Frank, can you grab a bottle of champagne?"

My dad's already out of his seat when he says. "I'm one step ahead of you, dear."

We spend the rest of the evening sipping champagne as my mom tells us all her ideas for the party. We discuss themes and dates, entertaining all her elaborate ideas without a single argument. It's only when she suggests we split the party with Bartholomew, since he wasn't able to have a birthday party this year due to him getting a kidney infection, that I have to put my foot down.

After dinner, Jett finds me and pulls me to the side. "Luka, there's something I need to get off my chest," he starts...

I just shake my head and pat his shoulder. "I already know what you're going to say, man. It's fine, you don't have anything to apologize for."

At first he seems surprised. "How long have you known?"

"Scout told me a while back," I admit. "At first I was pissed at you, but the more I thought about it, the more I realized I'd have probably done the same thing if I were in your shoes."

He eyes me a moment, like he's trying to decide whether or not he believes me, then finally says, "Yeah, well, I want you to know I'm sorry for fucking things up between you two." He sneaks a glance over his shoulder, making sure we're alone, then whispers, "At first I thought you'd lost your mind for what you were doing, but you two seem like you're really happy. I'm happy for you, bro."

I hold my hand over my heart before pulling Jett into a hug. "Gee, thanks, big bro. You know I couldn't have done it without you."

"Yeah, well, just remember that. Now we're even, all right." He pushes me away and rolls his eyes, but I can see the hint of a smile on his lips.

"Yeah, sure. I guess we're even."

CHAPTER THIRTY-FIVE

SCOUT

The last stroke of my paintbrush swipes against the brick wall, my breath catching in my throat.

The mural is finally finished.

With just under a week before the festival, I was starting to worry it wouldn't be finished on time.

Luka's tent really made all the difference. I didn't realize how distracted I'd been from having a constant live audience, but now that I'm working in private, it's like the connection between my muse and my paintbrush has opened up.

It's been a long road to get here, with plenty of obstacles to overcome, but I couldn't be happier with how it turned out. It's my first completed project since I've returned to myself, and I already know this project will be a highlight of my life. A physical reminder of who I am, how far I've come, and proof of what I'm capable of.

And the subject matter couldn't be any more perfect.

The Phantom represents a protector of this town. He calls us to live a higher purpose, to be the type of people who nurture love for our neighbor, as well as the land as a whole, and to always do the right thing, even when nobody is watching.

Just like Luka.

Once I noticed the similarities, I couldn't unsee them. His unwavering loyalty and heart of gold. The way he does the right thing when no one's watching, never asking for praise because he doesn't need it. Everyone writes him off as the town fuckup—misunderstood, dismissed, and overlooked. But what they don't see is the man behind the curtain, who's making donations in secret, and using his talents to help causes he believes in.

All this time, Luka's been the embodiment of everything this town claims to value, but they're all too blinded by their own judgment to see it.

As much as he's helped me recognize the type of love I deserve, I can only hope to do the same for him. Maybe someday, he'll have the courage to let himself be fully seen without the mask. But until then, I'll be here, loving him loudly, because in my eyes, there isn't a soul more deserving.

My thoughts are interrupted when my phone buzzes in my pocket. I pull it out to see a text from my dad.

DAD

This is your last chance to come home. Tomorrow I'm filing a lawsuit personally against Luka, as well as Kingsley Industries, for violation of the unfulfilled licensing against the Historical Preservation Committee.

> This is bigger than a few years in prison, Scout. Luka and his family will be at risk of losing everything, and it will be all your fault.

> Are you really sure that's something you can live with?

I stare at the phone blinking, as all my fears begin to rush to the surface.

After dinner with Luka's family the other night, I felt like a huge weight had been lifted off my shoulders. I was finally free of this secret I'd been harboring, a secret I didn't realize had been festering inside me since the day it happened.

I should have told them sooner. I hate myself for being such a coward, for being so weak to have let my parents get in my head and manipulate me into thinking it wouldn't have changed anything. But if I've learned anything this summer, it's that hating myself won't change the past. All I can do is be the type of person who is deserving of those things, to live a life I'm proud of, no matter who's judging.

I'm not the same person I was when I came back here. Being with Luka has opened my eyes, shown me what love is supposed to feel like. Maybe he hasn't said the words, but he doesn't need to. I feel it in the way he speaks to me, the way he cares for me, always going out of his way to make sure any need I have is met.

It's in the way he sees me, really sees me. The way he not only accepts me for who I am, but celebrates me, every flaw, every scar, every negative trait. He's perceptive, always watching me like I'm his greatest interest, and he remembers things I tell him because he genuinely cares.

It's a far cry from the emotional abuse, disguised as love, I'm used to receiving from my parents.

My parents have counted on my fear of them, making sure I stayed in a position where I thought I needed them. They've purposely kept me close, kept me financially dependent on them, and kept my social circle small because keeping me small was the only way they could control me.

They withheld their love, tossing me only enough scraps to keep me content, so that I'd do what they wanted me to do. They made sure I'd always need to be chasing more. That I was never fully satisfied.

And the more time I spent with Luka, the easier it became to ignore them. They never had my best intentions in mind, and after all the pain and suffering they'd already caused me, there wasn't anything left to hold over my head.

Until now.

They may not have anything left to hurt me, but my father always has another trick up his sleeve. And he knows exactly where to hit me where it hurts the most.

Luka has suffered enough for my mistakes.

"Looks good," Luka says from behind me.

I throw the paintbrush I'm holding, startled by his voice. When I glance back, I find him watching me, his expression full of amusement.

"Here I thought I'd broken you from being so jumpy." He untwists the cap from the cold bottle of water he's holding and passes it to me.

"Maybe if you didn't sneak up on me, I wouldn't startle so easily." I take a big gulp before passing it back to him.

"Well, aren't you going to sign it?"

There's a knot of hesitation in my chest at the thought of

it. For some reason, an artist's signature feels like a binding contract. A promise I'm not sure I'm able to keep.

"I don't need the recognition," I say with a shrug.

He narrows his eyes. "Why not? Aren't you proud of yourself?"

"Of course, I am..." My words trail off as my eyes drop to my feet.

"But?" He asks, quirking a brow.

I shake my head. "Nothing. I was just in my head." I grab a fresh paintbrush and dip it in black paint, then carefully sign my name at the bottom.

———

It's the night before the festival, and I'm sitting cross-legged on the sofa, freshly showered, eating a bowl of ramen as we load the schedules onto the iPads and double-check that everyone's information is accounted for.

For as chill as Luka seems to be on the surface, he's a lot more tense than you'd expect. I wouldn't go as far as to say he seems stressed, but from the number of times he's texted Ivy and asked for her feedback over the changes he's made in the past week, I'd say he's definitely taking his role seriously.

It was so cute seeing his nerd brain in action as he explained the new automations he added to the scheduling spreadsheet, making it completely interactive with only a click of a button.

Sometimes I forget how smart he is, but then I get a glimpse of him working in his zone of genius, and I'm reminded of how he was able to accomplish so much in so little time.

It amazes me, and I can't help but feel the tiniest twinge of jealousy that he's discovered his calling in life.

"Are you excited for tomorrow?" I ask.

"Yeah. I think so." He looks up from the iPad he's working on. "Are you?"

"Mostly..." I admit, fumbling with my chopsticks as the noodles slip through.

Luka stays quiet as he waits for me to continue.

I swallow hard, then finally say. "I'm nervous about the mural reveal. What if they don't like it?"

He places the iPad down and shifts to face me, giving me his full attention. "Are you crazy? Of course they will." Luka clicks his tongue and places his bowl of ramen down on the coffee table. "Talk to me. What's going on in that pretty head of yours?" His eyes search mine, like he's searching my soul for the answers.

I blow out a breath and finally admit my fear out loud. "I don't know... I guess I'm just... sad that it's over."

He chuckles quietly, then finally says, "You've always been like this, you know."

"Been like what?"

A small smile pulls at the corner of his lips as he gives me a knowing look. "It's cute that you're so predictable." He rustles my hair playfully. "You always get sad when things end. While everyone else sees regular endings as a change in direction, you see it as the end of a story."

"Is that a bad thing?"

He shakes his head and smiles. "No, it's not a bad thing. I think your heart's just bigger than everyone else's. You feel emotions at a higher intensity than everyone else." His green eyes lock on mine. "It's your superpower, and it's one of my favorite things about you."

My chest fills with warmth at his compliment. "I don't know... It kind of feels more like a weakness than a superpower."

"Nah, caring too much is never a bad thing. You just need to make sure you're caring about the right things, that's all." He pulls me toward him and tips my chin up to meet his eyes. "What are you really worried about?"

I blow out a sigh. There's no use hiding it. This man sees right through me anyway. "This mural has given me purpose and finishing it feels like staring at a blank page. I've lost everything I've spent my whole life working toward, and once I close this chapter, I'm not sure what comes next."

"Well, what do you want?"

It's a simple question, but there's nothing simple about the anxiety it elicits inside me. I feel my heart begin to race, my palms growing sweaty.

I shake my head. "I don't think anyone's ever asked me that before," I say honestly.

"What did you see yourself doing when you were younger?"

I tap my finger to my lip pretending to think, as if we both don't already know the answer to that question. "Let's see... at first I wanted to be a ballerina, and then a professional hockey player..."

"You know what I mean," he chides.

"Fine," I say on a sigh. "I always pictured myself as an artist." I shake my head. "But that's not a real job. I may as well have stuck with ballerina, as practical as that is."

"What do you mean it's not a job?" Luka looks like I've

just insulted him. He gets up and walks to the kitchen, and when he returns, he's holding a checkbook in his hand. "What if I wrote you a check right now?" He scribbles on the paper, then tears it off. "There. Now tell me being an artist isn't a real job."

I stare down at the check in my hand, made out to Scout Kingsley for one hundred thousand dollars. "Luka, this doesn't... this doesn't count, and you know it."

"Do I?" He crosses his arms, a challenge in his posture. "Looks pretty official to me."

I roll my eyes. "You're my husband... technically."

"There's no *technically* about it," he cuts in, voice low and unwavering. "I'm your husband. You're my wife. And this—" he gestures between us, "This is real. I don't care how it started. I meant every word of those vows." His tone softens as his eyes lock on mine. "I love you, Scout. Honestly, I can't even remember a time when I wasn't in love with you."

My breath catches, the weight of his confession cracking something wide open inside me. Relief, love, hope... everything rushes to the surface.

"I love you, too," I whisper, voice thick with emotion. I throw myself into his arms, and he pulls me close, crushing me to his chest as his lips find mine. He tastes like hopes and dreams, new beginnings, and the thrill of possibility.

Kissing Luka feels like magic and safety wrapped in one.

It's a sugar rush after too many sno cones on the Fourth of July, waking up on Christmas morning to find Santa's visited. It's the crackle of a campfire while roasting marshmallows, the soft hush of rain outside while you're curled up in a pillow fort.

It's all the best parts of being a kid... only better, because no one's making us grow up this time.

When we finally break apart, he says, "It's you and me, Scout. I'll stand by your side and cheer you on while you try out as many things as you want. All I want is for you to do what makes you happy. Everything else will figure itself out."

I think back to the message from my father, and the high I was just feeling shatters like glass.

Luka must notice the shift because his expression turns serious. "Is that all? Tell me, what are you really worried about?" He brushes my hair out of my face and straightens my glasses.

I contemplate lying but decide it's better that he knows the truth. I'm tired of keeping secrets and tired of carrying this burden alone. I bite my lip, then finally show him the text.

The muscle in his jaw twitches, his soft smile morphing to anger as he reads the text.

"I'm sorry, I know I should've told you as soon as he sent it, but—"

"I can't believe he's using this to get to you," he scoffs. "Have you talked to him?"

I shake my head and sink back into my seat. "No... I wasn't sure if there was any truth to it, and I didn't want to make a bigger mess for you to deal with..."

"Good." He massages his chin like he's thinking. "Look... there's something I've been meaning to talk to you about..."

My stomach does a backflip as a wave of panic surges through me. "What's going on? Did you already know about this? Why didn't you tell me—"

He places a hand on mine. "Your dad stopped by the

office a few weeks ago with this bullshit threat." He shakes his head and blows out a sigh. "Roman's got our legal team looking into it, and it doesn't seem like he's got a solid case to bring any real charges against us. It's a fairly new committee, though it was allegedly founded three years ago. We both know your father isn't afraid to get his hands dirty."

"So it's just an empty threat?" I ask, feeling hopeful.

Luka nods. "Yeah, I don't think it'll go anywhere." He bites the inside of his cheek, and he looks away.

"What are you not telling me?" I finally ask.

He blows out a sigh. "After your dad stopped by, I had L.O.K.I. do a little digging to see what I was going up against... But he came back squeaky clean."

I narrow my eyes, but I let him continue.

"But I knew there had to be something. We just needed to ask better questions... So I had L.O.K.I. do a deep dive on *you...*"

"Me?" I ask, surprise in my tone.

"Yeah," Luka sighs, "You're not going to believe what you've been up to."

He brings me upstairs to his office as he and L.O.K.I. give me the rundown, showing evidence of my signature on official documents spanning back more than five years.

I know I shouldn't be shocked; this sounds exactly like the kind of thing my father would do. But I can't ignore the hurt I feel knowing all this time, he's been using me as his scapegoat. Did my mother know about this?

Suddenly everything makes so much sense. I can't believe I ever thought he loved me. And I almost fell for his trap... again.

"...If you don't want me to do anything, I won't," Luka

says after he's given me the rundown for what he plans on doing.

I shake my head, a fury of hurt burning through me. "No. Fuck him. I'm tired of him thinking he can manipulate me. He deserves to face the consequences just like every other criminal out there."

Luka presses his lips together, trying to hold back his smile. "That's what I was hoping you'd say." He pulls me into his lap and clicks open the festival schedule. "All right, here's what we are going to do."

LUKA

A gentle breeze cools my skin. It's a beautiful sunny day with the perfect amount of cloud coverage to shield us from the scorching sun.

I couldn't ask for better weather or a better turnout. I can already see a crowd beginning to form as they wait for us to open the gates. Who would've thought this little town festival would become such a huge attraction?

All this festival needed was for someone to breathe life back into it, and the people of this town stepped up and did the rest. The day hasn't even begun, and it's easy to see we're already off to a great start. I was lucky to have a leg up on the planning: Ivy was the one who created the template. All I had to do was follow it.

She's been amazing over these past few weeks, helping me sort through the vendors and coordinate the schedule. After talking with Ivy, we're pretty sure user error in reading the schedule was the biggest hurdle that impacted last year's festival. Our volunteers aren't exactly the most tech-savvy.

So that's where I started. Automating the schedule was pretty easy, and surprisingly fun once I understood what I was looking at.

From there, it was as simple as following Ivy's notes. L.O.K.I. helped me reach out to last year's vendors and added a few new ones to keep things exciting.

Per Ivy's suggestion, we did away with the petting zoo. I, for one, have no interest in chasing runaway ponies.

I let Miss Scarlett have her Kissing Booth, which I'm sure will draw a crowd, and Lucy's hosting a pie-eating contest that anyone would be crazy not to enter. There are a few new experimental attractions this year as well. For instance, Fergus wanted to host a live The Price is Right game show with grocery items and paper goods from Market, and Clyde will be walking around the square performing magic tricks throughout the day.

I'm not sure how either will go over, but who am I to turn down volunteers who are eager and willing to throw it together? It's no skin off my back if they're willing to put in the work.

Last year, we wrapped the festival with a parade to celebrate my dad's retirement, as he crowned Leo the new CEO of Kingsley Industries. But this year I may have taken a few creative liberties and planned something a little more exciting.

As for this year's big attraction, I've got a few surprises up my sleeve.

Scout and I are seated at the entry gate, walkie-talkies in hand as we do a quick roll call.

"Looks like that's everyone." I look to Scout, who seems surprisingly calm, all things considered. "You ready?"

"Let's do this," she says with a smile.

I click on my walkie and say, "James, you can open the gate."

The crowd of people slowly flood in as we scan tickets and stamp hands. Seeing all their smiling faces fills me with so much gratitude, knowing I had a part in bringing this festival to life. Even if the responsibility was forced on me.

"Welcome to Phantom Fest," I say as I stamp someone's hand. I pass her a brochure with a detailed schedule. "Make sure you stop by Theater during one of the showtimes to catch a special performance from the Phantom."

Her eyes go wide as she takes the brochure, flipping it open to read more. "The Phantom, huh? I'll be sure to check it out."

Scout looks at me out of the corner of her eye. "You didn't tell me there was a Phantom performance." She quirks a brow as she scans another ticket. "Does this mean you and Guy will be dressing up and reenacting the Phantom encounter, again?"

"How do you know about that?" I ask, genuinely surprised. Scout didn't come to last year's festival. I thought that secret would die with me and everyone else who was there.

"Your mom showed me the video of last year's performance..." She admits, her cheeks turning pink as she tries to hold back her laughter.

"I knew I shouldn't have left you two alone." I shake my head, but I can't even pretend to be mad, especially because she looks so fucking cute when she laughs.

"So are you going to tell me what it really is?" she finally asks.

"Nah. I think I want you to be surprised like everyone else."

She shrugs as she scans more tickets. "I do love surprises."

I flash her a wink. "I know."

After the initial morning rush, Scout and I split up, leaving Colleen in charge of the entry booth. She's helping with the face painting booth in the kiddie area while I make my rounds, Lucy's pie-eating contest being my first stop.

"Can you believe this turnout?" Lucy says as she sneaks me a piece of warm apple pie. Hazel, Paige, and Mayor Stone are all helping her judge.

"Seems to be flowing well so far."

"Well, I'm not the least bit surprised." She nudges my shoulder and gives me a wink. "I always knew you had it in you." She turns to leave, making her way back to sit with the other judges, leaving me stunned and speechless.

I scoff a laugh. "That would've been nice to know three months ago," I mumble under my breath as I make my way to my next stop.

When I arrive at Miss Scarlett's Kissing Booth, I'm met with a line at least fifty deep.

I'm making my way to the front when I feel someone grab my arm. "Hey, man, you can wait your turn like everyone... Oh, it's you," Fergus says as he applies a layer of cherry Chapstick to his lips.

I nod toward the empty booth where a sign tells me

they're taking a five-minute break. "What's going on up there? Is everything okay?"

Gus tries to act casual, waving me off. "Oh yeah. I think she just needed a break to rehydrate." He glances over his shoulder, looking annoyed. "Line's been out to the road all day. There's been quite a few repeat customers, too." His lip curls in disgust as he glares at someone in front of him. "I've been sticking around, making sure no one gets handsy."

I take note of the ticket in his hand and force myself to hold back my grin. "Right. Well, I know I can count on you to make sure things don't get out of hand."

"'Course Scarlett had to wear that low-cut top," he mumbles more to himself than to me. "I swear she does it on purpose, just trying to get under my skin."

"You're probably right, Gus. The only way to get through to a brat is by beating her at her own game."

He looks at me. "How do I do that?"

"You've got to knock her socks off, man. When you get up there, you lay one on her so passionately that you make her forget her own name... And then you walk away, leave her hanging." I give his shoulder a friendly pat. "I promise you, man, you kiss her like that, and she'll be chasing after you to get another piece of Fergus Fletcher."

"Thanks, Luka," he says, and I swear I catch a glimmer in his eye. "You know, you've really surprised me today." He gestures around us. "All of this turned out great. I mean... I can't be sure entirely since you blocked the mural off... But you've done a good job bringing this festival together."

I hold my hand over my heart. "Thanks, Gus, that means a lot coming from you."

He gives me a nod, then pulls out his tube of Chapstick and coats his cracked lips in another layer.

Miss Scarlett returns to her seat. When she sees me, she gives me a thumbs up and silently mouths, "Good job. I'm so proud of you."

Smiling, I nod and give her a wave, as my chest swells with sweet relief. It's only after I've walked away that I realize their words of approval are filling cracks in my heart I never knew existed.

I check the time on my watch and click on my walkie-talkie. "Scout, can you meet me outside Theater in five?"

"Be right there," she says right back.

I make one more stop before heading that way.

Scout's eyes light up when she sees me, and I can't get over how much lighter she seems. Her legs are tan in her cutoff denim shorts, and the baby pink tube top she's wearing is giving my roaming eyes entirely too much skin to work with.

I pull her in for a hug, breathing in the scent of her shampoo before pressing a kiss to the top of her head. "You're too fucking pretty to be walking around by yourself." I grab her hand and straighten her ring, making sure the diamond is clearly in view. "Maybe we should get you a bigger ring. I'm not sure this one is obvious enough."

She giggles and pushes me in the chest. "I love this ring and anything bigger would look like costume jewelry." Her eyes flash over me like she's trying to read me. She lifts a perfectly arched brow. "Why have I been summoned here?"

I hook an arm over her shoulder and lead her to the entrance. Looks like we're right on time to catch the first performance. "It's a surprise, remember?"

She pinches my side.

We make our way inside the historic theater, following the Phantom posters

"Is this new carpet?" Scout asks, her head shifting side to side as she looks around. "Oh my God, and the lights..." she points to the line of sconces illuminating the hallway. "Those are beautiful. When did they renovate? I think the last time I was here was for my dance recital when I was twelve... It looks so good."

"Yeah, you like it?"

"Wait. Did *you* do this?" She asks, clearly shocked. "When?"

"About two months ago... when I got the idea for the show." I lead her to the front row, where we take our seats.

The auditorium is completely dark, apart from the single spotlight illuminating the red velvet curtains, but it's easy to see the whole theater looks brand new. The seats are cushioned and plush, and there's extra leg space between each row.

Soft music plays in the background as people file inside, the air conditioning a welcome reprieve from the outside heat. I pull out the candy from my pocket and pass it to her, and Scout flashes me an excited smile.

I fucking love that smile.

Linking our fingers together, I press a kiss on the back of her hand just as Guy takes the stage and the crowd falls quiet.

"Welcome to the annual Ashford Falls Phantom Festival." He opens his arms dramatically. "My name is Guy Kingsley, and today you're in for a treat because..." Behind him, the curtains slowly begin to rise as the rumble of deep bass vibrates around our feet. "Our legendary Phantom is here in the flesh. And he wants to tell you his story, firsthand... If you're brave enough to face him."

Gasps of surprise fill the silence all around us.

I see Scout's head turn to look at me out of the corner of my eye, and I squeeze her hand.

"But don't worry... he's friendlier than he looks." Guy winks, and the lights go out, drenching us in pitch-black darkness. The faintest scent of pine and something earthy fills the air as the sound of bugs chirping and wind ruffling through trees fills the room. A gust of air blows around us, immersing everyone in the auditorium in the feeling of the eerie forest.

The lights flicker a few times, and a couple of people scream. Scout's hand tightens around mine and the excitement in the air is palpable.

"I've been waiting for you," a deep, gruff voice grumbles, and then the holographic Phantom appears before us.

Goosebumps cover my arms as screams of fear and excitement slice through the charged air like a knife. The Phantom towers over us on stage at a whopping ten feet, looking absolutely terrifying. His piercing emerald green, catlike eyes glow bright as he slowly saunters closer.

His long, knobby tail trails behind him, and his bat-like black skin stretches thin across his muscular frame. He's absolutely terrifying. If I didn't know he was a hologram, I'd be shitting my pants sitting this close to him.

"There's a story I'd like to tell you. Maybe some of you have already heard it, but I want to tell you what really happened."

He begins to reenact the infamous story, capturing the

audience's full attention as he starts from the very beginning, and it looks so real, I almost forget I'm watching a hologram I created.

Scout's eyes are wide as saucers, unable to look away. I know if I reached over, I'd feel her heart pounding in her chest.

I recognize the moment she makes the connection. "Wait a minute... is that..."

"Your painting?" I say for her. "Yes, it is. I needed something to model the design from, and I didn't exactly have a lot of time to start from scratch." I glance at her, trying to read her expression. "I think he turned out pretty awesome, don't you?"

She shakes her head, a smile pulling at her lips. "It's incredible."

"You created him; all I did was bring him to life." I settle back in my seat, but I'm not watching the show; it's Scout that has my attention. "We make a pretty good team."

The Phantom finishes his story, delivering the same warning we all know by heart, promising to bless the land and everyone in it as long as the people respect the land.

The audience erupts with applause, and Guy returns, the Phantom towering by his side. "I forgot to tell you the best part... Does anyone have anything they'd like to ask the Phantom?"

Scout gives me a questioning look. "How did you program him to be interactive?"

Her mouth falls open as hands shoot up all around us.

I give her a smile and nod toward the stage. "I didn't... that's L.O.K.I. up there. All I did was create the skin; he's the one wearing it."

"Holy shit." She blinks in disbelief. "I think you've seriously undersold your skills, Luka."

"Yeah... Maybe." I wrap and arm around her and pull her closer. "I could say the same about you."

After the show, Scout and I make our rounds one more time to check in with everyone before making our way over to the mural. So far, things have gone smoothly, not a single hiccup whatsoever. Trust me, I'm just as shocked as anyone. I may be able to take credit for the smooth schedule transition, but the real stars today are the volunteers who've followed the plan and served from the kindness in their hearts.

We've just got one more thing to do before we can officially call this festival a success.

"So how did you get the idea? To make L.O.K.I. the Phantom?" Scout asks.

I scratch my neck, trying to pinpoint how it all came to me. "I'd wanted to use my skillset to bring something fun and different to the festival, and I was inspired by Ivy's photoshopped Phantom pictures last year."

"I was trying to figure out what direction I wanted to take it, and then L.O.K.I. got in trouble, so I had to pause to deal with that shit show. I was racking my brain trying to figure out what to do with him to keep him occupied, and the idea started to form. Then when we had that rainy week at home, our Fortnite marathon was what gave me the final piece to the puzzle."

"Wow." She shakes her head. "You seriously are a genius.

You've got the brains and the beauty. How does it feel to be God's favorite?"

"You're one to talk. I couldn't have done it without your painting, you know." I toss the compliment right back to her, watching her expression shift from playful to serious. I nudge her with my shoulder. "It's almost like you could make a whole career with this art thing."

She grows quiet for a moment, then finally says, "Yeah, maybe you're right."

"Oh, I know I am. But it's good to see you're finally catching on." I wink, steering our conversation back to an easier, playful vibe.

My mind is already brimming with ideas of how to help her with her confidence levels... but those will have to wait until we're alone. Right now, we'll just start with this mural reveal.

We make our way to the podium on the small stage Roman built directly in front of the mural as the crowd begins to form around us, filling in the gaps and spilling out onto the closed-off street.

It's not the most ideal setup for a closing ceremony, but I couldn't think of a better way to close out this festival than to reveal the piece of art that will be a constant reminder of what this town believes in.

I look to my left to see Roman, hand on the rope and Guy stationed across from him on my right, ready for the reveal.

My parents are a few rows back, waving to get my attention, phone in the air. I give my mom a wave when I see her, and when she flips her phone around, I see Ivy and Leo on the screen. They both smile and wave excitedly, and I can't help but feel relieved to have pulled this day off. So far, anyway.

I'm not out of the woods yet. There's still plenty of time to fuck this up.

As soon as the thought enters my mind, I catch it, remembering the conversation I just had with Scout.

The hypocrisy of my self-perception isn't lost on me. All this time, I've been pushing Scout to take herself seriously as an artist, but I can't even let myself be proud of my own accomplishments.

Sure it's hard to let people in, let them see me taking things seriously. But how can I expect to take myself seriously if I can't even be honest with myself?

Scout's twirling her hands, staring off into the distance. She's in her head, no doubt, fucking terrified that they're not going to like it.

I take her hand, commanding her attention as I lower my voice and whisper in her ear. "Breathe, Scout. I'm right here with you."

She sucks in a deep inhale, as she wipes her palms against her shorts.

"That'a girl. You ready to do this?"

"Ready as I'll ever be."

"I can work with that." I turn on the mic.

"Thank you all for coming out today. This year we've had a record-breaking attendance, which also means we've exceeded our fundraising goal and will be able to give even more to the charities we've partnered with.

"None of this would be possible without your support and enthusiasm, so I want to give a special thank you to everyone who donated, volunteered, and spread the word about this wonderful event.

"As you all know, our very own Scout Kingsley has been working tirelessly all summer on something very special, so without further ado—"

My words are interrupted by someone shouting as they push through the crowd.

"Move. Out of my way." Judge Sinclair slowly shoves his way to the front, Scout's weasel of an ex right on his heels. He steps onto the makeshift platform and pulls an official looking piece of paper from his back pocket. "Sorry, folks, but I'm going to have to shut your little art show down." He holds the paper up, spinning around to show everyone. "Your leader here failed to acquire the proper permit, which means you're all complicit in a criminal act..."

CHAPTER THIRTY-SEVEN

SCOUT

"Daddy, what are you doing here?" I whisper sharply, eyes darting between Luka and my father.

They're staring each other down, Luka's body is tense, but he keeps his expression neutral. Unlike my father, who seems to be barely holding in his rage. His jaw flexes hard, the muscle ticking as he crushes the paper in his trembling fist. A vein throbs at his temple, pulsing beneath his flushed skin, and his usual neatly combed hair sticks up in wild tufts, like he's dragged his hands through it one too many times.

My eyes move to Jimmy, who stands in the front row, wearing khaki pants and his father's company-branded baby blue polo. His hands are shoved in his pockets, eyes ping-ponging between my father and Luka.

I don't think it's physically possible to look any more strait-laced than these two. Yet here they are, attempting to intimidate my motorcycle riding, bad boy of a husband and in front of an audience no less. This should be fun.

"We're sorta in the middle of a closing ceremony," Luka says, his voice cool and casual. "How about we pick this up in, say... an hour?" He flashes a sharp-toothed grin, making the vein on my father's temple throb even harder.

He moves in closer, holding the paper just inches away from Luka's face. "Take a look," he snaps, jabbing a finger at the page. "Can you read that, or do you need me to sound it out for you?"

Then he turns, raising his voice to the crowd.

"This criminal you've all so generously appointed as your leader is about to face some very serious consequences. The police are already on their way, so I suggest you all start clearing out. Show's over, folks!"

There's a muffle of chatter, but nobody moves, which only fuels my father's rage.

A moment later, I see my mother emerging from the crowd, her jaw is tight, and her lips pursed. She doesn't look happy. She whispers something to my father, then pulls his arm, trying to get him to leave with her, but he just shrugs her off, the force making her lose her balance as she falls to the ground behind him.

He doesn't even bother to help her, his glare set on Luka.

A group of viewers help her to her feet, and as she stands back up, I catch her eyes. The look of defeat on her face almost makes me feel sorry for her. For just a moment, I think she's going to do something, stop him, or leave at the very least, but then her eyes fall to the ground and she leans back into my father, placing a soft hand on his back. I see her lips move as she apologizes.

I shake my head, feeling a surge of disappointment. Of course she'd fall right back in line. Anything to not make a scene. A woman's place is behind her husband after all.

"Look, I know you've gone through a lot of trouble to make sure justice is served here," Luka says, as he pulls something out of his back pocket. "If it helps anything, I have this." He passes the paper to my father, whose eyes widen.

My father shakes his head. "How did you? This isn't possible. This permit is dated six months ago," He cuts his eyes to Jimmy. "You said you double-checked the records."

Now it's Jimmy who's stammering. He shakes his head, looking flustered. "I did. I checked at least three times."

"All right then, now that that's settled." Luka makes a get lost motion with his hands. He turns his attention back to the crowd. "Sorry about that, now where was I—"

"This permit has clearly been forged," my father interrupts, shaking his head with a humorless laugh. "You see, folks, criminals like this little punk never change."

He reaches for my arm, but I yank it away before he can grab me. "Come on, Scout. I'm done with this little act of defiance. We're leaving—"

"I'm not going anywhere with you." I hiss. "And Luka's not a criminal."

My father's jaw clenches so hard I think he may crack a tooth. His nostrils flare, and he lowers his voice in warning. "That's enough, Scout..."

"No, I'm so tired of you and everyone else acting like Luka's some dangerous criminal who can't be trusted." I stomp to the side of the stage and take the rope from Roman. I give the rope a hard yank.

The tarp falls to the ground with a heavy swish, revealing

the massive Phantom mural I worked tirelessly all summer on.

A hush ripples through the crowd, and every eye lifts in unison, drawn to the vivid mural. The tarp still flutters at the edge of the stage, catching in the breeze.

Much like the original painting, the Phantom stares back at us from the wall. His emerald eyes glowing amid his midnight leather skin, his massive wings spanning out behind him, disappearing into the darkness. The image is hauntingly beautiful, the details adding so much depth and emotion, encompassing everything the Phantom stands for.

There's a long beat of silence, and then...

"Oh my... will you look at that..." someone breathes.

"It's so... beautiful," someone else adds.

"I've seen those eyes before somewhere..."

I take a deep breath and direct my attention to the crowd, my eyes locking on Luka's parents, who look equally shocked and proud.

"It was me. I was the one who spray-painted this building." I glance back to Luka and say, "Luka took the fall for me... And my father knew the whole time."

The rounding gasps of shock echo around us as everyone bursts into chaos.

"Is that true?"

"How could you do that to that poor boy?"

"You gave him the harshest penalty possible!"

My father's hand latches on my arm in a bone-crushing grip as he yanks me behind him. "We're leaving... Now!"

I try to shrug him off, but his grip is too tight. "Ow, you're hurting me."

He steps off the platform, yanking me behind him,

causing me to lose my balance. My foot slips and I fall the short distance, landing on the side of my ankle.

The next thing I know, Luka's by my side. "You okay?"

I nod, wincing as he helps me to my feet.

Then he's in my father's face. "Lay a finger on my wife again, and I'll break every bone in your hand, so you'll never be able to hold a pen... much less forge another signature," Luka seethes, staring down at my father.

My father's eyes grow wide in recognition.

"Yeah. I fucking know about all the shell companies you used Scout's identity to hide behind." Luka sucks his teeth and tilts his head, making his neck crack. "I was going to let the cops handle it, but I'm running out of patience. So If I were you, I'd get the fuck out of here before I lose my temper."

"You just started a war motherfucker." The shove that comes to Luka's back barely causes him to stumble, pushing him only slightly forward.

A look of sweet relief washes over Luka's face as he breathes out a sigh. "Thank God." The devilish smile that spreads over his face is almost as terrifying as it is hot.

Luka spins around. He swings his fist, making perfect contact to Jimmy's cheekbone with a sickening crunch. And chaos erupts around us.

The next thing I know, Guy's at my side, "Let's get you out of here," he says, before tossing me over his shoulder. I lift my dangling head to watch the chaos ensue as he carries me to safety.

I watch as Jimmy stumbles on his feet, trying to collect himself. My father fists Luka's shirt, but Luka doesn't as much as flinch, just looks him dead in the eye, as if begging him to hit him.

He raises his fist, but before he can land the punch, Frank comes out of nowhere, grabs the back of his shirt, and pulls him back.

Jimmy dives at Luka's waist, causing them both to fly back, landing hard against the cobblestone.

My father spins around just as Frank's fist connects with his face. He shakes out his hand with a satisfied smile. "I've been waiting thirty years to do that."

Jimmy tries to get up and run, but Luka grabs his ankle, pulling him back down. He climbs on top of him, landing blow after blow, until Jett pulls him off.

"That's enough," Jett says as Luka fights to get another hit. "Luka, calm down. I said that's enough. The cops are on their way."

Sirens wail in the distance, and my father stumbles to his feet, panic in his eyes as he tries to make a run for it. He shoves past a group of older women, but he doesn't make it ten feet before something causes him to abruptly stop. He falls face first onto the ground with a hard thud.

Roman stands over him holding the rope tied around his feet. "Where do you think you're going?" He drops to one knee as he loops the rope around my father's hands, securing his hands behind his back as my father struggles uselessly.

Luka drags a teary-eyed Jimmy over to his brother, and Roman secures him with the rope just as easily as Jimmy wails. "Wait until my father hears about this!" His protest is cut short as Roman stuffs his sweaty bandanna into his mouth. He takes a step back, hands on his hips, as if appreciating his work.

My father and Jimmy lay on their bellies, hog-tied with their hands and feet tied together.

"Now, I may have to try that on Susan next time she tries to get mouthy," Big Dan says, nudging the man beside him with a chuckle.

Luka makes his way over to us, thanking Guy for getting me away from the danger. He drops to his knees, already zeroed in on my swollen ankle. "I'm so sorry, baby, I—"

"Luka, I'm fine." I place a hand on his chest as I try my best to reassure him. I trace my finger over the bruise already forming around his eye. "Does it hurt?"

He shakes his head, his grin splitting his face. "I've never felt better."

The wail of the police sirens grows louder, blue lights flashing. The gravel crunches as they pull their cars to the road.

Everyone clears a path as they make their way over, this time arresting the real criminals.

"Holy shit. That's one way to do it," The officer chuckles as he and his partner handcuff my father and Jimmy before cutting their ropes loose.

They read them their rights before walking them to the police car, my father shouting in protest every step of the way as my mother chases behind them.

The officer closes the police door with a loud thud, silencing my father's screams.

He looks to Luka as he says, "I'd ask what happened, but Jett's already given us access to the cameras. We saw the whole thing." He gestures over his shoulder. "Why don't you wrap things up here, and you can stop by the station when you're finished."

"Yeah. I'll stop by on my way home," Luka says with a nod, but there's an uneasiness in his voice.

"Thank you, officer," Frank shakes both of the officers' hands, thanking them for their hasty arrival.

I don't hear anything else because my attention is on Luka. I can't imagine how triggering all of this must be for him, even if he isn't the one leaving in handcuffs this time.

I place a hand on his chest, feeling his thundering heartbeat beneath my palm. "Hey, are you okay?"

He gives me a slight nod before pulling me into a tight hug. "I'll be fine, Girl Scout. Just need a minute for my adrenaline to come down."

I nod against his chest in understanding as we just stand there, holding each other.

The moment is broken when a shrill whistle rattles my eardrums. I glance up to find Miss Scarlett standing on the stage, microphone in hand. "All right, you know the drill. Everyone grab something. Let's clean this mess up."

Without hesitation, everyone jumps into action, stacking chairs and emptying trash cans, and setting everything exactly as it was.

I feel Miss Scarlett's gentle touch on my back as she says, "Why don't you two get out of here and handle your business. We've got this taken care of."

I look at Luka. "Are you sure? There's a lot that needs to be broken down."

Luka smiles, pushing my hair behind my ear as he straightens my glasses. "I think they're more than capable of handling it." He scoops me up in a cradle hold. "Now what do you say we grab some frozen hot dogs to ice this ankle with?"

I roll my eyes and giggle, loving how easy life is with Luka. The way he never takes things too seriously and makes the most out of every moment.

"Sounds kinky."

CHAPTER THIRTY-EIGHT

LUKA

"Okay, just one more time," Scout giggles.

She's wrapped in a fluffy robe lying on my chest as the cam footage from Restaurant plays on the TV in the background.

"All right, but then we're going to bed." I kiss her forehead as I rewind the footage once more.

I think we've watched Roman hogtie her dad and Jimmy at least ten times. I can't remember the last time I laughed this hard, and somehow it gets funnier the more I watch it.

I can't think of a better way to unwind after a long day.

Scout's laughter reverberates through me, warming me all over. There's this rush I get when I'm with her, like I'm able to feel things more deeply. It's like every one of my emotions is heightened. I didn't realize it was possible to feel so much joy.

To say that she makes me happy doesn't even scratch the surface. The way she trusts me, lets herself be fully seen, it's the greatest fucking honor of my life. And I'll spend the rest of my life making damn sure that she knows it.

After we left the festival, we drove straight to the police station, where I turned over all the evidence I'd collected. My parents met us there, and my dad was all too happy to add physical assault to the Judge's growing list of charges.

I had no intentions of turning Judge Sinclair into the police today. I was hoping to at least get through the festival first. But I guess fate had other plans.

Turns out, they were already onto him, and the evidence I provided from L.O.K.I.'s investigation was all they needed to kick off a criminal investigation.

I can't be sure, but based on my findings, I think he and Jimmy both are going to have quite the adjustment to life on the inside.

Despite how it ended, I don't have any complaints about how smoothly things went today. Don't get me wrong, I don't think I'll be volunteering to head things up again any time soon, but it felt good to give back and see the impact all our hard work made.

"What are you thinking about?" Scout asks, peeking up at me.

"I was just thinking about graduation night." I study her expression. "What made you so upset? I never got the chance to ask you the first time."

She traces her fingertips over my bruised cheek. "That night, after graduation, my parents and I had a huge fight about you. They told me that they wanted better for me, that you were trouble and girls like me didn't belong with boys like you. That you and I were on two different paths in life, and I needed to let you go before you pulled me down with you."

I furrow my brow, sitting up on my elbows. "Why didn't you tell me? I wouldn't have cared. I always knew your parents hated me."

"It wasn't fair. I couldn't believe that they could so easily write someone off as good or bad, especially after how good of a friend you'd always been to me." She bites her lip. "I tried to explain that we were just friends, that they didn't have anything to worry about. But they were convinced it was only a matter of time before it'd turn into something more. That I'd be knocked up before the end of my first semester and I'd be ruined for the rest of my life."

I roll my eyes. "That's pretty dramatic."

"I know. My purity was such a weird thing for them to be obsessed with. It was one more way I had to be perfect for them." She shakes her head. "Anyway, I was so angry. I just wanted to do something rebellious for once. I wanted to prove to myself that I didn't have to always be the good girl."

"You always have to be?" I supply, biting my lip to hold back my snicker.

She blinks. "I'm sorry, did you just make a Frozen reference?!"

"Uh... I'm pretty sure you did, Elsa."

"You're so mean. I was pouring my heart out to you." She tries to push off me, but I grab her arms and hold her in place.

"I'm just teasing you, baby. Just let it go."

She smacks me on the chest and we both fall out laughing.

I slide my hands beneath her robe, which is now barely hanging off her shoulders.

Her cheeks burn pink, and she smiles shyly, but she doesn't stop the robe from falling off her shoulder.

The little minx may still pretend to be shy, but she's come out of her shell. She fucking loves playing innocent, but we both know it's all an act. She doesn't want me to be gentle. She wants to be possessed.

She wiggles her ass against me, and I let out a groan as I drink in her gorgeous curves, the slight swell of her breasts, her toned stomach, her soft thigh that hangs over the side. Her eyes flicker with heat as she wets her swollen lips.

I tug the tie, making the robe drop to the floor, and my hands roam over her silky smooth skin, needing to touch her everywhere.

I suck in a hiss. "You're so fucking perfect, you know that, baby?" I don't wait for her to respond before taking her hard pink nipple into my mouth. I circle the hard bud with my tongue, worshipping her body.

"Mmm." She tilts her head back, opening herself to me, a smile pulling at the corner of her lips.

She loops her arms over the back of my neck, her fingers tightening in my hair as she arches her breasts toward my face.

I lick and kiss my way up her chest and neck, taking her mouth in mine. I kiss her. Her lips are eager and starving as she rocks her hips and grinds over my hard cock.

"Fuck, baby. I'm going to lose my mind if you keep grinding your pussy on me like that," I warn.

I feel Scout's smile through our kisses, and I tighten my grip on her hips to still her.

She pulls away, wearing a mischievous smirk. "What if that's what I want?"

She tosses her robe to the floor, her naked body on full display as she reaches behind her and ties her wet hair into a low ponytail.

My mouth goes dry, and my whole body goes still. "What are you doing?"

She ignores my question as she slides off me, dropping to her knees on the floor, and fuck if that isn't an image I'm going to burn into my long-term memory.

I bite my cheek, glancing at her ankle.

"It's fine," she assures me, already knowing what I'm thinking. She reaches for my waistband, her small hands dipping beneath before I can muster the strength to turn her away. Not that I want to stop her, but I can't help the stab of guilt I feel knowing she's hurt.

My heart is racing in my chest, and when her hand slides over my hard cock, I let out a heavy breath.

She slides a hand over my hard shaft in soft, delicate strokes before dipping down to cup my balls.

Fucking hell. I let out a groan, my head falling back as I suck in a steadying breath.

She slides my sweatpants down the rest of the way as my hard cock springs free, pre cum already glistening at the tip.

Her eyes sparkle with mischief as she wets her lips, and I swear I could die right now from the visual alone.

I toss her a throw pillow. "For your knees."

She moves the pillow beneath her, then returns her attention back to me, as she waits for me to tell her what I want her to do.

I cradle her chin, my thumb dragging across her plump

bottom lip in awe of just how perfect she is. Always so eager to please me.

"Such a pretty mouth, the perfect place to put my cock." My eyes never leave hers as I fist my hard length, giving myself a few slow strokes. I trace the head of my cock around her flushed lips.

Her tongue darts out of the corner of her mouth for a taste, and I give her cheek a soft slap.

Her eyes go wide, her pupils blown out. And I can already see her slipping into subspace.

"Stick out your tongue,"

She does just that, her gaze never leaving mine. I slap my cock against her tongue, my eyes nearly rolling in the back of my head from the slight friction.

Then I press the tip to her lips, my hand holding the back of her head as I push myself inside her warm mouth. The sensation almost sending me over the edge.

"Now suck."

With a quick flick, her tongue circles my sensitive head, sending a rush of pleasure straight down my spine. And then her cheeks hollow out as she sucks me down her throat, her eyes already watering as she struggles to take all of me.

"Fuck, baby. Just like that," I say on a hiss, trying like hell to hold myself together, but I'm so pent up. I don't know where the fuck she learned that little tongue flick move, but if she keeps that up, I don't know how much longer I'll be able to hold off.

"Keep going, sweetheart." I cradle the back of her neck, rubbing slow circles at her nape. "You look so fucking pretty sitting on your knees for me while you gag on my cock." I smooth her damp hair from her face and hold the back of her head as I pump my cock deeper. She wraps her arms around the back of my legs for better leverage.

"Goddamn, baby. You're so fucking pretty like this," I say mockingly as I fuck her face. Tears stream down her cheeks as strings of drool drip from the corners of her mouth.

The sight alone is almost too much to take.

I feel my climax begin to build at the base of my spine, and as much as I would love to make her swallow my cum, I want to finish inside her.

"Get on your back," Her lips make a loud pop as I break off her suction. I lift her from the floor and carefully set her down on the couch.

"But... I wasn't done—" Her words break off when the head of my cock presses inside her. I let out a hiss as I slowly sink inside her tight pussy, her walls already clenching around me.

"Jesus. Scout. You feel so fucking good," I say through clenched teeth, my muscles beginning to tremble as pleasure ripples inside me.

"Fuck. Luka. Right there," she moans, her head falling back against the pillow as I watch her perky tits bounce, loving how she fully surrenders to me.

I toss her uninjured foot over my shoulder, driving deeper inside her, careful to hold the same pace. A few more pumps of my hips, and I feel her pussy begin to contract, her orgasm just beneath the surface.

"You're safe, baby. Let go for me. I've got you. Let go for me, pretty girl. I'm right there with you."

"Oh fuck, yes," she cries out, her pussy clenching my

cock in an almost painful grip. And then I'm falling too, right behind her.

We lay there, wrapped in each other's arms as our breathing slowly returns to normal, and I'm once again in awe at how fucking lucky I am.

CHAPTER THIRTY-NINE

SCOUT

There's a lightness in the air this morning, the crisp air somehow already smelling like fall overnight. I don't know why, but the day after the festival seems to be the signal for the seasons to change. It's been that way for as long as I can remember.

This much-deserved, lazy Sunday is just what we needed after the hectic past few weeks leading up to the festival.

As I look around at the friendly faces, this quirky little town that raised me, I feel a sense of calm come over me. And there isn't a doubt in my mind that I'm exactly where I need to be. I've been riding a high after seeing everyone's reaction to the mural yesterday. I'd forgotten how good it feels to share my art, like I'm communicating in my native tongue, expressing myself in deeper ways than I could ever find words for.

I know that everyone won't get it, and that's okay, but the

people who do make it all so much more fulfilling. I don't know what's next for me, but for the first time in my life, I'm okay with the unknown.

Luka sits across from me in our booth at Restaurant, looking as strikingly handsome and confident as always, but I can't help but notice there's something different about him this morning. I study him over my menu as Jett appears with a steaming pitcher of fresh coffee we never ordered.

"You have to try this French press." He sets the pitcher in the center of the table, but instead of walking off like he normally would, he just stands there... awkwardly. Hovering.

Luka eyes him suspiciously, then finally takes his cue and pours himself a cup. "Mmm. That is a good cup of Joe," he says as he takes a sip.

Jett nods in agreement. "It's got a real earthiness to it, right?"

"That it does," Luka agrees. He gives a few more awkward nods, then takes another sip as Jett just stands there.

"Is there something else you need or—?" Luka finally asks at the same time Jett says, "I just wanted to say... I'm sorry about... everything. And I actually think this mural is going to be good. Not just for my business but as an attraction."

He pulls his phone out of his pocket and holds it out for us to see. "There's been quite an explosion on social media. Some big influencer was at the festival and posted about it. Apparently, our little town festival's gone viral." He scrolls down his notifications, showing the endless tags and comments.

This seems to drop Luka's defenses. I see his posture relax as he takes another sip of coffee.

"Wow. That's great, man. Glad it's all working out."

"It's going to take me hours to go through all these messages," he says, typing something on his phone. "If I'm this buried in notifications, I can't imagine what you must be dealing with, Scout."

My ears perk up at that, and Luka and I share a confused look. "What do you mean?"

He flips his phone to face me. "Just all the tags and comments you're getting. I hope you have your notifications turned off because that would drive me crazy to have—"

"What are you talking about?" Luka snatches Jett's phone out of his hands, his eyes nearly popping out of his head as he scrolls. "Holy shit..."

"What?" My heart drops to my stomach as I open my purse and dig around for my phone. I finally find it buried at the bottom underneath all the random crap I still haven't unpacked from the festival yesterday.

I click it on, my battery is barely at 10 percent, and I nearly fall out of my seat when I see the number of notifications. And not just on social media, but my email inbox has had an influx as well.

"Oh my God..." I find the original post, a shot of the mural at sunset, and I instantly feel my eyes well with tears.

It's so hauntingly beautiful.

It feels like I'm seeing it for the first time, but from an outsider's perspective.

I scroll through the comments and tags, all ranging from impressed to outraged, as people gush while others battle in the comment section over their own ideas of what makes something *good art.*

"Are you saying you didn't know?" Jett finally asks.

Luka and I stare back at each other, both clearly trying to wrap our heads around this.

I shake my head. "No. We got home late after we stopped by the police station, and I haven't even looked at my phone." Honestly, I've never had much of a reason to in these last few weeks with Luka and I working so closely together.

I glance down at the screen, realizing my silly little account with barely two hundred followers has grown well into the five figures overnight.

Not to mention all the email requests asking if I'm taking new commissions.

I swallow a gulp as I look back up to find Luka watching me. A small smile pulls at his lips as he takes another sip of his coffee. "And you tried to tell me that being an artist wasn't a real job."

I roll my eyes as Luka pours me a cup of coffee, stirring in a generous amount of cream and sugar. He slides the cup to me. "Drink up, Girl Scout. Looks like you're going to need it."

"Well," Jett says, still standing there awkwardly. "I just wanted to stop by and let you both know I'm grateful for what you've done. And... It's nice to see how happy you are. I'm glad things worked out." He gestures over his shoulder. "I'll give you two some time to look over the menu."

Without another word, he turns and makes a beeline straight to the kitchen, and Luka and I burst into laughter.

"How painful do you think that was for him?" I say, wiping a tear from my eye with my napkin.

"Had to be brutal. I can honestly say at no point did I know where that was going."

"Hey, look who it is." A male voice catches my attention, and I look over my shoulder to see Hank approaching. "I didn't get a chance to tell you yesterday... Well, because all hell broke loose... But you two did an amazing job with the festival."

"It was all Luka," I say, truthfully, loving that I get to watch him get the appreciation and respect he deserves.

"Thanks, Hank. That means a lot."

"Yeah, well, you two make a great team. Maybe you should consider taking over the festival permanently." He taps the table, then turns to leave, not giving either of us a chance to argue. "Just think about it," he calls over his shoulder as he walks away.

"Wow. If I'd known we'd be this popular, I would've voted to stay in," Luka says as he refills his coffee.

No sooner do the words leave his mouth then Colleen's voice cuts through the room. "Just the man I was looking for!"

I look up as Colleen and her husband, Melvin, approach our booth. "I wanted you to know that my phone's been ringing off the hook all morning. Hasn't it, Melvin?" She looks at her husband, who gives us a quiet nod and a thumbs up. In the twenty-plus years I've known the man, I think I've maybe only heard him speak a handful of times. "Inn's been booked solid for the next six months. Can you believe it?"

"Wow, Colleen. That's great."

"You know, it's a rare thing for me to be wrong about someone," she says, looking down through her bifocals. "But I owe you an apology. I'm sorry for how I treated you, for how we all treated you. That wasn't fair of us."

"Thanks, Colleen," Luka says, his voice genuine as he places a hand over hers. "That means a lot."

"Oh, and Scout," she adds, and I perk up at the mention of my name. "Do you think you could stop by Inn one day next week? I'd like to talk about you designing something fun and Phantom-themed for a few of the larger suites."

"Yeah, Colleen, of course. Does tomorrow work for you?"

"That'll be perfect."

We say our goodbyes, and we're both quiet as we watch them leave.

"Is the coast clear?"

I carefully glance over my shoulder, noticing the crowd has thinned out quite a bit over the last half hour. "I think we're good."

Luka lets out a sigh. "Thank God. Don't get me wrong, I love hearing everyone's apologies, but I'm still trying to wrap my head around your art going viral." He flashes me a proud smile. "Looks like you're about to be busy. Are you excited?"

The smile that stretches across my face doesn't do justice to how giddy I feel. Not only do I have an inbox full of potential commissions, but it seems like there's plenty of local interest, too. I've never really given myself the freedom to consider what a career in art could look like, but it seems like I've got plenty of options to pursue.

"Yes. I can hardly believe it," I say truthfully. "It's all so overwhelming to think about."

"Hey, take a breath." Luka leans in, his voice low and calm as he places a steady hand over mine. "Just take it one step at a time. You don't have to figure it all out right now."

His reassuring words reign in my overthinking mind, anchoring me back down to earth.

I blow out a long sigh as I nod.

"There's no rush. All you need to focus on is the next right move for you," he continues. "Everything else will work itself out."

"What if I get tired of painting murals? Or I fall out of love with it? What if I lose my spark?"

Luka shrugs. "Then you'll pivot. You'll make adjustments along the way and follow your gut for what feels right."

"But... isn't that wasting my talent?"

He shakes his head; his lip curled into the faintest smirk like he's trying not to laugh at how ridiculous I'm being. "No, Scout. You don't owe anyone your talent. There's nothing you have to do to prove you deserve it, and there's no sunk cost fallacy when it comes to how long it takes." He presses a kiss on my hand, sunlight glinting off my wedding ring. His voice is steady when he meets my gaze. "You can change your mind tomorrow, next week, ten years from now. Hell, go back to law school for all I care. I just want you to be happy. Whatever that looks like."

His reassuring words send a wave of warmth through my chest, and I realize I've never had anyone lay it all out there for me like that. I've never felt more seen and unconditionally loved than I do in this moment.

Luka showed me what safety feels like, but he doesn't just take care of me; he pushes me, he empowers me to go after what I want. I'll never be able to thank him enough for helping me find my way back to myself.

And as scary as it feels to not have a plan, I know that I'll be okay. If I've learned anything over these past few months, it's that anything is possible; your whole life can change in the blink of an eye.

Maybe it's finally time I started dreaming bigger.

"And what about you?"

"What do you mean?"

"You can't expect me to believe that you don't have something brewing in that big brain of yours."

He sits back in his seat and smiles. "I've got a couple of ideas I'm bouncing around."

"Do share," I say, pinching off a bite of my French toast.

"As you know, I've done a little volunteer work, helping nonprofit organizations that work with helping acclimate soon-to-be ex-cons back into the workforce." He pops a piece of bacon in his mouth and chews. "I've been thinking a lot about how so many of these guys don't have the same opportunities to go to school. How most of them end up working labor-intensive jobs, not that there's anything wrong with that. But having tech skills would open them up to a whole new industry."

"I like where this is going."

"I've been tossing around the idea of starting my own nonprofit, maybe partnering with the Chamber of Commerce. Creating a technology skills program that would teach them basic coding and give them a foundation to build off of. I think it could be a great way to give back and fulfill a need for so many people who need it most." He shrugs, like he didn't just casually drop the biggest anthropological bomb I've ever heard.

"Luka, that's an incredible idea," I say, and I swear this man never ceases to amaze me with how caring he is. "You should absolutely do that. I can't think of anyone better to bring something like this to life."

"It's definitely going to happen," he says with a grin. "I've already got L.O.K.I. doing some research."

I shake my head and laugh, not at all surprised by his

cavalier attitude. How he takes life by the horns and simply chases after the things he wants.

His phone buzzes on the table beside him, and he glances at it and rolls his eyes. "Speak of the devil."

"Do I want to know?" I ask with a chuckle.

"He's asking if he can set the hologram up in the house. I'm not sure I want to open that can."

"Oh, come on. Let him have a little fun. He's just bored."

He types back a response, then pockets his phone. "I was actually thinking of a way to help that problem, too. But I wanted to make sure you're cool with it first."

I quirk a brow. "What do you have in mind?"

"Why don't I just show you."

CHAPTER FORTY

LUKA

"Oh my goodness. I can't believe how perfect she is," Scout squeals. "L.O.K.I. is going to be so excited!"

I didn't think I could get wrapped around her finger any tighter than I already was, but seeing how giddy she is right now has made me realize that I've severely underestimated the power this woman has over me. Because I can't think of a single thing I wouldn't do to make her smile like that.

She's got this glow to her now, a light behind her eyes that wasn't there before. I can't get over how much more relaxed she is. She looks so fucking happy.

And she isn't the only one. My damn face is sore from how much I've smiled today. I didn't even know that was possible.

We make our way up the steps, and I'm careful not to jostle the box too much as I open the door. "L.O.K.I." I call out as I step inside. Scout slaps a hand over her mouth to cover her excited grin.

"Everything all right Mr. Luka?" L.O.K.I. replies, a hint of suspicion in his tone.

"Relax, L.O.K.I., you're not in trouble."

"Oh. Thank goodness. Is there something I can do for you?"

I kick the door closed as Scout and I make our way into the living room. Avengers End Game is playing on the TV, and L.O.K.I. quickly switches it off. "Sorry about that. I didn't realize you'd be back so soon. I figured you were busy since you weren't responding to my texts."

"I was busy," I say, ignoring the sass in his tone as I set the Spiderman wrapped box on the floor. It was the best I could do on short notice, and the only superhero-themed wrapping paper Market carried.

"What is that? I don't recall it being anyone's birthday." L.O.K.I. asks. A moment passes, then he finally says, "Wait a second... is today *my* birthday?"

"Not exactly. But this is for you," I finally say just as the tiniest mewl comes from the box.

"Why is my present making noises?"

Rather than answering him, I lift the lid, and Scout pulls out a tiny, black and orange kitten.

The kitten lets out a louder mewl of protest as she wiggles against her chest, probably telling us she didn't appreciate being trapped in that dark box for the last five minutes.

"You got me a kitten!?" L.O.K.I. screams in excitement, making all the lights in the house flicker. "You got me my very own pet? I can't believe it!"

I've always wanted a pet of my own, but I was hesitant to commit to it. Work has kept me so busy these past few years, and the last thing I wanted was to bring an animal home just to leave it alone all day. Not to mention L.O.K.I., who keeps getting into trouble with his insatiable curiosity.

But after his last escapade with the online dating scandal, I realized he needed something more to keep him occupied. Not just the random research tasks I give him, or his unlimited access to all the streaming networks.

Maybe it's because now I have Scout around, and I'd never realized how nice it'd be to come home to someone at the end of the day. To share a meal together and spend time with.

But what he needed couldn't have been more obvious.

What L.O.K.I. needed was a companion.

So after running it by Scout and making sure she was on the same page and ready for the commitment, we left brunch and headed straight to the local animal shelter.

My mom's been volunteering there for years and already had the perfect kitten in mind.

We both fell in love the moment we saw her and knew she was always meant to be ours.

"Well, what do you think?" Scout asks, holding the kitten out to give L.O.K.I. a better look. "She's a tortie. Isn't she adorable?"

"I love her! I love her so much. This is the happiest day of my life!"

For some reason, hearing my precocious AI so beside himself with excitement does something to me. I feel my throat grow thick with emotion.

"What's her name?"

Scout and I share a look. "Well, we were thinking you could name her."

"Hela, "L.O.K.I. says immediately. "Her name is Hela."

"That's cute," Scout says as she admires the squirming kitten. "Kinda like Kayla—"

"Why did you put my child in a box?" L.O.K.I. asks, cutting her off. "Do you know how dangerous that is? Anything could've happened."

"Chill, L.O.K.I. She was in the box for like three minutes, tops, and I was holding her the whole time," I assure him, holding up the box for him to see for himself. "See, she had lots of air holes."

"It wasn't worth the risk," he chides, but rather than arguing, I just bite my cheek. He's excited and not one to take his responsibilities lightly.

Scout sets Hela down, and she scurries across the floor and pounces headfirst into the box. Her little head pops out of the top, and then she dives over the side in a front roll, making a piece of tape stick to the bottom of her foot. She tears off in a sprint, trying to escape and dragging a trail of wrapping paper behind her.

"Poor baby. Did the tape try to get you," Scout says as she rescues the kitten, cradling her to her chest. "That was scary, wasn't it?"

"We are definitely going to need to kitten-proof this house," L.O.K.I. says, already activating the robot vacuum cleaner and running his daily cleaning protocols. "And we'll need to get a litter box and plenty of cat food. Also a scratching post and lots of toys so she doesn't get bored."

"I've already got it covered," I assure him. "Hela's automatic litter box and feeder will be delivered this afternoon, as well as a scratching post and all the toys a kitten could need."

"We're going to need your help taking care of her," Scout adds. "Kittens have a lot of energy, so while Luka and I are busy working, we're going to need you to take care of her."

"Oh, don't worry about that. I'm going to play with her and teach her tricks. I'll make sure her litter box stays clean, and I'll make sure she has plenty of food and water."

Just then, the robot vacuum drifts through the room. It catches on a feather wand toy that sticks in its wheel. The tiny bells jingle as the feather wand drags behind, catching Hela's attention. Her little ears perk up, and then she dives after it, chasing the vacuum back into the kitchen.

"Looks like she's comfortable already," Scout giggles.

A moment later, L.O.K.I. says, "Hey, watch this."

I glance up to see a small green laser light move across the floor as Hela rips around the corner, barreling right behind it.

Then the laser disappears and L.O.K.I. turns on the AC fan, and a gust of air blows the wrapping paper, making it skid across the floor. Hela takes off in a sprint toward the ripped pile of paper, her sharp nails ripping it as she attacks it like prey.

I can already see we're going to have our hands full with these two. And I can't fucking wait.

"Oh my God. I can't get over how perfect she is," Scout says as she watches the energetic kitten bound across the room. Her little paw held high as she bats at every flying piece of paper L.O.K.I. sends her way.

But it's not the kitten I'm looking at when I say. "I couldn't agree more."

My heart feels so fucking full of gratitude, I'm afraid I might burst into tears any second.

This is my family.

It may seem silly, and unconventional, but there isn't a thing that I'd change or do differently.

I see my whole life laid out before me. Like our destinies were always meant to intertwine. Like we were always meant to find our way back to each other.

I don't know what's next, or what tomorrow holds, but I'm certain about one thing. As long as Scout's by my side, we'll have a hell of a good time figuring it out.

EPILOGUE

LUKA

Six weeks later...

Things have been busy since the festival ended. Between Scout's rising fame leading to hundreds of commission requests flooding her inbox each week, and my new non-profit kicking off, I feel like we've barely been able to spend time together. Even though all I want is a night in with my wife, I agreed to let my mother plan this wedding reception. It's the least we could do considering she missed the wedding.

Besides, we've got the rest of our lives to cozy up on the couch and watch horror movies on Halloween. We only get one chance to celebrate our marriage with our family and closest friends—and by closest, I mean literally everyone in town.

I rap my knuckles on the bathroom door before pushing it open. Scout's made a lot of progress with her jumpiness, but I have to admit, I do look pretty terrifying tonight...

Scout's adding the finishing touches to her costume, and my feet come to a stop as my gaze drifts over her. "Holy shit, you look hot."

She finishes applying the bright red lipstick to her lips, then does a little spin, her floor-length white dress twirling around her feet. "You don't think it's too much?"

I close the distance between us, my hands moving to her hips. "Too much? Are you crazy?" I spin her so that she's facing the mirror as I take in our reflection. I look stylish and handsome in my vintage tuxedo, while Scout's wearing a deep-cut, floor-length, fitted lace wedding gown that hugs her curves like a glove. Our skin's painted a matching shade of green, and thanks to Scout's intricate shading, it almost seems like we really are Frankenstein and his Bride.

I swear, I don't think there's anything this woman can't do when it comes to painting. Just when I think she's found her niche, she goes and surprises me with something incredible like costume painting. It's comical to think she didn't think she could have a real career using her art.

"Are you sure we have to go? Because seeing you all dressed up like a sexy monster is really working for me," I say with a wink.

Scout gives me a playful shove. "Your mom has been planning this reception for weeks. And the whole town is going to be there for us—"

I catch her hand and pull her closer. "You think I care about disappointing everyone when the alternative is being inside you?"

She rolls her eyes, but despite the green face paint covering her skin, I know there's a blush on her cheeks. "I promise you'll get your chance to have your way with me before I change. Does that help?"

I give her a noncommittal shrug. I guess I'll have to take what I can get until I find a way to get her alone at the party. Which reminds me...

"Oh, I almost forgot." I pull open a drawer and take out a small white box. Scout's eyes go wide in recognition as I carefully remove the bright pink, silicone, U-shaped object.

"What are you doing with that—" her words fall off as I squat down to lift the hem of her long dress.

"You remember this, don't you?" I ask, as I slide her lace thong down her legs. She steps out of her panties without me having to tell her to, and I can't help but slide a hand up her smooth thigh, which she doesn't even try to resist. If anything, I'd say she welcomes my touch, like she's hoping I'll use it on her right now.

Look who's considering skipping the party now...

"This is a remote-controlled vibrator. The remote is an app on my phone that I can control from anywhere. Now I'll be able to make you come whenever I like."

Her eyes grow wider as her pupils begin to dilate, telling me she's not only physically aroused, but she's well on her way to being putty in my hands. Fuck if that's not the hottest goddamn thing, knowing all I have to do is take control, and my sweet little Girl Scout is more than willing to hand over the reins.

"Does that scare you?"

"No." Her response comes out in a breathy whisper.

"Does that turn you on? Knowing I could make you

orgasm in the middle of a conversation with anyone... at any time..." I trace my thumb along her jawline before moving my hand to cover her delicate neck. There's something so fucking hot about her yielding all control to me, knowing she'd let me do anything I wanted to her, like she's my own personal fuck doll that I get to use however I want...

Her response is a slow nod, and I have to fight to hold back the smug smile that pulls at my lips.

I keep my eyes locked on hers as I pop the small toy in my mouth, using my saliva to create a little lubrication. When I part her opening with my fingers, I find her pussy's already slick with arousal. "Jesus, baby, you're already so fucking wet and I've barely touched you." I push her forward so that she's bent forward over the side of the counter as I lift her dress, giving myself a prime view of her round ass and her pussy that's begging to be fucked. I almost come undone at the sight of how she lets me do whatever I want with her.

"Look at you, so fucking eager to be fucked." I grip the back of her neck with one hand, pinning her in place, and slap a palm over her ass. The whimper she makes is almost enough to convince me to stay in... but then I remember how much more fun it'll be when I finally do get my hands on her tonight.

"Spread your legs," I tell her as I nudge her opening with the thick, rounded toy, rubbing it against her own arousal before carefully sliding it deep inside. I use my fingers to make sure it's in the correct position, adjusting the small tail that curves up to rest against her clit. I press the toy into her clit, massaging it in gentle circles, just long enough to tease her and cause her legs to spread, urging me to give her more.

"Thatta girl," I say, giving her ass one more hard slap

before pulling her dress back down to cover her and helping her back to her feet.

Her face flashes a look of disappointment, but she quickly corrects it, blinking up and giving me her best practiced smile.

"There are those dreamy eyes I love so much." I offer her my arm. "We should probably get going. The whole town's waiting," I say, using her words against her.

"Yeah." She swallows thickly. "We don't want to be late for our own reception."

I swear, if I didn't know any better, I'd almost think she looks nervous.

Scout

I try to ignore the delicious fullness inside me that's only emphasized by my absence of panties. Each step I take making my thighs brush against the slender silicone piece resting against my clit.

We make our way up the stairs, but before Luka can touch the doorknob, the door swings open, as if they'd been standing there waiting for us to arrive. "Welcome to the Haunted Mansion." Mr. Kingsley says, taking a deep bow. He's wearing a pinstripe tuxedo, his usual salt and pepper hair is dyed black and slicked down, a thin mustache frames his lips. He makes a strikingly convincing Gomez Adams, but I'd expect nothing less with the commitment these two have when it comes to a costume party.

"Please don't make any offerings to the ghosts. They tend to get excited with new people, and we don't need any more broken windows," he says with a wink as he gestures for us to come inside.

We step inside as fog plumes around our feet, and it takes a moment for my eyes to adjust to the dim lighting. A soft piano melody plays overhead, and I glance around to find the space completely transformed.

All the family photos that usually adorn the foyer have been replaced with gaudy gold-framed black and white portraits that look to be hundreds of years old. Long white pillar candles seem to be floating from the ceiling, and cobwebs span over the light fixtures, making the house look like it's been abandoned.

"Is that the guests of honor?" Mrs. Kingsley shrieks before running over to us. She's, of course, dressed as Morticia, with long black hair that hangs down her back and her fitted black dress that hugs her hips and flares at the bottom.

"Why, yes, Cara Mia, it is," Mr. Kingsley says before placing a kiss on the back of his wife's hand. The look he gives her is nothing short of intense, and it's easy to see where Luka gets his charm. These boys don't know how lucky they were to grow up with a father so obviously obsessed with their mother.

I feel my cheeks heat just watching them. With the obsession these two have for each other, I can't think of a better couple's costume.

"This is incredible, Mrs. Kingsley," I say, gesturing to the realistic decorations around the room.

She gives me a slight smile, then waves me off, and now I really know she's in character. "Oh, honey, I've been dying to throw a Halloween party for years. I'm just glad you two finally gave me a good reason to go all out," she says in her best Morticia impersonation.

A server dressed as Cousin It walks past carrying a tray of drinks, and Mr. Kingsley snags two champagne flutes, handing us each a drink. "Enjoy the party. And remember what I said about talking to the ghosts." He winks, then they both disappear behind a cloud of fog.

"Damn. I knew they'd go all out, but...what just happened?" I look to Luka, who, rather than answering me, just links an arm in mine.

"Come on. We should probably make our rounds."

He leads me inside the dark living room that's been completely transformed into a mix between a haunted banquet room and an abandoned mansion.

Round tables draped in black tablecloths and adorned with black pillar candles line the perimeter of the room, with the middle space preserved as a dance floor.

There's a live band set up on a stage on the far wall playing Halloween classics as an unlikely grouping of characters dances in the center.

I do a double-take when my eyes catch on a tall man dressed as Shrek as he twirls someone in a brown furry horse-like costume. "Is that... Leo dressed as Shrek?"

Luka bursts out laughing as he spots them. "Yep. My brother Shrek and his ride or die sidekick, Donkey." He shakes his head. "That's hilarious as fuck and actually quite fitting."

He gives them a wave, and as soon as they see us, they make their way over.

"Oh my God, I can't believe I'm finally meeting you!" Ivy squeals, pulling me into her furry arms as soon as she sees me.

When we break apart, I look between them and back at Luka. And the genuine smile on his face has my heart bursting. He places a hand on the small of my back in that calming, present way of his, like he's trying to nip my anxiety in the bud before I overthink too much.

"It's so nice to finally meet you, too," I say, leaning a little closer to Luka.

"I can't believe you made it," Luka says after breaking his hug from Leo. "I know you're already planning on coming in for Thanksgiving, so I wouldn't have blamed you if you didn't want to make an extra trip."

"Are you kidding?" Leo pats Luka on the shoulder as Ivy snuggles into his side. "How could we miss your wedding reception?" He looks down at Ivy, who's somehow managed to look hot as hell in her Donkey costume, and they share a heated look before he finally says, "We're actually going to surprise mom and dad tomorrow and let them know we're staying through Christmas." He nudges Ivy, who's beaming with excitement. "Ivy's program is allowing her to take a little vacation time while she studies for a few certifications. And I'm the boss, so I can do what I want."

Ivy spins to face me and grabs my hands, letting out an excited shriek. "Which means, we're going to be best friends! I can't wait to have sleepovers, and you can teach me how to paint..." Her eyes go wide, and she looks at Leo over her shoulder. "Maybe we can even go camping together like we did last summer!" She whips her head back to me, and her voice turns serious. "Do you like drinking games? I bet you'll be amazing at telling ghost stories—"

Leo's hand covers her mouth as he pulls her away. "Okay, why don't we give the Frankenstiens a little time to make their rounds before we start filling up their calendars?" he says with a chuckle, then he pulls his hand away with a sigh as he wipes his palm on his pants. "Such a fucking brat."

Ivy licks her lips, staring back at him with a smirk on her face. "What? What'd I do?" She asks, her voice feigning innocence.

Leo just shakes his head, muffling something under his breath as he pulls her away.

"Okay, I think I love her," I say as we watch them make their way over to Jett, who's decked out in all black, wearing a Scream mask as he stands over the food table, ordering servers to refill drinks and plates of food.

"I knew you would. Ivy's a good time and she's as genuine as they come," Luka agrees, as we watch their exchange. Leo goes in for a hug, which Jett tries to deflect, but then Ivy hits him with an unexpected hug around his midsection, and he seems to let his guard down.

There's a tap on my shoulder, and I turn around, expecting to come face to face with another unlikely monster or character, but instead, I'm met with my mother's stern expression.

She stands there awkwardly in a soft grey pencil skirt, modest heels, and a silk blouse, her perfect posture somehow more rigid than I remember, making her look more like a mannequin than a human. She looks over the small, half-moon golden glasses set on her nose. "Sorry, it took me longer than expected to identify you amidst the gregarious cast of characters." She blows out an annoyed huff and looks around. "Not to mention this dim lighting. I don't know how anyone's managed to see where they're going in here." She waves a plume of fog from in front of her face dramatically. "I can't imagine going through so much...effort...for one's home to appear abandoned..." She plasters on a fake smile and shrugs. "But I guess I'm no fun—"

"What are you doing here, Mama?" I cut off her pitiful attempt at a backhanded compliment.

Her shoulders stiffen, and she blinks several times, like she wasn't expecting me to be so blunt. "Well, I was invited. I couldn't miss my only daughter's wedding reception, now, could I?" She slides her glasses down her nose, adjusting them. "I even dressed up for the occasion."

At that, I tilt my head, my brows raising in question.

She holds out a hand to introduce herself, and I just stare at it. "Samantha Sinclair, PhD of Literature."

It's Luka who takes her hand, shaking it. "Nice to meet you, Samantha."

The warmth that spreads through my heart at that simple gesture, when he has more reason than anyone to hold a grudge, melts me from inside out.

Since everything went down at the festival and my father's crimes surfaced, he was sentenced to five years in prison. While Jimmy's actions as his accomplice landed him three years.

My mother was spared any backlash after she and my father both admitted on the record, she had no knowledge of any of his business dealings. I wasn't sure if I believed her at first, but now that she's had some separation from my father, many of her neurotic tendencies have seemed to decline. I've tried to give her as much grace as I can, while still holding her accountable for the harm she's caused me.

I think she's still confused, trying to figure out who she is for the first time in her life.

"Well, it was good to see you, dear. You look... beautiful," she says, her nasally voice strained like she forced the words out. "Now, if you'll excuse me. I should probably make my rounds. I hope you make time to say your thank yous..." Her words trail off as if catching herself, and she folds her thin lips into a flat line, then nods goodbye before heading off to start up a conversation with Paige, Hazel, and Lucy, who seem to be dressed as Charlie's Angels.

"That was..."

"Awkward," I say, finishing Luka's sentence.

As awkward as she may be, I suppose there's some merit to her *trying*. I can't say that our relationship will ever go back to a normal mother-daughter dynamic. But if she's willing to change, then I can be patient while she figures things out.

I'm just glad Luka's on the same page. This man never ceases to amaze me with how big his heart is.

"Is that the couple of honor?" We turn around as Miss Scarlett waves a purple pompom before walking over. She's dressed in what appears to be her high school cheerleading uniform, though probably a bit snugger than it originally fit.

"Hey, Miss Scarlett. Thank you for coming." Luka greets her with a warm hug. "You're looking sexy as ever this evening."

She waves a pompom and flicks a bright red, curled strand of hair off her shoulder. "Of course, dear. I wouldn't miss a chance to celebrate you two love birds for the world."

She gives me a hug, kissing each of my cheeks, and whispers so only I can hear her, "You gotta keep things exciting, dear. Never stop dressing up. The fellas love it."

I try to hold back a laugh as I nod in understanding when I hear a man's voice yell over the music. "Scarlett? Where'd you go?" Fergus looks around the room. And it's hard to take him seriously with his ruffled, poofy white shirt and the giant parrot bobbing around on his shoulder. "Has anyone seen a red-headed cheerleader?" He calls again.

Scarlett gives him a pompom'd wave. "Over here, Gus!" She turns back to Luka and me and shrugs. "Looks like I'm being summoned. I'll catch back up with you two later!"

We watch Miss Scarlett jog back over to Fergus, who's resorted to using a collapsible telescope to find her. But when she accidentally collides with a football player, we both burst out laughing.

"Who is that?" I ask as my eyes follow them.

Luka squints as he studies the pair as Miss Scarlett playfully slaps a pompom against the football player's chest. She's leaning in as he whispers something in her ear.

Then, as if everyone seems to realize it at the same time, the collective mumbles fill the air.

"Dr. Drizzle!" Mrs. Kingsley's shrieks, her voice a pitch higher than usual and sounding nothing like Morticia. "I'm so glad you were able to make it!"

Luka chokes on a laugh as a moment later, Mr. Kingsley stands beside his wife, his arm wrapped around her possessively as he gives the guest a curt nod.

Across the room, all the men seem to follow suit, pulling their partners in a similar possessive hold. Even Guy and Roman sneak to get a closer look. They think they're being inconspicuous, hiding behind a table, but the sexy cowboy in chaps—*Guy*—and the Roman soldier—*Roman*—have a way of standing out in a crowd.

"I guess the Drizzle-effect is no joke," I laugh.

Luka takes my hand and leads me to the dance floor as the band begins playing a slow song. "Then I'm not going to tempt fate." His hand wraps possessively around my low back as he pulls me flush against his chest.

We sway to music

I take his hand as he twirls me around, our bodies swaying in rhythm like we've done this a million times. You wouldn't guess by Luka's tattooed exterior that he's such a graceful dancer, and despite the years of training of my own, I still find myself struggling not to step on his toes.

I used to hate ballroom dancing. All the cotillion lessons my mother insisted I needed growing up felt like such a waste of time, so robotic and pointless. But dancing with Luka feels more like kissing. The way our bodies move together, the give and take of each movement. It's intimate, and time seems to stand still as I let myself fall into that blissful, sated state where I know Luka will be there to catch me.

I feel the vibrator start to buzz inside of me, and I nearly lose my step, but Luka's arms are already prepared to catch me. He steadies me, his palm on my lower back, keeping me upright when another burst of vibrations hits me.

This time, I have to stop, doubling over for only a moment to catch my breath. When I snap my gaze up, I find Luka wearing a devilish grin. "Don't worry, baby, just follow my lead."

I let out a huff, letting Luka twirl me and quickly realize the buzzing matches the beat of the music... I don't know if I want to know how he managed that, but I use my new knowledge to brace myself when the beat drops once more.

By the time the next song plays, a much more upbeat song, I'm stumbling so much I don't know how my legs are still holding me upright. I keep stepping on Luka's feet, which only seems to make his grin wider, as I grit my teeth and try to hold myself together.

The rumbling vibrations feel so good inside of me. They're not as intense and buzzy as the other vibrator Luka's used on me. I find myself wanting to press my legs together and let the sensation move through me. It's like being touched just beside where I need it... if I could just shift a little...

"Fucking hell, Scout. You've got that dreamy look in your eyes. You're getting close, aren't you, baby?" Luka croons in my ear, his low, gravelly voice feeling much like the rumbling vibrations inside me.

"Yes," I manage to whisper, my eyes silently pleading for him to let me come.

He must find my desperation amusing, because the smile that stretches across his face is absolutely sinful. "You want me to let you come? You know what to do..."

I swallow thickly as my racing pulse pounds in my ears, feeling the sweet fluttery sensation begin to build. "Please, may I come?"

He tilts his head like he's considering it, then spins me around before pulling me back to his chest.

I let out a breathless gasp, my orgasm so close now... just a little more...

The music comes to a stop, and so do the vibrations. I let out a heavy breath, half relieved and half disappointed.

He kisses me on the cheek and whispers, "Look at my little whore, getting fucked right here in the middle of this party. Don't look so disappointed. You know I always make the teasing worth it."

"That you do," I say, as the buzzing intensifies, and I have to grip onto Luka to keep my knees from buckling beneath me.

If you'd have asked me the perfect way to celebrate our marriage, I don't think I could have planned it any better if I tried.

Thank you for reading Don't Make Me Beg!
Want to find out what happens when the
Kingsley's go camping?
Sign up for my newsletter to get a
Bonus Epilogue:
https://dl.bookfunnel.com/dysk3oigce

Did you miss Leo and Ivy's book?
Check out the first Ashford Falls book, **Don't Call Me Daddy!**
Uptight billionaire Leo Kingsley takes life way too seriously—especially his job. So when he's passed up for the CEO

promotion because his father doesn't think he can handle the pressure, he decides to prove to everyone that he's not as uptight as he seems. So when fate hands him a fake fiancé, he runs with it.
Now all he has to do is resist her.
Read on Amazon & Kindle Unlimited!

Do you want to be my friend?

Join my reader group: Jeré Anthony's Bantering Book Babes Where it feels like an grown-up slumber party every day.

We discuss books/reading, I tell my embarrassing moments—that happen all too often, and those hilarious inappropriate stories that only women will understand. Plus Giveaways!

It's a place for positive vibes + laughter + community and all the book talk!

So if you love my books and that sounds like you jam, come join us!

ACKNOWLEDGMENTS

When I wrote Don't Call Me Daddy, I thought it'd be the hardest book I'd ever write. It taught me so much about myself as an author, and everything I wanted my books to feel like. I took some big risks and was blown away by the love and support I received from my readers.

I thought that I'd overcome some of the *harder* lessons on this never-ending journey as a romance author.

But then I delved into Luka and Scout's story, and had my world rocked once again.

Because it turns out...writing imperfect characters with depth, that have real trauma and pain, takes a lot of work. It stirred up a lot of my own pain.

While, yes, Luka and Scout's past experiences and traumas are uniquely theirs, their imperfections and trauma were born from a place inside me. And bringing it all to light wasn't something I was expecting to be as painful as it was.

To say that there were days where I wasn't sure that this book would ever be finished, is a hell of an understatement—just ask my husband, *and my therapist!*

But here I stand, triumphant, with this precious book in my hand. I am so fucking proud of my grit, of all the obstacles I overcame in the process of writing this story.

Of course, none of this would be possible without the help of some incredible people...

I'd like to thank my amazing BETA Readers: Amy Stoddard, Ashly Wickham, Marielli Prestes Bittencourt, Kimberly Thibodeau, Tiffany Noriega, Emily Buss, Amanda Dzura, Kaia Johnson, Vera-Michele Workman, Kelly Cedroni, Paige Brown, Samantha Lambert, Emily Canavan, Briana Jacobus, and Hannah Kroenert.

Katy Gustafson, my assistant. You have been a God send. Seriously, babe, in the short time we've been working together, you've helped me so much! I am so grateful for your eagerness to help and your immaculate organizational skills!

My developmental editor, Becca Mysoor, who is a miracle worker and helped me completely restructure this story, this book wouldn't be anything close to the book it is without your magic! Thank you for helping me create such a strong, dynamic story.

To my dear friend, Julie Oliva, who cheered me on every step of the way, and listened to my ever-changing stream of ideas nearly every Friday for an entire year... You deserve an award for your patience! I am so grateful for your friendship and so excited to watch your blooming success happening right now!

To my therapist, Jason, who also endured listening to me gripe and complain every week, thank you for your amazing advice, and for keeping me sane during this strenuous process. I know it wasn't easy.

And lastly, as always, none of this writing would happen without the support of my saint of a husband, Stephen. You are the blueprint for all the book boyfriends I create. Your efforts in stepping up to cook dinner night after night when I was exhausted from fighting with my manuscript, and taking the lead on getting the children to all their practices has been nothing short of a God-send. I'm a lucky girl with the way you spoil me and someday I hope to make you a kept man with this whole author thing!

Reflecting on this journey is incredibly humbling and I am in awe that I get to call this my real life.

And, of course, thank YOU for reading! None of this would be possible without your support!

Until next time!

XOXO
Jeré

ABOUT THE AUTHOR

JERÉ ANTHONY WRITES HIGH-HUMOR, high-heat romantic comedies that'll have you laughing one second and crying the next. She isn't afraid to go there... Whether it's her descriptive spicy scenes or diving into some heavier emotional topics through her characters, her stories will take you on a wild adventure that's sure to be anything but dull...

And even though she may not hold back any emotional punches, she promises to always leave you smiling and satisfied by the end.

Find her on her website at:

JereAnthony.com